I0831673

LOVE, POWER, AND GENDER IN SEVENTEENTH-CENTURY FRENCH FAIRY TALES

Women and Gender in
the Early Modern World

SERIES EDITORS

Allyson Poska
Abby Zanger

Love, Power, and Gender in Seventeenth-Century French Fairy Tales

BRONWYN REDDAN

UNIVERSITY OF NEBRASKA PRESS LINCOLN

Portions of chapters 1 and 2 first appeared as "Scripting Love in Fairy Tales by Seventeenth-Century French Women Writers," *French History and Civilization* 7 (2017): 93–107, and appear courtesy of the George Rude Society. An earlier version of chapter 4 first appeared as "Gift-Giving and the Obligation to Love in *Riquet à la houppe*" in *Emotion, Ritual and Power in Europe, 1200–1920: Family, State and Church*, ed. Merridee L. Bailey and Katie Barclay, 23–41 (Cham, Switzerland: Palgrave Macmillan, 2017). Portions of chapter 5 first appeared as "Losing Love, Losing Hope: Unhappy Endings in Seventeenth-Century Fairy Tales," *Papers on French Seventeenth Century Literature* 42, no. 83 (2015): 327–39.

Library of Congress Cataloging-in-Publication Data
Names: Reddan, Bronwyn, author.
Title: Love, power, and gender in seventeenth-century French fairy tales / Bronwyn Reddan.
Description: Lincoln: University of Nebraska Press, 2020. | Series: Women and gender in the early modern world | Includes bibliographical references and index.
Identifiers: LCCN 2020007547
ISBN 9781496216151 (hardback)
ISBN 9781496223937 (epub)
ISBN 9781496223944 (mobi)
ISBN 9781496223951 (pdf)
Subjects: LCSH: Fairy tales—France—History and criticism. | French fiction—Women authors—History and criticism. | French fiction—17th century—History and criticism. | Women and literature—France—History—17th century. | Courtship in literature. | Marriage in literature. | Love in literature.
Classification: LCC PQ637.F27 R43 2020 | DDC 398.209/44—dc23
LC record available at https://lccn.loc.gov/2020007547

Set in Arno by Mikala R. Kolander.
Designed by N. Putens.

For Ric

CONTENTS

ILLUSTRATIONS

TABLES

NOTE ON SOURCES AND TRANSLATIONS

All quotations from seventeenth-century fairy tales are from the Bibliothèque des Génies et des Fées series published by Honoré Champion unless otherwise indicated. For quotations from other seventeenth- and eighteenth-century French texts except the *Dictionnaire de l'Académie française,* I have modernized spelling, punctuation, and capitalization. All translations are my own unless stated otherwise.

ACKNOWLEDGMENTS

This book is the result of several years of research and thinking, and I am indebted to the many scholars, colleagues, and friends who have supported it, and me, during this time. It began as a PhD supervised by Charles Zika, to whom I am profoundly grateful for his generosity, close reading, and insightful comments. I would also like to thank the members of my advisory committee at the University of Melbourne, Véronique Duché and Catherine Kovesi, for sharing their time and expertise in providing valuable comments on various drafts, as well as my honors supervisor, Jenny Spinks, for her support of the early stages of this project and her ongoing interest in my research. I am grateful to my examiners, Lewis Seifert and Sarah Ferber, for providing invaluable feedback on the daunting task of transforming thesis into a book. Anne Duggan and Theresa Kennedy read this book for the University of Nebraska Press, and I am grateful for their incisive comments, which, along with editorial support and guidance from the team at the press, in particular Bridget Barry and Alisa Plant, helped to shape the final form of the book. I would also like to thank the series editors, especially Abby Zanger, for supporting this project.

During my thesis and in the murky early career waters beyond, my colleagues in the Australian Research Council Centre of Excellence for the History of Emotions have been a wonderful source of intellectual and emotional energy. I would like to thank Katie Barclay, Stephanie Trigg, and Sarah Randles for reading and commenting on my work and Claire Walker, Grace Moore, Stephanie Downes, Merridee L. Bailey, Carly Osborn, Aleksondra Hultquist, Giovanni Tarantino, Lisa Beaven, and Gordon Raeburn for their interest in my research. Katie deserves special acknowledgment for her generous advice on all manner of topics, and this book has benefited enormously from her input. I would also like to thank the center's administrative team, especially Leanne Hunt and Jessie Scott, for its practical support.

To my fellow graduate students in the School of Historical and Philosophical Studies, especially the intrepid inhabitants of the Old Quad, thank you for being such a vibrant postgraduate community. My PhD experience would not have been half as enjoyable without your friendship and camaraderie, in particular Jean McBain, Charlotte-Rose Millar, Bethany Phillips-Peddlesden, and Rhys Cooper. I am also grateful to the many generous scholars with whom I have exchanged ideas and friendship at conferences and presentations in Australia and abroad, especially Heather Kirk, Charlotte Trinquet du Lys, Volker Schröder, and Katherine Ibbett.

The research for this book has been supported by several grants and awards. I am very grateful to the Australian Research Council Centre of Excellence for the History of Emotions (project number CE110001011) for a Research Support Scholarship that funded travel during my PhD and a Project-to-Publication Fellowship that supported the initial stages of transforming that research into this book. My PhD research was funded by an Australian Postgraduate Award from the University of Melbourne, as well as a number of travel and research bursaries. I am particularly grateful to Helen Davies for funding the French History Research Higher Degree Scholarship, which allowed me to travel to Paris to review original editions of the *conteuses'* tales held at the Bibliothèque Nationale de France and the Bibliothèque de l'Arsenal. I would also like to thank the Max Planck Institute for Human Development and Concepta for their financial support of my attendance at their 2014 summer school, which helped develop my thinking about the methodology of this book. Travel funding from the Faculty of Arts at the University of Melbourne and the Alison Patrick Memorial and Elizabeth and Nicholas Slezak Scholarships have allowed me to discuss my research and engage with a broad network of scholars within Australia and internationally, especially the wonderful members of the Society for Interdisciplinary French Seventeenth-Century Studies and the North American Society for Seventeenth-Century French Literature. This book is far richer for this exposure.

My family and friends have been a constant source of the right blend of encouragement and distraction. I would like to thank my parents and siblings for their love and support, especially my sister for sharing the PhD experience with me, and my in-laws for welcoming me into their family. I am very grateful to the lovely friends who have listened to my ideas, asked thoughtful questions, and read portions of the manuscript, and I owe a very big thank you to Natasha Sung, Lydia Wong, Bree Saunders, and Clare Parsons. To my husband, Ric, thank you for listening to me, for wrangling our energetic toddler to give me time to write, and, most importantly, for keeping me supplied with sufficient quantities of pasta and chocolate. This book is dedicated to you.

LOVE, POWER, AND GENDER IN SEVENTEENTH-CENTURY FRENCH FAIRY TALES

Introduction

Reimagining Fairy-Tale Love

Imagine a situation in which you are blessed with extraordinary wealth, intelligence, and beauty. Would life be complete, or would you feel like something was missing? This is the scenario examined by Henriette-Julie de Castelnau, Comtesse de Murat, in her 1698 tale "Anguillette" (Little Eel). The heroine of this tale is rewarded with good fortune when she rescues a fairy, Anguillette, from being served as the king's dinner after Anguillette is captured by a fisherman while metamorphosed as an eel. As a mark of her gratitude, Anguillette offers the young princess the choice between three wishes: perfect beauty, a brilliant mind, or infinite wealth.[1] Despite desiring beauty, our heroine wisely chooses intelligence, and the generous fairy rewards this choice by giving her beauty and wealth as well. One might think that the lovely princess Hébé now has everything she needs for a charmed existence, but her heart is troubled by a malaise she cannot understand. When Anguillette asks Hébé what else she could possibly desire, the melancholy princess declares: "I don't know what I desire . . . but I feel . . . that I lack something, and that this lack is absolutely necessary to my happiness."[2] It is not difficult for Anguillette to solve this mystery. She immediately identifies love as the cause of Hébé's distress: "'Ah!' cried the fairy. 'It's love you desire. Passion is the only thing that can make you think so strangely. Dangerous inclination. . . . If you want love, you will have it, hearts are only too willing to seize it. But I warn you that you will invoke my name in vain to end this fatal passion you believe to be a happiness so sweet, my power does not extend that far.'"[3]

Anguillette's warning about the dangers of love is prescient. As soon as Hébé returns to her father's court, she falls hopelessly in love with the feckless Atimir, who, unbeknownst to her, had already paid certain tender attentions to her sister. The resulting love triangle ends in disaster. The inevitability of this outcome is foreshadowed by the emotional intensity of Hébé's first encounter with Atimir: "never were two hearts so promptly and profoundly touched."[4] Almost immediately, Hébé abandons herself to passion and loses a tranquility of which she was not aware. She is unable to resist her heart's desire for love despite Anguillette's prediction that it will cause her unimaginable pain. Her courtship with Atimir proceeds rapidly, and the charming young prince wastes no time in securing permission for their marriage from their respective fathers. Atimir's affections are, however, rather less constant than Hébé's tender passion. When he accidentally discovers that Hébé's sister, Ilérie, is also in love with him, he convinces himself that to love Hébé is to be unfaithful to Ilérie, whom he saw and flirted with first. Atimir confesses his feelings to Ilérie, and the pair elopes after Ilérie announces her intention to kill herself rather than see Atimir marry her sister. It is the force of their mutual passion that drives this dramatic action. Neither can resist their desire for the other despite the social consequences of their illicit romance. For Ilérie, love is an irresistible force that compels her to act irrationally by entrusting her fate to an unfaithful lover. Like Anguillette, she anticipates the suffering this passion will cause but she is unable to resist her unhappy destiny.

The idea of love as an inescapable restriction on freedom is a key theme in Murat's reworking of the folkloric motif of two sisters in love with the same man. In "Anguillette," neither reason nor fairy magic can moderate the heart's desire for love. The fatal consequences of this desire fulfill Anguillette's melancholy prediction about the danger of passion even though she tries to use her powers to thwart fate by sending Hébé to an enchanted island with the ability to cure unhappy passions. Hébé's sojourn on Peaceful Island (l'Île Paisible) restores the tranquility of her heart and the princess follows Anguillette's advice by allowing herself to be wooed by the prince of Peaceful Island. In a stereotypical fairy tale, this would be the end of the story, with both sisters achieving a happy ending after marrying handsome princes. But when Murat continues her tale beyond this point, their happiness is short-lived. Hébé is unable to resist her desire to see her former lover when she learns that he and Ilérie have returned to her father's court. She convinces her reluctant husband that they should visit her parents, and her disobedience of Anguillette's injunction never to see Atimir again seals her unhappy fate. The sight of his former beloved reignites Atimir's passion, and his obvious displays of tender feeling for Hébé leads to a duel in which he is killed and Hébé's husband is wounded. Upon arriving at the fatal scene, Hébé believes both men to be dead and throws herself on Atimir's sword to avenge their sacrifice with her own life. This blood-soaked ending fulfills Anguillette's warning, and she transforms Hébé and Atimir into a pair of beautiful trees as a monument to unhappy lovers.

Murat's pessimistic representation of the suffering caused by love offers an intriguing counterpoint to the "love conquers all" stereotype associated with the fairy-tale genre. None of the characters in "Anguillette" can escape their desire for love, and the only character who achieves the semblance of a happy ending is Hébé's husband, who manages to forget his passion by returning to Peaceful Island. Murat's tale was first published in 1698, and it is one of a number of tales created by the French women whose literary production was central to the first French fairy-tale vogue. Between 1690 and 1709, Murat and her literary contemporaries, Marie-Catherine Le Jumel de Barneville, baronne d'Aulnoy; Louise de Bossigny, comtesse d'Auneuil; Catherine Bernard; Catherine Durand (née Bédacier); Charlotte-Rose de Caumont de La Force; and Marie-Jeanne Lhéritier de Villandon, whom I refer to collectively as the *conteuses*, produced two-thirds of a corpus of tales known as *contes de fées*. These tales are important literary ancestors of the modern fairy tale as they initiated many of the conventional features of the genre. But their significance has been overshadowed by the better-known tales from Charles Perrault including "Sleeping Beauty," "Little Red

Riding Hood," and "Cinderella." The conteuses' tales offer an important contrast to modern idealization of love as the ultimate fairy-tale ending as they represent love as a disappointing or disastrous experience as well as a source of joy. In doing so, their tales develop a nuanced and complex theory of love that critiques the gender politics of courtship and marriage in seventeenth-century France.

This book focuses on the relationship between love, power, and gender in the fairy tales written by the conteuses.[5] Love is the most important theme in the tales they wrote for the elite, adult audience of seventeenth-century literary salons, but it does not function simply as a necessary narrative element in the journey toward marriage. The conteuses' tales represent love as a passion with positive and negative consequences and emphasize its importance as an essential part of human life. It is essential as the conteuses' characters cannot find happiness without love, but, as Murat shows in the tale of "Anguillette," desire for love disrupts the lives of the conteuses' heroines. While falling in love offers the promise of a blissful union, it also gives rise to agitation and the destructive effects of jealousy. The conteuses' representation of the complex nature of love continued a conversation begun in mid-seventeenth-century salon literature published by authors including Madeleine de Scudéry; Marie-Catherine Desjardins, madame de Villedieu; and Marie-Madeleine Pioche de la Vergne, comtesse de Lafayette. I argue that the conteuses' tales do not simply replicate the *précieuse* code of love developed in seventeenth-century literary salons.[6] Their tales reinterpreted salon conversation about love to develop a range of different perspectives that engaged with early modern intellectual debate about the nature of the passions, early feminist criticism of courtship and marriage, and ongoing conflict about the status of women and women's writing. In making this argument I suggest that the conteuses' tales mark an important moment in the history of love because the diversity in their representations of how love shaped the lives of their heroines offers insight into the gendered power dynamics of courtship and marriage in seventeenth-century France. Their tales show how the category of gender shapes how emotions are experienced and expressed and question the idea of love as an emotion with a constant or universal human experience. Their critique of love compels revision of the "happily ever after" narrative so often associated with both the experience of love and the fairy-tale genre.

PROBLEMS OF DEFINITION AND GENRE

> There is no such thing as *the* fairy tale; however, there are hundreds of thousands of fairy tales. And these fairy tales have been defined in so many different ways that it boggles the mind to think that they can be categorized as a genre.
> —Jack Zipes, *The Oxford Companion to Fairy Tales*

Fairy tales, even literary versions crafted by a single identifiable author, are not unique or original stories. They migrate and mutate across national borders and time periods to produce a dizzying array of narrative variations. Angela Carter suggests that determining the origin of fairy-tale plots is akin to the search for a definitive recipe for potato soup. There is not one version of this classic dish but multiple variations produced by the cultural and social contexts in which it is made.[7] To complicate matters further, fairy-tale conventions often wander from their narrative home to cross-pollinate a diverse range of literary and cultural genres including novels, television, popular music, and advertising. Consequently, the term *fairy tale* also functions as a powerful epithet applied to situations and people—one might experience a fairy-tale romance, encounter a fairy-tale villain, or long for a fairy-tale ending.[8] In this book, I suggest that it is our familiarity with the form and elements of fairy tales that gives them their power. To tell a fairy tale is to engage with a long history of storytelling in which meaning is created by constant revision of a classic formula. New ingredients are added, traditional components are modified or omitted, and it is the combination of old and new that allows each taleteller to distinguish their version of a story from those told by their ancestors and future descendants. This process of remaking means that the flavor of each tale is unique even though we might be familiar with its structure and constitutive elements.

In the modern popular imagination, fairy tales are imaginative stories for children about the marvelous adventures of beautiful princesses, handsome princes, and powerful fairies. They are short, simple tales with a moral message in which virtue is rewarded, evildoers are punished, and true love's kiss is the ultimate protection against misfortune. As readers we often intuitively feel that we know whether a story is a fairy tale or not when we read it, but defining the boundaries of the genre is an almost impossible task. Like the wonders of which they tell, fairy tales are elusive: they shape-shift, take flight in our imagination, and transform themselves and us, their spellbound audiences. Nevertheless, countless folklore and fairy-tale scholars have proposed definitions of the fairy tale as both a distinct narrative form and an umbrella category encompassing a range of forms.[9] Despite the plethora of alternatives, none is entirely satisfactory in encapsulating the essence of the genre. Rather than attempting to provide a comprehensive definition of the fairy-tale genre, a goal Jack Zipes and Angela Carter suggest is unattainable, the following discussion examines features of the genre that differentiate it from other narrative forms.

Reflection on the nature of fairy tales by Zipes, Cristina Bacchilega, Maria Tatar, and Marina Warner offers insight into the distinctive characteristics of the genre. For Zipes and Bacchilega, the desire for transformation is a crucial element of our attraction to fairy tales. They interpret the genre as speaking to a longing for change by providing a narrative form that gives us permission to wonder about what could be and how we might remake ourselves and the world we live in.[10] Tatar also emphasizes the importance of transformation in her identification of magic and metamorphosis as key features of fairy tales.[11] To this, one might add Warner's six defining characteristics of fairy tale. She too emphasizes the importance of wonder and magic in shaping the plots and pleasure offered by fairy tales and identifies five other elements relating to the form, origins, and cultural status of the genre. Warner describes fairy tales as short, familiar stories drawn from folklore that shift between oral and literary traditions. They evoke a sense of the past and operate as instruments for imagination. Last but not least, Warner argues that fairy tales offer hope: the promise that a happy ending is possible and that miracles can work to redress violence, injustice, and misfortune.[12]

Another response to the challenge of definition is to distinguish literary fairy tales from oral folk or wonder tales but this approach is not without controversy. While Zipes argues that literary fairy tales borrow motifs, plots, and characters from oral storytelling traditions (and a range of literary texts) in order to invent sophisticated narratives that transform their source material into new stories, Ruth Bottigheimer claims that there is no evidence that popular oral storytelling traditions inspired the creation of the fairy-tale genre.[13] Although it is impossible to provide conclusive support for either position, allusions to popular fairy-tale storytelling practices in the tales published by seventeenth-century French authors, some of which I discuss further in chapter 1, suggest that speculation about which tradition came first is less productive than recognition of their mutual influence.[14] Regardless of the position taken on the origins of the literary fairy tale, the birth of the genre dates to sixteenth- and seventeenth-century Italy, following the publication of Giovan Francesco Straparola's *Le piacevoli notti* (*The Pleasant Nights*) in 1550–53 and Giambattista Basile's *Lo cunto de li cunti overo Lo trattenemiento de peccerille* (*The Tale of Tales, or Entertainment for the Little Ones*) in 1634–36. As Nancy Canepa explains, this does not mean that Straparola and Basile invented the narrative form of the fairy tale, as there is a long history of literary and oral antecedents, including Apuleius's *The Golden Ass* and Giovanni Boccaccio's *Decameron*.[15] But these Italian collections of tales do mark an important moment in fairy-tale history as the beginning of a process that established the literary fairy tale as an independent genre.[16] The literary fairy-tale genre did not, however, capture the imagination of reading publics until it was popularized by the conteuses in late seventeenth-century France. It was Marie-Catherine Le Jumel de Barneville, baronne d'Aulnoy, who initiated this vogue for fairy tales when she published the first French literary fairy tale, "L'île de la félicité" in 1690. She was also responsible for coining the term *contes de fées*, and it is from this phrase that the term *fairy tale* was born as a translation of the title of d'Aulnoy's 1697–98 collection of tales *Les contes de fées* as *Tales of the Fairies* in 1699.[17]

Traditional methods of analyzing fairy tales such as folklorist, structuralist, and psychoanalytic approaches tend to overlook the sociohistorical significance of fairy tales as a source of insight into the conditions of the lives of fairy-tale tellers. Instead, such methods read fairy tales as sources of universal truths about human experience.[18] This interpretation of the cultural significance of fairy tales is influenced by the close connection between fairy tales and folklore. It is premised on the notion that fairy tales are written versions of oral folk wisdom inherited from popular storytelling traditions.[19] As Elizabeth Wanning Harries argues, the fairy-tale canon established by this definition privileges tales created by male authors such as Charles Perrault and the Brothers Grimm as exemplars of what fairy tales should look like. This classic or, to use Harries's term, "compact" model of the genre defines fairy tales as short, simple stories that draw on a shared set of basic plot motifs and stock characters. It reads fairy tales as foundational origin stories for children, bookended by opening and closing formulas that mark the transition from stability to conflict and back: "once upon a time" and "happily ever after." The tales written by the conteuses do not fit within this narrow definition of fairy tales. They are, as Harries observes, "complex," self-referential tales that are intertextual, playful, and digressive.[20] The conteuses' tales are not timeless classics as they unapologetically engage with contemporary social debate about the role and status of women. Their tales are provocative and political in their reworking of conventional romance plots, and their critique of early modern gender norms forces us to rethink the gender politics of love and the boundaries of the fairy-tale canon.

Despite their traditional exclusion from the fairy-tale canon, the conteuses' tales played a significant role in defining key features of the modern fairy tale. Their tales inaugurated conventions we now recognize as stereotypical elements of the fairy-tale genre including the use of folkloric plots and motifs, the presence of fairies or a marvelous setting, and the marriage closure happy ending.[21] If you apply Warner's six characteristics to the conteuses' tales (length, familiarity, presence of the past, imagination, wonder, and hope), the results are both illuminating and frustrating. This is because the extent to which individual tales satisfy Warner's list of features varies by author and by tale. The first and second criteria are often challenging: many but not all of the conteuses' tales are short and relatively few are familiar to modern readers, whose sense of the genre has been shaped by Disney films and is now closely tied to the tales published by the conteuses' male counterpart, Perrault.[22] The third element is satisfied by the conteuses' paratextual and metatextual commentary emphasizing the legacy of oral storytelling traditions in shaping their tales, as well as their evocation of a distant medieval past in which encounters with fairies were a perfectly ordinary part of life. This fictive past is created by acts of imagination that establish a magical reality offering the conteuses' readers the pleasure and consolation of wonder, thus fulfilling Warner's fourth and fifth criteria. The sixth element, hope, is the most difficult to satisfy, as a significant proportion of the conteuses' tales end unhappily, and others suggest that happiness in love exists only in the marvelous contes de fées universe. The generic instability highlighted by this analysis is both a hallmark of the fairy-tale genre and a powerful example of the way the conteuses' tales resist categories they helped to inaugurate.

WRITING THE CONTEUSES INTO FAIRY-TALE HISTORY

The fluidity of the fairy tale as a hybrid genre shaped by a range of literary and oral antecedents has important implications for fairy-tale history. If scholars cannot agree on the defining characteristics of the genre, how should we approach the task of determining which tales are included in this history? Even the most cursory review of fairy-tale scholarship reveals a range of different responses to this question. Studies undertaken by scholars working in the fields of folklore and narrative theory focus on identifying patterns of structure and form to identify immutable elements that can be used to analyze the geographic and temporal spread of the genre. Influential examples include the Aarne-Thompson-Uther (ATU) classification system that catalogues tales according to type in an index based on historical and comparative folk narrative research, Vladimir Propp's thirty-one basic functions of folktales, and A. J. Greimas's actantial model.[23] This type of analysis has contributed to the formation of the "compact" model of the fairy-tale genre, which excludes tales that do not fit within a predictable narrative structure.[24] This traditional view of fairy-tale history privileges tales by well-known (male) authors and has had a strong influence on contemporary popular culture through the ubiquitous presence of the Disney versions of tales such as Cinderella, Sleeping Beauty, Snow White and the Seven Dwarfs, and the Little Mermaid.

Only in recent decades have scholars examined the conteuses' corpus as a significant moment in fairy-tale history. The watershed moment for reexamination of the fairy-tale canon was the publication of two groundbreaking studies by Jack Zipes and Raymonde Robert in 1979 and 1982, respectively. Both studies used social history methodologies to highlight the cultural and historical significance of fairy tales. Zipes's *Breaking the Magic Spell* called for a radical reorientation of folklore and fairy-tale scholarship to expose the appropriation of wonder and enchantment by the culture industry's production of stories for mass consumption. Zipes argues that fairy tales must be read in reference to their historical context because their meaning is inextricably linked to the sociopolitical conditions in which they are produced.[25] Robert's *Le conte de fées littéraire en France* emphasizes the historical significance of fairy tales as texts produced in a particular social context. Her masterful interdisciplinary analysis of the social history of the French fairy tale identifies the conteuses as important contributors to the development of the genre, emphasizing their role as the creators of a significant percentage of the corpus of tales published in France between 1690 and 1778.[26] This scholarship challenges the compact model of the fairy-tale genre by illustrating the historical value of fairy tales, including those created by the conteuses, as cultural practices that show how people construct meaning in response to the social and political conditions in their lives.

The legacy of Zipes's and Robert's scholarship is evident in feminist fairy-tale scholarship emphasizing the subversive nature of the conteuses' corpus as a female literary genre in the 1990s and early 2000s. Scholars including Warner, Harries, Lewis C. Seifert, and Patricia Hannon answered the call to examine the social and material contexts in which fairy tales are produced. Their revisionist cultural histories argue that the conteuses' tales disrupted norms of gender and sexuality in seventeenth-century France.[27] Warner's *From the Beast to the Blonde* situates the conteuses' tales within a long tradition of female storytelling. She suggests that the conteuses' tales should be read as an attempt to reclaim a space for female voices and challenge prejudices and practices that confined and defamed women.[28] In *Fairy Tales, Sexuality, and Gender in France,* Seifert demonstrates the importance of the marvelous as a performative aesthetic that allows authors to look back at an idealized past while simultaneously imagining a utopian future. He interprets the seventeenth-century conte de fée as a gendered form of writing that the conteuses used to develop ambiguous definitions of gender and sexuality.[29] Hannon's *Fabulous Identities* also reads the conteuses' tales as exploratory spaces that allowed seventeenth-century aristocratic women to imagine alternative identities, but she suggests that this process was forward-looking rather than nostalgic.[30] Both Seifert and Hannon agree that the conteuses' tales provide evidence of the development of a group consciousness that distinguished their tales from those written by male authors in the same period.[31] In *Twice upon a Time,* Harries uses a feminist formalism to reread the history of the fairy-tale canon to include tales written by women, including those by the conteuses.[32]

This scholarship is part of a broader push to expand the French literary canon to include texts created by women writers. The significant literary contribution made by seventeenth-century French women writers, especially the role and influence of the salon, has been demonstrated by scholars including Joan E. DeJean, Faith E. Beasley, and Elizabeth Goldsmith. DeJean's influential study *Tender Geographies* illustrates the role of salon women writers in the creation of the modern novel.[33] In *Revising Memory,* Beasley examines the role of women writers in the creation of alternative histories that reconfigured the conventional focus on military and political events to include women's experiences.[34] The contribution of women writers to the formation of the public sphere in seventeenth- and eighteenth-century France, along with the political implications of the decisions made by French women to publish their work, is the focus of *Going Public,* a collection of essays edited by Goldsmith and Dena Goodman. Essays in this collection, along with monographs by Goldsmith, Goodman, and Beasley, emphasize the importance of the salon as a space in which women writers exercised significant cultural influence in seventeenth-century France.[35] More recently, Allison Stedman's *Rococo Fiction in France* identifies the conteuses as key figures in the transformation of salon sociability from an oral-collective mode of literary production to exchanges mediated by text.[36]

During the same period, a number of French scholars began examining the aesthetic and ideological significance of the conteuses' tales. A number of these studies concentrate on d'Aulnoy as a key figure in the development of the literary fairy-tale genre in seventeenth-century France. Anne Defrance and Jean Mainil analyze particular aspects of d'Aulnoy's oeuvre in studies published in 1998 and 2001, respectively. Defrance reads d'Aulnoy's tales as mirrors inscribed with multiple social codes that reflected the values of her aristocratic audience, whereas Mainil focuses on d'Aulnoy's subversive use of humor and irony to critique the ancien régime.[37] Nadine Jasmin's *Naissance du conte féminin* suggests that d'Aulnoy's tales were representative of the genre the conteuses created at the end of the seventeenth century.[38] The most important study from this period is Sophie Raynard's *La seconde préciosité*, which interprets the conteuses' tales as a second wave of the literary phenomenon of *préciosité* developed in Parisian literary salons in the mid-seventeenth century. Raynard's reading of the conteuses' corpus argues that feminism is inherent in préciosité, and emphasizes the significance of the conteuses' tales as a mode of writing that is original, imaginative, and very different to Perrault's tales.[39] Most recently, Charlotte Trinquet's *Le conte de fées français (1690–1700)* reiterates the link between the conteuses' tales and seventeenth-century salons, as well as the influence of sixteenth-century Italian authors Giovan Francesco Straparola and Giambattista Basile.[40]

This book contributes to revision of the fairy-tale canon by offering a cultural history of fairy-tale love that builds on the important work of feminist and literary scholars in writing the conteuses back into fairy-tale history. This is an important project because the legacy of the conteuses' tales continues to shape our ideas about love and marriage in the present due to their inauguration of stereotypical features of the fairy tale such as the marriage conclusion. As the following discussion shows, existing fairy-tale scholarship has not examined the significance of this legacy, nor has it considered how the multifaceted treatment of love in the conteuses' tales challenges ahistorical definitions of fairy-tale love as a timeless or universal emotion.

INTERROGATING FAIRY-TALE LOVE

Love is a classic narrative element of the fairy-tale genre. It drives the development of a romantic relationship between the heroic couple and the "happily ever after" ending characterized by a wedding. While scholars frequently acknowledge the presence of a love story as a stereotypical feature of fairy-tale narratives, surprisingly little attention has been given to the meaning of fairy-tale love and the related question of whether this meaning varies over time and across different fairy-tale traditions.[41] Studies of the conteuses' tales have focused on the extent to which their tales recreated the code of love developed in seventeenth-century literary salons. Nadine Jasmin identifies five précieuse themes in the conteuses' representation of love: love at first sight, marvelous love and fairy magic, salon sociability and conversation, passions rhetoric, and misfortunes of love. Her analysis emphasizes variation in the conteuses' representation of love as a natural, innocent sentiment fulfilled by the triumphant union of lovers, as a powerful emotion beyond the control of fairy magic, and as a sociable emotion expressed using the gallant code of salon conversation.[42] Seifert and Domna Stanton also emphasize the interplay between medieval traditions of courtly love and salon sociability in the conteuses' use of conventional ideas about love such as the virtuous and civilizing power of love, the pain of unrequited passion, and male subservience to female beloveds.[43] Trinquet and Marcelle Maistre Welch associate the conteuses' tales with early feminist criticism of love and marriage in seventeenth-century salon literature and conversation.[44]

Raynard and Seifert offer the most detailed examination of the conteuses' treatment of love. Raynard's contextual literary analysis in *La seconde préciosité* suggests that differences in the conteuses' representation of love offer evidence of variation in their interpretation of the précieuse code of love.[45] Seifert's *Fairy Tales, Sexuality, and Gender in France* interprets the conteuses' representation of love in romantic quests and marriage closures as an expression of the myth of heterosexual complementarity.[46] Like Raynard, Seifert reads the conteuses' take on love as a literary reworking of discourse inherited from folkloric and chivalric romance traditions: "almost all of the *contes de fées* construct an idealized vision of past discourses of love as a counter-reality for the present."[47] Seifert identifies two literary models of love as particularly influential in understanding the conteuses' representation of love: a neoplatonic or tender love associated with early seventeenth-century romances and made famous by Madeleine de Scudéry's *Carte de Tendre* (Map of Tenderness), and a gallant or courtly love incompatible with virtue. Hannon draws on both models in her reading of d'Aulnoy's tale "L'Oiseau Bleu" as an example of the development of an egalitarian or reciprocal model of love as a private negotiation between the heroic couple.[48] Seifert, Raynard, and Hannon all contextualize the conteuses' representation of love by reference to the literary context in which their tales were written, but they do not examine the significance of love as an emotion with a history that reflects the gendered power dynamics between men and women at the time it is felt and expressed. This book suggests that the conteuses' tales shaped and were shaped by gendered social codes for the performance of love in seventeenth-century France.

The methodology of this book is based on the idea that emotions have a history that provides insight into the cultural and social dynamics of the society in which they are expressed. Examining this history provides a method for increasing our understanding of how people develop strategies to negotiate the power structures that shape their lives by managing how and when they expressed emotion.[49] In adopting a history of emotions methodology to analyze the conteuses' tales, I draw on Barbara Rosenwein's concept of emotional community and Monique Scheer's theory of emotion as a form of practice to explore the ways in which the conteuses' tales contributed to early modern understanding of the nature of love as an emotion with social, political, and gendered effects. In doing so, I aim to focus attention on the social significance of their literary corpus as important historical sources for understanding the development and expression of cultural norms of love in seventeenth-century France. The methodological frameworks developed by Rosenwein and Scheer emphasize the performative nature of emotion as instruments that influence and are influenced by cultural and social norms. I use Rosenwein's concept of emotional community as a framework to read the conteuses' tales as a conversational exchange between a group of writers. Scheer's theorization of emotion as a form of practice helps explain how the conteuses' tales produced emotion norms as accounts of "things people do *in order to* have emotions."[50] This book conceptualizes the accounts of love in the conteuses' tales as emotion scripts for the performance of love in courtship and marriage in seventeenth-century France.

The term *emotion script* is designed to focus attention on the relationship between the conteuses' tales and gendered social norms governing expectation about the role of love in courtship and marriage in seventeenth-century France. It is influenced by Rosenwein's and Scheer's theories of emotion as it is based on the idea that it is not possible to separate the embodied experience of emotion from the social context in which that experience occurs. Rosenwein briefly discusses the idea that the expression of emotion creates scripts in her 2005 article "Problems and Methods in the History of Emotions." She uses the term *script* in a discussion emphasizing the social role of emotions as interactions that negotiate social relationships.[51] For Rosenwein, emotion scripts provide evidence about the norms shaping emotional expression at a particular moment in time in the sense that multiple emotional responses are always available to us, but our choice of response is influenced by our social relationships. She suggests that the emotional communities to which we belong "help determine which responses win out—and which ones are never tried."[52] The key issue for Rosenwein is not whether a particular emotional response is authentic but why certain norms of emotional expression are preferred over others. The script metaphor focuses attention on this question by emphasizing the connection between individual emotional responses and social norms for the expression of emotion. The strength of this approach is that it focuses attention on variation in patterns of emotion in different historical communities. It does, however, struggle to provide a coherent explanation of how emotion norms change over time. Rosenwein suggests that emotional communities are agents of change in that they influence shifts in emotion norms when they change or become less dominant or when they are replaced by a new or previously marginal emotional community.[53] But this does not explain how emotional communities become ascendant, nor how or why emotional communities change their emotion scripts.[54]

My use of the term *emotion script* goes beyond Rosenwein's focus on social communities to draw attention to the fact that individual people perform emotion norms and that this performativity provides space for individual agency in the development of emotion norms. In choosing to perform an emotion script, an individual might replicate the script in accordance with its terms and thus reinscribe the emotion norms expressed in that script. Another person might choose to deviate from an emotion script and therefore challenge or question the script's emotion norms. In deviating from a script, an individual may modify or adapt the script and thus revise the emotion norms expressed by it, or they might completely rewrite the norms and create a new emotion script. If other people accept the new emotion script, the emotion norms in that emotional community change. The degree of change is determined by whether the script is revised or reinterpreted: revisions modify emotion norms; reinterpretations transform them. Scheer's idea of emotions as practices shares the idea that people perform rather than merely possess or passively experience emotions. This theory applies Pierre Bourdieu's concept of *habitus* to emotion to focus attention on the *doing* of emotions rather than the *having* of emotions. This approach to emotion historicizes the body by arguing that emotions are "acts of consciousness," and that emotional practices are "things people do *in order to* have emotions."[55] This approach to emotion rejects the Cartesian mind/body and reason/emotion dichotomies as it conceptualizes the body as an active participant in the construction of feelings rather than the external conduit for the expression of internal feelings produced by the mind.[56]

In this book, the concept of emotion scripts combines key elements of the methodologies developed by Rosenwein and Scheer to suggest that emotion scripts are norms of emotional expression learned by members of an emotional community. They are the ways in which groups of people articulate the shared system of feeling that transforms them from a social community to an emotional community. To use Rosenwein's description, emotional communities are "groups in which people adhere to the same norms of emotional expression and value—or devalue—the same or related emotions."[57] Emotion scripts play a vital role in the formation of emotional communities because they are, to use Scheer's terminology, "the things people do" to show their membership of an emotional community. Performance of an emotion script allows members of an emotional community to embody the emotional response expected by that community. Emotion scripts are practices in the sense that they are learned behaviors that produce emotion. Scheer describes this process as akin to the way a pianist learns to play a piece of music. At first the techniques of expression must be taught and require concentration of effort, but after sufficient practice the body begins to move without the need for conscious thought or effort.[58] This idea of emotions as skillful behaviors that are practiced until they become automatic suggests that we are taught how to experience emotion; it is not a natural or instinctive process. One of the ways in which we are trained how to express emotion is by being taught to perform emotion scripts.

The concept of emotion scripts suggests that emotions are the result of interaction between biology and culture because they are produced by the combined effect of our affective or physiological reaction to a situation and the social norms that determine the range of possible responses available to us. When we examine historical scripts of emotion, we ask why certain responses (emotion scripts) are preferred over others and how the preferred response changes over time.[59] Asking these questions allows us to interrogate the relationship between social attitudes and beliefs about emotion and the embodied experience of emotion. In other words, this book examines the extent to which the conteuses' emotion scripts replicated, modified, or critiqued gender norms for the performance of love in courtship and marriage in seventeenth-century France. This project is motivated by the goal of understanding how their tales contributed to contemporary debate about the nature of love and how it ought to be expressed. I suggest that the emotion scripts in their tales should be read as social commentary on expectations about the performance of love that provide insight into the ways early modern women and men negotiated the gendered power dynamics of courtship and marriage.

In using the concept of emotion scripts to examine the conteuses' tales, I argue that their tales drew on a shared vocabulary of emotion to critique the role of gender in shaping the experience of love by early modern French women. This argument expands on the work of Beasley and Goldsmith in foregrounding the integral role of salon conversation and networks of women writers in cultural and literary life in seventeenth-century France.[60]

My aim is to illustrate how the texts produced by the conteuses shared common features and contributed to the same political project and also facilitated the development of a literary conversation featuring multiple distinct voices. Whereas Beasley and Goldsmith emphasize the importance of collaborative processes of literary creation and criticism in seventeenth-century salons, this book focuses on how the conversational aesthetic in the conteuses' corpus locates their work within networks of salon literary production while also allowing each author the opportunity to develop her own perspective on the gendering of love. I argue that each of the conteuses contributed to the development of a shared lexicon of emotion in their creation of scripts for love that proposed a range of strategies for negotiating the power dynamics of courtship and marriage. The conteuses' articulation of a range of responses to love illustrates the nature of love as an emotion with a history that reflects the political and social context in which it is felt and expressed. The system of feeling that underpinned the conteuses' emotional community was a reinterpretation of seventeenth-century discourses on love that identified the heart as the source of desire for love. The conteuses' fairy tales contributed to these discourses by using a shared emotional vocabulary to imagine different situations for the performance of love in courtship and marriage.

GENDERING LOVE IN THE CONTEUSES' TALES

Love is the most important theme in the conteuses' tales, but their heroines do not always find love with a handsome prince and live happily ever after. Their tales represent courtly or romantic love between heterosexual couples as a multifaceted emotion rather than simply a necessary narrative element in the achievement of a fairy-tale wedding. The conteuses' scripts for love challenge the gender politics of courtship and marriage in seventeenth-century France by articulating a series of different answers to the following questions: How should love be performed in courtship and marriage? How does love affect the negotiation of gender relationships between courting couples and husbands and wives? I interpret the conteuses' different perspectives on love as a series of emotion scripts developed by members of a literary emotional community engaged in a

Part 1

Formation of a Literary Emotional Community

1

The Creation of a Female Literary Community

> Fairy tales [Les Contes de Fées] have become fashionable, and many people of great wit [esprit] and reputation do not disdain using their time to give us many in the simple and natural style that this type of narrative requires.[1]
> —*Le Mercure Galant,* April 1698

In the last decade of the seventeenth century, a craze for fairy tales captured the imagination of the French literary public. More than one hundred tales were produced between 1690 and 1709, and contemporary accounts suggest that this literary fashion grew out of storytelling games popular in salons and Louis XIV's court in the preceding decades.[2] The above report in *Le Mercure Galant,* the worldly literary periodical edited by Jean Donneau de Visé, identifies 1698 as a key moment in the popularity of the fairy-tale genre. It is impossible to precisely delineate the relationship between oral storytelling practices and the emergence of the literary fairy tale, and folklorists and fairy-tale scholars continue to debate the place of oral tales in fairy-tale history.[3] But the significance of the seventeenth-century French fairy-tale vogue as a key moment in the history of the modern fairy-tale genre is undeniable. Charles Perrault, an author often identified as one of the founders of the genre, published his famous collection of tales *Histoires, ou Contes du temps passé* (Stories or Tales of the Past) in 1697. The tales included in this volume are firmly established in contemporary popular culture as classic fairy tales, especially "Sleeping Beauty," "Cinderella" and "Little Red Riding Hood." But Perrault's tales were not produced in isolation, nor was he the first French author to publish fairy tales. His female contemporaries, the conteuses, produced more than two-thirds of the tales created between 1690 and 1709. Not only were authors such as Marie-Catherine d'Aulnoy and Henriette-Julie de Murat more prolific than Perrault during the 1690s fairy-tale vogue, but d'Aulnoy and Murat, along with Catherine Bernard and Marie-Jeanne Lhéritier, were instrumental in establishing the aesthetics and purpose of the emerging literary genre.

Lhéritier was the primary theoretician of the fairy-tale genre in seventeenth-century France. Her "Lettre à Madame D.G.***," which was published in 1696, immediately before the high point of fairy-tale vogue, articulates an origin story for the genre as a collaboration between the "charming ladies" (*charmantes dames*) of the salon tradition and gallant twelfth-century Provençal troubadours.[4] According to Lhéritier, this collaboration breathed new life into an ancient Gallic tradition by expressing the virtuous sentiments of the troubadours' tales using the sophisticated, delicate language of salon conversation.[5] In doing so, salon women used the conversational aesthetic of salon sociability to reimagine the troubadours' tales of courtly love according to *mondain* salon culture. Lhéritier emphasizes the collective nature of this endeavor by instructing her readers to interpret her tales as the first examples of a broader literary phenomenon involving other authors: "But warn your friends not to judge this fashion [fairy tales] merely by the works it made me produce, for they would do it an injustice. They will see a variety of works with different refinements. I am only showing the way to others. Isn't that already doing a lot to be among the first to tread new routes?"[6]

Lhéritier's framing of her tales as an example of work produced by a modern literary community is an important feature of the conteuses' representation of their identity as writers involved in the creation of a new literary genre. The female nature of this genre and its association with the literary salon tradition are key elements of the conteuses' self-identification as a community of readers and writers. The influence of the salon as the locus of female literary creativity in seventeenth-century France, especially the collaborative nature of literary production by networks of women writers, is emphasized in work by scholars including Joan E. DeJean, Faith E. Beasley, and Elizabeth C. Goldsmith.[7] The importance of the conteuses in shaping seventeenth-century literary culture is illustrated by Allison Stedman's identification of them as key figures in a shift in the nature of social interaction in late seventeenth-century France. Stedman argues that the conteuses' tales transformed salon sociability from an exchange of conversation in the physical space of the salon into a socioliterary interaction based on the exchange of written texts.[8] This chapter builds on Stedman's thesis by suggesting that the strategies of authorship the conteuses used to frame their tales created a modern community of readers and writers connected by a shared literary sensibility.

In this chapter I examine the social and literary connections between the conteuses that suggest their tales should be read as the work of a literary community. The first section outlines the chronological development of the contes de fées genre and the conteuses' role in shaping it. The second and third sections examine the relationship between the conteuses and their modern readership of salon women. In doing so, I read the conteuses' framing of their tales as creative works contributing to a shared literary project as evidence of the creation of an authorial identity that reshaped the aesthetic of salon conversation. This framing, which appeared in the letters, dedications, and other metatextual and paratextual material that accompanied the publication of the conteuses' tales, emphasized their identity as modern female writers. The conteuses' self-identification as a modern literary community engaged in the creation of a new literary genre reimagined the principles of salon sociability developed by midcentury *salonnières* to defend the contribution of women writers to the literary field.

MAPPING THE FAIRY-TALE VOGUE IN LATE SEVENTEENTH-CENTURY FRANCE

The first French literary fairy tale, "L'île de la félicité," was published by Marie-Catherine d'Aulnoy in 1690 as a story interpolated in her first novel,

Histoire d'Hypolite, comte de Duglas. "L'île de la félicité" recounts the adventures of Adolphe, a Russian prince taken by the son of the God of the winds to an enchanted island ruled by the beautiful Princess Félicité. The story is told by Hypolite, the novel's protagonist, who introduces it as a story "like a tale of fairies."[9] This story, as Nadine Jasmin observes, is an allegorical or mythological story rather than a true fairy tale.[10] It does, nevertheless, mark the beginning of the 1690s fairy-tale vogue as the first published example of the type of tales popular during this literary craze. The publication of "L'île de la félicité" in 1690 was followed by Perrault's entry into the genre. His famous collection of tales, *Histoires, ou Contes du temps passé*, was circulated in manuscript form under the title *Contes de ma Mère L'Oye* in 1695, before being published at the height of the vogue in 1697.[11] The manuscript of Lhéritier's *Œuvres meslées*, a heterogeneous collection of letters, prose, and verse, including the first three of her five fairy tales, was also completed in 1695.[12] This volume was published in 1696, the same year Bernard published her two tales as stories told by characters in her novel *Inès de Cordoue*.

The years 1697 and 1698 saw a rapid acceleration in the popularity of the fairy-tale genre in France, with the majority of the tales published during the 1690s vogue appearing between 1697 and 1699. This period also saw an expansion in the range of authors to include Charlotte-Rose de La Force, Louis de Mailly, Henriette-Julie de Murat, Jean de Préchac, and Catherine Durand. It also saw the publication of commentary on the origins, poetics, and moral intent of the genre by Lhéritier, Murat, d'Aulnoy, and Bernard. The status of fairy tales as a literary fashion popular with women readers and writers was the subject of multiple reports in *Le Mercure Galant* from the mid-1690s to the early 1700s, several of which appeared in 1698. In February 1698, a note on the publication of d'Aulnoy's *Contes Nouveaux, ou les Fées à la mode* remarked on the favorable public reception of tales published by same author the previous year in her four-volume *Les Contes des Fées*.[13] The same report announced the publication of La Force's *Les Contes des Contes* and praised the literary reputation and good taste of their author.[14] Similar references to the fashion for fairy tales appeared in the April and July editions of 1698. The April 1698 edition referred to the great number of tales produced by people of great reputation and esprit.[15] The particular success of d'Aulnoy's *Contes Nouveaux, ou les Fées à la mode* was reported in July 1698.[16]

The production of tales slowed from 1700, with only a small number of tales created by authors including Louise d'Auneuil, Durand, Lhéritier, and Murat until the end of the vogue in 1709. In 1703 *Le Mercure Galant* published a report announcing the publication of d'Auneuil's first collection of tales, *La tyrannie des fées détruite,* as a work created in the style popular among women in the recent past. Significantly, this report remarks on an important difference in d'Auneuil's representation of the figure of the fairy. Unlike the tales that preceded it, d'Auneuil's tale critiques the absolute power exercised by fairies as a form of tyranny.[17] Like several of her fellow conteuses, d'Auneuil also represents love as a destructive passion, but her negative depiction of the fairy protagonist in the tale "La tyrannie des fées détruite" marks a shift in the genre away from celebration of fairies as muses or sources of female knowledge and wise counsel.

French authors created 104 tales between 1690 to 1709: 63 were produced by the conteuses, 35 by male authors (collectively the *conteurs*), and 6 by anonymous authors. This figure is based on a broad definition of the contes de fées genre as a modern genre of salon literature that used marvelous elements, most often the figure of the fairy, to create stories of romantic love that reflected contemporary debates about marriage and gender. This definition is influenced by a literal English translation of the phrase *contes de fées* as "tales of or about fairies," analysis of the style and key themes of the tales published between 1690 and 1709, and the conteuses' own commentary on the origins, purpose, and intended audience of their tales.[18] I have deliberately adopted a broad definition of the genre because I agree with Jack Zipes that the "volatile and fluid" nature of fairy tales means that attempts to provide a comprehensive definition are likely to fail.[19] My definition therefore includes tales that do not feature fairies or a marvelous setting if they engage with the style inaugurated by d'Aulnoy's "L'île de la félicité" or the gender politics of the conteuses' scripts for love. For example, Murat's "Le père et ses quatre fils" does not feature a fairy, but this was a deliberate authorial strategy by Murat to test whether she could create a happy ending without relying on supernatural intervention.[20]

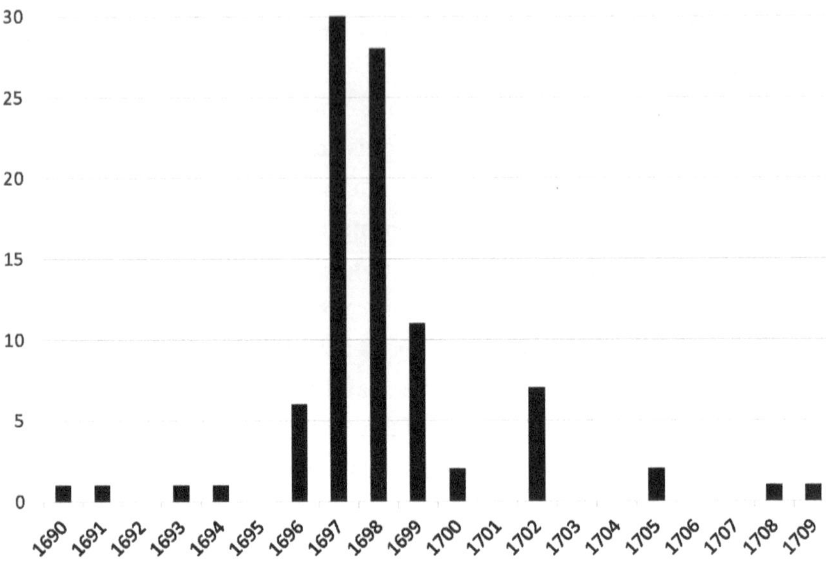

FIG. 1. Publication of tales by year, 1690–1709. Created by the author.

I have provided a list of the tales included in this definition of the contes de fées genre in appendix 1. This appendix is a chronological list of tales that identifies their author and the title of the volume in which they were first published. Figure 1 provides a visual representation of this data. It illustrates the chronological development of the popularity of the contes de fées genre by showing the number of tales published each year from 1690 to 1709. Figure 1 differs slightly from appendix 1 in that it is based solely on date of publication. It does not include multiple entries for tales that were republished or circulated in manuscript form before publication, nor does it include unpublished or undated tales.[21]

Figure 1 illustrates the significance of 1697 and 1698 as the peak years of the seventeenth-century French fairy-tale vogue.[22] Of the 104 tales produced between 1690 and 1709, more than half were published in 1697 and 1698. Fifty-eight tales were published in this two-year period: 30 in 1697 and 28 in 1698. The years 1697 and 1698 were also important in terms of the number of authors contributing tales. Figure 2 demonstrates this by showing the number of tales produced by each author participating in the

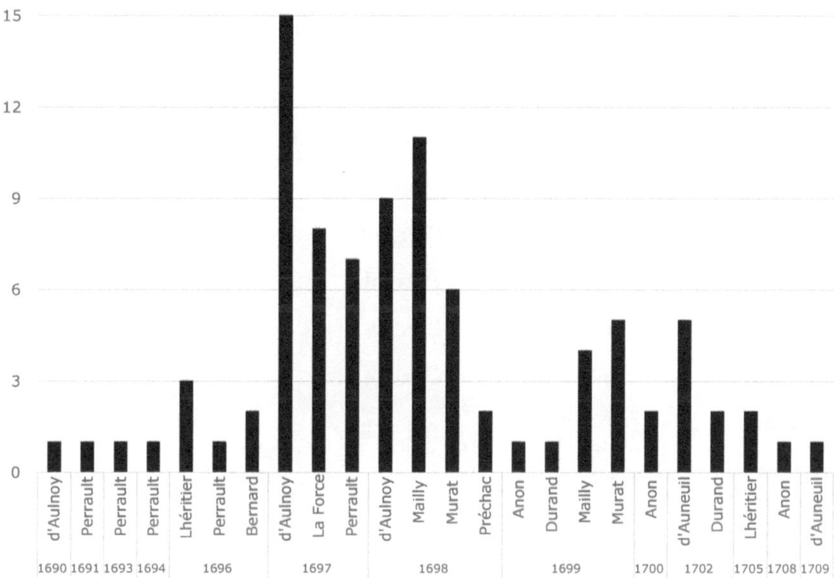

FIG. 2. Publication of tales by year and author, 1690–1709. Created by the author.

vogue between 1690 to 1709.[23] This figure reinforces the importance of 1696–99 as a period in which the largest number of authors participated in the contes de fées genre. Ten authors published tales between 1696 and 1699, including six of the seven conteuses and three of the five conteurs. D'Auneuil is the only conteuse who did not publish any tales between 1696 and 1699. It is not known when François-Timoléon de Choisy and François de Salignac de la Mothe-Fénelon produced their tales.

Figure 2 also offers insight into author productivity. D'Aulnoy was the most prolific author, with 25 tales, 24 of which were published in 8 volumes between 1697 and 1698. Mailly, with a total of 15 tales, is the most prolific of the conteurs. His contributions appeared in 2 collections published in 1698 and 1699. In general, the conteuses' productivity is higher than that of the conteurs, both in terms of individual corpus size and total number of tales. Table 1 sets out a comparison of the relevant figures for each group of authors. This table provides an important illustration of the impact of the conteuses on the development of the fairy-tale genre. This influence is further demonstrated by analysis of the timeline of tale production in figure 3.

TABLE 1. Comparison of the number of tales by conteuses and conteurs, 1690–1709

Tales by conteuses		*Tales by conteurs*	
d'Aulnoy	25	Mailly	15
Murat	14	Perrault	11
La Force	8	Fénelon	6
d'Auneuil	6	Préchac	2
Lhéritier	5	Choisy	1
Durand	3		
Bernard	2		

Figure 3 illustrates the active involvement of the conteuses in the development of the contes de fées genre across the duration of the 1690s vogue. A complete list of the tales produced by the conteuses between 1690 and 1709 is included as appendix 2. Appendix 2 and figure 3 show that as a group, the conteuses produced tales from the beginning to the end of the first French fairy-tale vogue. The majority of tales were published between 1696 and 1699; this period is also significant as a time when participation in the vogue was highest in terms of the number of active authors. The period 1696–99 is also notable for the publication of commentary on the nature of the emerging genre by Lhéritier, Murat, d'Aulnoy, and Bernard, which I discuss in the final section of this chapter.

CONNECTING A MODERN COMMUNITY OF SALON WOMEN

Fairy-tale scholars have engaged in much speculation about the biographical connections between the conteuses.[24] Although conclusive evidence is elusive, it is likely that the conteuses knew each other, at least by reputation, as several of them moved in the same social circles. The connections between the conteuses include family ties and interpersonal and literary relationships. Murat, La Force, and d'Auneuil were cousins, and Durand and Murat were friends and literary collaborators. There is also evidence that d'Aulnoy, Bernard, La Force, and Murat frequented the weekly salon of the

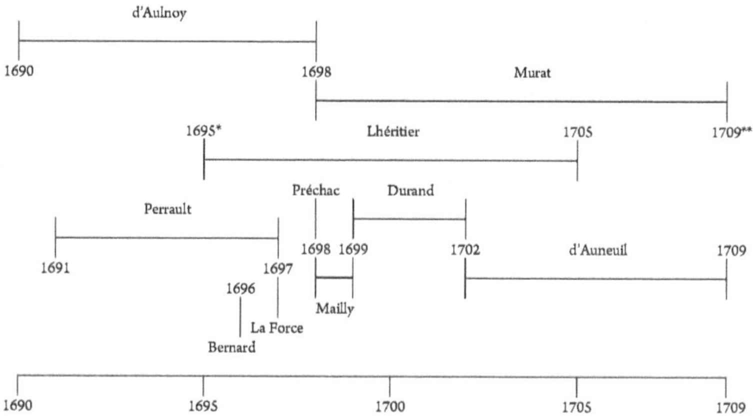

FIG. 3. Timeline of author participation, 1690–1709. Created by the author.

Marquise de Lambert during the 1690s, though it is suggested that she did not appreciate their tales.[25] Lhéritier, d'Aulnoy, and d'Auneuil also ran their own salons. D'Aulnoy's salon was located on Rue Saint-Benoît in Paris and was attended by Murat, whose journal includes an evocative description of d'Aulnoy composing tales in the midst of her salon gatherings.[26] It is also suggested that Bernard attended the twice-weekly salon Lhéritier inherited from Madeleine de Scudéry after Scudéry's death in 1701.[27] The authorial notice in Charles Joseph Mayer's *Le cabinet des fées* describes d'Auneuil's salon as being open to *beaux-esprits* and women writers, although little is known about the attendance at this salon.[28]

The conteuses were also connected by their knowledge of each other's work. Intertextual references to other tales, especially to those by d'Aulnoy, appear throughout the conteuses' corpus. The same characters and motifs also appear in multiple tales. Two of Murat's tales, "Le roi Porc" and "Le Turbot," rework the plots of d'Aulnoy's "Le prince Marcassin" and "Le Dauphin" respectively. In "Anguillette," Murat creates a hero who is a descendant of the eponymous heroine in d'Aulnoy's "La princesse Carpillon." La Force's "Tourbillon" reimagines the relationship between Zéphyr and

Princess Félicité in d'Aulnoy's "L'île de la félicité."[29] D'Auneuil's "La tyrannie des fées détruite" refers to characters from d'Aulnoy's "La Grenouille bien-faisante," "La Biche au bois," and "La Chatte Blanche," as well as those from her own tale "La princesse Léonice."[30] D'Aulnoy and Lhéritier both use the name Finette for two of their most independently minded heroines in "Finette Cendron" and "L'adroite princesse ou les aventures de Finette." Durand's "Le prodige d'amour" inverts the opposition of female beauty and male intelligence in the "Riquet à la houppe" tales by Bernard and Perrault by featuring a handsome but stupid hero transformed by love.[31] Ten proverb comedies composed by Durand are published at the end of Murat's *Voyage de campagne*, and Durand continued her literary collaboration with Murat by revising and paying homage to *Voyage de campagne* in her 1702 *Les Petits Soupers de l'année 1699, ou Avantures galantes avec l'Origine des fées*.[32] Several of the conteuses also used the same Parisian publishing houses. D'Aulnoy, Bernard, Durand, Lhéritier, and Murat published tales with Claude Barbin, a publisher closely associated with modern literary texts including works by Perrault, Desjardins, and Jean de La Fontaine.[33] Lhéritier, Bernard, Durand, and d'Auneuil published with Pierre Ribou between 1680 and 1735.[34]

Like Patricia Hannon, I read instances of textual solidarity in the conteuses' tales as evidence that their literary production was part of a female literary tradition involving both collaboration and individual creative effort.[35] An example of this sense of community can be found in Murat's journal, which is framed as a series of letters to her cousin, Mademoiselle de Menou, between April 1708 and March 1709.[36] In it, Murat tells Mademoiselle de Menou that she has read d'Aulnoy's *Histoire d'Hypolite* with pleasure and recommends that she read it and the tale it frames, "L'île de la félicité."[37] Murat also praises d'Aulnoy's writing style as "natural" and notes that even though she does not have the "elevation" of La Force or the "purity" of Bernard, she writes about "modern women" in an "inimitable" fashion.[38] This comparison suggests that, at least according to Murat, the conteuses were a group of writers connected by their shared interest in fairy tales but distinguished by their particular literary talents. They are the "modern fairies" (*fées modernes*) to whom she dedicated *Histoires sublimes et allégoriques* in

1699. This dedication explicitly distinguishes the tales by Murat's female contemporaries from those by Perrault, which Murat dismisses as the stories of ancient fairies amusing only to nurses and servants. By contrast, Murat praises the tales of modern fairies for "giving esprit [wit] to those who have none, beauty to the ugly, eloquence to the ignorant, riches to the poor, and light to the most obscure things."[39]

The conteuses' contemporary reputation is further illustrated by the literary prizes they won. Bernard and Durand were awarded poetry prizes by the *Académie française*: Bernard in 1691, 1693, and 1697, Durand in 1701. Bernard also received prizes from the Académie des Jeux Floraux in Toulouse in 1696, 1697, and 1698.[40] Lhéritier was accepted into the Académie des Lanternistes in Toulouse in 1696, an honor awarded after she won poetry prizes from that academy and from the Académie des Palinots in Caen.[41] Another literary academy to which the conteuses were awarded honorary membership was the Accademia dei Ricovrati of Padua. D'Aulnoy and Lhéritier were elected as members in 1697, and Bernard, La Force, and Murat received the same honor in 1699. In 1699 and 1701, *Le Mercure Galant* published a list of the academy's muses that celebrated the literary talents of d'Aulnoy, Bernard, Lhéritier, La Force, and Murat along with those of prominent salonnières Madeleine de Scudéry and Antoinette Deshoulières.[42]

Reports on the popularity of fairy tales in *Le Mercure Galant* provided further recognition of the conteuses as a talented group of writers. Early reports announcing the publication of new works by d'Aulnoy and La Force emphasized the popular success of the contes de fées genre as a recent phenomenon and identified the conteuses as the key players in it.[43] Although neither d'Aulnoy nor La Force are identified by name in these reports, the elliptical signing practices used by the conteuses means that it was likely that readers of *Le Mercure Galant* knew or could guess with reasonable certainty the identity of each author.[44] Informed readers knew, for instance, that Madame D** was d'Aulnoy, that Mlle L'H*** referred to Lhéritier, and that La Comtesse de M*** was a coded reference to Murat.[45] The effect of this pseudo-anonymity created a sense of exclusivity that invited readers to participate in a guessing game about the true identity of the author and contributed to a sense that they were members of a select group able to identity and appreciate the conteuses' writing. It did not, as Seifert and Hannon observe, represent an attempt to disguise their authorship, as the conteuses' partial signatures functioned as a means of identifying themselves as a group of women writers.[46] *Le Mercure Galant* reports on the conteuses' role in the fairy-tale vogue reinforced this sense of community and provide evidence of their contemporary reputation as a group of talented writers.

Dedications: Aiming to Please an Illustrious Female Audience

One of the most important ways the conteuses identified themselves as a literary community was in the dedication of their tales to an elite female audience. These dedications share common features: they are addressed almost exclusively to royal or literary women and use similar language to articulate a desire to entertain a sophisticated salon audience. D'Aulnoy, Bernard, Durand, Murat, and d'Auneuil all dedicated their work to royal patrons. Lhéritier's dedications addressed a personal audience and La Force's single collection of tales, *Les Contes des Contes,* contains no dedication. The conteuses' dedications are an example of how seventeenth-century authors responded to uncertainty about the reception of their texts by creating what Roger Chartier describes as a reading protocol (*protocole de lecture*) providing guidance to readers about how to interpret their writing.[47] The conteuses' reading protocols are contained in the paratextual material published with their tales, in particular their dedications. Felizitas Ringham identifies this type of paratext as a typical feature of literary texts published in late seventeenth-century France. Like Chartier, she interprets such texts as attempts to establish generic boundaries, identify the text's ideal reader, and provide interpretative guidance to that reader.[48] In light of this scholarship, I read the conteuses' dedications as evidence of a conversation between author and reader about the aesthetics and function of their tales.

Dedications by d'Aulnoy, Murat, Durand, and d'Auneuil address several of their tales to royal patrons. D'Aulnoy's *Histoire d'Hypolite* and Murat's *Contes de Fées, Les Nouveaux Contes de Fées,* and *Voyage de campagne* are dedicated to Marie Anne de Bourbon, princesse de Conti, the daughter of Louis XIV and Louise de La Vallière and the widow of Louis Armand, prince de Conti. D'Aulnoy's letter of dedication in *Histoire d'Hypolite* expresses her wish that taking a few moments to read the novel will give the princess pleasure.[49] Each of Murat's dedications is a rondeau that extravagantly praises the beauty, charm, and esprit of the princess, whom Murat likens to Venus, the mother of Cupid.[50] The second of Murat's dedicatory poems, which was published in *Les Nouveaux Contes de Fées*, offers her tales to the princess as a fairy gift designed to give her pleasure. This dedication claims that Murat's work has been endorsed by a fairy who encourages her "to make Tales of Us" ("[d]e faire des Contes de Nous").[51] D'Aulnoy's dedication of *Les Contes de Fées* and *Contes Nouveaux, ou les Fées à la mode* follows the same pattern. She expresses a desire to please and entertain in her letter of dedication to Élisabeth-Charlotte de Bavière, the second wife of Louis XIV's brother, Philippe de France, who was known as both Princesse Palatine and the Duchesse d'Orléans.[52] Durand's *Les Petits Soupers de l'année 1699* and d'Auneuil's *La tyrannie des fées détruite* are dedicated to Princesse Palatine and Marie Adélaïde de Savoie, duchesse de Bourgogne, the wife of Louis XIV's grandson, Louis, duc de Bourgogne respectively. Neither Durand nor d'Auneuil comment on the reason for these dedications.

The articulation of a desire to please female readers appears in Murat's dedicatory epistle in *Histoires sublimes et allégoriques*. This dedication is addressed to Murat's fellow conteuses and likens their role as authors to the role played by modern fairies in transforming the lives of the ugly, ignorant, and poor.[53] This dedication echoes the language d'Aulnoy used in her 1697 dedication to Princesse Palatine, which compared the marvelous qualities of the princess to those possessed by fairy queens.[54] Both dedications suggest that there is a close association between the women for whom d'Aulnoy and Murat wrote—fairy-like royal queens and female fairy-tale writers—and the marvelous atmosphere of the "Empire de Féerie" (fairy empire) in their tales.[55] Ruth Bottigheimer and Sophie Raynard claim that the "flowery language" of d'Aulnoy's dedications is characteristic of the style of dedications from this period.[56] However, the hyperbolic language used by d'Aulnoy and Murat does not lessen the significance of their identification of their dedicatees with the powerful female figure of the fairy. In doing so, d'Aulnoy and Murat identified an illustrious female audience as their intended readers. They aimed to entertain these readers by writing stories they would be interested in reading.

Bernard dedicated her *Les malheurs de l'amour* novel series to royal patrons, but the style and tone of her dedications differ from those of d'Aulnoy and Murat. The first two novels in the series, *Éléonor d'Yvrée* and *Le comte d'Amboise,* are dedicated to Marie-Anne Christine de Bavière, madame la Dauphine, the wife of Louis XIV's eldest son. The third and final novel, *Inès de Cordoue,* in which Bernard includes the tales "Le prince Rosier" and "Riquet à la houppe," is dedicated to Louis XIV's six-month-old grandson.[57] Bernard's dedications, like those by d'Aulnoy and Murat, express a desire to please her royal patrons, but Bernard's praise of her patrons is more restrained than the effusive compliments proffered by d'Aulnoy and Murat. Bernard does not draw any comparison between the characters in her novels and the personal qualities of her royal patrons. The dedication in *Éléonor d'Yvrée* refers to Bernard's respect for her royal patron and her fear that her work will not receive the approval of the princess.[58] The dedication in *Le comte d'Amboise* expresses Bernard's gratitude for the princess' goodness toward her first novel and asks for her continued patronage.[59] This dedication appeals to Bernard's royal patron as a sympathetic audience and suggests that the subject matter of the novel will be understood by few people, namely, royal persons in whose souls one can find "great emotion" (*les grands sentiments*).[60] These differences in style may be due to the fact that Bernard's first two novels were published in 1687 and 1689, which was before the increased popularity of the figure of the fairy in the 1690s. Moreover, Bernard's third novel is dedicated to a baby, Monseigneur Le Prince de Dombes, a dedicatee whose age and sex did not invite comparison to the figure of the fairy.

Lhéritier's dedications are addressed to a diverse personal audience. The first three tales published in *Oeuvres meslées* are dedicated to Mademoiselle Perrault, daughter of Charles Perrault ("Marmoisan"); one of Lhéritier's patrons, Madame la Duchesse d'Épernon ("Les enchantements de l'éloquence"); and Murat ("L'adroite princesse"). The precise relation between Lhéritier and Perrault remains unclear, although it is generally accepted that they were related. According to Seifert, Lhéritier's mother,

Françoise Le Clerc, was either the niece or sister of Perrault's mother, Paquette Leclerc.[61] Very little is known about Perrault's daughter. There is no record of her in the Church of Saint-Eustache, where Perrault's three sons were baptized, and Lhéritier's dedication of "Marmoisan" to Mademoiselle Perrault is traditionally cited as the only contemporaneous document referring to her existence.[62] However, recent archival work by Volker Schröder has uncovered notarial documents in the Archives Nationales that confirm Mademoiselle Marie-Madeleine Perrault did indeed exist, as well as evidence of an ongoing dispute within the family about her inheritance.[63] Lhéritier's final two tales, which are embedded in a framing narrative in her 1705 *La tour ténébreuse et les jours lumineux*, are dedicated to her primary patron, Madame la Duchesse de Nemours Marie d'Orléans de Longueville.[64]

Like d'Aulnoy, Murat, and Bernard, Lhéritier uses her dedications to articulate a desire to give pleasure to her readers. She also explicitly evokes the salon milieu from which the 1690s fairy-tale vogue emerged. In her dedication to Mademoiselle Perrault, Lhéritier states that the tale of "Marmoisan" was inspired by a salon storytelling session in which Perrault's tales were praised and new tales invented.[65] She describes her version of the tale as a spontaneous embellishment of a story she heard from her nursemaid as a child.[66] In the preface to "Les enchantements de l'éloquence" and the afterword to "L'adroite princesse," Lhéritier identifies stories told by medieval Provençal troubadours as her source material.[67] In doing so, Lhéritier represents fairy tales as a collaboration between salon women writers and the medieval troubadours who reimagined medieval tales of courtly love according to the conversational aesthetic of salon sociability. But even as Lhéritier's commentary on the fairy-tale genre associated it with oral traditions of tale-telling, her insistence on her identity as a writer and the nature of her stories as literary texts gave literary form to the aesthetic of salon conversation. Lhéritier's dedications make it clear that she aims to entertain an audience of readers rather than a circle of listeners. The final section of this chapter explores the relationship between this transformation in salon sociability and the strategies of authorship the conteuses use to frame their tales as individual creative works.

SALON SOCIABILITY AND FEMALE LITERARY CREATIVITY

> We write to instruct and to entertain ourselves; we also write to instruct and entertain our friends. . . . What does it matter if people without taste are not pleased with works that are not made for them?[68]
>
> —Lhéritier, "Lettre à Madame D.G.***"

Lhéritier's bold assertion that she and her female contemporaries write for themselves and not for the benefit of unsympathetic critics offers important insight into their motivation and intended audience. Lhéritier's use of the plural pronouns "we" and "our" and her rejection of the opinion of "people without taste" identifies this shared literary project with the "charming ladies" (*charmantes dames*) of the literary salon tradition.[69] Yet even as Lhéritier evokes the collaborative mode of literary production in seventeenth-century French salons, she insists on the literary nature of fairy tales as modern texts produced by individual writers. She identifies her ideal audience as a network of readers and correspondents connected by a shared literary sensibility that emerged from the seventeenth-century literary salon, a circle broader than the salon audience who listened to her tales in person. Stedman argues that the tales created by Lhéritier and her literary contemporaries functioned as instruments of sociability that replaced physical interaction in the space of the salon as the locus of literary creativity in seventeenth-century France. She reads their tales as markers of a transition from an oral-collective mode of collaborative literary production in spaces such as the salon, to acts of individual literary creativity mediated by the exchange and discussion of texts.[70]

Lhéritier's representation of herself as a modern author engaged in the creation of literary texts for a sophisticated female audience marks a key shift from d'Aulnoy's emphasis on the oral origins of the fairy-tale genre in *Histoire d'Hypolite.* D'Aulnoy's framing of "L'île de la félicité" as a spontaneous storytelling performance functions as an example of what Stedman has described as a tradition of "literary orality" in seventeenth-century salon literature.[71] D'Aulnoy's evocation of salon storytelling games sees the novel's protagonist, Hypolite, who entered a convent disguised as a painter's assistant in search of Julie, the novel's virtuous heroine, tell the tale to entertain an abbess sitting for her portrait. Hypolite is reluctant to satisfy the abbess's demand to be entertained with a story until he realizes that his silence risks displeasing the woman who has the power to determine his social position within the convent. The story he tells, "L'île de la félicité," pleases the abbess so much that she immediately sends him to Julie's chamber, thus ending the separation of the lovers and facilitating a happy ending to the novel.[72] The abbess's delight upon hearing "L'île de la félicité" characterizes her as the ideal audience for appreciating this first literary telling of a fairy tale. Hypolite's mastery of conversation is the reason for her delight. She praises him for his manner of speaking, and then sends him directly to Julie as a form of entertainment more amusing than a book.[73]

D'Aulnoy's framing of "L'île de la félicité" as a tale told in a setting reminiscent of a salon identifies it as a textual recreation of the conversational aesthetic of the salon. Stedman suggests that this framing sought to reinvent salon conversation by transforming the oral eloquence of the salon into a socioliterary exchange mediated by text.[74] One of the few documented accounts of the presence of fairy tales in salon conversation is the oft-cited letter by Marie de Rabutin-Chantal, marquise de Sévigné, to her daughter dated August 6, 1677: "Madame de Coulanges . . . was willing to share with us an example of one of the stories used to amuse women of Versailles [women of the upper nobility] . . . and told us about a green island, where a princess more radiant than the sun was being brought up; it was the fairies who breathed life into her at every moment. The Prince of Delights was her lover: both of them arrived one day in a crystal ball . . . It was a magnificent spectacle."[75] This account of the migration of tales from salon to salon through the person of the storyteller emphasizes the importance of the physical space of the salon as a place of conversation and the popularity of tale-telling as a form of entertainment. A fictionalized account of this type of tale-telling appears in d'Aulnoy's 1691 pseudo-memoir *Relation du voyage d'Espagne*, which is comprised of a series of letters addressed to the narrator's cousin in Paris.[76] D'Aulnoy's text includes several references to stories the narrator is told during her travels.[77] Her third letter recounts a

TABLE 2. Framing structure in volumes 3 and 4 of d'Aulnoy's *Les Contes des Fées* (1697)

VOL. 3	**Saint-Cloud**	**Don Gabriel Ponce de Leon**	Le Mouton
			Finette Cendron
			Fortunée
VOL. 4		Babiole	
		Don Fernand de Tolède	Le Nain Jaune
			Serpentin Vert

conversation in which she is told the fairy-tale like story of Mira, a princess so beautiful that all who see her fall in love with her.[78] Although d'Aulnoy's narrator does not herself believe the story, she nevertheless takes pleasure in telling it and tailors her version of the tale to suit her audience by omitting details she fears will bore her cousin.[79] In this account of the narrator's ambivalent response to the tale she recounts, d'Aulnoy creates a figure who embodies the authorial anxieties she articulates in her dedications. D'Aulnoy as narrator and d'Aulnoy as author both seek to transpose oral fairy tales into entertaining literary texts.

D'Aulnoy's transfiguration of salon sociability into a new literary mode is further developed in the Saint-Cloud narrative in volumes 3 and 4 of her 1697 *Les Contes de Fées*. As in *Histoire d'Hypolite*, d'Aulnoy presents the tales in these volumes as stories read aloud to an appreciative audience. However, the character who recounts tales in the Saint-Cloud narrative marks a shift in d'Aulnoy's representation of the contes de fées genre as she replaces the male protagonist in *Histoire d'Hypolite* with Madame D, a celebrated author who reads stories aloud from her notebook. In writing herself into the Saint-Cloud narrative, d'Aulnoy creates a double frame for her tales that reinforces their status as literary texts by offering a fictionalized account of her literary process. The first part of this framing sees Madame D read two Spanish novellas, "Don Gabriel Ponce de Leon" and "Don Fernand de Tolède," to her companions during an excursion to the chateau of Saint-Cloud. The second part of the framing sees characters within the novellas read tales to a circle of listeners. Table 2 provides a visual representation of this framing structure.

The salon-like environments created by d'Aulnoy in *Les Contes des Fées* differ from the storytelling scene in *Histoire d'Hypolite* in their representation of the process of creative inspiration. Unlike Hypolite, who searches his memory for a story he can recount, Madame D and the characters in her novellas read stories that have been produced by prior creative effort and written down. In creating the character of Madame D, d'Aulnoy emphasizes her ability to exercise control over her stories as their author. It is Madame D who decides when and how to share her creative efforts with the group visiting the chateau of Saint-Cloud. When the group first arrives, Madame D sends her companions away to explore the grounds of the chateau and while she waits by a fountain hoping to be visited by one of her literary muses. Before leaving, one of Madame D's companions, Monsieur de Saint-P——, gives her a copy of *Contes des Fées* to amuse her if the woodland creatures she anticipates do not appear. In a not so subtle act of self-promotion, Madame D agrees that the book would indeed amuse her if she had not written it. The gesture proves unnecessary as Madame D is visited by the nymph of Saint-Cloud, but the nymph disappears when she hears Madame D's companions returning. In interrupting the exchange between Madame D and the nymph, d'Aulnoy withholds the details of her source material from her audience. Madame D is the only person privy to her the exact nature of her conversation with her muse, and when her audience requests to hear a fairy tale, Madame D reads them stories already written in her notebook, one of which she claims is an original tale.[80]

D'Aulnoy's representation of her tales as texts read aloud to a salon-like gathering appears again in the novella of "Le Nouveau Gentilhomme Bourgeois," which frames the tales in volumes 2, 3, and 4 of *Contes Nouveaux, ou les Fées à la mode* (1698).[81] In each framing narrative, praise of d'Aulnoy's literary talents by their first (fictional) audience foreshadows the laudatory tone of *Le Mercure Galant*.[82] The characters in "Don Gabriel Ponce de Leon," "Don Fernand de Tolède," and "Le Nouveau Gentilhomme Bourgeois" respond enthusiastically by thanking the teller for the pleasure the tale has given them. In "Don Gabriel Ponce de Leon," Doña Juana applauds

"Le Mouton" as "the most beautiful romance in the world."[83] The tale she tells, "Finette Cendron," is received as "gallant" and "well told," although it remains an open question whether this praise is sincere as Doña Juana is not a sympathetic character.[84] The teller of "Fortunée" is praised for her ability to create value from the "smallest trifles."[85] The tales interpolated in the "Don Fernand de Tolède" novella, "Le Nain Jaune" and "Serpentin Vert," are received with pleasure by their listeners, but their appreciation is quite subdued in comparison to the enthusiastic responses in "Le Nouveau Gentilhomme Bourgeois."[86] In this novella, the charm of "La Chatte Blanche" provokes a death-like reverie of rapture, whereas "Belle Belle, ou le chevalier Fortuné" elicits tender tears.[87] "Le Pigeon et la Colombe" is applauded as a perfect work, and enthusiastic admiration of "La princesse Belle Étoile et le prince Chéri" ends with the physical comedy of listeners tumbling into each other and falling to the ground.[88] "Le prince Marcassin" makes the company forget that they are waiting for dinner, and "Le Dauphin" is effusively praised by all.[89]

D'Aulnoy's creation of a fictional community of readers and writers who express appreciation for fairy tales models the response of her ideal reader. Bernard, Durand, and Murat use similar framing strategies by introducing their tales in the midst of conversation about the merits and aesthetic purpose of fairy tales. It is through these conversations that each author offers her take on how readers should interpret her contribution to the contes de fées genre. Bernard's *Inès de Cordoue* presents "Le prince Rosier" and "Riquet à la houppe" as stories told by rival ladies-in-waiting for the amusement of their queen. This royal audience, Elisabeth of Valois, the third wife of Philip II of Spain, articulates two aesthetic principles for judging the success of the tales: implausibility and naturalness of emotion.[90] Durand's *La Comtesse de Mortane* frames her first tale, "La Fée Lubantine," as a story told by a marquis impersonating a conteuse from Gascony in order amuse the eponymous heroine of the novel. This narrator offers his tale as a reflection on the corrupting influence of the absolute power wielded by fairies.[91] Murat's *Voyage de campagne* frames her fairy tale without a fairy, "Le père et ses quatre fils," as a story told to a small group of aristocrats gathered in a country chateau a day's journey north-east of Paris. Murat's narrator presents this story as her version of a text she had heard recounted in a well-known salon.[92]

In their recreation of salon conversation as a frame for their published tales, d'Aulnoy, Bernard, Durand, and Murat reimagine salon sociability as a literary practice. This shift in the mode of salon literary production is illustrated by Murat's description of d'Aulnoy's practice of writing during salon gatherings: "she [d'Aulnoy] wrote as I do now according to her whim and in the midst of the noise of a thousand people who came to her home."[93] In contrast to the collaborative mode of salon literary production in the middle of the seventeenth century, d'Aulnoy and Murat write as individual authors surrounded by salon conversation. They create texts to entertain their salon audience, and the role of this audience is to appreciate their work rather than contribute to its production. The relationship between audience and author is exemplified by the narrators created by d'Aulnoy, Bernard, Durand, and Murat. In d'Aulnoy's and Bernard's framing narratives, interaction between narrator and audience is limited to discussion of a tale after it has been told. The audience to whom each narrator speaks does not contribute to the composition of the tale. In Durand's *La Comtesse de Mortane,* in which the telling of "La Fée Lubantine" is interrupted by conversation with the audience, the narrator claims the tale as his own creative work. He responds to the first interruption, a suggestion that the fairy figure in the tale "perfectly resembled" the marquise he is trying to woo, by identifying a particular difference between the marquise and the fairy.[94] He then interrupts the tale himself in order to make sure that he gives his hero a form that is pleasing to the marquise.[95] In each instance, Durand's narrator asserts control over the form and content of his tale. In *Voyage de campagne,* Murat's narrator offers to share a fairy tale with a circle of listeners on the condition that her audience accept her right to make changes to and embellish her source.[96]

The paratexts and metatextual commentary produced by Lhéritier and Murat provide the strongest advocacy for female literary creativity. Their tales offer a vision of salon sociability that promotes the literary activities of salon women as modern, creative authors. Lhéritier represents herself as a translator and a historian bringing medieval sources to a modern literary audience.[97] She identifies two different sources as her inspiration: oral stories inherited from Provençal troubadours and medieval manuscripts. In *Œuvres meslées,* Lhéritier names chronicles and stories she heard as a child as the sources for her tales.[98] In *La tour ténébreuse,* she claims that the tales interpolated in this volume are stories told by Richard the Lionheart to Blondel de Nesle and recorded in a fourteenth-century manuscript.[99] In identifying historical texts as her sources, Lhéritier represents herself as an impartial truth-teller. In "Les enchantements de l'éloquence," Lhéritier emphasizes her fidelity to her source texts: "I recount only what is in my chronicle; I am a historian, and a historian must not take sides."[100] However, Lhéritier's approach to her sources belies this denial of her creative agency. In "Les enchantements de l'éloquence," Lhéritier continually interrupts the tale to comment on the characters, explain the troubadour origin of the tale, and assert her status as an historian recounting a tale recorded by a source she describes as a *chronique.*[101] In the preface to the 1717 republication of "Marmoisan" under the title "L'Amazone française," Lhéritier openly acknowledges the changes she has made to her source in omitting and adding facts according to her perspective on the subject.[102] Lhéritier also acknowledges the legacy of oral traditions of storytelling but insists on the literary nature of her work. In "Lettre à Madame D.G.***," Lhéritier states that she does not merely transcribe tales told by grandmothers and governesses; she writes to entertain her salon audience, an audience for whom she refines the troubadours' tales by removing the impurities introduced by the "mouths of the lower classes."[103]

Murat emphasizes her credentials as a modern author and the distinctive nature of the conteuses' tales as the work of "modern fairies" in her dedication of *Histoires sublimes et allégoriques* in 1699. This dedication distinguishes between the conteuses' eloquent tales and those by Perrault, which Murat dismisses as the stories of ancient fairies. Murat's criticism of Perrault rejects popular traditions of storytelling as sources for the conteuses' tales. She identifies the sixteenth-century tales of the Italian writer Giovan Francesco Straparola, as well as her own imagination, as the inspiration for her tales.[104] Murat explicitly claims ownership of her tales as their creator; she feels a "fatherly love" (*amour de père*) for them and is willing to defend them against any criticism.[105] Murat attributes any similarities between her tales and those of the other modern fairies (a veiled reference to d'Aulnoy's "Le prince Marcassin" and "Le Dauphin") to their common use of the source text of Straparola.[106] In publishing her collection of tales, Murat responds to Lhéritier's invitation to contribute her own tales to the emerging genre in the rhyming moral at the end of "L'adroite princesse."[107] Murat's representation of the fairy-tale genre as the work of talented women writers reinforces the sense of community created by the conteuses' transformation of salon conversation into literary texts exchanged by salon readers and writers.

Murat's emphasis on the creative role of the author is particularly pronounced in the conversation surrounding the telling of "Le père et ses quatre fils" in *Voyage de campagne*. Her narrator introduces the tale as one she has known for a long time and is willing to share if her audience does not require her to follow the source exactly.[108] When the narrator has finished telling this tale, it receives the obligatory praise from the audience. But the more pressing topic of discussion is the changes the narrator has made to the tale. It is at this point that Murat, speaking through the voice of the narrator, asserts her credentials as a writer who creates stories "in her own style."[109] In this instance, she has lengthened the tale, given names to the heroic couple and other characters, and removed the supernatural elements often present in this type of tale. Murat defends these aesthetic choices as a deliberate authorial strategy designed to test the limits of the fairy-tale genre. In asking whether the presence of a fairy was necessary for the happy resolution of her tale, Murat establishes the role of the modern author as the most important influence on the content of the text.

Unlike the rest of the conteuses, La Force and d'Auneuil do not comment on the nature of the contes de fées genre, nor do they emphasize their identity as female writers. A notice in La Force's *Les Contes de Contes* makes a claim of creative ownership by identifying a source text for "L'Enchanteur" and then stating that the rest of the tales are the author's own invention.[110] D'Auneuil does not represent herself as the author of literary texts. She frames her four volumes entitled "Nouvelles du temps" or "Nouvelles diverses du temps" with authorial commentary evoking the conversational tone of *Le Mercure Galant*.[111] Each volume is dated according to the month of publication, and d'Auneuil positions her literary project as akin to that of the *Le Mercure Galant*. But d'Auneuil distinguishes her reports on salon activities for her female correspondent from *Le Mercure Galant*'s reports on the exploits of Louis XIV.[112] She does not claim authorship of her writing, and she refers to *l'auteur* (the author) of her tales as someone separate from herself.[113] While it is possible that d'Auneuil is referring to herself, this type of distancing strategy does not appear in the work of the other conteuses.

One of the reasons underpinning the different authorial strategies adopted by La Force and D'Auneuil might be that they published their tales after the popularity of the genre was established. This idea is supported by the notice to the reader added by the publisher of La Force's 1697 *Les Contes de Contes,* which refers to the success of the genre as the motivation for publishing tales La Force had composed some time ago.[114] All of d'Auneuil's tales were published toward the end of the vogue from 1702 to 1709, and the entries referring to d'Auneuil in *Le Mercure Galant* suggest that her tales were published posthumously, as a notice of her death was published in January 1700.[115] This did not prevent *Le Mercure Galant* publishing a positive review of d'Auneuil's writing in February 1703. As I discuss above, this report praised *La tyrannie des fées détruite* as an "ingenious fiction" written in a style that had, of late, been popular among women.[116] This review distinguished d'Auneuil's tales from the rest of the conteuses by identifying a thematic shift her representation of the figure of the fairy. This comparison provides further evidence that the conteuses were viewed by their literary contemporaries as a group of writers connected by their shared interest in the contes de fées genre.

The conteuses' reflection on their status as creative authors and women writers offers insight into the ways their literary production was underpinned by their self-identification as a community of modern authors. This sense of community drew on preexisting networks of personal and literary relationships as well as a desire to actively shape the emerging contes de fées genre. The conteuses' engagement with the popularity of fairy tales in

1690s France reshaped the conversational aesthetic of seventeenth-century salon sociability from an activity located in a particular place, the salon, to a literary conversation disseminated by text. The conteuses' insistence on the literary nature of their tales as texts to be read, circulated, and discussed by a network of salon readers is a particularly important feature of this shift. In the paratexts to their tales, d'Aulnoy, Bernard, Lhéritier, and Murat used sociable reading practices to identify their ideal readers and talk to each other about the nature of the genre they were creating. In framing their work as texts created by creative, modern authors for a sophisticated audience of salon readers and writers, the conteuses sought to expand the definition of literary value to include stories by and about women. The following chapter examines the content of these stories, namely their focus on the definition and effects of love. In doing so, it draws on the methodological framework outlined in the introduction of this book to explore the emotion norms developed by the conteuses' scripts for love. These norms are articulated by the ways the conteuses drew on seventeenth-century emotions terminology and engaged with the legacy of influential texts such as Scudéry's *Carte de Tendre*. The vocabulary of love featured in the conteuses' tales emphasizes the significance of the heart as the locus of emotion and reflects the shared system of feeling that underpinned their contributions to seventeenth-century debate about the social and moral codes for courtship and marriage.

2

A Shared Vocabulary of Love

> One cannot have perfect happiness without love, [but] love that is not ruled by virtue causes all the misfortunes in life.[1]
> —Catherine Durand, "La Fée Lubantine"

> Love is one of those turbulent passions that we can rarely hide under the veil of discretion.[2]
> —Marie-Jeanne Lhéritier, "Ricdin-Ricdon"

Love is the central theme in the conteuses' tales, and their scripts for love are underpinned by the idea that love is an essential and inescapable part of human life. It is essential in the sense that life is not complete and happiness not possible without love, inescapable to the extent that to be human is to be susceptible to love. Susceptibility to love comes from the heart, which the conteuses represent as a sensible organ predisposed to seek love. Love at first sight, or a variation on this motif, is the most common way the conteuses' characters fall in love. Love is inspired when the heart is moved by beauty, and this involuntary movement is made visible by the body. Love enters hearts through the senses; it is a bodily experience engaging eyes, ears, mind, heart, and soul. This conceptualization of love as a movement of the heart legible on the body combines elements of the vocabulary of embodiment in René Descartes' *Les Passions de l'âme* and Madeleine de Scudéry's framing of love as *tendresse* in *Clélie, Histoire romaine* (1654–60). The shared vocabulary of emotion in the conteuses' tales provides an example of the semantic clustering Joan E. DeJean identifies as a feature of semantic innovation in seventeenth-century French emotions discourse.[3] In using a variety of nouns and verbs to refer to love—*amour, passion, tendresse, sentiment, inclination, ardeur, désir*—the conteuses' tales develop different perspectives about the nature and effects of love. The language the conteuses use to define and describe love is the focus of this chapter.

The conteuses' tales use a range of seventeenth-century emotions vocabulary to emphasize the importance of the heart in understanding love. Tales by d'Aulnoy and Murat frequently describe love as a *passion* of the heart.[4] D'Aulnoy, Murat, La Force, Durand, and d'Auneuil conceptualize love as a change in or movement of the heart.[5] La Force, Murat, d'Aulnoy, and d'Auneuil also explain love as an *émotion* or *tendresse* felt in the heart.[6] In tales by Bernard, Murat, and Lhéritier, love is a *sentiment* or *ardeur* inspired by beauty.[7] And with only a few exceptions, the conteuses' heroic couples fall in love with a heterosexual partner of equal social rank: most often princes or kings with princesses or queens.[8] Of their corpus of sixty-three tales, only one, Lhéritier's "L'adroite princesse ou les aventures de Finette," features a heroine whose fate is not affected by love; she does not fall in love and is not courted by any suitors motivated by love. Lhéritier's Finette is an intelligent and resourceful heroine who uses her wit, courage, and virtue to rescue herself from the villain of the tale, Riche-Cautèle. It is Finette's creativity and mastery of conversation that shapes her destiny; her agency is not limited by magic or love.[9] Although she does, as one might expect, marry a prince at the end of the tale, this decision is motivated by filial duty rather than affection for her husband.[10] Finette's heart remains untouched by love and her story is an important exception to the usual structure of the conteuses' tales in which development of a romantic relationship between the heroic couple drives the narrative. This narrative structure reflects the pattern identified by Raymond Robert, namely that valorization of the exemplary destiny of the heroic couple functions as a key element of the aesthetic of seventeenth- and eighteenth-century fairy tales.[11] The conteuses' representation of a perfect love between the heroic couple is an important aspect of this aesthetic.

The conteuses' scripts for love developed a shared vocabulary of emotion that reflected the influence of debate about love in seventeenth-century literary and philosophical texts. Their representation of love as a tender, turbulent passion and a social instrument for the negotiation of gender politics engaged with contemporary debate about emotion. The conteuses' choice of affective vocabulary to describe the embodied experience of love has important conceptual implications. Most importantly, it provides evidence of the influence of multiple theories of emotion on their scripts for love. The conteuses' emotion scripts do not embrace the passions theory of emotion articulated by Descartes to the exclusion of Scudéry's psychological definition of love as a rational social act. Their tales draw on aspects of both theories of emotion, thus illustrating the extent to which change in emotion scripts is not a linear progression but an unpredictable process in which old and new norms mingle and overlap. I argue that each of the conteuses draws on different elements of the seventeenth-century emotional lexicon to develop her own perspective on love and marriage and that their tales should be read as contributions to a conversation about the effects of love on the lives of early modern women, as well as individual stories. This conversation about love provides evidence that the community created by the conteuses' socioliterary exchanges was an emotional community. According to Barbara Rosenwein's definition, emotional communities are social communities underpinned by systems of feeling based on shared emotion norms.[12] The system of feeling underpinning the emotional community created by the conteuses' tales was a theory of emotion based on the emotional agency of the heart as the source of human desire for love. The conteuses' tales express this system of feeling by using a shared vocabulary of emotion to define and describe the consequences of love.

This chapter examines the conteuses' conversation about love from three perspectives. The first section analyzes the extent to which the conteuses' scripts for love draw on seventeenth-century emotions terminology, especially the language of embodiment associated with the passions theory of emotion. The second section considers the influence of salon literature, in particular Scudéry's *Carte de Tendre,* in the development of an emotional vocabulary that articulated a shared system of feeling. The third section reflects on the different ways the conteuses used this vocabulary to explore the nature and effects of love and the strategies available to their characters to regulate the expression and experience of love.

PASSIONS DISCOURSE AND THE EMBODIED EXPERIENCE OF LOVE

The conteuses' tales define love using a range of seventeenth-century emotions terminology. The common theme in their descriptions of love is the importance of the heart as the location or source of love. It is the heart that is affected by love, and once touched by love, it exercises a subjectivity of its own separate from that of the body in which it resides. Love moves, animates, and inspires hearts, but it also disorders, enflames, and injures hearts. These metaphorical descriptions of love express several different ideas about what love is and how it is manifested. They characterize love as a human weakness to which even fairies succumb, as a tyranny that cannot be escaped, and as a fire, flame, or poison that animates or injures the heart.[13] The choice of this vocabulary to describe the nature and effects of love is not simply a matter of semantics. As DeJean observes, it marks a shift in the conceptualization of emotion in seventeenth-century France from a passion of the soul to a sentiment of the heart.[14]

The conteuses' preoccupation with love was shared by many of their literary contemporaries. Obsession with love was a typical feature of seventeenth-century French literature such as poetry and novels, especially those by Scudéry, Lafayette, and Villedieu, as well as in non-literary texts including medical, religious, and emblem treatises.[15] Love was identified by Descartes as one of the most important of the passions, and his *Les Passions de l'âme* (1649) contributed to an intellectual tradition that emphasized the importance of love.[16] Other examples of this tradition can be found in Nicolas Coëffeteau's *Tableau des passions humaines, de leurs causes et leurs effets* (1620), Jean-Pierre Camus's *Traité des passions de l'âme* (1614), and Jean-François Senault's *De l'Usage des passions* (1641). In seventeenth-century French literature, the association between the heart and emotion is exemplified by the eponymous heroine in Scudéry's *Clélie,* who cites her heart as the source of her authority on the subject of emotion: "If it is true that I do not speak badly about it . . . it is because my heart taught me to speak well; it is not difficult to say what one feels."[17] The heart is the source of passion in other seminal seventeenth-century texts including Lafayette's *La princesse de Clèves* and Villedieu's *Les Désordres de l'amour.*[18] DeJean argues that identification of the heart as the "control center" of the emotions is a key feature of semantic innovation in French emotions discourse in the seventeenth-century. She identifies three phases of innovation that developed a vocabulary of feeling in which the heart replaced the soul as the seat of the emotions.[19]

Each of the phases of semantic innovation outlined by DeJean introduced new terms into the seventeenth-century emotional lexicon. During the first phase in 1649, Descartes proposed the term *émotion* as a replacement for the term *passion.* Scudéry's concept of *tendresse* or *tendre* emerged during the second phase, 1650–70, as a means of creating an affective typology of courtship underpinned by the notion of *amitié* (friendship).[20] The terms *sentiment* and *sensibilité* became the dominant affective vocabulary in eighteenth-century French literature, but they were not widely used in seventeenth-century texts until the latter part of the century, 1670–95. DeJean associates this third phase of innovation with a consolidation in seventeenth-century affective vocabulary that saw the gradual replacement of *passion* as a synonym for love with a semantic cluster of the terms *sentiment, sensibilité, sentir, tendresse, tendre, amour, aimer.*[21] The conteuses' tales were produced during this period and reflect the linguistic diversity of the emotions vocabulary popular in the third stage of innovation. In my analysis of the conteuses' vocabularies of emotion, I have italicized emotion terms to distinguish between their historical usage and their modern English equivalents. This distinction is particularly important for *émotion*/emotion. The modern concept of emotion as a psychological category of analysis is the legacy of eighteenth- and nineteenth-century debates about the physical and mental states that seventeenth-century French theorists referred to as *passions,* or, with less frequency, *affections.*[22] I have not translated the term *tendresse* and its adjectival and verbal forms as there is no equivalent in English that captures the nuance of this concept.

The semantic innovation proposed by Descartes in his 1649 *Les Passions de l'âme* was unsuccessful in the sense that the term *émotion* never played a significant role in French affective vocabulary.[23] The same is true in the conteuses' tales. The term *émotion* appears infrequently, and when it does, it refers primarily to a strange or elusive sensation in the heart.[24] The term is virtually non-existent in the conteurs' tales. The verb *émouvoir* and the participle *ému(e)* appear only a handful of times in Perrault's tales, and he is the only author to use the term to refer to an effect on the soul.[25] This is at odds with Descartes's preference for *émotion* as a replacement for the term *passion* on the basis that *émotion* conveyed a sense of change or alteration in the soul, as well as the force of emotion as something that agitates or shakes the soul.[26] In making this case, Descartes's treatise drew on the etymological origins of *émotion* as a term referring to political or social agitation (*émotion populaire*), or bodily movement.[27] The conceptualization of emotion as a force that agitates the feeling subject appears frequently in the conteuses' tales. Unlike Descartes, the conteuses use the term *passion* to describe the embodied experience of love as a force difficult to govern, and their emotion scripts cast doubt on his claim that *passion* can be tamed by reason and will.[28]

Another crucial difference between the conteuses' conceptualization of emotion and Descartes's thinking is their insistence on the heart as the location of *passion*. This reflects a long tradition of belief about the affective role of the heart in which the heart functions as both a symbol of passion and the source of vitality and life.[29] This tradition is linked to humoral theory, in particular Galenic medical principles, and can be traced back to classical thinkers including Plato, Aristotle, and Hippocrates.[30] For Plato the heart was the guardian of feeling and the source of the heat of the passions.[31] Aristotle and Hippocrates identified the heart (not the soul or the mind) as the location of consciousness.[32] Robert Erickson and Lucie Desjardins show that early modern views about the heart were influenced by a Galenic-Aristotelian framework that identified the heart as the source of cognition, feeling, desire, and volition.[33] However, Descartes explicitly rejected the heart as the location of the passions. He claimed that the only reason for this idea is that the passions are felt as though they are located in the heart. Descartes argued instead that the feeling of alteration in the heart caused by the passions is produced by a nerve descending to the heart from the brain. He concluded, therefore, that the passions are located in the pineal gland.[34] This critique seems to have had little effect on seventeenth-century French literature, which frequently represented the heart as the locus of emotion.[35]

Ambivalence toward Cartesian dualism and objectivity is further illustrated by the reception of Descartes's work by seventeenth-century salonnières. As Erica Harth has shown, Anne de la Vigne, Marie Dupré, and Catherine Descartes, who were recognized as "cartésiennes" by their contemporaries, challenged the separation of thought and emotion in Cartesian dualism, even though the separability of mind and body supported the intellectual project of the salon and recognition of women as thinking subjects.[36] Moreover, Descartes's critique of the term *passion* does not appear to have influenced the conteuses, as it is one of the most important terms in their shared vocabulary of emotion. In the epigraph to this chapter, Lhéritier describes love as a "turbulent passion" that cannot be concealed from observation.[37] Durand warns that one is not the master of one's self when agitated by the *passion* of love.[38] Bernard blames *passion*, which she defines as the jealousy caused by love, for destroying the marriage of the hero and that of his parents in "Le prince Rosier."[39] This conceptualization of emotion as a turbulent force that agitates the body echoes Descartes's definition of *émotion* as a movement or change affecting the feeling subject. This theory of emotion, which I refer to in this chapter as the passions theory of emotion, was an important influence on seventeenth-century emotions discourse.[40] It emphasized the power of love as an uncontrollable force and is associated with a long literary tradition exemplified by love at first sight and the figure of Cupid and his arrows.[41]

The conteuses' representations of the bodily effects of emotion, in particular the power of the eyes to reveal, express, and provoke passion, are key features of their emotion scripts about the experience and expression of love. Like many of their early modern contemporaries, the conteuses interpreted the body as a surface on which traces of the passions appeared as external signs of interior agitation.[42] This understanding of emotion theorized the body as a site for the physical expression of the passions such as changes in complexion like blushing or paleness, and in the bodily movements of trembling, fainting, tears, and sighs. Movement of the eyes and eyebrows, opening of the mouth, and other physical actions including gesture, posture, and tone of voice were also interpreted as signs revealing the passions.[43] The conteuses' characters display many of the external signs of the passions. Eloquent or expressive eyes that reveal love appear in tales by Murat, Lhéritier, La Force, and d'Auneuil. In Murat's "La fée Princesse," the presence of *tendre* in the hero's eyes convinces the heroine that his heart is not insensible to her.[44] The expression of tendresse in the regard of female characters reveals the *inclination* of their hearts in Murat's "Anguillette" and "Le père et ses quatre fils."[45] Eloquent eyes allow lovers communicate with looks rather than words in Murat's "L'Aigle au beau bec," Lhéritier's "Ricdin-Ricdon," and La Force's "Tourbillon."[46] A mutual expression of joy in the eyes of Prétintin and Nirée, who first meet as children in La Force's "Tourbillon," foreshadows their enduring love.[47] In d'Auneuil's "La princesse Léonice," the heroine's jealous sister sees the prince's secret love for her sibling and his distaste for her in his eyes.[48]

Involuntary bodily reactions such as blushing, fainting, and tears are represented as signs of love in tales by d'Aulnoy, Lhéritier, La Force, Murat, and Bernard. The face is the site of revelation in tales by d'Aulnoy. In "L'Oiseau Bleu," Charmant's love for Florine is broadcast by his joyful expression when the courtiers instructed to disparage her character to him change their abuse to praise.[49] Constancia's blushes and lowered eyes reveals the presence of love in her heart in "Le Pigeon et la Colombe."[50] Blushes are also depicted as signs of love in d'Aulnoy's "La princesse Carpillon," Lhéritier's "La robe de sincérité," La Force's "Plus Belle que Fée," and Murat's "Le père et ses quatre fils."[51] Heroines faint at the unexpected sight or sound of their lovers in d'Aulnoy's "Le prince Lutin" and Murat's "La fée princesse."[52] And in Bernard's "Le prince Rosier," the heroine's tears reverse the hero's metamorphosis as a rosebush by providing physical proof of her love for him.[53]

The conteuses' representations of the embodied experience of love reflect the theory of emotion prominent in early modern passions treatises that emphasized the power of love as an uncontrollable force. Except for two of Lhéritier's female characters, Léonore in "Marmoisan" and Anaxaride in "La robe de sincérité," the conteuses' tales portray the bodily expression of emotion as an involuntary revelation. In d'Aulnoy's "Le Pigeon et la Colombe," Constancia's face betrays the secrets of her heart.[54] And as we saw above, eloquent eyes speak of love without a conscious decision by the feeling subject to reveal the sentiments of their heart in Murat's "Anguillette" and "Le père et ses quatre fils."[55] The bodies of characters in the conteurs' tales also function as eloquent surfaces on which the passions are made legible. Eyes and sighs are more eloquent than words in communicating the heroic couples' mutual affection in Choisy's "Histoire de la princesse Aimonette."[56] The loss of appetite caused by a young prince's lovesickness in Perrault's "Peau d'Âne" makes his parents unable to refuse his request to marry the woman whose finger fits the ring he found in the cake made for him by the eponymous heroine.[57]

The influence of the passions theory of emotion is particularly evident in the conteuses' representation of love at first sight. This emotion script is underpinned by the idea of love as an involuntary and immediate passion. The typical scenario involves a meeting between the heroic couple in which both are struck by the beauty of the other. The heart is moved by admiration, which is quickly followed by love.[58] A version of this scenario appears in tales by all the conteuses. The most common variation to it is love inspired by the sight of a beautiful portrait.[59] La Force's "L'Enchanteur" includes multiple versions of how one might fall in love at first sight. In this tale, the hero falls in love with the sleeping Adelis and cannot resist seizing her in his arms. Fortuitously, the beautiful Adelis had already fallen in love with the prince's portrait, and thus her distress upon waking in the arms of a strange man is short-lived.[60] Significantly, the fact that Adelis's passion preceded that of the prince shows that it is not only the conteuses' male characters who are susceptible to falling in love at first sight. In the conteuses' scripts for love, male beauty is just as important as female beauty, and tales by d'Aulnoy, Murat, La Force, and Durand foreground the importance of the female gaze in their descriptions of the heroines whose passion is inspired by the sight of a beautiful other. As I discuss further in chapter 3, heroines who initiate declarations of love in d'Aulnoy's "La Belle aux Cheveux d'Or" and "La princesse Printanière" do so after admiring the physical beauty of their chosen beau. La Belle aux Cheveux d'Or tells Avenant that she finds him "more beautiful than the sun."[61] Princesse Printanière dates her passion for the ambassador to the moment she saw him mounted on his beautiful horse.[62] Murat's "Jeune et Belle" reverses the gender of the sleeping beloved in La Force's "L'Enchanteur," as it is the heroine who falls in love with a handsome shepherd sleeping in the woods.[63]

Lhéritier is the only conteuse who questions the force of love by suggesting that it is an emotion that can be managed by the feeling subject. In "La robe de sincérité," Anaxaride's "noble education" means that she has an unusual degree of self-control. She maintains a dignified silence in response to unjust treatment by her jealous spouse and gives "no external sign of her thoughts."[64] In "Marmoisan," Léonore "knows how to rule her passions."[65] Although her heart is not insensible to the prince who falls in love with her, she refuses to succumb to the weakness of loving someone whose social status means she cannot admit her feelings without damaging her reputation.[66] And as discussed above, Finette in "L'adroite princesse" does not fall in love but marries to fulfill her filial obligations. Lhéritier also expresses doubt about the immediacy of love. She interrupts the narrative of "Les enchantements de l'éloquence" to question whether, as her source text recounts, Blanche's beautiful eyes did indeed wound the hunter from the first moment he saw her.[67] In questioning the representation of love at first sight in her source text, Lhéritier suggests that if this story is true, the hunter is "as easy to ignite as his gun."[68] Lhéritier's distrust of love at first sight aligns her views on love with those of Scudéry, whose concept of *inclination*, as I discuss below, reframes love as a code of behavior as opposed to the involuntary nature of love at first sight.

Love at first sight is the primary way in which the conteurs' characters fall in love, but the experience and vocabulary of love do not feature prominently in their tales.[69] This does not mean that love is absent from the conteurs' tales, as their characters frequently fall in love and marry, but that their stories include little discussion or reflection on the nature of love aside from references to the association between hearts and love.[70] Most often, love functions as a plot device that either sets the scene for, or resolves, conflict. In both scenarios, descriptions of the cause and effects of love are perfunctory and conventional. In Perrault's tales, a gendered model of love structures the relationship between his beautiful heroines and the male suitors who woo them. This model is most clearly articulated in "Grisélidis," in which a misogynist king demands absolute obedience from the eponymous heroine as a condition of their marriage.[71] Although an extreme example, this tale points to a broader trend in the conteurs' representation of love and marriage as processes of female acquiescence to male desire.[72] For example, in the tales "Peau d'Âne," "Cendrillon," and "La belle au bois dormant," Perrault's heroines do not fall in love so much as they respond to the passion of men who fall in love with their beauty. Their emotional response is given comparatively little attention aside from Peau d'Âne's sadness at her father's incestuous passion for her.[73] The relative passivity of Perrault's heroines, which has been the subject of critique by feminist scholarship, reflects the gendered distribution of power in early modern marriages that allowed fathers and husbands to exercise control over their children and wives.[74] Préchac's allegorical homage to Louis XIV's court in "Sans Parangon" and "La reine des fées" reinforces this gender dynamic by representing marriage as a political negotiation motivated primarily by dynastic considerations.[75] Fénelon's tales contain no substantive discussion of love aside from fairy advice to the effect that too much or too little love is undesirable in a marriage in "Histoire d'une vieille reine et d'une jeune paysanne."[76]

Perrault's representation of male love as passion and female love as obedience frames male volition as the primary factor in the initiation of romantic relationships. A similar pattern appears in Mailly's "Blanche Belle," "Le prince Roger," and "Fortunio" in which heroines respond to questions about their affections by deferring to the authority of their fathers. In each of these tales, the heroines express indirect approval of their suitor by indicating that she would not be unhappy with, or unwilling to obey, her father should he approve of the union.[77] These responses, which I discuss further in chapter 3, provide insight into the filial obligations owed by early modern women to their fathers. Unlike the conteuses' heroines, Mailly's heroines do not use the vocabulary of passion to express their emotions, and the extent to which they exercise influence over the choice of their husband depends on whether their preference aligns with the wishes of their father. This is made explicit by a conversation between the eponymous hero, and the first princess he attempts to woo in "Le prince Roger." Already engaged to another man, the princess is resigned to her fate and tells the prince when he asks her to consult her heart that doing so would only serve to make her more unhappy as she has no choice but to submit to her father's will.[78] Female characters who fail to adhere to this model by actively pursuing the object of their passion are punished for their subversion with unrequited love in Mailly's "Constance sous le nom de Constantin" and Choisy's "Histoire de la princesse Aimonette."

REVISING THE SALON LEGACY OF *GALANTERIE* AND *TENDRESSE*

Salon literature was a particularly important influence on the conteuses' scripts for love. The sociable code of love associated with the literature produced by midcentury salonnières, a code often described as either précieux or *galant*, reinterpreted ideas associated with the courtly love tradition for the modern, female audience of the seventeenth-century salon.[79] Salon reformulation of ideas such as the civilizing effect of love, male subservience to the female beloved, and the suffering of love challenged seventeenth-century gender roles by emphasizing the agency of women in courtship and marriage. It is no coincidence that this reformulation of the gender politics of love and marriage coincided with the second stage of semantic innovation identified by DeJean in which *sentiment, tendre,* and *tendresse* were proposed as possible replacements for the term *passion*. Salonnière reformulation of marriage drew on the development of a new vocabulary of emotion, in particular Scudéry's articulation of tendresse or tendre, to redefine the emotional dynamic between men and women. Consequently, Scudéry is a key figure in development of a vocabulary of emotion that replaced the focus on passion with a psychological definition of emotion as a shared experience affecting subject and object. In Scudéry's ten-volume novel, *Artamène, ou le grand Cyrus* (1649–1653), and *Clélie,* characters are affected by the bodily upheaval of *émotion,* but they also feel, and strive to control, the *sentiments* in their hearts.[80]

Scudéry's suggestion that emotions can be controlled or regulated by the feeling subject is an important divergence from the passions theory of emotion that emphasized the turbulent, disruptive force of emotion as an involuntary bodily experience. It is different from Descartes's suggestion that people can learn to control their passions by the exercise of virtue and reason because his theory of emotion starts with the idea that the passions are fundamentally unruly.[81] By contrast, Scudéry represents love as an emotion produced by the performance of a set of practices.[82] She develops her theory of love in *Clélie,* in which she represents tendresse as a practice that created "a certain sensibilité of the heart."[83] In transforming love into tendresse, Scudéry redefined love as a rational social performance enacted by individuals rather than a powerful force onto which control must be imposed. In *Clélie,* Scudéry proposed *tendre amitié* (tender friendship) as the ultimate goal of courtship, and she created her influential *Carte de Tendre* as an allegorical map that articulated her method for negotiating the passion of love to achieve this goal.[84]

Scudéry's *Carte de Tendre* represents courtship as a journey through a series of towns starting from Nouvelle Amitié (New Friendship).[85] Her allegorical map explores the affective dimensions of love and friendship in the context of a conversation about how to distinguish between the different emotions the characters in *Clélie* feel for different people. In a fictionalized account of a conversation in Scudéry's *samedi* salon, Clélie declares that she does not call all of her friends her "tendres amis" (tender friends) and offers the *Carte de Tendre* as a method for distinguishing between amour and amitié.[86] Significantly, Scudéry uses the term *tendresse* to describe relationships between men and women that are distinct from amitié and amour but nevertheless influenced by both concepts. The association between friendship and tendresse is an important aspect of Scudéry's reformulation of the emotional relationship between husbands and wives. In identifying friendship as the model for tendresse, Scudéry sought to incorporate a sense of reciprocity and equality into the marital relationship. This represented a critical departure from the courtly love tradition that emphasized the fatality of love. Marriages produced by following the path laid out in the *Carte de Tendre* transformed desire into a tendre relationship between equals based on mutual inclination.[87]

Scudéry's cartographic representation of the routes to tendre represents love as a negotiation between male suitors and the women with whom they seek tender friendship. Tendre exists only insofar as it is produced by the actions of the male suitor: he must choose the correct path and regulate his desire by passing through the towns leading to tendre. Significantly, tendre cannot be achieved by suitors who do not follow the courtship practices in Scudery's map, and the power to decide whether a suitor has enacted these practices correctly is vested in the woman being courted.[88] This is represented by the routes to towns of tendre in the *Carte de Tendre* that require suitors to follow a particular mode of conduct. The overland route to Tendre-sur-Reconnaissance requires male submission to the female friend with whom he seeks tender friendship. He must pass through the towns of Soumission (Submission), Petits Soins (Small Attentions), Grands Services (Great Services), Obéissance (Obedience), and Constante Amitié (Constant or Faithful Friendship), and other related destinations, before he can arrive at Tendre-sur-Reconnaissance.[89] In order to reach Tendre-sur-Estime, the male lover must demonstrate his mastery of social activities and character traits prized in salon interaction: Grand Esprit (Great Wit), Jolis Vers (Pretty Verse), Billet Galant (Gallant Letter), Billet Doux (Love Letter), Grand Cœur (Great Heart), and Bonté (Goodness).[90] The river of Inclination, a metaphorical representation of desire as an attraction to or disposition toward a particular suitor, flows through the center of the *Carte de Tendre* and creates a direct route to Tendre-sur-Inclination. However, if a suitor fails to stop at this town, the river continues until it meets the Mer Dangereuse (Dangerous Sea), beyond which lies the mysterious Terres Inconnues (Unknown Lands).

The semantic innovation in Scudéry's *Carte de Tendre* had an important influence on the conteuses' vocabulary of emotion. The terms *sentiment* and *tendre* appear frequently in their scripts for love and both terms are associated with the affective role of the heart.[91] *Sentiment* is used as a term describing a variety of emotional states, whereas *tendre* refers specifically to love. *Tendre* appears as an adjective modifying love, lovers, hearts, eyes, sentiments, and spouses.[92] For instance, the ending to Murat's "Le parfait amour" describes the rare good fortune of the heroic couple's enjoyment of a love that was "as tendre and constant" in good times as it had been ardent and faithful during their misfortunes.[93] In d'Auneuil's "La princesse Léonice," the strength of the emotional connection in the hearts of the heroic couple is attributed to their tendre love.[94] The hero in d'Aulnoy's "Le Rameau d'Or" laments the loss of his beloved, the "tendre object of his love," in a verse he carves into the bark of a tree.[95]

The presence of *tendresse* in the heart or the susceptibility of the heart to *tendresse* is used to describe the effect of love in tales by d'Aulnoy and Murat. In d'Aulnoy's "Babiole," the heroine's heart, which was not affected by her metamorphosis as a monkey shortly after her birth, is overtaken by tendresse for the cousin with whom she was raised.[96] The heroine in Murat's "Le père et ses quatre fils" cannot contain the sadness and tendresse she feels in her heart in response to her father's wrath upon discovering her feelings for the fisherman with whom she spent a year alone on a deserted island, so she confides in one of her ladies' maids.[97] The hearts of the heroic couple are moved first by admiration and then by tendresse in Murat's "Le palais de la vengeance."[98] A heart capable of responding to tendresse is identified as an essential quality in a potential lover in Murat's "Le roi Porc."[99]

The definition of *tendre* as a faithful, constant love that leads to eternal happiness is a particularly strong theme in tales that end with the celebration of a wedding or, on occasion, multiple weddings. Couples whose faithful love survives persecution or tests of separation are united in marriage at the end of tales by d'Aulnoy, La Force, and Murat. For example, metamorphosed lovers are returned to their ordinary human form and marry their respective beloveds in d'Aulnoy's "L'Oiseau Bleu," "L'Oranger et l'Abeille," "Le Rameau d'Or," and "La Biche au bois." Lovers separated by parental disapproval of their relationship are reunited at the end of Murat's "Le père et ses quatre fils" and "La fée princesse" and in d'Aulnoy's "La princesse Carpillon" and "La princesse Belle Étoile et le prince Chéri." The fidelity of virtuous lovers is rewarded with the celebration of a wedding in La Force's "Plus Belle que Fée" and "Tourbillon," in Murat's "Jeune et Belle," "Le parfait amour," and "Le prince des feuilles," and in d'Aulnoy's "Gracieuse et Percinet," "La Belle aux Cheveux d'Or," and "La Grenouille bien-faisante." Multiple weddings are celebrated at the end of La Force's "L'Enchanteur," "La Bonne Femme," "Plus Belle que Fée," and "L'île de la magnificence," and Murat's "Le Sauvage." In each of these tales, the representation of tendre as an emotion that can be managed by the feeling subject is an important element of the depiction of love as a positive experience. It is the cultivation of tendresse that allows heroic couples to transform their mutual inclination into a successful union.

The concept of *inclination* is the key to understanding the subversive nature of the gender politics of tendre. According to DeJean, inclination can be translated as a "penchant" or "propensity" that is related to, but distinct from, love at first sight. In *Clélie,* inclination is a force that justifies resistance to arranged marriages by allowing women the agency to choose between admirers.[100] The distinction between inclination and love at first sight is an important one. Unlike love at first sight, which emphasizes the violent nature of love as an immediate and involuntary passion that seizes the hearts of both partners, inclination allows women to exercise a measure of control over their interpersonal relationships by reinventing courtship as a contractual negotiation controlled by women.[101] Identifying inclination as the foundation for courtship provides women with a justification for rejecting suitors, as Clélie does when she resists her father's choice of Horace as her intended husband.[102] It also provides a method for developing a code of conduct governing the behavior of suitors, as Scudéry does in the *Carte de Tendre.* And while inclination might predispose a woman to prefer one suitor over another, her choice is not inevitable.

The reformulation of marriage and courtship based on the concept of inclination is one of the most important emotion scripts in seventeenth-century salon literature. However, the term *mariage d'inclination,* which DeJean identifies as the legacy of salon criticism of arranged marriages, did not enter the French lexicon until its appearance in the Robert Dictionary in the nineteenth century.[103] This is reflected in the conteuses' tales, which contain only a small number of references to the terms *inclination* or *mariage d'inclination*, even though the reformulation of marriage on the basis of personal choice is a key theme in their scripts for love.[104] The subversive potential of inclination as a justification for extramarital liaisons is demonstrated by La Force's use of the term in "L'Enchanteur" to describe the adulterous relationship between Isène la Belle and the enchanter who seduced her on her wedding night. After being lured from her marital bed by a secret (magical) power, Isène feels such a "great inclination" toward the enchanter that La Force concludes that it is a "natural sentiment" that could not have been produced by magic.[105] This distinction is important as the conteuses' scripts for love emphasize the inability of magic to control love. In "Anguillette," Murat suggests that love is more powerful than fairy magic; once it has seized control of a heart, it is extremely difficult to displace.[106] In "L'Enchanteur" Isène is punished by her husband and son when her infidelity is revealed, but she is eventually reunited with the enchanter. Their "long, ardent and faithful love" is rewarded with permission to marry at the end of the tale.[107] Without the concept of inclination to legitimize Isène's adulterous relationship as a faithful, loving union, it is difficult to see how La Force would have been able to produce this unconventional ending.

The tendre theory of love does not play an important role in the emotional lexicon in the conteurs' tales. The terms *sentiment* and *tendre* appear less frequently in their vocabularies of emotion than in the conteuses' vocabularies of emotion, but their usage of the terms is similar in the sense that both emphasize the affective role of the heart.[108] The term *inclination* appears rarely in the conteurs' tales, and their usage of this term conforms to a more conventional meaning than the one introduced by Scudéry and adopted by the conteuses. It appears primarily as a general term denoting a preference or disposition rather than a justification for the heroine's choice of suitor.[109] For example, in Mailly's "La princesse délivrée," the heroine's father does not follow his inclination for a particular suitor for his daughter, a sentiment he suspects she shares, due to political considerations.[110] This use of the term *inclination*, though it hints at consideration the heroine's personal preferences, reinforces the patriarchal dynamic of marriage by emphasizing the king's role in choosing for his daughter. This use of emotional vocabulary is reflective of a broader trend in Mailly's tales, in which the subversive potential of the tendre theory of love is subsumed within a patriarchal framework. This is most evident in Mailly's deference to the authority of fathers in the negotiation of marriage. The gender politics in his tales, and in the conteurs' tales more broadly, reflect the legal structure of early modern marriage; they do not engage with Scudéry's redefinition of love as tendresse.

The semantic innovation produced by Scudéry's concept of tendre also had relatively little impact on the vocabulary of emotion in the work of Lafayette and Villedieu. *Passion* is by far the most important emotion term in Lafayette's *La princesse de Clèves,* and the maxims around which Villedieu's *Les Désordres de l'amour* are organized emphasize the force of love as a destructive passion. In both texts, love is conceptualized as a passion that seizes the heart and is not subject to control by the feeling subject. The terms *tendre* or *tendresse* appear less frequently than they do in the conteuses' tales, and like the conteurs, Lafayette and Villedieu use *inclination* to denote a general preference or disposition for a particular suitor, either male or female.[111] They also pair the adjective *violente* with *inclination* as a synonym for passion.[112] In their use of emotions vocabulary and their thematic treatment of love, Lafayette's and Villedieu's texts exemplify the passions theory of emotion. We see this especially in Lafayette's representation of the emotional struggle of the virtuous heroine in *La princesse de Clèves.* Although the princess ultimately refuses to marry her lover, even after her husband's death means that she is free to do so, she cannot displace passion for Monsieur de Nemours from her heart. She chooses to retreat from society rather than continue to struggle with the conflict between her emotions and her sense of duty.[113] Unlike Scudéry's *Clélie,* who sought to redefine the emotional framework of courtship and marriage, the characters in Lafayette's and Villedieu's novels struggle against passion and the emotional restrictions imposed on women by the integration of love within the patriarchal framework of marriage. Chapters 4 and 5 discuss the presence of this struggle in conteuses' tales.

THE LANGUAGE OF LOVE IN THE CONTEUSES' TALES

Reflection on the nature, manifestation, and regulation of love is one of the key features of the conteuses' emotion scripts. The importance of this theme is illustrated by the significant role played by the development of a romantic relationship between the heroic couple in almost all the conteuses' tales. Tales by d'Aulnoy and Murat show the greatest variety in the representation of how this love is negotiated by the heroic couple. Idealization of love as a perfect union between faithful, virtuous lovers is a prominent theme in tales that end with the celebration of a marriage, and beauty is an essential precondition to love for all their heroes and heroines.[114] Murat's "L'île de la magnificence" is illustrative of the hyperbolic representation of perfect love. The tale features several couples, and it ends with the celebration of multiple weddings. Murat begins the tale with the birth of two sets of triplets who are raised by the fairy queen Plaisir. The triplet brothers are named Esprit, Félicité, and Histoire, and they each find their perfect match with one of the triplet sisters, Mémoire, Entendement, and Prudence. The brothers are required to leave their chosen partner when they neglect their duties in Plaisir's palace. In the course of their adventures, they reunite three other couples who were separated from their respective beloveds. They also help king Antijour successfully woo queen Plaisir. All seven couples marry at the end of the tale.[115] Similarly, at the end of d'Aulnoy's "Le prince Lutin," all of the heroine's ladies-in-waiting, nymphs from the Île des Plaisirs tranquilles (Island of Tranquil Pleasures), find husbands among the soldiers attending the wedding of the heroic couple within twenty-four hours of meeting.[116]

Several tales by Murat and d'Aulnoy challenge the idealization of love as the ultimate happy ending. As I discuss further in chapter 5, d'Aulnoy's "L'île de la félicité," "Le Mouton," and "Le Nain Jaune" suggest that perfect love is an unattainable ideal that exists only in a marvelous fairy realm. A more profound pessimism emerges in Murat's "Anguillette," "Le palais de la vengeance," "L'Aigle au beau bec," and "Peine Perdue." In these tales, love is a dangerous passion that is more powerful than magic and an inevitable source of suffering for anyone who has the misfortune to fall in love. Murat's fairies lack the power to inspire love in unwilling hearts or extinguish genuine passion; they can only make people worthy of love by giving them beauty and esprit. Such gifts do not always produce a positive outcome for the heroic couple, as we saw in Anguillette's warning about the fatal passion of love in the introduction. D'Aulnoy and Murat also express doubt about the desirability of love in tales that exaggerate the script of love at first sight. In d'Aulnoy's tales, characters who fall in love with a peacock, a slipper, fancy clothes, or a pot of carnations subtly ridicule this emotion script.[117] The dangers of falling in love with a portrait are the subject of discussion in Murat's "Le roi Porc." In this tale, Miris, the heroine's companion, advises the heroine that she cannot be sure if the prince whose portrait she admires has the qualities required to animate his beauty: birth, esprit, and a heart capable of responding to her tendresse.[118] The heroine rejects this challenge to the neoplatonic association between physical beauty and virtue as she declares it impossible that the prince would not be as perfect as his charming exterior.[119]

La Force and Lhéritier present the most consistent emotion scripts in their tales but their representation of the nature of love differs. Love is an instinctive inclination of the heart in La Force's tales, all of which feature at least one instance of a couple falling in love at first sight. Each of her tales ends with the union of the heroic couple, or in the case of "L'Enchanteur" and "La Bonne Femme," the union of multiple couples. Love is an essential element of these unions, and it is the triumph of love over conventional sexual mores that challenges the patriarchal politics of female chastity in "Persinette" and "L'Enchanteur."[120] By contrast, love plays a comparatively unimportant role in Lhéritier's tales. Her heroines use their virtue and education to exercise a degree of control over their emotions, and to the extent that they express love, it conforms to Scudéry's concept of tendre. Herminie in "La robe de sincérité" loves the husband she marries "as much by inclination as by reconnaissance," Léonore in "Marmoisan" is able to control her passion for the prince.[121] Rosanie in "Ricdin-Ricdon" does not love the prince who loves her until his ardent declarations convince her that his love is "sincere and pure."[122] Blanche's eloquence is identified as her most attractive quality in "Les enchantements de l'éloquence," and she feels benevolence and curiosity toward the hero after their first meeting.[123] It is the heroes in "Ricdin-Ricdon" and "Les enchantements de l'éloquence," who fall passionately in love at first sight, although, as discussed above, Lhéritier herself doubts whether love at first sight truly exists.[124]

Distrust of or skepticism about love is a prominent theme in tales by Bernard, Durand, and d'Auneuil. But Durand and d'Auneuil also represent love as a positive, transformative force. In Bernard's "Riquet à la houppe" and "Le prince Rosier," tales I discuss in chapters 4 and 5 respectively, the act of falling in love causes misfortune. Bernard's characters are not able to resist love, and love inevitably leads to jealousy and infidelity. D'Auneuil's "L'inconstance punie ou l'origine des cornes" emphasizes the inevitability of infidelity. In this tale, a king who breaks his promise of faithful devotion to a sylph is cuckolded by a wife who loves his title more than his person.[125] The false illusion of love tricks a princess into marrying a cruel ogre who exploits her labor to amass the wealth he craves in d'Auneuil's "La princesse patientine dans la forêt d'érimente."[126] Jealous love provokes violence in Durand's "La fée Lubantine" and d'Auneuil's "La princesse Léonice," with spurned lovers attempting to kill their rivals in both tales. Unlike Bernard's tales, which present an overwhelmingly negative image of love, a positive view of love appears in Durand's "Le prodige d'amour" and "L'origine des fées." Love cures the stupidity of the hero in the former tale and tames the wandering heart of Jupiter in the latter. Faithful, reciprocal passion between the heroic couple is rewarded with a happy ending in d'Auneuil's "La tyrannie des fées détruite," "Agatie princesse des Scythes," and "La princesse Léonice."

The most important element of the conteuses' emotion scripts is their representation of love as an essential element of the human condition that must be negotiated by the heroic couples in their tales. All but the most exceptional lovers struggle to regulate their passion, and they are unable to rely on magic to produce, resist, or control love. Their hearts seek love without their conscious knowledge or consent, and once moved by love, the body and the senses are implicated in the embodied experience of love. This representation of love does not conform to the "love conquers all" script associated with the contemporary fairy-tale genre. Nor does this reading of the conteuses' tales sit comfortably with the idea that fairy tales offer a timeless perspective on love that can be distilled into a single emotion script. The distinct nature of the conteuses' conversation about love is emphasized by comparison to the comparative absence of reflection on the nature of love in the tales by their male contemporaries. Although the same emotion terms are used by both groups of authors, the conteurs' tales do not engage with contemporary debate about the nature of love or the semantic innovation introduced by Scudéry's concept of tendresse.

The shared vocabulary of emotion in the conteuses' tales reflects a long tradition of debate about the relationship between reason and passion, but this is not resolved by their conversation about love. Nor do they offer a definitive answer to the question of whether love has a positive impact on the lives of seventeenth-century women. Some of the conteuses' heroines successfully negotiate a reciprocal emotional bond with their chosen spouse, but others are disappointed in their choice or fail to achieve the union they desire. The following chapter examines examples of the ways the conteuses' characters use the vocabulary of emotion discussed in this chapter in declarations of love designed to create an emotional connection with their desired marriage partners. This emotional model of courtship identifies love as a prerequisite to marriage, thus reversing the order of priorities in the traditional model of courtship as a social and economic negotiation conducted by the families of the couple. However, the conteuses' emphasis on the emotional dimensions of courtship did not materially affect the distribution of power or the operation of gender stereotypes in early modern courtship and marriage. The form and content of declarations of love used by the conteuses' heroes and heroines reflect gendered scripts about how men and women ought to express love, with male suitors overwhelmingly choosing to speak first and most directly about their love. Female suitors rarely initiate courtship, and their emotional agency is primarily limited to choosing whether to reciprocate a declaration of love. The gendered patterning of these declarations highlights the role of courtship as a social ritual illustrating the patriarchal framework within which early modern couples negotiated their relationships.

Part 2

Conversations about Love

3

Courtship, Consent, and Declarations of Love

The revelation of love is a dramatic moment in the conteuses' tales. It is a crucial turning point in the development of an emotional bond between the heroic couple and a vital stage in their courtship. A favorable response, as illustrated by the following exchange from d'Aulnoy's "La princesse Carpillon," means that a marriage between a courting couple is likely, subject, of course, to successful negotiation of the economic and social prerequisites to marriage:

PRINCESS: Do you love a heart that loves you?

. . .

PRINCE: By thousands and thousands of fires I feel myself inflamed.

. . .

PRINCESS: Enjoy the extreme happiness
Of loving and seeing yourself loved in return.[1]

But if a declaration of love is not reciprocated, the relationship between the couple cannot progress any further. This is a crucial departure from traditional courtship practices in early modern France in which parental consent was most important factor in determining whether a couple would marry. In the conteuses' tales, negative responses to declarations of love identify either a lack of reciprocal emotional affection, or disparity in social status of the couple as the reason for rejection. Whether a suitor can overcome these obstacles depends on the gender of the person making the declaration and whether the author of the tale approves of the match.

In seventeenth-century France, as in the conteuses' tales, courtship was a social and emotional negotiation in which declarations of love constituted performances of social power.[2] Courtship was both a rite of passage marking the transition from youth to adulthood and a series of strategic material and symbolic exchanges between the couple and their families. Marriage was the ultimate goal of courtship, and Pierre Bourdieu's theorization of marriage as the "outcome of a *strategy*" is a particularly apt description, as early modern courtship involved the performance of gendered scripts designed to achieve the best possible match for the couple and their families.[3] The legal definition of marriage as an economic and social transaction subject to parental consent meant that courtship was a public negotiation often arranged by the couple's respective parents.[4] Scudéry's literary representation of courtship as a journey toward tendre amitié in the *Carte de Tendre* challenged this paradigm by emphasizing the performative nature of courtship as a set of practices designed to produce a particular emotional response. In doing so, she represented love as a negotiation between men and women: male suitors could only reach the destination of tendre by performing the emotion scripts of courtship, and the women they courted decided whether they had reached that destination.[5] A similar representation of the performativity of courtship appears in the conteuses' tales. The material exchange of property and other gifts associated with the traditional model of marriage as a socioeconomic transaction is preceded by expressions of love designed to create a reciprocal emotional bond between the couple. This chapter examines the cultural and social significance of declarations of love as gendered emotion scripts performed by courting couples. Chapter 4 focuses on the emotional significance of gift exchange by prospective marriage partners.

Seventeenth-century debate about marriage had an important influence on the representation of courtship by the conteuses. In the majority of their tales, courtship is a private, intimate negotiation between the courting couple. Their emphasis on love as a crucial element of courtship developed an emotional model of courtship based on personal choice of the spouse. The key elements of this model are illustrated by the following narrative sequence. A couple of equal social rank (usually a prince and a princess) and equal physical beauty meet and fall in love at first sight. The couple develops an emotional bond by performing courtship rituals such as declarations of love and the exchange of gifts. After proving their fidelity and mutual affection, the couple obtains parental consent to marry, and the tale ends with a joyous celebration of their union. In this chapter, I argue that this emotional model of courtship is associated with the companionate model of marriage promoted by seventeenth-century salon debate about marriage.[6] The development of an emotional bond between the heroic couple is the most important feature of the conteuses' emotion scripts for courtship, and this goal shapes the way in which their tales engage with seventeenth-century debate about marriage reform. The gendered patterning of declarations of love in their tales illustrates the importance of courtship as a negotiation that established the nature of the marital relationship between early modern couples. The additional of an emotional component to courtship reshaped the way such a relationship was formed but did not fundamentally alter the distribution of gender and class privilege.

NEGOTIATING PARENTAL CONSENT

The strategic significance of marriage as a social and economic transaction had a significant influence on the practice of courtship in seventeenth-century France. Parental consent was the most importance component of this transactional model of marriage. It was codified by the French state as a legal requirement of all marriages in 1639 and enforced judicially throughout the seventeenth century.[7] According to Sarah Hanley, the marriage pact produced by the "Family-State compact" in sixteenth- and seventeenth-century France overruled canon law in order to protect family interests. Clandestine marriages, secret marriages made by consenting couples without parental consent, were prohibited and penalized by deprivation of assets, confiscation of goods, disinheritance, and criminal liability for the capital crime of *rapt* (seduction or abduction).[8] Derogation laws punished *mésalliances,* namely marriages between nobles and their social inferiors, with the loss of noble status.[9] Most marriages therefore involved couples from the same socioeconomic background, who were often also from the same geographic area. Couples did not marry until they had the financial means to set up a separate household, and the median age of first marriage rose from 22 for women and 24–25 for men in the sixteenth century to 25–26 for women and 27–28 for men in the eighteenth century.[10]

The legal definition of marriage as an institution that transferred legal and social control over women from fathers to husbands meant that courtship negotiations focused primarily on economic matters such as property arrangements and the exchange of gifts.[11] Notarized contracts recorded the details of the property transfer agreed by the families of the couple and were ordinarily signed in the presence of relatives and friends in the house of the bride's parents.[12] The role of marriage as a social alliance between kinship groups, which I discuss further in chapter 4, meant that parental consent was more important than love, particularly with regard to the selection of marriage partners. Although parental influence was often exercised in the form of advice or encouragement rather than coercion, parents retained the legal right to refuse consent.[13] Courtship was therefore often conducted in the house of the bride's family after a suitor obtained permission from her father to visit (*la hanter*).[14] When courtship was conducted at rural *veillées* (evening work-gatherings), the presence of family and other members of their community acted as a form of social control over the choice of marriage partner.[15] Early modern couples were not free to choose their marriage partner without performing these social rituals.

Love was not considered an important element of early modern courtship, but couples did expect to develop an emotional connection with their spouse. This might happen during meetings between courting couples in the weeks and days before their marriage, but falling in love was not a prerequisite of marriage.[16] Identification of love as an important feature of courtship was connected to the development of the companionate model of marriage in the seventeenth and eighteenth centuries. This alternative to the traditional, transactional model of marriage redefined marriage as an individual personal commitment to a spouse chosen for the purposes of intimacy and companionship as well as material support and reproduction.[17] The emphasis on love as the proper motivation for marriage challenged parental control over marriage in seventeenth-century France. This had significant implications for the practice of courtship, as it shifted the focus from the social implications of the union to the emotional connection between the couple. However, as Katie Barclay and Nicole Eustace have observed, an increasing emphasis on love did not replace the social and economic dimensions of early modern courtship. In eighteenth-century Scotland, love was a "tool in negotiations of power" that was expressed in accordance with strict gendered scripts. Men offered love to women, and women did not express emotion until agreeing to marry.[18] The gendered performance of love, in particular the active man/passive woman dichotomy, was also an important feature of public declarations of love in courtships in eighteenth-century Philadelphia.[19] In both early modern Scotland and North America, expressions of love were strategic social performances designed to mask the social and economic realities of courtship.

The issue of partner choice was a key topic in discourses challenging the traditional model of marriage in seventeenth-century France. Midcentury salonnière criticism of marriage as loveless unions of convenience that benefited men and oppressed women rejected parental control of courtship and promoted marriage reform allowing free choice of spouse.[20] As we saw in chapter 2, Scudéry's *Carte de Tendre* provided a fictional model for how a courtship based on personal choice might proceed. This model used the concepts of *inclination* and *tendre* to justify the right of women to choose their spouse. It identified the development of an emotional relationship between a woman and her suitor as the reason a woman might choose one suitor over another, and, more importantly, it claimed that the absence of such a relationship was legitimate grounds for rejecting a suitor chosen by a woman's father. In this emotional model of courtship, love is a mechanism for enabling choice of spouse and resisting parental control of marriage. However, the emancipatory potential of love as a panacea for structural power imbalances in early modern courtship is limited. The rhetoric of *inclination* did not increase the agency of women beyond the ability to accept or reject suitors. Courtship remained a male prerogative, and male suitors retained responsibility for initiating courtship and declaring love.[21]

Choice of partner and the tension between female agency and patriarchal authority were key issues in marriage discourse published in 1690s France. This decade saw a proliferation of polemical marriage texts that echoed the mid-seventeenth-century crisis in marriage DeJean identifies as the inspiration for fiction by women writers including Lafayette and Villedieu.[22] Claire L. Carlin suggests that the "nuptial imaginary" of the 1690s fostered a literary creativity in which women writers promoted free choice of spouse by illustrating the tragic consequences of forced marriages. In contrast to the stark pro- and anti-women perspectives adopted by their male contemporaries, who represented marriage as either paradise or hell, women writers promoting choice of spouse, including d'Aulnoy, Murat, and Anne Bellinzani Ferrand, developed a nuanced approach to the issue of marriage reform.[23] Their support for an increase in the agency of courting couples was often accompanied by pessimism about marriage as a source of misfortune for women.[24] This pessimism was particularly pronounced in tales by d'Aulnoy, Bernard, Murat, and d'Auneuil, whose unhappy endings question the idealization of marriage as a loving union.[25]

The most significant feature of the emotional model of courtship in the conteuses' tales is their identification of love as a prerequisite to marriage. Only suitors motivated by love can succeed in the conteuses' tales, and money or property arrangements are not discussed before the development of an emotional connection between the couple. For example, the resourceful heroine in d'Aulnoy's "Finette Cendron" negotiates the return of her parents' kingdom as a condition of her consent to marriage after the hero's parents beg her to marry their lovesick son.[26] Characters who fail to adhere to this emotion script by marrying in order to increase their wealth or status are punished for their mercenary motives. The ogre who marries a princess because of a prediction that she will make him wealthy loses his wife and his life at the end of d'Auneuil's "La princesse patientine dans la forêt d'érimente."[27] An unfaithful, social climbing wife is forced to flee the vengeance of her wronged husband in d'Auneuil's "L'inconstance punie ou l'origine des cornes."[28] Fairies who attempt to seduce heroes with promises of wealth are rejected, as material inducements are considered to offer inadequate compensation for the absence of love.[29] By contrast, the conteurs' tales do not focus on love as a prerequisite to marriage. Although several of their characters seek to marry people with whom they are in love, love does not displace parental consent as an essential precondition to marriage.[30] There is a similar pattern in Lafayette's *La princesse de Clèves,* in which the absence of a reciprocal emotional bond does not prevent the marriage between Mademoiselle de Chartres and the Prince de Clèves. This is despite the prince's desire for a loving wife and his knowledge that his future wife's heart is unmoved by affection for him.[31]

The conteuses' sympathy for an emotional model of courtship does not replace socioeconomic factors as important influences on the conduct of courtship. Most heroic couples marry social equals with the blessing of their parents, and parental consent is almost always sought and rarely refused. Consent is reluctantly given for marriages in d'Aulnoy's "La princesse Carpillon," "Le prince Lutin," "Le prince Marcassin" and Murat's "La fée Princesse." In "La princesse Carpillon" and "Le prince Lutin," parental consent is forthcoming only after intervention by a fairy supporting the union of the heroic couple.[32] The father of the heroine in "La fée princesse" convinces his estranged wife to consent to their daughter's marriage.[33] In "Le prince Marcassin" the hero's mother objects to the inferior birth of his bride, who is the daughter of an impoverished noblewoman and therefore lacks the royal lineage expected of a prince's wife.[34] But the queen does eventually consent to the union because of her love for her son.[35] Couples rarely marry in secret, with La Force's "Persinette" and Murat's "Le père et ses quatre fils" the only tales that feature marriages constituted by physical consummation rather than an official ceremony.[36] The heroines in d'Aulnoy's "Le Dauphin" and "L'Oranger et l'Abeille" refuse to marry without obtaining permission from their parents.[37] The conteurs' tales also emphasize the importance of parental consent, especially for women. Except for Perrault's "La belle au bois dormant," the couples in their tales do not marry without first seeking consent from their parents. Moreover, in Mailly's tales love is unable to overcome the obstacle of a lack of parental consent. In "Le prince Roger," the princess of Barcelona laments her fate as she prepares to marry a man she does not love, but she refuses to act against her father's wishes despite her preference for the hero.[38] The king's decision to kidnap the princess he is in love with in "Le roi magicien" inspires hatred rather than love.[39]

The representation of courtship in the conteuses' tales rarely questions the status of marriage as a socioeconomic union negotiated by families of equivalent social status. Mésalliances appear in only a small number of tales, and the conteuses' heroines are extremely reluctant to marry suitors who are not from the right social class. Potential mésalliances are frequently resolved by the revelation of royal status, much to the relief of parents in d'Aulnoy's "La princesse Carpillon" and in Murat's "Le père et ses quatre fils."[40] In both tales, the heroine attempts to resist her love for a suitor she believes is her social inferior. The eponymous heroine in d'Aulnoy's "Gracieuse et Percinet" objects to the hero's declaration of love until she learns that he is a prince rather than a page.[41] In Murat's "Le Sauvage," the princess heroine flees her father's attempts to marry her to one of his officers.[42] In tales where the threat of mésalliance is not resolved by the revelation of highborn status or the substitution of a more suitable suitor, it is explained as the result of love rather than a deliberate rejection of the social codes of marriage. And even in this scenario, the inequality of rank is most often limited to degrees of nobility, namely to alliances between royals and nobles rather than alliances between nobles and commoners. For example, queens and princesses fall in love and marry men of lower rank in d'Aulnoy's "La Belle aux Cheveux d'Or" (courtier) and Murat's "Jeune et Belle" (shepherd), and both heroines use their social power to elevate their husbands to the status of a king. Kings and princes love brides of inferior social rank in d'Aulnoy's "Belle Belle, ou le chevalier Fortuné" (daughter of a seigneur) and "Le prince Marcassin" (daughter of a noblewoman), in Lhéritier's "Marmoisan" (daughter of a seigneur), and in La Force's "Persinette" (daughter of commoners) and seek to justify their actions by reference to their love and the virtue of their chosen spouse.[43] We see a similar pattern in the conteurs' tales. Mésalliances are rare, and

Fénelon warns against them as a source of unhappiness in "Histoire d'une vieille reine et d'une jeune paysanne."[44]

DECLARATIONS OF LOVE AND THE CREATION OF INTIMACY

Declarations of love are a key element of the conteuses' development of an emotional model of courtship. Whether a public declaration, inadvertent disclosure, or private epistolary confession, the revelation of love is a performative act designed to produce a reciprocal emotional response in the person to whom the revelation is made. The performative nature of declarations of love provides an example of the dynamic nature of emotion scripts as tools of social communication that shape and are shaped by the people who use them. In the conteuses' tales, the form and content of declarations of love are influenced by social expectations about how love should be expressed. In other words, emotion scripts provide guidance to suitors about how to articulate the emotion of love in a socially acceptable form. The extent to which a suitor's declaration of love conforms to norms of emotional expression provides insight into how emotion scripts change over time. Declarations that replicate emotion scripts for the expression of love reinforce the role of emotion norms in shaping the way courtship is conducted. Declarations that modify or refuse to adhere to social norms for the expression of love raise questions about the status of these norms by offering an implicit or explicit critique of their relevance. But this is not the end of the story. Irrespective of how a suitor expresses their love, it is the response of the recipient that determines whether a performance of love is successful. Even declarations of love that perfectly adhere to the emotion norms of the emotional community to which a suitor belongs fail if they are not reciprocated. The way recipients respond to declarations of love is influenced by emotion scripts about who is worthy of love, as well as their own emotional response, or lack thereof, to their suitor. The characteristics of successful declarations of love in the conteuses' tales illustrate the extent to which gender norms shaped the expression of love in early modern France.

In the conteuses' tales, declarations of love are a strategic emotional performance enacted with the aim of creating intimacy between courting couples. The emotion scripts governing this performance develop a strictly gendered code for the expression of love. This code shapes both the style and content of declarations of love by male and female suitors. Significantly, it is almost always the hero of the tale who speaks first, and most directly, about his love for the heroine. Heroines rarely speak of love unless they are responding to a declaration by a male suitor. Declarations by heroes focus almost exclusively on their passion for the heroine. Heroes use the emotion vocabulary identified in chapter 2 to confess their love, offer promises of service and eternal fidelity, and lament the suffering caused by their passion. When heroines do speak first, they focus on marriage as often as they speak of love or passion. Their declarations are more often private than declarations by heroes, with fewer public performances and more whispered confessions. A similar pattern appears in the conteurs' tales. Heroes almost always speak first, and the heroines who respond to declarations in Mailly's tales express their wishes indirectly by stating a willingness to obey their father's wishes.[45] These gendered differences in the expression of love points to the existence of gendered emotion scripts shaping declarations of love in early modern courtship. My analysis of these scripts examines the extent to which they illustrate the relationship between love and power in early modern courtship. In doing so, I am not concerned with whether these declarations were intended to be read as genuine performances of love but with how they illustrate the operation of gender norms in early modern courtship practices.

Bold Confessions by Male Suitors

Heroes initiate declarations of love much more frequently than heroines in the conteuses' tales. This gendered pattern is particularly pronounced in tales by d'Aulnoy, Lhéritier, and La Force, in which male suitors are responsible for the overwhelming majority of declarations. Sixteen of d'Aulnoy's 25 tales, 4 of Lhéritier's 5 tales, and 7 of La Force's 8 tales feature declarations of love by heroes. Tales created by Murat and d'Auneuil also feature active male suitors, although they also include several examples of couples whose mutual love is not explicitly declared.[46] In the relatively small number of tales written by Bernard and Durand, two and three respectively, male suitors court female characters with declarations more often than not, although love is missing from Riquet's proposal of marriage in Bernard's "Riquet à la houppe," a tale I discuss in detail in chapter 4. Appendix 5 lists the conteuses' tales featuring declarations of love by heroes. Almost all these declarations succeed in producing a reciprocal emotional response in the women to whom they are directed. They invariably include a confession of love, but the form of their confessions does not otherwise conform to a particular pattern. The circumstances of declarations vary, including private conversations, letters, public statements, and the recitation of verse or performance of songs. Private conversations are by far the most common method for declarations of love; although letters reveal love in d'Aulnoy's "Le prince Lutin" and Durand's "Le prodige d'amour." A small number of heroes confess their love to a third party rather than directly to their beloved in tales by La Force, Lhéritier, and Durand.

Declarations by d'Aulnoy's heroes show the most variation in style and content. In "L'île de la félicité," Adolphe throws himself at the feet of Princess Félicité to offer her his admiration and love: "I have crossed the world to admire your divine beauty, I offer you my heart and my best wishes."[47] The rhetorical question with which Adolphe concludes this declaration, "would you refuse them?," illustrates his expectation that his declaration will prompt a favorable response from Félicité.[48] In asking whether the princess would refuse his heart, Adolphe is subtly suggesting that she has no good reason to refuse his love. D'Aulnoy's use of the conditional form of the verb *vouloir* (*voudriez*) emphasizes the role of declarations of love as invitations to perform a reciprocal emotional response. This invitation is often accompanied by an articulation of a desire to possess or be possessed by one's beloved. Adolphe offers his heart to Félicité, an offer that is also made by the hero in "Le prince Marcassin": "I love you, and I am offering to share my heart and my crown with you."[49] Percinet in "Gracieuse et Percinet" explicitly states that he belongs to the heroine: "I am yours, and I want to belong only to you."[50] Charmant in "L'Oiseau Bleu" gives the heroine exclusive possession of his love, declaring that he is "an unfortunate king who loves you and will never love anyone but you."[51] These promises seek to reassure the heroine that she will not regret accepting the hero's invitation to love him as she is the only person who has captured his heart.

The role of male suitors as instigators of courtship is emphasized in d'Aulnoy's "Serpentin Vert" and "Le prince Lutin," and in Bernard's "Le prince Rosier." The heroes in these tales use declarations of love to convince heroines who are uninterested in love to marry them. In "Serpentin Vert," the long-suffering Laideronnette, whose name reflects the effects of a curse of ugliness inflicted on her by a vengeful fairy, is seduced by sweet words whispered to her at night.[52] A mysterious voice repeatedly declares his adoration, and his assurance that he has seen Laideronnette and loves her anyway overcomes her resolution never to love: "I have seen you, Madame. . . . I do not find you as you represent yourself. . . . I repeat, I adore you."[53] Laideronnette agrees to marry her unseen suitor even though she is prohibited from looking at him.[54] She thus unwittingly marries a king metamorphosed as a green serpent. This marriage is not, however, the end of the tale. Laideronnette does in fact look at her husband, and both are punished for her disobedience, although they are eventually reunited after Laideronnette fulfills a series of impossible tasks. The eponymous hero in Bernard's "Le prince Rosier" develops an emotional connection with the heroine, Florinde, by recounting the sad story of his persecution by a fairy who transformed him into a rosebush until the day he is loved by the most beautiful person in the world.[55] His reverences and laments convince Florinde to allow him to speak to her of love, and his eloquence persuades her that she is tenderly loved.[56] This belief causes Florinde to utter tender words of her own, and the prince's metamorphosis is reversed when the threat of separation transforms Florinde's pity for him into passion. Her tears allow the prince to regain his human form by providing physical proof of her love and their emotional courtship culminates in marriage.[57] Both Laideronnette and Florinde fall in love despite their better judgment, and the declarations of love by their gallant suitors are a key factor in overcoming their reluctance to marry.

The hero in d'Aulnoy's "Le prince Lutin" infiltrates a utopian island to court a beautiful and eternally youthful princess raised by her fairy mother to shun the society of men. Men are banned from this island, but Lutin's power to make himself invisible gives him the access he needs to cultivate an emotional relationship with the princess.[58] He falls in love with her despite his vow never to love, and his gallant courtship thwarts the efforts of the princess's mother to shield her from love. Lutin declares his love on multiple occasions and in doing so gradually overwhelms the princess's desire to avoid love. He sings to her in the voice of a canary praising love, begging her to choose a lover.[59] He also gives her a poem lamenting his loss of liberty in an elaborate present.[60] He paints a portrait of himself gazing adoringly at a portrait of the princess while holding a scroll inscribed with the text: "She is more beautiful in my heart."[61] Finally, Lutin writes the princess a note telling her that he is an unhappy lover who does not dare to appear before her eyes.[62] When Lutin finally appears before the princess singing of his surrender to love, she faints. It is not until after Lutin defeats a king trying to force the princess to marry him that the princess sees the true form of her invisible lover. Her quiet admiration of his sleeping body is disrupted by her mother, whose disapproval of love is unmoved by Lutin's promises of eternal fidelity or by her daughter's avowal that she will not be content without him. The princess's mother refuses her consent to their marriage until she is persuaded by a fellow fairy that Lutin will remain faithful to her daughter and that their union will bring her satisfaction.[63]

Declarations of love to third parties are an interesting feature of the courtships conducted by male suitors in tales by La Force and Lhéritier.[64] In La Force's "La Bonne Femme," Finfin, who is Lirette's childhood sweetheart, indirectly admits his love for Lirette to their adoptive mother. His description of Lirette's effect on his internal emotional state reveals his love: he is moved by her presence, alternatively troubled and pleased by her regard, touched by her scolding, and overjoyed when her words are sweet and gentle toward him.[65] Lhéritier's suitors speak more directly about their love. In "Les enchantements de l'éloquence," the prince declares his "ardent passion" for the heroine to a fairy before he tells his beloved about the impression she has made on his heart.[66] Cléarque, one of the many suitors in Lhéritier's "La robe de sincérité," confesses his ardent and tender love for Célénie to her brother Téléphonte.[67] Both these suitors speak candidly of their love using the first-person pronoun, *je*, and their use of the noun *ardeur* emphasizes the strength and sincerity of their love. Other male suitors in Lhéritier's tales, Téléphonte and Léandrin in "La robe de sincérité" and the prince in "Marmoisan," declare their love directly to the women they adore. Téléphonte asks for Elismène's consent before he speaks to Cléarque, her brother and the king, to obtain permission for their marriage.[68] Léandrin seizes the first opportunity available to him to confess to Herminie that in attempting to secure her liberty he has lost his own.[69] The prince in "Marmoisan" makes a speech to Léonore in which he describes his fear that she will not reciprocate his love for her as a wound that is more dangerous than a wound from a sword.[70]

Male suitors in La Force's tales also declare their love directly to the women they court. Like Adolphe in d'Aulnoy's "L'île de la félicité," the prince in "Persinette" and the Enchanter in "L'Enchanteur" fall to their knees before confessing their love.[71] Phraates in "Plus Belle que Fée" tells the eponymous heroine that he is not Cupid but that he has "more love than there is in heaven or on earth" and that he loves and wants to help her.[72] In "La puissance d'amour," Panpan informs Lantine, a princess who was created by Cupid to tame Panpan's wayward heart, that he has nothing to give her: "you have everything when you have my heart."[73] The adventuring hero in "Le pays des délices," whose journey to the island of pleasures (*délices*) is a metaphorical exploration of Scudéry's *Carte de Tendre*, declares his submission to Queen Faveur: "since I was struck by the radiance of your charms, I cannot love anyone but you."[74] Prince Vert, the heroine's perfect opposite in "Vert et Bleu," is inspired by the sight of the heroine bathing to impetuously reveal his feelings to her.[75] Princess Bleu interprets the prince's declaration as evidence of his noble and natural sentiments and believes that he has been created by heaven to make her happy.[76] The eroticism of this scene is unusual. References to sexual desire are rare in the conteuses' tales, with this scene and the declarations in La Force's "Persinette" and "L'Enchanteur" notable exceptions.[77]

Unsuccessful declarations of love play an important role in Murat's "Le palais de la vengeance" and "L'Aigle au beau bec," and in d'Auneuil's "Le prince curieux." In Murat's tales, inducements to love including gifts and acts of services are incapable of inspiring reciprocal affection in heroines who are already in love with someone else. In "Le palais de la vengeance," Pagan the enchanter, a rival to the hero, offers the heroine, Imis, his love and his fortune: "I offer you a heart a thousand times more grateful, a heart deeply touched by your charms, and a fortune large enough to be desired by all except you."[78] Pagan prefaces this declaration with a criticism of the hero for not being sufficiently cognizant of the good fortune of being loved by Imis.[79] Neither statement has the intended effect. Pagan's declaration of love is not reciprocated, and Imis does not accept his criticism of her beloved. It is "pointless" for Pagan to love Imis because she has already given her heart to Philax, a hero who is "too worthy of love to cease being the master of it."[80] Despite Pagan's best efforts, he cannot persuade Imis to love him.[81] A similar fate befalls the hero in "L'Aigle au beau bec." His attempts to convince the beautiful Belle to marry him fail because she is in love with someone else. Unlike other metamorphosed lovers, the king is unable to speak to Belle. An enchanter speaks to her on his behalf, telling her that he is a grand king who has given her refuge in his palace from her hateful stepmother, but this information has no effect on Belle's heart.[82] In "Le prince curieux," the heroine rejects a declaration of love by the eponymous hero because she cannot return his love. She does not have another suitor, but she feels nothing for him and rejects his declaration because he deserves "a whole heart."[83]

Cautious Revelations and Assertive Statements by Female Suitors

It is unusual for female suitors to initiate courtship in the conteuses' tales. Only seven of their heroines, and a small number of secondary characters or antagonists who are almost always fairies, declare their love for a male suitor without waiting for him to speak first. Appendix 6 lists tales by d'Aulnoy, La Force, and Murat that feature declarations of love by heroines. In d'Aulnoy's "La Belle aux Cheveux d'Or," "La princesse Printanière," and "Babiole," and in Murat's "Jeune et Belle," heroines initiate courtship with a suitor of their choice. Moufette in d'Aulnoy's "La Grenouille bienfaisante," Isaline in Murat's "Le père et ses quatre fils," and Adelis in La Force's "L'Enchanteur" also choose their preferred marriage partner but reveal this preference after their future spouses have made their intentions clear. When heroines declare their intentions to male suitors, they are less likely to speak of love than the conteuses' heroes and are more likely to use indirect language. By contrast, the fairy antagonists who attempt to seduce heroes in tales by d'Aulnoy, Durand, and Murat use the direct language favored by the conteuses' heroes, as do secondary female characters in tales by d'Auneuil and Murat. None of Lhéritier's or Bernard's heroines initiate courtship, and the fairies in their tales do not intervene in the courtship between the heroic couple.

In d'Aulnoy's tales, heroines use indirect or oblique language to express their desire to marry a man of their own choosing except for the bold heroine in "La princesse Printanière." In "La Belle aux Cheveux d'Or," "Babiole," and "La Grenouille bien-faisante," heroines express their desire to marry the spouse they have chosen without mentioning love. In "La Belle aux Cheveux d'Or," Belle's conditional declaration to Avenant is made en route to her marriage to another suitor: "If you had wanted, I would have made you king, and we would not have to leave my kingdom."[84] Her desire to marry Avenant rather than the king who sent him to woo her on his behalf is subject to her deference to Avenant's wishes. Avenant rejects this declaration due to his loyalty to the king, even though he thinks that Belle is "more beautiful than the sun."[85] Belle's declaration is wholly ineffective in the sense that it does not convince Avenant to marry her. The pair does not marry until she is widowed by an unfortunate accident caused by the king's jealousy of Avenant's place in his wife's heart.[86] Although Belle identifies Avenant as her preferred husband, she lacks the social power to arrange this union. Her agency in courtship is limited by her inability to marry the suitor of her choice until his higher ranked rival is dead.[87]

Declarations by Babiole and Moufette also defer to male volition. The eponymous heroine in "Babiole" confesses to her cousin that he is the only one she could wish as her spouse after she is threatened with an arranged marriage to King Magot, ruler of the kingdom of Monkeys.[88] The prince ridicules her revelation because he is unable to see past Babiole's metamorphosis to love the princess trapped in monkey form.[89] The couple do not marry until after her metamorphosis is reversed and rumors of Babiole's beauty attract the prince to her kingdom, where he falls in love with her without knowing her true identity. In "La Grenouille bien-faisante," Moufette's father takes the unusual step of allowing his daughter to choose her own husband. He tells prince Moufy that he will impose no conditions on Moufette's choice because he wants to please his daughter and make her happy.[90] When Moufy informs Moufette of her father's decision, she declares: "if he was not her spouse, she would never have another."[91] Moufette does not initiate her courtship with Moufy, and it is perhaps for this reason that her declaration of her desire to marry him is successful. Her declaration, like that of Belle in "La Belle aux Cheveux d'Or," is conditional, and her deference to Moufy's authority does not challenge the active male–passive female dynamic in early modern courtship.

The heroines in "La princesse Printanière," "L'Enchanteur," "Jeune et Belle," and "Le père et ses quatre fils" do not conform to the script of female deference. In d'Aulnoy's "La princesse Printanière," the eponymous heroine declares her love to the ambassador sent to court her on behalf of the son of King Merlin: "I have feelings for you that you would never guess if I did not explain them to you myself. . . . know then, Mr Ambassador, that I admired you when I saw you on your beautiful, dancing horse, and I regretted that you came here on behalf of another. We will not give up finding a remedy, if you have as much courage as me: instead of marrying you in the name of your master, I will marry you."[92] Although this declaration is whispered by Printanière, it uses the direct language favored by male suitors to offer the ambassador her love. He accepts, and her declaration is a success in that it convinces the ambassador to elope with her. But this elopement is a complete disaster. Printanière ends up killing the ambassador and marrying the prince who sent him to court her on his behalf. This ending erases Printanière's unconventional courtship: the prince is not informed about her premarital adventures, and a suitor approved by her parents replaces her initial choice.[93]

The reversal of traditional gender roles is an important feature in La Force's "L'Enchanteur." This unconventional tale features two couples whose courtships do not conform to seventeenth-century codes of female behavior. Adelis boldly declares her love to the handsome Carados and informs him of her intention to marry him: "Here is your portrait. . . . As soon as I saw it, I loved you. And as soon as I loved you, I intended myself for you, and I made my brother agree that I would never have another husband."[94] Adelis's repeated use of the first-person pronoun, *je*, emphasizes her agency in courtship negotiations to which Carados was not a party. Adelis's declaration makes no apologies for her choice of husband, nor does she defer to his judgment or authority. This declaration is made in response to Carados's passionate reaction to Adelis's beauty. After falling in love with the sleeping Adelis, Carados kisses her hand and takes her into his arms. Upon waking, Adelis screams and tries to escape the strange man in her tent, but when she learns his identity, she declares her love for him. Adelis's feelings for Carados predate his passion for her, and she states her desire to marry him in unequivocal terms. The other relationship featured in the tale is an adulterous liaison between Carados's mother, Isène la Belle, and his father, the Enchanter. As we saw in chapter 2, this relationship was initiated by the Enchanter on Isène la Belle's wedding night. Her acceptance of his extramarital declaration of love is clear breach of moral codes of female chastity and fidelity, as well as the script of female restraint.

The courtship in Murat's "Jeune et Belle" inverts the sleeping beauty motif in La Force's "L'Enchanteur." Murat's heroine, Jeune et Belle, is a princess and a fairy who uses her magic to seduce a young shepherd with whom she fell in love when she saw him sleeping in the woods.[95] Alidor, the sleeping shepherd, is woken by charming music to find himself wearing magnificent clothing embroidered with interlaced letters (*chiffres*) of Jeune et Belle's name.[96] Jeune et Belle also uses her magic to decorate the shepherd's flock and gives his sheepdog a golden collar inscribed with a verse about burning ardor, tender hearts, and fidelity as a requirement of happiness.[97] Alidor falls in love with Jeune et Belle but he does not learn her true identity until he has passed her tests of his fidelity.[98] She finally reveals herself to Alidor after he has ardently declared his love. She promises him that they will both be happy if he remains faithful to her.[99] Like Adelis, Jeune et Belle declares her love in response to the revelation of passion by a male suitor, but she initiates their courtship and controls how it is conducted. Isaline in "Le père et ses quatre fils" also takes matters into her own hands in a rather unconventional way. When she finds herself stranded on a deserted island guarded by a dragon with only the handsome Delfirio for company, she is the one who suggests they consummate their union with the gods as their witnesses.[100]

Declarations by fairies and secondary female characters in the conteuses' tales are almost always unsuccessful. Fairies declare their love using the direct language favored by the conteuses' heroes, and their offers of love are often accompanied by promises of power or material advantage associated with the traditional model of courtship. Mordicante in Murat's "Jeune et Belle" offers Alidor the chance to seek vengeance on his enemies.[101] Ragotte in d'Aulnoy's "Le Mouton" promises to substantially increase the wealth of the hero.[102] Berlinguette in Murat's "L'île de la magnificence" promises prince Verdelet that if he marries her, he will be "the happiest and richest prince in the world."[103] But the material advantages offered by these fairies cannot compensate for their physical appearance. Their bold declarations of love are rebuffed because they are old and ugly and therefore not desirable. Their physical appearance is incompatible with the notion that only the young and beautiful are worthy of love. However, young and beautiful fairies are also rejected by heroes already in love with other women in Durand's "La Fée Lubantine" and "Le prodige d'amour."[104] These tales suggest that love cannot be bought by material inducements or created by magic; it arises spontaneously when the requirements of the script for falling in love are satisfied.

Female characters who initiate courtship by revealing their love in d'Aulnoy's "Belle Belle, ou le chevalier Fortuné," d'Auneuil's "L'inconstance punie," and Murat's "Anguillette" struggle to achieve a successful outcome. The vindictive queen in "Belle Belle, ou le chevalier Fortuné" punishes the heroine, who is disguised as a chevalier, for failing to reciprocate her passion. But her attempt to have the chevalier executed for refusing her proposal of marriage backfires spectacularly by causing the revelation of the heroine's true identity, thus allowing the king to marry her. Doucereuse in "L'inconstance punie" unintentionally drives her lover away when he becomes bored with his good fortune.[105] Only Ilérie in "Anguillette" obtains a reciprocal response to her passionate declaration, but she loses her fickle husband in the tragic ending to the tale. One reading of these failed courtships is that courtship cannot be successful when initiated by women. But this does not account for the fact that rival male lovers are equally unsuccessful in their attempts to woo women whose hearts already belong to another man.[106] The failure of these courtships suggest that there is also an element of luck or fate involved in securing a successful outcome. Characters in the conteuses' tales cannot successfully navigate courtship without replicating gendered emotion scripts for the expression of love, but they must also have the good fortune of meeting an unattached partner suitably matched to their social status and personal charms.

GENDERING THE EMOTIONAL AGENCY OF COURTING COUPLES

The declarations of love in "La princesse Carpillon" exemplify the gender politics of courtship in the conteuses' tales. This lengthy tale has a complex narrative structure with two courtships in which two diametrically opposed suitors declare their love for the beautiful Princess Carpillon. The first suitor, Bossu, is a tyrannical, hunchbacked prince whose name reflects his physical deformity.[107] He commands the princess to reconcile herself to their marriage and reproaches her for refusing to accept the honor of his courtship.[108] The princess rejects Bossu's forceful suit and the traditional model of wifely obedience he attempts to impose on her.[109] Her heart is touched by the charms of her second suitor, a shepherd prince who is Bossu's younger, handsome brother. Abandoned in the woods as an infant to safeguard Bossu's claim to the throne, the unnamed prince is cared for by an eagle and then raised by Sublime, a shepherd who is a king dispossessed of his kingdom.[110] Sublime is also the father of the heroine. Her parentage and the royal lineage of the hero are unknown when they meet.

The courtship between Princess Carpillon and the shepherd prince is an exemplary illustration of the emotional model of courtship. After falling in love at first sight, the shepherd prince perfectly embodies the role of a courtly lover. He assists the princess with her chores, brings her gifts of flowers, and sings verses he has composed about love. For her part, the princess displays no outward signs of encouragement to the shepherd prince, and he interprets her emotional restraint as a sign of indifference.[111] The princess's interior monologue reveals that she is both pleased and troubled by the shepherd prince's obvious affection for her.[112] The emotional connection between the couple is developed in a series of personal exchanges. The first exchange culminates in a declaration of love by the shepherd prince. After courting the princess with acts of service and songs of love, he carves a verse lamenting his inability to find refuge from Cupid into a tree he knew the princess would visit.[113] When the princess appears, he pretends to be embarrassed before declaring: "You see an unfortunate shepherd who offers complaints to the most unfeeling things [trees], for a suffering he should lament only to you."[114]

Despite the princess's affection for the shepherd prince, she does not perform the emotional response invited by his declaration of love. The reason the princess gives for her refusal is that she does not want to love.[115] The real reason is the apparent disparity in their social rank. The princess fears entering into a mésalliance and therefore believes that she cannot accept the shepherd prince's love. He accuses her of favoring a rival, and this accusation implies that the only legitimate reason the princess has for rejecting his love is that her heart already belongs to someone else. The princess admits the existence of a rival lover but assures the shepherd prince that she despises her other suitor.[116] The princess's attempts to discourage the shepherd's courtship are undermined by this assurance, so he continues to court her affection with gifts of flowers and ribbons and by reciting verses and songs praising her beauty. His attentions are noticed and praised by their social circle, all of whom approve their courtship.

The princess scrupulously follows the emotion script of female restraint until a wild bear threatens the shepherd prince's life. The sight of his blood causes her to confess her feelings: "Shepherd, if you die, I will die with you. In vain I have hidden my secret sentiments from you; know them, and know that my life is joined to yours."[117] This declaration is soon followed by another, which is carved into a tree after the princess's revelation of her royal status threatens to separate the lovers. She uses the indirect language characteristic of female declarations to initiate the exchange by asking a question, "Do you love a heart that loves you?" The prince's passionate reply confesses his love: "By thousands and thousands of fires I feel myself inflamed." The princess's response is decidedly more restrained. She confirms her reciprocal emotional attachment without using the first-person pronoun: "Enjoy the extreme happiness / Of loving and seeing yourself loved in return."[118] Significantly, the princess's revelation of her love is prompted by threats to her relationship with the shepherd prince. It is the physical danger posed by the bear and the pain caused by the separation ordered by her parents that overwhelm her ability to follow the emotion script of restraint. She does not intend to admit her feelings for the prince but is overwhelmed by the emotional impact of circumstances beyond her control.

The conteuses' rejection of forced marriages is an important element in the unsuccessful courtship between Bossu and Princess Carpillon. This courtship is an exaggerated version of courtship as the negotiation of a social alliance between royal families. This type of courtship, as the princess's governess observes, is an affair of state arranged without reference to the princess's inclination or consent.[119] Unlike a traditional royal courtship, it is initiated by Bossu after he falls violently in love with the princess when he captures her during a military campaign. His father, the king, consents to their marriage if the princess does not have an aversion to it.[120] In this model of courtship, the heroine's agency in the negotiation of her marriage is expressed solely in terms of her emotional connection to her suitor. She can reject Bossu if she does not love him but not on any other basis. The king's support for a companionate model of marriage is representative of parental involvement in courtship in the conteuses' tales. When parents, or fairies assuming the role of parents, are involved in the courtship of a heroic couple, their role is most often restricted to offering advice to their children. Bossu's father follows this model by warning his son that he will be unhappy if he marries a woman who does not love him.[121]

Bossu's harsh treatment of Princess Carpillon seals his fate as an unsuccessful suitor. She does not reciprocate his love because he speaks to her as a master and reproaches her as his slave.[122] This thinly veiled criticism of the coercive powers of early modern husbands emphasizes Bossu's moral deformity as the reason for the princess's aversion to him. She identifies the "bad qualities of his heart" as the reason she cannot bear to marry him.[123] Bossu's father supports the princess's resistance to his son's attempts to court her, but his attempts to protect her from Bossu's tyranny fail. Bossu forces his father to consent to the marriage by entering into a seditious alliance with the army and threatening to seize the throne. The king then attempts to reconcile the princess to the marriage by suggesting that it would be a union based on love. He assures her that Bossu's lack of respect is a sign of his ardor because he would have found a more willing bride if he did not love her.[124] But the king's remark that Bossu "wants no one but you" is telling.[125] Bossu's desire to marry the princess is a desire to possess a beautiful object that he believes is rightfully his. He is not motivated by a desire to create an emotional connection with the princess, nor does he care whether she loves him or not.

The strategic role of declarations of love in courtship makes the question of whether such declarations are sincere expressions of genuine feeling irrelevant. The social implications of a successful declaration, namely a marriage negotiated by a consenting couple, mean that assertions of sincerity must be read in light of the social and economic realities of courtship. Even in the emotional model developed by the conteuses, courtship is not simply a matter of personal feelings. Declarations of love are expressions of social power that illustrate the gender dynamics in early modern courtship. The gendered expression of love in declarations made by heroes and heroines in the conteuses' tales offer insight into how different characters adopted different strategies for negotiating social codes for the expression of love in seventeenth-century France. Heroes express their love in accordance with the vocabulary of emotion outlined in chapter 2: their hearts are moved by love, the heroine's beauty is the inspiration for their passion, and they lament their status as unhappy lovers. Heroines reveal their feelings indirectly, and they defer to the volition of their preferred spouse when broaching the subject of marriage. But for a declaration of love to be successful, it must be directed to the right person. Only certain people are deemed worthy of love, and declarations of love are limited in their power to produce a reciprocal emotional response: they cannot create love in a heart opposed to the suitor.

In d'Aulnoy's "La princesse Carpillon," the most important distinction between Princess Carpillon's suitors is the way they court her. Although each courtship represents a break from tradition in the sense that it is initiated by a suitor motivated by love rather than arranged by the parents of the couple, d'Aulnoy establishes a clear distinction between Bossu's coercive approach and the shepherd prince's tender love. Bossu's attempts to force the princess to marry him fail because he makes no attempt to develop an emotional connection with her. He is unwilling to follow his father's advice to work to earn her love through acts of service, and his escalating acts of violence are met with resistance rather than acquiescence. The absence of love is an insurmountable obstacle in Bossu's courtship as the princess is willing to die rather than marry him. This representation of a heroine prepared to choose death over marriage to a man she hates makes a strong case for free choice of a marriage partner. However, d'Aulnoy's advocacy for the ability of women to choose their spouse does acknowledge the social limits on the agency of her heroines. Princess Carpillon exercises emotional agency in her courtship with the shepherd prince in the sense that she chooses him as her preferred spouse, but she is unable to marry him without parental consent. Their objection to the match as a mésalliance causes the princess to terminate the courtship, and the couple is unable to marry until the fairy Amazon instructs Sublime and his wife to consent to their union. It is this intervention that eliminates this obstacle to the princess's choice of spouse.[126]

A successful courtship in the conteuses' tales features characters who fall in love with people who satisfy the requirements of a traditional marriage partner. Although the focus on love reflects a shift in the nature of courtship, it does not displace the social and economic role of marriage in seventeenth-century France. The key difference between the conteuses' representation of courtship and the traditional model of courtship is a reversal of the order of priority: love comes first and is a prerequisite to further discussion. Love is negotiated between women and their male suitors, and declarations of love make a crucial contribution to the creation of an emotional connection between courting couples. These declarations are performed in accordance with gendered emotion scripts. Active male suitors are expected to initiate courtship and declare their love using bold, direct language. Heroines are expected to refrain from expressing emotion unless they are responding to a declaration of love by a male suitor. Their emotional agency in courtship is limited to deciding whether to accept or reject the suitors who court them; the emotional model of courtship does not allow them to initiate courtship. Reformulation of courtship as a negotiation based on love does not, therefore, empower women to resist the patriarchal structure of marriage. In shifting the balance of power from fathers to suitors, it reinforces the power structure of marriage as an institution supporting male power and frames female desire as a passion to be controlled by marriage.

The conteuses' critique of the patriarchal structure of early modern courtship and marriage is further developed in the following chapter's analysis of the emotional significance of gift-giving as a courtship ritual. Like declarations of love, the exchange of gifts creates an obligation of reciprocity designed to develop an emotional bond between couples before their marriage. In the "Riquet à la houppe" tales by Bernard and Perrault, the hero's gift of intelligence in exchange for the heroine's promise to marry him imposes an implied obligation of love as a term of their marriage. The ability (or lack thereof) of the heroine to fulfill this emotional obligation determines whether her marriage is successful. While the balanced gift exchange in Perrault's tale produces a model companionate marriage sustained by loving union between husband and wife, the asymmetrical exchange between the unhappy couple in Bernard's tale provides another example of the failure of a coercive approach to love. Although less outwardly villainous than d'Aulnoy's Bossu, Bernard's Riquet embodies the role of a traditional patriarchal husband in his attempts to control his wife's person and movements. Unsurprisingly, this does little to persuade Riquet's wife to love him, and their marriage is a source of misery to them both. As we see in the following chapter, this critique of marriage as a source of unhappiness for women illustrates structural limits on the ability of women to negotiate the gender politics of courtship and marriage in seventeenth-century France.

4

Marriage, Gift-Giving, and the Obligation of Love

The exchange of marriage gifts is a long-standing ritual in many cultures. In Charles Perrault's 1697 tale "Riquet à la houppe," Riquet's offer of intelligence in exchange for a promise of marriage defines marriage as a reciprocal relationship imposing emotional obligations on husbands and wives: "I have the power, Madame, to give as much intelligence as one can have to the person I love the most. And since you are, Madame, that person, it is up to you whether you have that intelligence, it is yours if you are willing to marry me."[1] The implied condition of the gift, that Madame will reciprocate the love Riquet offers her by accepting his proposal, emphasizes the emotional significance of gift-giving as an emotion script creating an interpersonal relationship between gift-giver and gift-recipient. Although Perrault identifies love as the motivation for Riquet's gift, it is, like all gifts, not a disinterested or benevolent offer but part of a social system of exchange that imposes a reciprocal obligation on Madame.[2] This obligation requires that Madame match the generosity of Riquet's gift by giving him what he desires: a loving wife. A similar offer is made to the heroine in Catherine Bernard's 1696 version of the Riquet tale. Her Mama is offered intelligence if she agrees to marry the ugly Riquet, but unlike Perrault's Madame, Mama is unable to reciprocate her husband's generosity. Her inability to perform the emotional obligation of marriage by reciprocating her husband's love reflects the pessimistic view of love and marriage that appears in a number of the conteuses' tales.[3]

In seventeenth-century France, the "right" emotion associated with marriage was the subject of much debate. In the 1690s salon milieu in which the conteuses composed their tales, this debate proposed a reformulation of marriage that challenged the French state's definition of marriage as a civil contract subject to parental consent.[4] This counter-discourse engaged with conversation about marriage in mid-seventeenth-century salons that reinterpreted the medieval courtly love tradition to propose an alternative model of marriage as a personal choice based on love. Such conversation rejected the traditional definition of marriage as an economic and social transaction on the basis that it was incompatible with love and imposed unjust restrictions on the liberty of women.[5] As we saw in chapter 3, the companionate model of marriage favored by salon writers stressed the importance of creating an emotional bond between courting couples before marriage. The exchange of gifts was one of the ways in which couples could create such a bond, and this chapter examines the emotion scripts for gift-gifting as a way of exploring the obligation of love in early modern marriage.

The growing influence of the companionate model of marriage in the seventeenth and eighteenth centuries represents a significant moment in the history of marriage in early modern Europe.[6] The reformulation of marriage as a reciprocal relationship imposing emotional obligations on husbands and wives plays a key role in the conteuses' representation of marriage. The central case study in this chapter analyzes this shift through a comparative reading of two versions of the Riquet tale by Perrault and Bernard. In writing different versions of the marital relationship created by the exchange of gifts, each author offers a different interpretation of the obligation of love associated with marriage. The reciprocal exchange in Perrault's tale creates a companionate marriage in which the emotional bond between husband and wife softens the transactional nature of marriage. But Bernard's Riquet, who offers the same gift as Perrault's Riquet but imposes an emotional obligation his future wife cannot fulfill, finds himself in an unhappy marriage in which the asymmetrical exchange of gifts produces resentment rather than love. In tales by d'Aulnoy, Murat, Lhéritier, and Durand the emotion scripts for gift exchange explore the agency of women to negotiate power imbalances in their relationships with men in early modern France.

GIFT-GIVING AS A RECIPROCAL EMOTIONAL PRACTICE

The strategic exchange of gifts in early modern France was used to sustain relationships between friends, neighbors, kin, and co-workers, and create relationships of obligation such as marriage and patronage.[7] As a social ritual illustrating the power relations of the society in which gifts are exchanged, gift-giving creates a contract between the gift-giver and the gift-recipient based on the norm of reciprocity.[8] This contract imposes three obligations: the obligation to give, the obligation to receive, and the obligation to reciprocate. Of these three obligations, the obligation of reciprocity is critical to understanding the social implications of gift-giving. When performed correctly, the obligation of reciprocity creates a continuous cycle of exchange between the gift-giver and the gift-recipient. In offering a gift, the giver indicates their intention to create a personal relationship with the recipient and their willingness to be bound by the obligation of reciprocity. When a recipient accepts a gift, they accept the reciprocal obligation to return the gift. A gift is therefore never "pure" or "freely given" but a strategic social instrument that establishes a social bond between the giver and the recipient.[9] This social bond obliges the giver and recipient to act in accordance with the social expectations governing the relationship established by their exchange. In this context, Riquet's gift to his future wife does more than provide her with intelligence; like all gifts exchanged between prospective marriage partners, it offers him to her as a husband. Her acceptance of the gift indicates her willingness to accept Riquet as her husband. This exchange negotiates the terms of the marriage by foregrounding love as the reciprocal obligation expected by Riquet.

The significant role of marriage as a mechanism for the transfer of property in early modern Europe meant that, particularly in aristocratic families, parents or close relatives of the couple negotiated the exchange of dowry gifts. These negotiations focused on the social status and wealth of the bride and groom and emphasized the definition of marriage as an economic and political alliance sealed by the exchange of property such as land, animals, equipment, cash, clothing, and household goods.[10] The details of this property transfer were recorded in marriage contracts that stipulated the types of gifts exchanged between husband and wife and the terms upon which the exchange occurred.[11] This reciprocal material exchange transformed the couple into a separate economic unit with shared property as the basis for the establishment of a separate household. Their alliance was designed to create a strategic social alliance between the couple and their kin. While love was not the primary motivation for marriage, early modern husbands and wives did expect to develop an emotional connection with their spouse.[12] But any emotional connection created by the mutual exchange of dowry gifts did not establish marriage as an equal partnership as early modern husbands continued to exercise legal authority over their wives' property and person.[13]

Natalie Zemon Davis's superb study of gift-giving in sixteenth-century France highlights the social significance of gift-giving as a compulsory, reciprocal practice.[14] According to Davis, the ritual exchange of marriage gifts included gifts recorded in the marriage contract formalizing the union of the couple, namely the dowry provided by the bride's parents and the husband's counter-gifts of promises to give his wife clothing and jewelry, as well as coins or rings exchanged by the bride and groom during the marriage ceremony.[15] Davis uses Marcel Mauss's essay on gift-giving to conceptualize the metaphorical or symbolic aspect of gift-giving as "gratitude engendering obligation."[16] Unlike Mauss, Davis argues that there is no universal model of the stages of gift-giving. She proposes instead that gift-giving is a relational mode shaped by the status, gender, and wealth of the individuals exchanging gifts.[17] Jane Fair Bestor identifies a similar pattern in Renaissance Italy, where the payment of a dowry was legally interpreted as a payment to the husband that replaced a daughter's inheritance. In this context, the husband's reciprocal obligation to present his bride with wedding ornaments was interpreted by jurists as a loan for a specific, limited use rather than as a gift.[18] However, Christiane Klapisch-Zuber argues that the Renaissance dowry was only one part of the exchange of marriage gifts. She suggests that this exchange was reciprocal only in a symbolic sense, as the gifts provided to the bride remained the property of the husband and his heirs.[19] These examples illustrate the extent to which the exchange of marriage gifts in early modern Europe defined marriage as a strategic social and economic alliance between husband and wife, their families, and the broader community. Gift exchange functioned as a symbol of the bond created between husband and wife, but the precise nature of this bond varied depending on how the couple negotiated the patriarchal framework underpinning early modern marriage.[20]

Marie-Jeanne Lhéritier emphasizes the power relations underpinning relationships of exchange in her 1705 tale "Ricdin-Ricdon." In her version of a tale we might recognize as a variation of the Rumpelstiltskin plot, a disguised demon offers to lend a magic wand to the heroine, Rosanie, on the condition that she remember his name and say, "take it Ricdin-Ricdon, here is your wand," when he returns to collect it.[21] This transaction, which Ricdin-Ricdon frames as a gift by characterizing it as a "favor" (*faveur*) he is pleased to offer, creates a relationship of obligation between Ricdin-Ricdon and Rosanie. Ricdin-Ricdon's offer is not a disinterested act of goodwill. He uses the rhetoric of gift-giving to trick Rosanie into accepting a disadvantageous condition: if she cannot remember his name, he will become her master and she will be obliged to follow him.[22] The motivation for Ricdin-Ricdon's offer is the acquisition of power over Rosanie as he uses the exchange of "favors" to bind her future to his. In this tale, as in the Riquet tales, a male giver initiates a gift with the intention of creating a relationship of obligation with the female recipient. Fortunately, Rosanie manages to escape Ricdin-Ricdon's trap with the help of a devoted suitor who overhears Ricdin-Ricdon bragging about his entrapment of dozens of beautiful girls. When this suitor recounts his adventures to Rosanie, he writes Ricdin-Ricdon's name on a slate, and Rosanie uses this knowledge to return the wand to its demonic owner.[23]

Evidence that the practice of gift-giving in early modern France created personal bonds between gift-givers and gift recipients is an example of how the performance of emotion scripts can be used to produce a particular emotional response. For example, the traditional exchange of dowry gifts was often preceded by the exchange of small tokens of affection by courting couples, such as flowers or items of personal clothing. The gifts exchanged by Riquet and his future bride exemplify the use of a more personal form of gift-giving to create an emotional relationship between the couple before the formal negotiation of their marriage contract. These efforts to develop an affective connection between husband and wife represented a shift in the definition of marriage from a purely economic model toward the companionate model discussed in chapter 3. This emotional definition of marriage was not incompatible with traditional marital duties of material support and reproduction because marrying for love and marrying for economic reasons were not mutually exclusive ideals.[24] The difference introduced by the companionate model was an identification of love as the proper motivation for marriage.[25] But as we see in Perrault's Riquet tale, the emotional model of marriage did not displace the traditional role of marriage as a moment of material exchange. The marital relationship in Perrault's tale is negotiated by the reciprocal exchange of gifts, and it is this exchange that makes it possible for the heroine to love Riquet. He gives her the intelligence she desires, and her love transforms him into a handsome husband. This interpretation reads the reciprocal obligation of gift-giving in light of seventeenth-century expectations about the marriage relationship and the idea of love associated with it. Enactment of this reciprocal obligation is not a natural or instinctive performance but a set of learned behaviors that change as the social definition of marriage changes.

FULFILLING THE OBLIGATION OF LOVE IN "RIQUET À LA HOUPPE"

"Riquet à la houppe" is a seventeenth-century literary fairy tale without any known folkloric antecedents.[26] Although there is debate about whose version of the Riquet tale came first, it is likely that both Bernard and Perrault were aware of each other's tale due to frequent circulation of salon tales in oral form before their publication. This chapter adopts Elizabeth Wanning Harries's position that the tales should be interpreted as rival stories told in a salon one afternoon.[27] In both versions of the tale, the narrative is structured around the gift exchange between Riquet and the heroine. Each tale commences with the birth of two characters with opposing character flaws: a beautiful but stupid heroine and an ugly but intelligent prince.[28] The prince, Riquet, attempts to woo the heroine by offering her the gift of intelligence in exchange for a promise to marry him in one year. Once the heroine accepts Riquet's gift, her personality is transformed, and her sudden mastery of the art of conversation attracts a rival suitor who is handsome and charming. A year elapses, and when Riquet returns to collect his bride, she is unable to decide whether to fulfil her promise to marry him. It is at this point that ideological differences between the two versions of the tale emerge. In Perrault's tale, Riquet informs the heroine that she has the (magical) power to physically transform the person she loves. When the princess declares her love for Riquet, he becomes the most handsome and charming man she has ever seen, and the tale ends happily with the celebration of their wedding.[29] Bernard's heroine, Mama, lacks the power to transform Riquet into a more desirable husband and is forced to accept marriage to an "odious husband."[30]

Riquet, the male hero, initiates the gift-giving ritual in both versions of the tale. As the gift-giver, Riquet has the power to create a personal relationship with the gift-recipient, a power he uses to acquire a beautiful and intelligent wife. Bernard and Perrault present different ideas about the nature of this exchange. Perrault's Riquet anticipates the gift of his beloved's hand in marriage as an exchange that will make him "the happiest of men."[31] Bernard's Riquet adopts a more pragmatic view of his relationship with the heroine. At their first meeting, Bernard's Riquet commands Mama to stop (*arrêtez*) and informs her that he has something unpleasant to tell her and something agreeable to promise her.[32] Unlike Perrault's Riquet, he does not approach Mama politely or compliment her beauty. The unpleasant thing Riquet tells Mama is that despite her beauty, the inferiority of her mind causes people to disregard her. He promises to give Mama the intelligence she desires if she agrees to marry him. All the advantage of the exchange belongs to Riquet: he gets a beautiful and intelligent wife, while Mama's intelligence causes her nothing but unhappiness. She does not have any attachment to her husband other than the relationship of obligation created by her acceptance of his gift and her intelligence makes her acutely aware of his defects.[33] When Riquet is confronted with Mama's reluctance to fulfill her promise to marry him, he tells her that she has a simple choice to make: either marry him or return to her former (stupid) state.[34] Unlike Perrault's heroine, Mama is unable to love Riquet and therefore cannot transform her ugly suitor into a more desirable husband. She agrees to the marriage only because she cannot bear to endure the social isolation she will experience if she gives up her intelligence.

The ability of Perrault's princess to love her husband is the key difference between the two heroines. Both are offered the gift of intelligence in exchange for a promise of marriage, but only Perrault's princess fulfills the implied obligation of love this promise entailed. In resolving his tale with a companionate marriage established by the exchange of gifts, Perrault represents marriage as a social contract with economic and emotional implications. As we see in the opening paragraph to this chapter, Perrault's Riquet follows the model of courtship outlined in chapter 3 by declaring his love and initiating an exchange of gifts. This courtship successfully creates a reciprocal emotional bond between the couple, due in no small measure to the fact that both are blessed with symmetrical fairy gifts that allow them to give the other the quality they lack. As I discuss further in the conclusion to this section, the ambiguous morals to Perrault's tale suggest that love, rather than fairy magic, is responsible for giving the princess her intelligence and Riquet his handsomeness. It is the mutual exchange of affection that is crucial to the tale's happy ending. It is love that motivates Riquet's gift of intelligence, and it is only by loving Riquet that the princess fulfills her obligation of reciprocity by giving him her heart. Bernard's Mama cannot give her heart to her husband and her inability love him creates a destructive asymmetry in their marriage.

The direct language of Riquet's proposal to Mama in Bernard's tale illustrates his expectation that his gift will allow him to obtain a loving wife. If Mama wants to have intelligence, she *must* love Riquet, and she *must* marry him. Bernard's Riquet invokes the language of obligation (*il faut*) to express the conditional nature of his gift. It is more difficult to untangle the precise nature of Mama's reciprocal obligation. When Riquet offers the gift, he identifies two separate obligations: "[1] you must love Riquet of the Tuft, that's my name; [2] you must marry me in one year." He then immediately refers to the condition being imposed on Mama in singular terms: "that's *the condition* that I impose on you."[35] The fact that Riquet's reference to "the condition" immediately follows his articulation of Mama's obligation to marry him suggests that marriage is the condition imposed on Mama and that an obligation of love is subsumed within the condition of marriage. Riquet's response to Mama's subsequent infidelity supports this definition of her reciprocal obligation. He takes away Mama's intelligence during the day (time she was spending with her lover) because Mama has breached the spirit of her reciprocal obligation. Mama fulfills the literal terms of the exchange by agreeing to marry Riquet, but in using his gift of intelligence to engage in adultery, Mama fails to fulfill the obligation to love him by giving her heart to her lover instead.[36] Mama's failure to love her husband aligns her experience with salon counter-discourse on marriage that questioned the compatibility of love and marriage.

The transactional nature of the gift exchange between Riquet and Mama illustrates the asymmetrical power relations embedded in the traditional model of marriage as a socioeconomic transaction. Riquet's blunt proposal emphasizes the material advantage of the match, and, unlike Perrault's Riquet, he does not express any emotional investment in Mama's acceptance of his proposal. However, Riquet's wounded reaction to Mama's obvious revulsion for him after their marriage suggests that he did expect that his gift would create an emotional bond between himself and Mama.[37] Read in this context, Riquet's gift was successful insofar as it created a relationship of obligation between himself and Mama, but it failed to produce an emotional bond between husband and wife. This failure is due to a lack of reciprocity. The exchange that provided Mama with intelligence in return for her promise to marry Riquet was not truly reciprocal because Mama acted out of ignorance and fear rather than generosity or gratitude.[38] When she accepted Riquet's proposal, Mama's stupidity meant that she could not appreciate the consequences of her acceptance. She was unable to comprehend the implications of the gift until after she had repeated the verse that Riquet told her would teach her how to think:

Love can surely inspire me
To shed my stupidity,
One need only know how to love:
Here I am, ready.[39]

Mama's repetition of these four lines of verse puts her in an impossible situation. The act of repetition gives Mama the intelligence she needs to decide whether to accept Riquet's gift of intelligence, and she therefore accepts the gift before she can decide whether she should accept it. Mama is thus bound by the obligation of reciprocity to someone whose gifts she does not want to return.[40]

Mama's inability to perform the right emotional response demanded by her acceptance of Riquet's gift means that their relationship is unbalanced: she resents his generosity, and he despises her lack of reciprocity.[41] Mama cannot fulfill her reciprocal obligation to love Riquet as his physical deformity means that he does not satisfy the emotion script for falling in love. An emotional bond between the couple cannot form, and Mama is not able to reconcile herself to the marriage by magically transforming her spouse. Paradoxically, it is the verse Riquet tells Mama to repeat that seals his fate as an unhappy, unloved husband. Mama's faithful repetition of it inspires her to love, but, contrary to Riquet's intention, she is not inspired to love him. Riquet's attempt to create a particular emotional response in Mama fails because she is unable to match his gift of intelligence with an equivalent act of generosity. By agreeing to marry Riquet without any intention to love him, Mama only partially fulfills her reciprocal obligation. She cannot give him a heart that already belongs to another, and Riquet punishes Mama for her lack of reciprocity.

When Riquet discovers his wife's adultery, he takes away Mama's intelligence during the day to deprive her of the ability to converse with her lover while retaining for himself the benefit of an intelligent wife. This punishment converts his gift from the register of exchange to the register of coercion.[42] His attempt to control Mama highlights the self-interested nature of his gift: "when I gave you intelligence, I presumed I would enjoy it."[43] Riquet's assertion of his power as Mama's husband reflects the patriarchal power structure of early modern marriage. By making Mama intelligent only at night—the time she is supposed to spend with him in their marital bed—Riquet exercises his patriarchal authority to control the movement of his wife. In seeking to limit Mama's sphere of movement, Riquet exercises the legal right seventeenth-century husbands had to demand obedience.[44] When this strategy fails, Riquet transforms Mama's lover into a hideous gnome so that she cannot distinguish between the man she loves and the husband she hates. His vengeance prompts Bernard to end her tale with a wry observation about the zero-sum nature of marriage for early modern women: "in the long run, all lovers become husbands."[45]

The optimistic ending to Perrault's tale does not share Bernard's pessimism that love inevitably leads to unhappiness. His tale concludes with two morals emphasizing the power of love as an emotional counterbalance to the transactional nature of marriage. The first moral, which claims Perrault's tale is not really a story because it is true, emphasizes the transformative power of love as an emotion that makes the object of affection beautiful and intelligent.[46] This moral suggests that the gift exchange between Riquet and Perrault's heroine is a metaphor for the transformative effect of falling in love. In other words, fairy magic is not responsible for Riquet's physical transformation; he becomes handsome because the princess loves him. The second moral characterizes love as an illusion that causes lovers to see what they want to see in their beloved. According to this moral, Perrault's Riquet is not actually transformed into a handsome prince, but the effect of love means the princess no longer sees his faults.[47] Regardless of whether love is a transformative or illusory force, the ending to Perrault's tale reinforces the patriarchal nature of early modern marriage. Like Bernard's Mama, Perrault's princess has no real choice about whether to marry as the intelligence she desires is only available to her as Riquet's wife. Her love for her husband makes submission to his authority more palatable, but it does not change the patriarchal nature of their relationship. Bernard's heroine is well aware of the gendered power imbalance in her marriage, and her intelligence is rendered worthless by her husband's vengeance.

GIFT-GIVING AND CHOICE OF MARRIAGE PARTNER

Choice of marriage partner, especially the ability of women to choose their husbands, is one of the most important themes in the conteuses' tales. The importance of this theme echoes salon counter-discourses questioning the patriarchal legal framework established by the French state's codification of marriage as an economic institution subject to parental control.[48] These counter-discourses proposed a reformulation of marriage to promote equality between the sexes and free choice of spouse. Marrying to satisfy family obligation or choosing a spouse based on his socioeconomic status rather than his personal merit was explicitly rejected by this critique of seventeenth-century marital convention.[49] A series of letters exchanged by Anne-Marie-Louise d'Orléans, duchesse de Montpensier, and Françoise Bertaut de Motteville between May 14, 1660, and August 1, 1661, exemplify this criticism of marriage. Montpensier, who was in the unusual position of being a single woman in control of substantial inherited wealth, refused several marriage proposals including one from her younger cousin Louis XIV.[50] In her letters to Motteville, she developed a vision of a utopian community without marriage in which women controlled their destiny and their property.[51] Marriage, which Montpensier rejected as a form of slavery from which women must deliver themselves, was allowed only on the basis of love, and people wishing to marry would be required to leave the community.[52] This pessimistic view of marriage as an institution that limited the liberty of women by granting power over their lives to men underpins Bernard's version of the Riquet tale.

The conteuses' tales engaged with salon criticism of arranged marriages in their use of gift exchange to explore the agency of women to choose their spouse. In tales by d'Aulnoy, Murat, and Durand, the role of male gift-givers as initiators of courtship is subverted by the agency of female gift-givers. This reversal of the gendered pattern of gift-giving in the Riquet tales emphasizes the relationship between the conteuses' tales and other 1690s texts that promoted marriage reform by advocating free choice of spouse.[53] In this context, a considerable number of d'Aulnoy's tales feature heroines who choose their own spouses based on personal inclination. The eponymous heroine in "La princesse Rosette" is determined to marry the King of Paons (Peacocks), and her brothers embark on a treacherous journey to fulfill her wish. Finette negotiates her own marriage contract with her future in-laws in "Finette Cendron." Gracieuse in "Gracieuse et Percinet" and Laideronnette in "Serpentin Vert" abandon their respective kingdoms to marry, without parental consent, men who have won their hearts. Serpentin Vert, the owner of the mysterious disembodied voice Laideronnette falls in love with, presents his future wife with a continuous stream of magnificent gifts while courting her each night with gallant words of love.[54] The hero in "Le prince Lutin" and the heroine in "La Chatte Blanche" use magical gifts to woo the objects of their respective affections. Prince Lutin uses his power of invisibility to overhear his beloved talking to her lady-in-waiting so that he can surprise her with gifts fulfilling her desires.[55] The heroine in "La Chatte Blanche" uses her fairy powers to provide her beloved with the objects he requires to fulfill his father's demands.[56]

In each of the following case studies, d'Aulnoy, Murat, and Durand use gift exchange to establish a personal relationship between husbands and wives before their marriage. The nature of these relationships reflects the scripts for love and marriage in the opposing versions of the Riquet tale by Bernard and Perrault. In d'Aulnoy's tales, elements of Perrault's representation of marriage as a reciprocal social contract and Bernard's critique of the patriarchal obligation of love appear alongside a strong call for freedom of choice in the selection of marriage partners. D'Aulnoy's tales reward faithful, virtuous love with perfect happiness, and the exchange of gifts between prospective marriage partners functions as a symbol of that love. Tales by Durand and Murat reverse gendered patterns of gift exchange during courtship. The fairy queen in Murat's "Jeune et Belle" courts a handsome shepherd by surprising him with marvelous gifts, and Durand's "Le prodige d'amour" inverts the gendered opposition of female beauty and male intelligence in the Riquet tales. The initial suggestion that each of these tales will adhere to a traditional model of marriage as a transactional exchange is undermined by the fact that it is the female characters who initiate the exchange of gifts.

D'Aulnoy's "La princesse Rosette" begins with a classic fairy-tale opening: a dire prediction of misfortune causing the heroine to be locked in a tower from which she cannot escape. The prediction that leads to Rosette's imprisonment is a fairy prophesy that Rosette "will cause a great misfortune to her brothers, and that they will die in an affair for her."[57] In order to protect their sons, Rosette's parents build a grand tower in which Rosette is confined, and they, along with Rosette's two brothers, visit her every day.[58] When Rosette's parents die, her brothers, who are unaware of the prophecy, decide to release their beloved sister and promise her that the new king, her eldest brother, will arrange for her to be married.[59] According to Rosette's brothers, marriage is her only destiny, and d'Aulnoy's tale recounts how this destiny is fulfilled. Before the death of the king, Rosette's eldest brother innocently asked his father whether there would soon be a wedding, as Rosette had just turned fifteen and was old enough to be married.[60] When Rosette's father dies, her brothers assume authority for the negotiation of her marriage.

The marriage arranged for Rosette by her brothers is a traditional royal marriage with a twist. Although d'Aulnoy employs conventional motifs such as love at first sight, the use of a portrait to negotiate the marriage of a beautiful princess, and the substitution of an ugly pretender for the true bride, her tale playfully reinterprets these tropes and subtly questions the patriarchal framework of early modern marriage by making a peacock the object of Rosette's affection.[61] When Rosette is released from her tower, a peacock is one of the first things she sees. She is astonished by the beauty of the bird, and she declares that she will marry no one but the king of the peacocks.[62] Despite misgivings about whether it is possible to fulfill the "unfortunate fantasy" of their sister, the brothers satisfy their filial duties by setting out to find the suitor she has imagined.[63] Upon finding the king of the peacocks, who is, luckily, a man rather than a bird, Rosette's brothers use her portrait to negotiate her marriage contract.[64]

Rosette's extraordinary beauty is the most important commodity in the negotiation of her marriage. It is her portrait that the brothers give to the king when asking if he wants to marry her. When the king consents to the union, he warns the brothers that he will kill them if Rosette is not as beautiful as her portrait. The king's affection for his future spouse is based solely on her beauty, and his promises to fulfill his spousal duties of material support and love are conditional on her body fulfilling the promise of her portrait.[65] The emphasis on Rosette's beauty, as well as the king's assessment of it as a valuable commodity, illustrates the transactional nature of early modern marriage as an exchange transferring authority over women from one patriarch to another. Despite Rosette's assertion of a right to choose her own husband, her marriage is arranged by her brothers according to the traditional model of marriage as a socioeconomic exchange. Rosette's brothers give the king her portrait as well as promises of gold and an assurance that Rosette will submit to his authority. In return, the king promises that he will love Rosette and that she will want for nothing as his wife.[66] This negotiation reduces Rosette to an object of exchange who is valued only insofar as she conforms to seventeenth-century gender norms that idealized chaste, beautiful female bodies. It is Rosette's perfect embodiment of the ideal of female beauty, as well as assistance from male guardians who agree to procure her chosen spouse, which allows the fulfillment of her choice of marriage partner.

The unconventional marriage negotiation initiated by the eponymous heroine in d'Aulnoy's "Finette Cendron" provides a more explicit assertion of the right of women to choose their husbands. At the end of this tale, which combines plot elements also present in Perrault's "Cendrillon" and "Le Petit Poucet," Finette negotiates the terms of her marriage contract with the parents of her future husband. Her consent to the marriage is conditional on the return of her parents' kingdom, a kingdom the prince's parents conquered at the beginning of the tale.[67] Finette's ability to negotiate on her own behalf comes from the power she obtains from her position as the only person able to prevent the death of the prince from lovesickness. This lovesickness, which is caused by the prince's discovery of Finette's petite slipper and his subsequent refusal to eat or to marry anyone but its owner, prompts his mother to promise to give him the woman he loves, regardless of her social rank.[68] Although Finette's royal lineage means that the threat of mésalliance is avoided, the queen's willingness to allow her son to choose his wife is significant in light of the legal requirement of parental consent enshrined in seventeenth-century marriage law.

From the perspective of Finette's future husband, love, or to be more precise, the love inspired by his discovery of Finette's slipper, is his sole motivation for marriage. Incapacitated by his emotional attachment to an unknown woman, the prince cannot conform to the traditional model of marriage as a socioeconomic transaction. Like the hero in both Riquet tales, he desires to marry the woman he loves, but, unlike the Riquet character, he lacks the capacity to initiate a reciprocal exchange of gifts with his beloved. With only his love to offer, the prince is dependent on his parents to provide the necessary material exchange. In the absence of Finette's parents, who abandoned her and her two sisters at the beginning of the tale, Finette is free to choose her husband and negotiate the terms of their union. Finette does not express any emotional attachment to her future husband, and he virtually disappears from the narrative once Finette agrees to marry him. Finette's primary concern in arranging her marriage is the restoration of her family's social status. After successfully reinstating her parents as the rulers of their kingdom, she presents her two (nasty) sisters to the queen and asks her to love them.[69] In her moral to the tale, d'Aulnoy praises Finette's magnanimous treatment of her sisters. She identifies Finette's generosity to them as the ultimate vengeance for their mistreatment of her.[70] The moral does not mention the prince or Finette's marriage to him.

D'Aulnoy presents two very different models of the marriage relationship produced by free choice of spouse in "Gracieuse et Percinet." After rapidly disposing of the perfect relationship between the heroine's parents at the beginning of the tale, d'Aulnoy develops two opposing versions of a nontraditional marriage relationship. The first model is the transactional union negotiated by the heroine's stepmother, Duchess Grognon.[71] The gift exchange negotiating the terms of Grognon's marriage to Gracieuse's father, the king, echoes the gift exchange in Bernard's Riquet tale with a few key differences. The first difference is that the gift exchange is initiated by the prospective bride, Grognon, rather than her future husband. When the king stops for a rest at Grognon's chateau while hunting on a hot day, she cunningly displays her wealth to him by causing valuable objects to appear from bottles of wine.[72] Dismissing the foreign and French gold coins, diamonds, and pearls covering her cellar floor as mere "bagatelles," Grognon offers them to the king in exchange for a promise of marriage. The direct language of her proposal, "I will make you the master of it [the gold and precious stones] on the condition that you marry me," invokes the language of obligation used by Bernard's Riquet.[73] This condition is not the only obligation attached to Grognon's gift. Like Bernard's Riquet, who expects his future wife to love him as well as marry him, Grognon attaches two obligations to her gift: the king must marry her, and he must give her complete control over his daughter, Gracieuse.[74]

Unlike the gift exchange in Bernard's Riquet tale, the exchange between Grognon and her future husband is a reciprocal transaction. She gives him control over her wealth, and in return he gives her control over his daughter. Neither husband nor wife are motivated by love, but neither expects their union to produce an emotional relationship with their spouse. The union between Grognon and the king exemplifies the traditional model of marriage, and when the king informs his daughter about his impending nuptials, he characterizes it as a conquest rather than a loving union by telling her, "I have captured a live dove."[75] In response to Gracieuse's literal interpretation of the hunting metaphor, he explains that he has taken Grognon as his wife, and he orders Gracieuse to love and respect her stepmother as if she were her mother.[76] This is the first time that love is mentioned in relation to the king's marriage to Grognon, and the king imposes this emotional obligation on his daughter rather than himself.

It is through the king's abdication of his parental authority over his daughter that d'Aulnoy develops a subtle critique of the patriarchal structure of early modern marriage. This critique is based on the opposition of Grognon's usurpation of patriarchal authority with the loving relationship between Gracieuse and Percinet. In this context, d'Aulnoy's obvious characterization of Grognon as the villain of the tale clearly indicates that her marital relationship is not the model d'Aulnoy intends to promote. Grognon, who is old and ugly with red hair, bad skin, one eye, and a big mouth, is physically deformed and morally suspect, as indicated by her name.[77] It is her unbearable jealousy of Gracieuse's beauty that motivates her desire to marry the king and her persecution of Gracieuse drives the narrative of the tale. The character of Grognon subverts elements of the patriarchal structure of early modern marriage by initiating the gift exchange with her future husband. She uses the exchange to obtain a power that is ordinarily exercised by the patriarch of a household. Grognon's abuse of her power to persecute Gracieuse, the more sympathetic character in the tale, undermines the subversive potential of her assertive courtship. Any alteration in the traditional model of marriage suggested by Grognon's relationship with her husband is overwhelmed by the unfavorable comparison between it and the relationship between Gracieuse and Percinet.

The second model of marriage proposed by d'Aulnoy in "Gracieuse et Percinet" is the loving union between the eponymous heroic couple. Their marriage, which is negotiated by the couple with encouragement from Percinet's mother, is based on their reciprocal emotional bond. There is no reciprocal material exchange. Percinet's courtly love for Gracieuse motivates him to save her repeatedly from the persecution of her stepmother and the eventual reward for his fidelity is Gracieuse's hand in marriage.[78] The relationship between Gracieuse and Percinet is based on d'Aulnoy's reinterpretation of the tenets of courtly love for a seventeenth-century audience. Percinet declares that Gracieuse is his *maîtresse* (mistress) and that he is therefore bound to obey her wishes in all matters.[79] He respects Gracieuse's scrupulous reluctance to spend time alone with him but magically appears whenever she needs his assistance. Gracieuse repeatedly tests Percinet's fidelity and initially refuses to accept his gifts because she is wary of the implied obligation of love they impose on her. When a magnificent fairy palace appears in the woods to which Grognon has exiled Gracieuse, she tries to run away: "Ah, it is too much! Let us get away from him [Percinet]. It is better to die than to love him."[80] After reluctantly accepting Percinet's hospitality, Gracieuse tries to leave almost immediately by telling him that she must account for her actions to her father.[81] Gracieuse's commitment to her filial duty means that she will not agree to marry Percinet. She does admit, however, that she would accept his proposal if she were in charge of her own destiny.[82] Gracieuse eventually gives her consent to the union after she is buried alive by Grognon. The tale ends with a joyous celebration of her wedding to Percinet.

Murat's "Jeune et Belle" and Durand's "Le prodige d'amour" also feature female gift-givers. Jeune et Belle uses her magic to make the fleece of the shepherd's flock "whiter than the snow."[83] She decorates his sheep with ribbons and gives his sheepdog a golden collar inscribed with a verse about burning ardor and tender hearts. Her gifts impose a reciprocal obligation of fidelity on the shepherd and Jeune et Belle does not reveal her true identity to him until he proves his fidelity to her. She appears before him in the guise of a shepherdess and gives him two portraits: one of herself and another of a person as young and beautiful as one could imagine. Jeune et Belle's portrait is inscribed with the following warning: "forget her charms, or your love will be fatal."[84] The shepherd passes the test of fidelity when he ignores this warning and ardently declares his love for Jeune et Belle. According to Murat, this relationship is not a mésalliance in the sense that it would be if Jeune et Belle was human. Fairies, Murat claims, have the same privileges as goddesses: "they love a shepherd when he is worthy of love as if he was the greatest king in the universe, because all men are beneath them."[85] The agency Murat allows her fairy heroines to choose their spouses is emphasized by Jeune et Belle's use of gift exchange to initiate and control courtship with the man she loves. She elevates the shepherd to the status of a king and promises him that they will be happy if he remains faithful to her.[86]

In Durand's "Le prodige d'amour," it is the hero of the tale who lacks esprit, and the heroine who has the power to transform a handsome but stupid prince into a desirable husband. Brutalis's lack of esprit means he is utterly uninterested in love or marriage, which is fortunate as he is rejected as a potential husband for the daughters of all the neighboring kings. Unlike Bernard's Mama, Brutalis is oblivious to his stupidity. His primary passion is hunting, and he is perfectly content to ignore any woman who might hope to marry him. Like Mama, love is identified as the cure to his lack of esprit, but he does not fall in love with the fairy who attempts to seduce him.[87] It is the heroine of the tale who inspires the love that gives Brutalis the gift of esprit. Brillante is a beautiful princess from l'Île Galante who has left her father's kingdom in search of faithful, virtuous love. She is destined to cure Brutalis's stupidity by a prediction in a nightingale's song that she will give a "precious gift" to a lover capable of giving her the faithful love she desires.[88] When Brutalis makes eye contact with Brillante, his ardor fulfills the nightingale's prophesy, and he uses his newfound esprit to court the princess.[89] This reciprocal exchange creates an emotional bond between the couple, and the tale ends with the celebration of their wedding.

The concept of marriage developed in tales featuring the exchange of gifts by courting couples is that of a relationship negotiated within a patriarchal framework. In writing different versions of the relationship between husbands and wives, d'Aulnoy, Bernard, Murat, Durand, and Perrault present different interpretations of the obligation of love associated with marriage. The tension between Bernard's critique of marriage as an inevitable source of misery and Perrault's optimistic interpretation of marriage as a reciprocal relationship offers insight into a sociopolitical shift in the concept of marriage in seventeenth-century France. Perrault's Riquet tale uses the successful gift exchange between Riquet and his bride to represent marriage as a reciprocal relationship in which the emotional bond between husband and wife softens the patriarchal structure of their relationship. Their companionate marriage relies on the exchange of gifts to create the loving union that sustains their relationship. The failed gift exchange between Bernard's Riquet and his reluctant bride illustrates the structural limits on the ability of early modern women to negotiate the gendered power imbalance inherent in the early modern marriage relationship. Their ability to choose their own marriage partner is circumscribed by the legal requirement for parental consent and the social limits on their ability to resist alliances arranged for them. The unbalanced gift exchange between Riquet and Mama illustrates this in Bernard's representation of marriage as an asymmetrical exchange causing unhappiness to both parties. Mama cannot reciprocate her husband's gift because she cannot love him, and this causes their marriage to fail. Their relationship is unbalanced due to Mama's inability to fulfil her obligation to love her husband, and she resents her husband for his power over her. But even if she were able to choose to marry her lover, Bernard suggests that this choice is illusory to the extent that he would become a husband whom she was obliged to obey.

In understanding the differences between the two versions of the Riquet tale, the emotional relationship produced by the performance of these emotion scripts is more important than the gifts exchanged. In offering a gift to his intended future wife, Riquet performs the emotion associated with the type of relationship he wishes to have with his wife, love. In accepting Riquet's gift, the obligation of reciprocity means that Riquet's wife is expected to reciprocate his love. If she fails to do so, she has failed to fulfill the reciprocal obligation she agreed to by accepting Riquet's gift. In Perrault's version of the tale, the heroine's fulfillment of her reciprocal obligation transforms her ugly suitor into the most handsome prince in the world.[90] According to the two morals to this tale, it is only by loving Riquet that Perrault's heroine can produce this transformation: her love either turns him into a handsome prince or it allows her to see him as one.[91] In Bernard's tale the issue of reciprocity is more complex. Although the heroine does marry Riquet, her newfound intelligence makes her unable to love him, and the tale ends with a pessimistic critique of marriage as a source of unhappiness for women.[92] Mama cannot return his love, and this exacerbates the asymmetrical nature of early modern marriage in which the balance of power was weighted in favor of husbands.

Bernard's critique of marriage appears in a more muted form in d'Aulnoy's tales. D'Aulnoy uses her tales to advocate for the right of women (and men) to choose their marriage partners, and her tales allow for the possibility of a successful marriage based on either the reciprocal exchange of material gifts or the mutual affection of husband and wife. In "La princesse Rosette," "Finette Cendron," and "Gracieuse et Percinet," the reciprocal exchange of material gifts reflects the traditional view of marriage as a socioeconomic transaction. In each tale, a marriage between persons of equal rank, either a princess and a king or a duchess and a king, is negotiated by a reciprocal material exchange: Rosette's beauty inspires her husband's love; Gracieuse's stepmother, Grognon, offers wealth in exchange for power; and Finette refuses to marry a lovesick prince until his parents return the kingdom they took from her parents. D'Aulnoy's tales also use gift-giving to comment on the obligation of love associated with the early modern marriage relationship. In "Serpentin Vert," "Le prince Lutin," and "La Chatte Blanche," the exchange of gifts operates in an analogous manner to the exchange in Perrault's Riquet tale in the sense that the moment of exchange created an emotional bond between husband and wife. But unlike the intangible gift offered by Perrault's Riquet (intelligence), d'Aulnoy's gift-givers offer material things to their respective beloveds. The recipients of these gifts are subject to the same reciprocal obligation as Perrault's heroine. The unspoken condition of each material gift is an implied obligation to reciprocate the love offered to the recipient by the giver and consent to a marriage consummating that love.

Bernard's criticism of love and marriage as sources of unhappiness for women is part of an explicit authorial strategy. In the preface to *Le comte d'Amboise*, Bernard articulates her motivation as follows: "I have declared . . . that my intention was to show only unhappy lovers to combat, as much as I could, the penchant we have for love."[93] This novel is the second in a series of three published by Bernard between 1687 and 1696 under the title *Les malheurs de l'amour* (The Misfortunes of Love). In the "Avertissement" to the first novel in the series, *Éléonor d'Yvrée*, Bernard explains that her decision to present the "malheurs de l'amour" is motivated by a desire to challenge the dangerous impression created by novels that reward virtuous and delicate lovers with happy endings. Instead, Bernard puts her heroes in situations so sad that no one will envy them.[94] Bernard's two fairy tales, her Riquet tale and "Le prince Rosier," appear as stories told by characters in the third novel in her series, *Inès de Cordoue*. As I discuss further in the following chapter, their pessimistic endings reflect Bernard's authorial intention to question celebration of love as the ultimate happy ending. According to Bernard, marriage means that all women will eventually be unable to distinguish between the men they once loved and their husbands. Love, whether an illusion, a transformative force or a source of unhappiness, does not alter the balance of power between husbands and wives. This critique of the distribution of emotional power within marriage problematizes the obligation of love expected of wives as an extension of their husbands' authority over them. The exchange of marriage gifts reinforces the structural imbalance in this distribution of power by reproducing the transactional definition of marriage as a socioeconomic exchange.

5

Love after Marriage

Moral Lessons and Unhappy Endings

The search for moral lessons in the conteuses' tales is a complex interpretative task. The rhetorical strategy of *plaire et instruire* (please and instruct) is a key feature of the conteuses' representation of the aims and aesthetics of their tales and one of the hallmarks of the fairy-tale genre.[1] However, contemporary critics, in particular Abbé Pierre de Villiers, interpreted the conteuses' framing of their tales as pleasurable stories as evidence of authorial disregard for the didactic poetics of marvelous literature.[2] With the exception of Charles Perrault's tales, which Villiers praises for imitating the style and simplicity of the nurses he claims invented the genre, Villers dismisses fairy tales as frivolous stories written by women and ignorant men.[3] This critique is based on two assertions: that fairy tales were written by authors who did not believe they required any talent and that the tales written by such authors failed to convey any instructive moral lesson.[4] The second accusation is the most damning. In Villiers's 1699 polemic *Entretiens sur les contes de fées,* good fairy tales are those that contain an instructive lesson.[5] He claims that the conteuses' tales do not satisfy this moral imperative because there is little rapport between the rhyming maxims and *sentences* at the end of their tales and the substance of the tales they conclude.[6] However, Villiers's attack on the conteuses' tales for lacking moral substance misreads the sophisticated framing strategies that delivered moral instruction under the guise of frivolous entertainment. It fails to recognize the didactic poetics that subtly framed the conteuses' tales as moral commentary on the gender politics of love and marriage in seventeenth-century France.

As I discuss in chapter 1, the aesthetic of conversation is a defining feature of the conteuses' tales. It shaped the representation of their work as a textual recreation of salon conversation and directed the emotion scripts in their tales to an elite female audience of salon readers and writers. This chapter focuses on the moral poetics intertwined with this conversational aesthetic. This poetics is articulated in the letters, prefaces, dedications, frame-tale narratives, and verse morals framing the conteuses' tales and reinforces their identity as an emotional community of modern female writers. My reading of the conteuses' moral poetics extends work by Sophie Raynard and Christine Jones. Like Raynard, I suggest that Villiers's accusation of frivolity tales misreads the conteuses' work by failing to recognize the moral messages encoded in their representation of eloquent fairies and sage heroines.[7] This misreading may be attributed to the fact that the models of moral poetics developed by the conteuses are subversive in the ways in which they question whether the marriage closure constitutes a happy ending for women. This reading of the conteuses' moral intent means that unlike Jones, I do not interpret the conteuses' aesthetic of frivolity as a rejection of didactic poetics but as a deliberate authorial decision to develop a distinctly female aesthetic that distinguished their tales from the conventional morality in Perrault's tales and Jean de La Fontaine's fables.[8]

This chapter argues that the moral critique of love in the verse morals, maxims, and endings in the conteuses' tales offer a set of emotion scripts about what happens after courtship and marriage. These scripts interrogate the emotional relationship between husbands and wives and valorize a modern morality distinct from the didactic poetics of Perrault's tales and La Fontaine's fables. This reading of the conteuses' tales interprets the conversational aesthetic of their writing as a sophisticated literary strategy designed to conceal a subversive politics of love and marriage as entertainment.[9] The poetics of frivolity established in the prefaces, dedications, and frame-tale narratives created by d'Aulnoy, Bernard, Lhéritier, and Murat reshaped the didactic poetics of seventeenth-century marvelous literature while simultaneously questioning the gender politics of love and marriage. The subversive nature of the conteuses' political scripts is illustrated by their production of tales that subtly undermined the marriage closure, a literary trope popular in the seventeenth-century fiction that influenced the development of the fairy-tale genre. In making this argument, it is importance to recognize, as Lewis C. Seifert observes, that the inaugural status of tales produced during the first French fairy-tale vogue means that the marriage closure was not an established convention of the fairy-tale genre at this time. This means that the inclusion or absence of the marriage closure in the conteuses' tales was a deliberate authorial choice.[10] In this chapter, I interpret the conteuses' choice of ending as a sociopolitical decision rather than a purely poetic one. This means that I read the ambiguous morality of tales that end unhappily or fail to punish social transgression such as adultery and premarital sex as moral instruction about the right way to love that undermined the patriarchal structure of courtship and marriage. This ambiguous moral poetic provided a new set of scripts for love after marriage for the sophisticated, modern audience to whom the conteuses directed their tales.

THE MORAL POETICS OF MARVELOUS TALES

The conteuses' comments on the didactic function of the fairy-tale genre appear in the frame-tale narratives in which d'Aulnoy, Bernard, and Murat embedded their tales and in the prefaces, dedications, letters, and avertissements that accompanied the publication of tales by d'Aulnoy, Bernard, Murat, and Lhéritier. The conteuses were not the only seventeenth-century writers to reflect on the moral poetics of the emerging genre. The moral utility of marvelous literature was a recurring theme in seventeenth-century debates about literary value, and one of the key issues of contestation in the *Querelle des Anciens et des Modernes.*[11] In the preface to a 1695 collection of verse tales, which contains three previously published tales, "Grisélidis," "Peau d'Âne," and "Souhaits ridicules," Perrault defends his stories from accusations of frivolity by arguing that they are modern tales with a superior morality to ancient tales. Like Villiers, Perrault emphasizes the importance of a moral imperative as a key feature of marvelous tales.[12] Although Perrault does not comment on the tales written by his female contemporaries, the model of morality identified by Perrault—the reward of virtue and punishment of vice—underpins much of the conteuses' commentary on their didactic intentions. However, as we will see in the second section of this chapter, the qualities identified as vices and virtues in the verse morals and endings to the conteuses' tales do not always accord with conventional seventeenth-century morality. But before I examine the ways in which the conteuses develop this subversive moral commentary, the following discussion analyzes how they articulate the didactic function of the fairy-tale genre.

The conversational framing of d'Aulnoy's tales as stories told by characters to an audience in a longer narrative allows d'Aulnoy to position her tales as entertaining stories and comment on their moral purpose. In "Don Gabriel Ponce de Leon," the frame tale to "Le Mouton," "Finette Cendron," and "Fortunée," d'Aulnoy uses the voice of one of the characters in the novel, Mélanie, to argue that fairy tales must amuse and provide some sort of moral.[13] D'Aulnoy reinforces this didactic poetics in the verse morals to "La bonne petite souris" and "Fortunée." In "La bonne petite souris," d'Aulnoy acknowledges the goals of pleasure and moral instruction as crucial elements of the purpose of the tale:

> All this is nothing but a fable,
> Made to amuse anyone who reads it;
> And yet in it we can find a true moral.[14]

The moral lesson of this tale praises the generosity of an imprisoned queen who shares her food with a fairy disguised as a mouse, thus earning fairy protection for her unborn daughter. It identifies gratitude as the most powerful virtue for winning a heart.[15] The moral concluding "Fortunée" argues that merit and virtue are the true markers of nobility and addresses this lesson to nobles whose pride in their ancient lineage means that they are unable to recognize other markers of status.[16] These rather conventional morals exemplify the "praise of virtue" and "punishment of vice" model of fairy-tale morality.

The paratexts to Lhéritier's tales contain the most explicit reflection on the moral poetics of the fairy-tale genre. In them, Lhéritier defends the aesthetics and morality of fairy tales and seeks to establish her authority as a scholar interpreting the moral virtue of medieval French tales for a modern audience. Lhéritier articulates this poetics in the moral to "L'adroite princesse," a tale she states her governess told her instead of animal fables.[17] This moral invokes the plaire et instruire model in La Fontaine's fables, but Lhéritier explicitly distinguishes her tales by stating that they are more amazing than his "acts of the monkey and the wolf."[18] Lhéritier's defense of the moral utility of fairy tales does, however, draw on many of the same arguments La Fontaine used to defend the pedagogical value of his fables. In 1668 La Fontaine dedicated his first book of fables, *Fables choisies mises en vers,* to Louis XIV's six-year-old son, Monseigneur le Dauphin. This dedication states that La Fontaine was presenting the Dauphin with fables inspired by Aesop because he was of an age at which he was in need of amusement and serious reflection.[19] It defends the childish appearance of fables on the grounds that their childishness disguises important truths.[20] La Fontaine promises the Dauphin that in reading his fables he will "learn . . . with pleasure, all that it is necessary for a prince to know."[21]

Lhéritier invokes the plaire et instruire dictum to defend the pedagogical value of her tales in *Oeuvres meslées.* Her letter of dedication to Madame D.G. praises the wisdom of adorning and embellishing maxims so that they might better instruct young people: "Everywhere in society we see little stories whose sole purpose is to confirm pleasantly the soundness of proverbs."[22] This reference to "little stories" (*petites histoires*) refers to the contemporary popularity of fairy tales and emphasizes the moral intent of the genre as modern retellings of tales inherited from the troubadours.[23] In representing fairy tales as a collaboration between the troubadours and educated salon women, Lhéritier sought to elevate the genre by linking it to an ancient Gallic literary tradition.[24] Lhéritier includes herself among the authors venturing to write tales based on ancient maxims, a task she praises for "seem[ing] to bring back the times of the fairies when there were so many perfect men and women."[25] In identifying the troubadours' tales as her source material, Lhéritier challenges the veneration of the classical Greek and Roman texts as the proper model for judging literary value. Lhéritier makes her intention to contribute to the *Querelle des Anciens et des Modernes* clear in "Les enchantements de l'éloquence." In commentary at the end of the tale, Lhéritier suggests that it is no more incredible than many stories from Ancient Greece and argues that ancient Gallic and ancient Greek tales have equal literary value.[26]

In the verse moral to "Marmoisan," Lhéritier reiterates her intention to use the principle of pleasurable didacticism to provide moral instruction.[27] The subtitle of this tale, "Nouvelle héroïque et satirique" (A Heroic and Satiric Tale), provides a subtle clue of Lhéritier's intention to use the tale to present a moral message to her readers. This intention is made explicit in the verse moral at the end of the tale in which Lhéritier praises "the wisdom of our fathers" for presenting moral instruction as "beautiful lessons" rather than "severe maxims."[28] The moral instruction Lhéritier provides rewards heroines who exemplify feminine virtues such as fidelity, chastity, discretion, and politeness. Her tales punish characters who display imprudence, vanity, and idleness.[29] In addition to developing moral standards for female behavior, Lhéritier presents her heroines as models of female eloquence and uses their exemplary behavior to advocate for female education. The moral to "Les enchantements de l'éloquence" idealizes the polite manners of the heroine and concludes that "sweet and courtly language is better than a rich inheritance."[30] In this tale, Lhéritier defends the moral poetics of fiction by suggesting it is more beneficial for young people to read novels instead of history because novels provide a better moral example. History, according to Lhéritier, shows the reality of human nature because is it "entirely subject to truth."[31] By contrast, novels offer an idealized version of how men "ought to be, and thereby encourage aspiration to perfection."[32] As compared to the rest of the conteuses, Lhéritier's tales provide limited moral instruction on love and marriage. Her tales do create an idealized version of seventeenth-century gender politics.[33] Her insistence on the moral character of the genre and her creation of active, eloquent heroines establishes a subversive moral poetic as a key feature of the modern aesthetic of the conteuses' tales.

Bernard comments on the purpose of the fairy-tale genre in the preface to *Inès de Cordoue*. Her take on the genre emphasizes the aesthetic function of fairy tales: "That the adventures should always be implausible, and the emotions always natural."[34] In the text of the narrative into which her fairy tales are interpolated, Bernard defines fairy tales as a new amusement for the ladies of the court that must be composed according to certain rules.[35] Bernard's aesthetic criteria means that *contes galants* are pleasing if they show what happens in the heart and are not restrained by the appearance of truth.[36] This aesthetic proposes an alternative moral poetic to the praise virtue–punish vice model used by d'Aulnoy and Lhéritier. Bernard seems to be suggesting that representing the reality of emotional experience is more important than providing a moral lesson. She describes the emotional truth she intends to represent in her tales in the prefaces to her *Les malheurs de l'amour* series. In the paratexts to *Éléonor d'Yvrée* and *Le comte d'Amboise,* Bernard expresses her intention to show unhappy lovers and the misfortunes of love. In expressing this intention Bernard distinguishes her writing from other contemporary literary works that end happily by rewarding delicate and virtuous lovers.[37]

Murat's perspective on the moral poetics of marvelous tales is more oblique than the explicit commentary by Lhéritier, Bernard, and d'Aulnoy about their didactic intentions. Murat published her first volume of tales in 1698 after Lhéritier urged her to turn her literary talents to the genre in the moral to "L'adroite princesse." In 1699 Murat offered her perspective on the fairy-tale genre in her dedication of *Histoires sublimes et allégoriques* to her fellow conteuses. Murat's "Aux Fées Modernes" emphasizes the superiority of modern fairies to the "base and childish" activities of Perrault's ancient muses.[38] She offers the great deeds of her modern fairies as superior moral exemplars to Perrault's *Contes de ma Mère l'Oye*.[39] Murat's critique of Perrault's claim that his tales are morally superior to La Fontaine's fables questions Perrault's credentials as a modern author. It establishes a clear distinction between his tales and those by the conteuses by identifying his source material as popular oral storytelling traditions designed to amuse servants and nurses. By contrast, Murat praises the conteuses' tales as modern literary creations designed to entertain a sophisticated, worldly audience. Like Lhéritier, Murat seeks to elevate the status of the fairy-tale genre by emphasizing the literary nature of her source material and the sophistication of her fellow authors. In doing so, Murat locates the moral poetics of the genre in the worldly milieu of salon conversation.[40] As we saw in chapter 2, salon debate about marriage rejected the idealization of courtship and love associated with pastoral texts such as Honoré d'Urfé's *L'Astrée*. Midcentury salonnières proposed a radical redefinition of marriage based on equality between the sexes and personal choice based on *inclination*.[41] The subversive nature of these ideas is reflected by the gender politics of the moral poetics in the conteuses' tales.

IRONY, AMBIGUITY, AND THE MARRIAGE CLOSURE

The conventional fairy-tale ending is the celebration of a marriage between the heroic couple.[42] This ending, which was established as a defining feature of the genre during the seventeenth and eighteenth centuries, is premised on the notion of marriage as the ultimate reward for couples who prove their virtue and overcome obstacles to their union. Raymonde Robert identifies the happy ending restoring order and fulfilling the exemplary destiny of the heroic couple as a central feature of the fairy-tale genre.[43] Her recognition of the generic importance of the happy ending draws on Vladimir Propp's work on the functions of Russian folk lore and fairy tales in which punishment of villains (U) and marriage and elevation in the status of the hero (W) are the final two functions.[44] As a symbolic representation of the heroic couple's triumph, the marriage closure became the dominant ending in the fairy tales published in France during the seventeenth and eighteenth centuries.[45] Nadine Jasmin, Sophie Raynard, and Patricia Hannon analyze the role of the happy ending in the seventeenth-century French fairy-tale vogue.[46] Jasmin and Raynard interpret unhappy endings in the conteuses' tales as challenges to the narrative logic of the genre.[47] Hannon goes further by suggesting that the conteuses' use of the marriage closure is, at best, an ironic gesture that cannot contain the subversive moral content of their tales.[48]

The conteuses' ironic or ambiguous use of the marriage closure is a central feature of the subversive moral poetic in their emotion scripts. Of their corpus of 63 tales, 44 end with the celebration of a wedding. Nineteen of d'Aulnoy's 25 tales end with marriage between the heroic couple. Three of the 6 tales that do not follow this pattern end unhappily due to denial of the marriage closure.[49] Of the remaining 3 tales, 1 reunites a separated married couple, 1 allows the heroic couple to live together in a marriage like relationship under fairy protection, and 1 sees the hero to marry three times in order to reverse his metamorphosis as a wild boar.[50] Both Bernard's tales feature a marriage between the heroic couple, but this marriage occurs during the course of the narrative, and each marriage fails by the end of the tale. All of Lhéritier's tales end with the celebration of a wedding, but love is not central to the plot in her tales. Marriage appears almost as an afterthought as the expected ending for heroines who have proven their virtue and intelligence.[51] Marriage is a prominent theme in tales by La Force and Murat. Six of La Force's 8 tales and 11 of Murat's 14 tales end with the celebration of a wedding. In La Force's "Persinette" and Murat's "Le palais de la vengeance" and "Le prince des feuilles," the heroic couples end up in a relationship akin to marriage. The marriage closure is used less frequently by Durand and d'Auneuil, with only 1 of Durand's 3 tales, and 5 of d'Auneuil's 9 tales ending with a marriage between the heroic couple.

Love plays an important role in the conteuses' use of the marriage closure. The verse morals at the end of tales by d'Aulnoy, La Force, and Murat, and the maxims in tales by Bernard, Durand, and Murat, reflect on the nature of love and the likely nature of the marriage between the heroic couple. If a tale ends with the celebration of a marriage, the verse moral often explains why the couple was rewarded with marriage. If the tale ends unhappily, the moral explains the reason for this unhappiness, most often a failure to love or a failure to love in the correct manner. Commentary on love in the verse morals and maxims in the conteuses' tales is particularly relevant to analysis of their emotion scripts for love. Shifts in the narrative voice used by d'Aulnoy, Lhéritier, and La Force suggest that they are directing their readers to pay particular attention to their verse morals. In the body of their tales, the dominant narrative voice is that of an omniscient third person narrator. In d'Aulnoy's and Lhéritier's verse morals, a switch to the first person, *je* (I), *mon*, *ma* (my), and *moi* (me), invokes their own experience to strengthen the truth claim of their commentary on love.[52] Along with La Force, d'Aulnoy and Lhéritier also use the second person, either the informal *tu, te, toi* (you), and *ton, tes* (your), or the formal *vous* (you), and *votre, vos* (your), to address the moral message in their morals directly to their readers.[53] La Force, d'Aulnoy, and Lhéritier use possessive pronouns, *nous* (we or us), and determiners, *nos, notre* (our), to emphasize the relevance of the moral to their seventeenth-century readers.[54]

The verse morals and maxims created by the conteuses develop three different models of moral poetics. The first model idealizes virtuous behavior by praising the hero or heroine for exhibiting virtuous qualities. It identifies those virtues as the reason the heroic couple is rewarded with a happy ending. For example, the verse morals in d'Aulnoy's "Gracieuse et Percinet" and La Force's "Persinette" identify the faithful, constant love of the heroic couple as the reason for their happy ending. In the moral to "Gracieuse et Percinet," d'Aulnoy declares constancy in love as the path to perfect happiness.[55] La Force advises spouses of the advantages of fidelity and mutual affection in the moral to "Persinette."[56] In both tales, virtuous lovers who remain true to their beloved are idealized as moral exemplars providing guidance on the right way to love. This script for happiness is repeated in the ending to Murat's "Le parfait amour" in which she observed that the heroic couple enjoyed the rare happiness of a tendre and constant love that was faithful and ardent during their period of misfortune.[57] Praise of love as a source of bliss appears in the verse moral to d'Aulnoy's "La princesse Belle Étoile et le prince Chéri," which identifies love as the origin of glory, and claims that hearts animated by love and glory do not fear misfortune.[58] The verse moral to d'Aulnoy's "Le Pigeon et la Colombe" adopts a more circumspect attitude to love. Although it identifies pure love as a guarantee of the most charming pleasures, it also acknowledges pain and agitation as an inevitable consequence of love.[59]

The second category of verse morals emphasize the dangers of love. These morals provide warnings about the consequences of failing to adhere to the emotion script for virtuous love, while simultaneously acknowledging the difficulties of regulating passionate love. D'Aulnoy, Durand, and La Force criticize behavior lacking in virtue by associating it with villainous characters. They identify a lack of virtue or reason as the explanation for why these characters are punished with unhappy endings. The verse moral in d'Aulnoy's "L'Oiseau Bleu" warns against entering into marriage in the absence of love, and she punishes the heroine's rival for trying to force the hero to marry her when he is in love with the heroine.[60] In the moral to "Le prince Marcassin," d'Aulnoy cautions that "it is better to lack love than to lack wisdom."[61] The maxim in Durand's "La fée Lubantine" advises that "love that is not regulated by virtue causes all the misfortunes in life."[62] In the maxim in "Le prodige d'amour," Durand acknowledges the force of passionate love, and the difficulties of acting reasonably when one is in love, in her warning that mastery of the self is not possible when one is agitated by love.[63] Warnings against love as a source of misfortune appear in the moral to La Force's "La puissance d'amour," which advises that for every happy lover there are a thousand unhappy lovers.[64] When read in light of the idealization of virtuous love in the first type of verse moral, these comments about the dangers of unregulated love offer a script for love that complements the script developed in the first model: that virtuous lovers will attain happiness if they are also governed by reason and virtue.[65]

The scripts for love established by the first two models of moral poetics are challenged by a third model comprised of ambiguous or ironic morals and maxims that question the gender politics of the marriage closure. These verse morals appear in tales that end unhappily and in tales in which there is inconsistency between the moral and the ending. The absence of a logical connection between the narrative of a tale and the verse moral purporting to explain the ending of the tale allows the conteuses to present a sophisticated understanding of the problems caused by love. It also allows them to subtly criticize conventional moral codes of courtship and marriage. This criticism takes a number of different forms. In "La princesse Printanière," d'Aulnoy's heroine does exactly what the verse moral warns the readers of the tale not to do. She loves without reason but she is not punished with an unhappy ending as she marries a prince who remains totally unaware of her premarital indiscretions. They then (presumably) live happily ever after.[66] In the moral to "L'heureuse peine," Murat questions whether the love of the heroic couple will survive marriage by suggesting that "weddings are almost always a sad celebration."[67] Other ambiguous morals, such as d'Aulnoy's exaggerated praise of faithful lovers in "La Grenouille bien-faisante" and "Le Mouton," suggest that faithful and virtuous lovers idealized in tales such as d'Aulnoy's "Gracieuse et Percinet" and La Force's "Persinette" could exist only in the distant chivalric past, as they do not reflect the behavior of couples in seventeenth-century France.

This third model of moral poetics also includes tales with endings and morals that appear to celebrate the virtuous love of the heroic couple but in fact question the conventional morality associated with the marriage closure. An example of this type of ambiguity appears in the verse moral to La Force's "L'Enchanteur":

> By different paths we arrive at happiness,
> Vice leads us there, as well as honor;
> . . .
> Blind deity, fortune too cruel,
> Improve the bestowal of all that comes from you;
> Overwhelm the wicked with eternal pain;
> Give the virtuous the sweetest happiness.[68]

The first two lines challenge the idea that virtue is the only path to happiness. The last two lines reflect the idea that fortune, namely the gods and goddesses of fairyland, should punish vice and reward virtue. In allowing for the possibility that vice, as well as honor, leads to happiness, La Force provides two conflicting viewpoints within the verse moral. This conflict raises the question of whether she is recognizing the reality of seventeenth-century life and calling for magical intervention to restore order or subtly proposing a subversive politics of love disguised by an appeal to conventional morality. The unconventional endings to "L'Enchanteur" and "Persinette," in which adultery and premarital sex do not preclude a happy ending, seem to support the latter interpretation, as do morally ambiguous endings in tales by d'Aulnoy, Bernard, and Murat.

UNHAPPY ENDINGS AND THE DISAPPEARANCE OF LOVE

As we saw in the previous section, one of the defining features of the fairy-tale genre is the orderly resolution of narrative conflict with a happy ending that rewards heroic characters with marriage.[69] However, endings that deviate from the marriage closure model form a small but significant proportion of the conteuses' tales.[70] As Charlotte Trinquet observes, these unconventional endings do not follow Propp's model of the happy ending. Instead of providing the anticipated marriage closure, unconventional tales end by rewarding characters who transgress moral or social norms or with a tragedy for the hero or heroine.[71] Approximately 20 percent of the conteuses' tales end unhappily with the heroic couple experiencing death or pain and suffering.[72] These endings appear in tales by d'Aulnoy, Bernard, Murat, and d'Auneuil. This percentage increases if it includes tales with unconventional endings, such as those that implicitly or explicitly question seventeenth-century moral codes for love and marriage. However, as Seifert argues, the inaugural status of seventeenth-century fairy tales complicates use of the term *conventional* to analyze tales written at a time when features of the genre were still being developed.[73] Like Seifert, I interpret the presence or absence of the marriage closure in the conteuses' tales as a deliberate choice, and therefore argue that their choice not to end all of their tales happily has sociopolitical as well as poetic implications.

The questions raised by a sociopolitical reading of the conteuses' unhappy endings encompass two key issues. First, what scripts for love does the absence of the marriage closure seek to convey? Second, what are the social implications of their representation of the disappearance of love as an inevitable outcome of romantic union? The answers to these questions are found in an analysis of the representation of love by each conteuse. Love, in particular the suffering caused by love, is a central theme in tales that mourn the disappearance or absence of the virtuous love idealized in verse morals celebrating marriage between the heroic couple. In d'Aulnoy's "L'île de la félicité," "Le Mouton," and "Le Nain Jaune," the union of the heroic couple is destroyed by the death of one, or both, of the lovers. Thwarted or unrequited love is the source of tragedy in Murat's "Anguillette," "Peine Perdue," and “L’Aigle au beau bec.” Loving union fails to produce eternal bliss for the heroic couples in Bernard’s “Le prince Rosier,” Murat’s “Le palais de la vengeance,” and d’Auneuil’s “L’inconstance punie ou l’origine des cornes.”

I read the unhappy endings written by d’Aulnoy, Bernard, Murat, and d’Auneuil as examples of a pessimism that questioned the gender politics of courtship and marriage in seventeenth-century salon literature. This politics, which advocated reformulation of marriage as a relationship based on mutual affection, idealized a reciprocal, gallant love that sought to reframe the ideals of courtly love for a modern, female audience.[74] The model of love proposed by this literary tradition rejected the patriarchal legal framework that defined marriage as an institution based on the transfer of control over women from fathers to husbands.[75] In the conteuses’ tales, this subversive moral code is reflected in tales that criticize forced marriages and allow heroines to choose their husbands on the basis of affection and consideration of personal merit.[76] However, the conteuses’ representation of love as an essential element of marriage does not constitute an uncritical celebration of love as an ennobling emotion with the capacity to emancipate women from structural gender inequalities in seventeenth-century French society.[77] Tales that subvert or refuse the marriage closure reflect an ambivalence about love that questions whether marriages based on love offer a better outcome for women than the traditional transactional model of marriage.

Separation, Death, and Disappointment

The first category of unhappy endings caused by the disappearance of love are tales in which the union between the heroic couple is denied by the disappearance of one of the lovers. In these tales, perfect love is an unattainable ideal that can only ever be temporarily experienced by men and women living in the human world. This type of unhappy ending is an interesting case study on the absence of the marriage closure as a deliberate authorial choice in d’Aulnoy’s tales. In “L’île de la félicité,” the hero of the tale is murdered by Father Time when he leaves the heroine to make his name in the world. This disappearance is reversed in “Le Mouton,” in which it is the heroine who does not return in time to prevent the hero dying from a broken heart. The ending in “Le Nain Jaune” sees the death of both the heroine and her intended husband. At first glance, d'Aulnoy's tragic endings seem to fit comfortably within a narrative formula celebrating marriage as the ultimate happy ending as they can be read as examples of what happens when the anticipated union cannot take place. But for the tragic death of the hero, one might imagine that the heroic couple would otherwise have lived happily ever after. A close analysis of these endings, however, reveals significant ambiguity in d'Aulnoy's depiction of the perfect love shared by each heroic couple. In each tale, a faithful, reciprocal love does not protect the heroic couple from tragedy. D'Aulnoy therefore seems to suggest that perfect love cannot exist outside of the marvelous world in her tales.

In "L'île de la félicité," Princess Félicité and Prince Adolphe experience perfect happiness for three hundred years, until Adolphe's desire to make a name for himself in the world causes him to leave Félicité and their utopian paradise in search for glory and fame. Once he leaves Félicité and her island, he is captured and killed by Father Time. But it is not Father Time who causes Adolphe's death. The epitaph dedicated to the unfortunate prince reveals d'Aulnoy's ambivalence about the ability of humankind to experience the perfect love depicted in her tale. The final two lines of this verse, which reappear in a slightly modified form at the end of the tale, express d'Aulnoy's doubt about whether eternal love (*d'éternelles amours*) or perfect happiness (*félicité parfaite*) can exist outside of the fairy utopia in her tale.[78] By making Father Time the instrument of Adolphe's death, d'Aulnoy suggests that love and happiness are transient, impermanent states that will inevitably be displaced by other human desires. Adolphe's death is therefore inevitable. He cannot remain forever in Félicité's island paradise because it is an enchanted state of stasis in which humans do not belong. The perfect love between Adolphe and Félicité exists only in this paradise, and it is lost as soon as Adolphe leaves.[79]

The tragic ending to "Le Mouton" echoes the tale of paradise lost in "L'île de la félicité." In this tale, the heroine, Princess Merveilleuse, is exiled to a forest where she meets and falls in love with the eponymous hero, a ram who is in fact a metamorphosed prince. In contrast to "L'île de la félicité," it is the heroine who decides to leave her lover to attend her sister's wedding. When she is delayed from returning, he dies of a broken heart.

Again, we have a tale of loss provoked by the intrusion of the outside world into the utopian paradise created by the heroic couple's love. The rhyming moral at the end of this tale raises questions about the role of love in this unhappy ending.

> Often the most beautiful gifts from Heaven
> Serve only to lead to our ruin,
> . . .
> The [hero] would have suffered less,
> If he had not sparked that fatal flame [love]
> . . .
> He hated honestly, he loved artlessly,
> Unlike the men of today.
> His death seems extraordinary to us,
> And not appropriate for a King:
> We no longer see in this part of the world
> A ram die because his sheep has run away.[80]

The moral to this tale is simultaneously nostalgic and fatalistic. D'Aulnoy's claim that the hero's faithful and sincere love does not resemble the sentiments of seventeenth-century men locates the tale in an idealized past, but her suggestion that blessings from heaven tend to cause suffering rather than happiness implies that such a past is simply a romantic fantasy. According to d'Aulnoy, the hero's love is a fatal flame that causes him to suffer a fate he does not deserve. But there is a note of humor in the final lines of this verse, with d'Aulnoy comparing the behavior of gallant lovers to that of a ram and his sheep. This burlesque parody locates the tale in an ideal past and characterizes the exaggerated devotion of the hero as an outmoded emotion script.[81]

Unlike Félicité and Merveilleuse, heroines to whom d'Aulnoy attributes no blame for the death of their lovers, the moral to "Le Nain Jaune" criticizes the heroine, Princess Toute Belle, for making a promise she had no intention of keeping. Toute Belle's promise to marry the eponymous antagonist, which she attempts to evade by becoming engaged to a more powerful suitor, is the subject of d'Aulnoy's censure:

But the destiny of Toute Belle
Warns you not to love
If the promises of your heart cannot be faithful.[82]

Although Toute Belle believed she would be killed by lions if she did not agree to marry the Nain Jaune, d'Aulnoy does not absolve her lack of fidelity. The ending to this tale is curious, given d'Aulnoy's idealization of the virtues of tender love in "L'île de la félicité" and "Le Mouton." Toute Belle's tender passion for the King of Mines d'Or, which is inspired by his merit, esprit, and delicate sentiments, as well as his "beautiful soul in a perfect body," is not mentioned in d'Aulnoy's moral even though it is the king's declaration of fidelity to Toute Belle that causes him to drop the magical sword he was using to defend them both from the Nain Jaune.[83] In essence, Toute Belle dies because she refuses to marry a spouse she does not love. This is an outcome that runs counter to the polemical rejection of forced marriages in 1690s fiction by women writers.[84] But if read as another example of the loss of perfect love as in d'Aulnoy's "L'île de la félicité" and "Le Mouton," Toute Belle's fate might also be interpreted as an illustration of the structural limits on the ability of seventeenth-century women to exercise control over their choice of marriage partner. Toute Belle cannot refuse to marry, and it is her resistance of her mother's desire that she choose a husband that initiates the chain of events that leads to her tragic end. In death d'Aulnoy allows Toute Belle and the king the union they were denied in life as their lifeless bodies are transformed into two beautiful palm trees whose embracing branches immortalize their tender, faithful love.[85] Like d'Aulnoy's unhappy couples in "L'île de la félicité" and "Le Mouton," their perfect love cannot survive in the imperfect human world.

Murat's tales of thwarted and unrequited love illustrate disappearances of a different nature. In "Anguillette," a love triangle between the heroine, Princess Hébé, her sister Princess Ilérie, and Prince Atimir results in a tragic duel in which Atimir is killed and Hébé's husband is wounded. As a consequence, Hébé kills herself by throwing herself on Atimir's sword. This tale provides a cautionary example of the unhappiness caused by love. Anguillette, the fairy who assists Hébé throughout the tale, advises Hébé against her desire for love by warning her that it is a dangerous passion that cannot be controlled. Despite Anguillette's attempts to protect Hébé from her fatal passion for the inconstant Atimir, Hébé's unhappy fate is sealed when she ignores Anguillette's warning never to see Atimir again. The tragic ending following their reunion illustrates the inability of conventional seventeenth-century morality to control passionate love: marriage to other loving spouses does not mean that Hébé and Atimir can resist their desire for one another. Hébé and Atimir are incapable of escaping the fatal lure of their passion and are released from their suffering only in death, when they, like d'Aulnoy's Toute Belle and the King of Mines d'Or, are transformed into a pair of beautiful trees.[86]

The bittersweet ending in "Anguillette" is echoed in Murat's "Peine Perdue," a tale of unrequited love that ends with the heroine finding refuge in the "country of Love's Injustices."[87] Peine Perdue's unhappy fate fulfills her fairy mother's premonition that she would suffer misfortune due to love when she is unable to make the object of her affection fall in love with her. Peine Perdue cannot escape her love, but her suffering is eased by the company of other people made unhappy by love.[88] But Murat does not ameliorate the pain of unrequited love for the unfortunate king in "L'Aigle au beau bec." He is punished by his initial aversion to marriage by falling hopelessly in love with a princess who is in love with another man and ends up married to the princess whose love he spurned at the beginning of the tale. The tale ends with the revelation that the king is not married to his beloved but to a princess disguised to look like her. This rather abrupt ending does not provide the king's reaction to this revelation. He, like Peine Perdue, is left to make the best of an unfortunate situation when it becomes clear that he will never be united with his beloved. In both tales, marriage causes all hope of a happy ending to disappear.

Marriage and the Disappearance of Love

The endings to Bernard's "Le prince Rosier," Murat's "Le palais de la vengeance," and d'Auneuil's "L'inconstance punie ou l'origine des cornes" are more overtly pessimistic than the tragic endings caused by denial of union between the heroic couple. In this second category of unhappy endings, it is the union between the heroic couple that causes suffering. In "Le prince Rosier," the marriage between the heroic couple is ruined by jealousy, and the hero of the tale asks the fairies to turn him back into a rosebush as he can no longer bear being married. "Le palais de la vengeance" shows the heroic couple faithfully enduring several tests of separation, but the fire of their passion is extinguished when they are eternally imprisoned in an enchanted palace with only each other for company. "L'inconstance punie" criticizes the inconstancy of male and female lovers: the hero quickly becomes bored with the perfect love offered to him by a sylph and foolishly replaces her with a wife who cuckolds him. Unlike d'Aulnoy's tales of "L'île de la félicité" and "Le Mouton," which create a utopian paradise in which the promise of love is denied, Bernard and Murat begin their tales with a prediction of misfortune that is fulfilled by the end of the tale. In d'Auneuil's tale, the sylph to whom the hero professes his love warns him that she will not tolerate infidelity, but he does not heed this warning.

In Bernard's "Le prince Rosier," a fairy predicts that the heroine, Princess Florinde, will suffer unhappiness if she loves a lover she cannot see:

> Florinde was born with many charms,
> But her misfortune will be extreme,
> If one day she loves
> A lover she cannot see.[89]

When Florinde falls in love with a talking rosebush who turns out to be a metamorphosed prince, the sincerity of her affection returns the prince to his true form. But when Florinde attempts to evade her destiny by testing the fidelity of her beloved before agreeing to marry him, she inadvertently seals her unhappy fate. After sending Prince Rosier to l'Île de la Jeunesse (the Island of Youth), Florinde suffers the pain of their separation for fifteen days before recalling her beloved and marrying him without asking whether he remained faithful to her.[90] Bernard suggests that it is this marriage that ends the pleasures in the heroic couple's life, just as marriage often ends all the pleasure in life.[91] She identifies the love shared by the couple as the reason their marriage is destined to fail: "people accustomed to loving are not as reasonable as others, and do not provide an example of a good household."[92] It is their passion that makes Florinde and her husband unable to act reasonably toward each other, and as a consequence, they make each other miserable. Unlike the deaths in d'Aulnoy's "L'île de la félicité" and "Le Mouton," and in Murat's "Anguillette," the tragedy in this ending is perfectly ordinary. When the prince admits to a flirtation with the queen of youth, Florinde's jealousy transforms the couple's love into hate. Their marriage fails and the prince asks the fairies to transform him back into a rosebush. In Bernard's tales, the representation of unhappy lovers is a deliberate authorial choice designed to question the emotion script of love as the ultimate happy ending.[93]

Bernard's decision to use her fairy tales to represent the "malheurs de l'amour" continues in "Riquet à la houppe." As I discuss in chapter 4, this tale features a beautiful but stupid heroine who is offered the gift of intelligence by an ugly gnome in exchange for a promise to marry him. This marriage, to which the heroine agrees despite her complete indifference to her husband, causes misery for both spouses. Riquet is wounded by his wife's obvious disgust for him, and she is trapped in a loveless marriage with full awareness of her husband's defects. Her attempts to ameliorate her misery by smuggling her lover into her husband's subterranean kingdom are discovered by her husband, and he punishes her infidelity by transforming his wife's lover into his mirror image so she cannot tell them apart. This tale does not warn against marrying without love; it warns against marriage as an inevitable source of unhappiness. The ending to the tale suggests that it does not matter that Mama married her husband rather than her lover because all lovers eventually become husbands.[94] In this tale, it is not love that disappears but the hope that it might be possible to experience love within marriage.

In Murat's "Le palais de la vengeance," the fate of the heroic couple, Princess Imis and Prince Philax, fulfills a fairy prophecy that Imis will become unhappy because of too much happiness. This cryptic destiny is achieved at the end of the tale when Imis and Philax are enclosed in an enchanted glass palace from which they cannot escape. Although their tender love survives several tests of their fidelity, it is destroyed when they are given the union they desire. As the moral to the tale explains, Imis and

Philax eventually become bored with their good fortune and each other once they achieve a state akin to marriage:

Before this fatal time, lovers too happy
Burnt always with the same fire;
Nothing troubled the course of their bliss.
Pagan made them discover the unhappy secret,
Of boredom caused by that same good fortune.[95]

The unfortunate king in d'Auneuil's "L'inconstance punie" provides another cautionary example of the curse of too much love. In this tale, as in Bernard's "Riquet à la houppe," an unbalanced or nonreciprocal love leads to infidelity and unhappiness. The hero of the tale, king Alcimède, falls in love at first sight with a beautiful sylph while hunting in a remote forest. She promises him that if he will experience great happiness if he loves no one but her but warns him that she will not forgive him if he is unfaithful because her vengeance is equal to her love.[96] In response, Alcimède throws himself at her feet and promises his eternal tendresse.[97] The lovers experience a year of happiness before Alcimède becomes bored with his good fortune. The sylph's fulfillment of his every desire causes him to become indifferent to her, and he is seduced by the charms of a less beautiful but magnetic princess who is courted by many other lovers.[98] Like the sylph, he loves his unfaithful wife more than she loves him. Both relationships end in recrimination and jealousy because the love felt by Alcimède and the sylph is not reciprocated by their chosen partners.

The models of moral poetics in the conteuses' tales illustrate an ambivalent attitude toward love and its capacity to produce the happy ending associated with the marriage closure. This moral framing rejected the model of didacticism defended by La Fontaine and Perrault and offered a distinctly feminine perspective on the experience of love after marriage. Tales by Murat, Bernard, Durand, and d'Auneuil suggest that the problem with love is that it is the enemy of reason and cannot be controlled. Even fairy magic is powerless to rescue hearts ruled by love as love is rarely displaced from a heart it has taken possession of. As we saw in the introduction, the pessimistic view of love as a dangerous passion that is nevertheless an essential element of human life is a powerful warning against love in Murat's "Anguillette." Hébé's charms cannot save her from the inevitable suffering of love and her unhappy fate fulfills Anguillette's warning about the fatal consequences of her desire for passion. The violence of thwarted passion leads to unhappy endings for the heroic couples in d'Aulnoy's "Le Nain Jaune," Bernard's "Le prince Rosier," and Murat's "Le palais de la vengeance." Unrequited passion motivates the vengeance sought by the fairy protagonist in Durand's "La fée Lubantine," who kills an eloping couple and then herself when she is unable to seduce the male half of the couple. The heroes in Murat's "L'Aigle au beau bec" and d'Auneuil's "L'inconstance punie" are punished for their failure to reciprocate the passion they inspire in the lovers they spurn. The former is tricked into marriage, while the latter marries a princess whose infidelities are publicly revealed by his former lover.

The verse morals in several of d'Aulnoy's tales propose reason and virtue as tools for managing passionate love.[99] But only in "L'Oranger et l'Abeille" does reason successfully cure the nascent passion of Linda, a fictionalized salonnière whose reluctance to marry is almost overcome by her encounter with the hero of the tale.[100] The moral to this tale also praises the heroine for listening to reason and regulating her passion with virtue while alone in the forest with the hero.[101] Reason does not prevent Laideronnette falling in love with her unseen suitor in d'Aulnoy's "Serpentin Vert," and d'Aulnoy criticizes Printanière's lack of reason in eloping with the ambassador who was sent to negotiate her marriage to a prince in the moral to "La princesse Printanière."[102] The eponymous fairy in Murat's "Anguillette" temporarily cures Hébé of her passion for the unfaithful Atimir by sending her to l'Île Paisible (Peaceful Island), but this cure is only effective if she never sees him again.[103] Like the king in d'Aulnoy's "La Grenouille bien-faisante," whose passion for the wife he believed to be dead increases when he sees her again, his passion is not extinguished; it is merely temporarily displaced.[104] In Murat's "Le Turbot," prince Fortuné convinces himself that he is cured of his passion for his first love, but his tendresse is reawakened when he hears of her death.[105]

This tension between passion and reason is not resolved in the conteuses' scripts for love. Nor do they offer a definitive answer to the question of whether love has a positive effect on the lives of women. While some of their heroines use love to justify their choice of spouse, others are disappointed in their choice or fail to achieve the union they desire. An optimistic view of love as an emotion that can be managed by reason, virtue, and fidelity appears in tales by d'Aulnoy, Lhéritier, and La Force. But d'Aulnoy questions this emotion script by implying that such love cannot exist in the world beyond her marvelous tales. She suggests that the perfect love experienced by her heroic couples is an unattainable ideal. A profound pessimism appears in tales by Bernard, Murat, Durand, and d'Auneuil, which represent love as a source of suffering that cannot be ameliorated or avoided. In Bernard's tales, it is love itself that leads to misfortune, but destiny is more important than love in determining the fate of Murat's heroines. Durand and d'Auneuil emphasize the violence of love as an unreasonable passion that causes death and destruction rather than a blissful union.

The conteuses' representation of the range of positive and negative experiences associated with love develops a nuanced set of emotion scripts that respond to the different ways seventeenth-century women negotiated the gender politics of courtship and marriage. Their tales develop a critique of love that challenges its idealization as an essential ingredient in the happily-ever-after narrative. As we saw in chapters 3 and 4, elevation of the importance of love did not fundamentally alter the patriarchal framework of courtship and marriage in early modern France. Early modern women, even the conteuses' most dynamic heroines, faced significant limits on their ability to exercise agency about their choice of spouse and the terms of their union. At best, the formation of a reciprocal emotional bond before marriage made a wife's submission to her husband's authority more palatable; it did not alter the legal authority of the husband as the head of their household. Nor, as we have seen in this chapter, did falling in love provide any guarantee of a happy ending. The ambivalence about love in the conteuses' models of moral poetics illustrates a tension between their idealization of perfect love and recognition of the gendered power imbalance inherent in early modern courtship and marriage.

Conclusion

Truth Finding in Fairy Tales

> Fairy tales are stories that try to find the truth and give us glimpses of the greater things
> —Marina Warner, *Once upon a Time*

> Different listeners, different readers will pull the storyteller towards affirming their point of view: a different audience, a different message. Every work is a "link in the chain of speech communication," and is made by source, narrator, receiver acting in conjunction.
> —Marina Warner, *From the Beast to the Blonde*

The enduring appeal of fairy tales lies in their ability to enchant and transform, to offer consolation and hope. But this is not all that fairy tales do. To inspire hope is to encourage belief in the possibility of change and invite imagination of a better future. To this end, fairy tales spark reflection about the shape of our lives and how things could be different by showing us truths about who has power and who does not and how those without power might negotiate the people and structures that restrict their choices. But the truths fairy tales offer are not timeless pearls of wisdom; they are, as this book has argued, shaped by the context in which they are expressed and the people with whom they are shared. Truth finding in fairy tales, as Warner suggests, is an act of cocreation by audience and author. Storytellers and their audience of listeners or readers exist in a symbiotic relationship in which both participate in the making of meaning. For Zipes this relationship extends the process of cocreation long after the teller has finished their tale as audiences read their lives into the fairy tales they hear as children and then use the genre as an interpretive lens through which they view their adult lives.[1] In writing the history of fairy tales, we seek to reverse this process. Instead of reading ourselves into fairy-tale narratives, we listen for echoes of the past we can weave into new narratives revealing truths about that past.

The truths in the conteuses' tales illustrate the operation of gender politics in courtship and marriage in seventeenth-century France. These truths challenge the popular axiomatic association between love, fairy tales, and happy endings. Love is the central theme in the conteuses' tales, but the conteuses develop a range of different scripts for the performance of love. The differences in their perspectives on love illustrate its nature as an emotion with a history that reflects the political and social context in which it is felt and expressed. This book has suggested that it is these differences, as well as the personal and literary connections between the conteuses, that mean the conteuses' tales should be read as a conversation about love as well as individual stories. As individual stories, each tale makes its own contribution to emotion scripts for the performance of love in courtship and marriage in seventeenth-century France. When read as a corpus of tales, the differences in the conteuses' perspectives on love contribute to a broader conversation about the gendered effects of love. This conversation developed a vocabulary of emotion to articulate scripts for love that reinterpreted conventional ideas in seventeenth-century literary and philosophical texts. The presence of this shared vocabulary in the conteuses' tales, as well as its absence in tales written by their male contemporaries, provides evidence of the creation of a literary emotional community of readers and writers connected by the contes de fées genre. The conteuses used this vocabulary and the dedications of their work to illustrious literary women to direct their tales to the modern audience of the literary salons in which conversations about love and marriage provided inspiration for the emotional truths offered by their tales.

In writing about the truths in the conteuses' tales, this book has focused on the conteuses' interest in love as a key feature of their writing and their connection to each other as a group of women writers. Their interest in love extends outwards from a shared vocabulary into emotion scripts that propose different methods for negotiating the gender politics of courtship and marriage in seventeenth-century France. D'Aulnoy's literary recreation of salon sociability emphasizes the need for support from a community of powerful women, whereas Lhéritier's cultivation of female eloquence advocates for the ability of women to make their own choices. The fatalism in Bernard's tales doubts the possibility of women achieving a happy ending without structural change to the patriarchal codes of courtship and marriage. La Force's emphasis on *inclination* offers a way for women to subvert conventional morality and choose a partner based on their personal feelings. Murat, Durand, and d'Auneuil emphasize the elusive nature of love—only some people are worthy of getting and keeping it, and it cannot be controlled or created by magic. These emotion scripts articulate a range of views on the ability of seventeenth-century women to navigate the patriarchal structure of courtship and marriage. This conversation about love resists the romantic wish fulfillment of the classic fairy-tale ending, in which the heroic couple marry and live happily ever after.

All the conteuses present love as an essential element of human life, but only some of their heroines successfully negotiate the challenges of courtship and marriage to obtain a happy ending. The fate of d'Aulnoy's heroines is shaped by their experience of love, but they do not achieve their romantic goals unless their union is supported by other more powerful figures. Heroines who find themselves operating outside of this paradigm do not achieve the happy ending they envisage as they are unable to escape the social expectations of obedience imposed on them as daughters and wives.[2] The key to success for d'Aulnoy's heroines is the ability to negotiate the social consequences of love by falling in love with appropriate partners whom their parents are happy for them to marry, although d'Aulnoy herself seems to doubt whether this possible outside of the marvelous fairy realm in her tales.[3] Bernard's heroines are unhappy in love, and the suffering it causes them is shared by heroines in tales by Murat, Durand, and d'Auneuil. These scripts for love emphasize the dark side of love as a destructive passion that causes women to act against their own interests. Love itself, rather than love gone wrong, is the cause of misfortune in these tales, and their heroines are unable to escape their unhappy destiny even with the help of powerful fairies. But this pessimistic representation of the disastrous consequences of love is reversed in tales by Murat, Durand, and d'Auneuil in which their heroines, like many of d'Aulnoy's heroines, experience perfect happiness after falling in love.

The extent to which women are able to exercise agency over their lives is an important theme in tales by Lhéritier and La Force, but they offer very different views on the extent to which love helps or hinders women. It is the personal qualities of Lhéritier's heroines, namely esprit and virtue, that determine their fate. Their destiny is not subject to love as Lhéritier allows her heroines exercise a measure of control over their emotions, although they do all end up married to handsome husbands at the end of her tales. La Force's subversive reinterpretation of the script of love at first sight uses love as a tool to expand the marriage closure ending to include unions based on an unconventional moral code. In her tales, love is both a cause and an effect of expansion in the agency of seventeenth-century women as it provides a mechanism that allows them to choose their own marriage partner. Her tales extend this agency even further by offering the possibility of a happy ending to adulterous and secret lovers.[4] These unions challenge both the traditional model of marriage as a socioeconomic alliance and the companionate model of marriage as an emotional relationship.

Making sense of the variation in the conteuses' range of scripts for love was one of the key interpretive challenges in writing this book. In focusing on the cultural and social significance of their tales as contributions to a conversation about how love was felt and expressed by seventeenth-century French women, I have sought to make space for the differences in the conteuses' perspectives on love as an important feature of a lively exchange between a group of writers. As an emotional community, the conteuses used a shared vocabulary of emotion to reflect on the gendered experience of love in courtship and marriage. In reaching different conclusions about the ability of seventeenth-century women to negotiate the gendered power dynamics of love, the conteuses' tales reflect the dynamic nature of the exchange of ideas in salon conversations and parlor games that inspired the contes de fée vogue. But the conteuses' conversation was a literary one conducted through the circulation of texts rather than the exchange of words by salon interlocutors. Their transformation of the form of salon conversation allowed them to reach out to networks of modern readers beyond those who attended the physical space of the salon, a project that was supported by *Le Mercure Galant*'s promotion of their works and the emerging fairy-tale genre.

The conteuses' critique of love challenges the idea that a single script for love underpins the fairy-tale genre. The gender politics of this critique simultaneously reflected and contributed to change in social attitudes to courtship and marriage in early modern Europe. The conteuses' emphasis on love as the proper motivation for marriage promoted a companionate model of marriage as an alternative to the traditional definition of marriage as a socioeconomic transaction. Their exploration of how such a model might work proposes an emotional model of courtship in which declarations of love and the exchange of gifts create a reciprocal emotional bond between courting couples and husbands and wives. But their corpus of tales does not uncritically celebrate love as a panacea for the patriarchal structure of courtship and marriage. The development of a subversive moral poetic in tales that question the emancipatory potential of love provides evidence of an ambivalence about the desirability of marriage as the ultimate goal for seventeenth-century women. The truths about love in the conteuses' tales suggest that love may lead to a happy ending, but not always, and often not in the way you might expect.

APPENDIX 1

French Fairy Tales, 1690–1709

The following table identifies 104 fairy tales produced by French writers between 1690 and 1709. Sixty-three of these tales are attributed to the conteuses, 35 to male authors, and 6 to unknown authors. Tales that circulated in more than one version are listed multiple times but counted only once. This table was created in reference to the table published by Raymonde Robert in the first volume of the Bibliothèque des Génies et des Fées series, the index in volume 5 of the same series, and a review of the holdings of the Bibliothèque Nationale de France.[1] My aim is resolve a number of small discrepancies between Robert's table and the index and to correct a few errors of attribution.[2] Any remaining errors are my own.

I have not included tales listed in Robert's table or the index that do not fit within the definition of the contes de fées genre outlined in chapter 1. Tales excluded on this basis are Murat's "L'origine des hérissons" and "Conte inachevé," and d'Auneuil's "La princesse des Prétintailles," "L'origine de l'occasion," "Les colinettes," "L'origine du lansquenet," and "Les chevaliers errants."[3]

	Date	*Author*	*Title*	*Tale*
1	1690	d'Aulnoy	*Histoire d'Hypolite, comte de Duglas*	L'île de la félicité
2	1691	Perrault	*La Marquise de Salusses, ou la patience de Grisélidis*	Grisélidis
3	1693	Perrault	*Le Mercure Galant,* novembre 1693	Les souhaits ridicules
	1694	Perrault	*Grisélidis, nouvelle avec le conte de Peau d'Asne et celui des Souhaits ridicules*	Grisélidis (duplicate)
4	1695			Peau d'Âne
				Les souhaits ridicules (duplicate)
5	1695	Perrault	*Contes de ma mère L'Oye*	La belle au bois dormant
6			(manuscript)	Le Petit Chaperon rouge
7				La Barbe bleue
8				Le maître chat, ou le chat botté
9				Les fées
10	1696	Lhéritier	*Œuvres meslées*	Marmoisan ou l'innocente tromperie
11				Les enchantements de l'éloquence ou les effets de la douceur
12				L'adroite princesse ou les aventures de Finette
13	1696	Bernard	*Inès de Cordoue*	Le prince Rosier
14				Riquet à la houppe

	1696	Perrault	*Le Mercure Galant, février 1696*	La belle au bois dormant (duplicate)
15	1697	d'Aulnoy	*Les Contes des Fées*	Gracieuse et Percinet
16				La Belle aux Cheveux d'Or
17				L'Oiseau Bleu
18				Le prince Lutin
19				La princesse Printanière
20				La princesse Rosette
21				Le Rameau d'Or
22				L'Oranger et l'Abeille
23				La bonne petite souris
24				Le Mouton
25				Finette Cendron
26				Fortunée
27				Babiole
28				Le Nain Jaune
29				Serpentin Vert
30	1697	La Force	*Les Contes des Contes*	Plus Belle que Fée
31				Persinette
32				L'Enchanteur
33				Tourbillon
34				Vert et Bleu
35				Le pays des délices
36				La puissance d'amour
37				La Bonne Femme

	1697	Perrault	*Histoires, ou Contes du temps passé. Avec des moralitez*	La belle au bois dormant (duplicate)
				Le Petit Chaperon rouge (duplicate)
				La Barbe bleue (duplicate)
				Le maître chat, ou le chat botté (duplicate)
				Les fées (duplicate)
38				Cendrillon
39				Riquet à la houppe
40				Le Petit Poucet
41	1698	d'Aulnoy	*Contes Nouveaux, ou Les Fées à la Mode*	La princesse Carpillon
42				La Grenouille bienfaisante
43				La Biche au bois
44				La Chatte Blanche
45				Belle Belle, ou le chevalier Fortuné
46				Le Pigeon et la Colombe
47				La princesse Belle Étoile et le prince Chéri
48				Le prince Marcassin
49				Le Dauphin

50	1698	Mailly	*Les Illustres fées. Contes galants, dédié aux Dames*	Blanche Belle
51				Le roi magicien
52				Le prince Roger
53				Fortunio
54				Le prince Guérini
55				La reine de l'île des fleurs
56				Le favori des fées
57				Le Bienfaisant ou Quiribirini
58				La princesse couronnée par les fées
59				La supercherie malheureuse
60				L'île inaccessible
61	1698	Murat	*Contes de Fées*	Le parfait amour
62				Anguillette
63				Jeune et Belle
64			*Les Nouveaux Contes des Fées*	Le palais de la vengeance
65				Le prince des Feuilles
66				L'heureuse peine
67	1698	Préchac	*Contes moins contes que les autres*	Sans Parangon
68				La reine de fées
69	1699	Anon	*Nouveau conte des fées*	Le portrait qui parle
70	1699	Durand	*La Comtesse de Mortane*	La fée Lubantine

71	1699	Mailly	*Recueil de contes galants*	Constance sous le nom de Constantin
72				Le palais de la magnificence
73				La princesse délivrée
74				Blanche
75	1699	Murat	*Histoires sublimes et allégoriques*	Le roi Porc
76				L'île de la magnificence
77				Le Sauvage
78				Le Turbot
79			*Voyage de campagne*	Le père et ses quatre fils
80	1700	Anon	*Le Gage touché*	L'apprenti magicien
81				L'oiseau de vérité
82	1701	Anon	(manuscript)	Le prince Michel et la princesse Sauvage
83	1702	d'Auneuil	*La tyrannie des fées détruite. Nouveaux contes dédiés à Madame la duchesse de Bourgogne*	La tyrannie des fées détruite
84				Agatie princesse des Scythes
85				La princesse Léonice
86				Le prince Curieux
87			*L'inconstance punie. Nouvelles du temps*	L'inconstance punie ou l'origine des cornes
88	1702	Durand	*Les Petits Soupers de l'année 1699, ou Avantures galantes avec l'Origine des fées*	L'origine des fées
89				Le prodige d'amour
90	1705	Lhéritier	*La tour ténébreuse et les jours lumineux*	Ricdin-Ricdon
91				La robe de sincérité

92	1708	Anon	?	Le mariage du prince Diamant et de la princesse Perle
93	1709	d'Auneuil	*Les Chevaliers errants, et Le Génie familier*	La princesse Patientine dans la forêt d'érimente
94	1708–9	Murat	*Journal pour Mademoiselle de Menou*	L'Aigle au beau bec
95				La fée Princesse
96				Peine Perdue
97	before 1709	Anon	*Recueil de Petits Contes* (manuscript)	Conte en vers (no title)
98	No date	Choisy	*Ouvrages de Mr. L. de Choisy qui n'ont pas été imprimes*	Histoire de la princesse Aimonette
99	No date	Fénelon	*Fables et opuscules pédagogiques*	Histoire d'une vieille reine et d'une jeune paysanne
100				Histoire de la reine Gisèle et de la fée Corysante
101				Histoire d'une jeune princesse
102				Histoire de Florise
103				Histoire du roi Alfaroute et de Clariphile
104				Histoire de Rosimond et de Braminte

APPENDIX 2

Tales Produced by the Conteuses, 1690–1709

	Author	Date	Title	Tale
1	d'Aulnoy	1690	*Histoire d'Hypolite, comte de Duglas*	L'île de la félicité
2		1697	*Les Contes des Fées*	Gracieuse et Percinet
3				La Belle aux Cheveux d'Or
4				L'Oiseau Bleu
5				Le prince Lutin
6				La princesse Printanière
7				La princesse Rosette
8				Le Rameau d'Or
9				L'Oranger et l'Abeille
10				La bonne petite souris
11				Le Mouton

12				Finette Cendron
13				Fortunée
14				Babiole
15				Le Nain Jaune
16				Serpentin Vert
17		1698	*Contes Nouveaux, ou Les Fées à la Mode*	La princesse Carpillon
18				La Grenouille bienfaisante
19				La Biche au bois
20				La Chatte Blanche
21				Belle Belle, ou le chevalier Fortuné
22				Le Pigeon et la Colombe
23				La princesse Belle Étoile et le prince Chéri
24				Le prince Marcassin
25				Le Dauphin
26	Bernard	1696	*Inès de Cordoue*	Le prince Rosier
27				Riquet à la houppe
28	Lhéritier	1696	*Œuvres meslées*	Marmoisan ou l'innocente tromperie
29				Les enchantements de l'éloquence ou les effets de la douceur
30				L'adroite princesse ou les aventures de Finette

31		1705	*La tour ténébreuse et les jours lumineux*	Ricdin-Ricdon
32				La robe de sincérité
33	La Force	1697	*Les Contes des Contes*	Plus Belle que Fée
34				Persinette
35				L'Enchanteur
36				Tourbillon
37				Vert et Bleu
38				Le pays des délices
39				La puissance d'amour
40				La Bonne Femme
41	Murat	1698	*Contes de Fées*	Le parfait amour
42				Anguillette
43				Jeune et Belle
44			*Les Nouveaux Contes des Fées*	Le palais de la vengeance
45				Le prince des Feuilles
46				L'heureuse peine
47		1699	*Histoires sublimes et allégoriques*	Le roi Porc
48				L'île de la magnificence
49				Le Sauvage
50				Le Turbot
51			*Voyage de campagne*	Le père et ses quatre fils
52		1708–9	*Journal pour Mademoiselle de Menou*	L'Aigle au beau bec
53				La fée Princesse
54				Peine Perdue
55	Durand	1699	*La Comtesse de Mortane*	La fée Lubantine

56		1702	*Les Petits Soupers de l'année 1699*	L'origine des fées
57				Le prodige d'amour
58	d'Auneuil	1702	*La tyrannie des fées détruite*	La tyrannie des fées détruite
59				Agatie princesse des Scythes
60				La princesse Léonice
61				Le prince Curieux
62			*L'inconstance punie*	L'inconstance punie, ou l'origine des cornes
63		1709	*Les Chevaliers errants*	La princesse Patientine dans la forêt d'érimente

APPENDIX 3

Publication Details of the First Known Editions of the Conteuses' Tales

Author	*Title*	*Place*	*Publisher*	*Date*
d'Aulnoy	*Histoire d'Hypolite, comte de Duglas*	Paris	Louis Sevestre	1690
Lhéritier	*Oeuvres meslées*	Paris	Jean Guignard	1696
Bernard	*Inès de Cordoue*	Paris	Martin et George Jouvenel	1696
La Force	*Les Contes des Contes*	Paris	Simon Benard	1697
d'Aulnoy	*Les Contes des Fées*	Paris	Claude Barbin	1697–98
d'Aulnoy	*Contes Nouveaux, ou Les Fées à la Mode* (vols. 1–2)	Paris	Veuve de Théodore Girard	1698
d'Aulnoy	*Contes Nouveaux, ou Les Fées à la Mode* (vols. 3–4)	Paris	Nicolas Gosselin	1698
Murat	*Contes de Fées*	Paris	Claude Barbin	1698

Murat	*Les Nouveaux Contes des Fées*	Paris	Claude Barbin	1698
Durand	*La Comtesse de Mortane*	Paris	Veuve de Claude Barbin	1699
Murat	*Histoires sublimes et allégoriques*	Paris	Florentin et Pierre Delaulne	1699
Murat	*Voyage de campagne*	Paris	Veuve de Claude Barbin	1699
d'Auneuil	*La tyrannie des fées détruite. Nouveaux Contes dédiés à Madame la duchesse de Bourgogne*	Paris	Veuve de R. Chevillon	1702
d'Auneuil	*L'inconstance punie. Nouvelles du temps*	Paris	Pierre Ribou	1702
Durand	*Les Petits Soupers de l'année 1699, ou Avantures galantes avec l'origine des fées*	Paris	Musier Rolin	1702
Lhéritier	*La tour ténébreuse et les jours lumineux*	Paris	Veuve de Claude Barbin	1705
d'Auneuil	*Les Chevaliers errans, et Le Génie familier*	Paris	Pierre Ribou	1709

APPENDIX 4

Publication Details of Literary Works by the Conteuses

Author	*Title*	*Place*	*Publisher*	*Date*
Bernard	*Frédéric de Sicle*	Paris	Jean Ribou	1680
Bernard	*Éléonor d'Yvrée*	Paris	M. Guérout	1687
Bernard	*Le comte d'Amboise*	Paris	Claude Barbin	1689
d'Aulnoy	*Mémoires de la Cour d'Espagne*	Paris	Claude Barbin	1690
d'Aulnoy	*Relation du voyage d'Espagne*	Paris	Claude Barbin	1691
Bernard	*Brutus*	Paris	Veuve de Louis Gontier	1691
d'Aulnoy	*Histoire de Jean de Bourbon, Prince de Carency*	Paris	Claude Barbin	1692
d'Aulnoy	*Nouvelles espagnolles. Par Madame D****	Paris	Claude Barbin	1692

d'Aulnoy	*Nouvelles ou mémoires historiques, Contenant ce qui s'est passé de plus remarquable dans l'Europe . . . , Par Madame D****	Paris	Claude Barbin	1693
Lhéritier	*Le Triomphe de Mme Des-Houlières, reçue dixième muse au Parnasse*	Paris	Claude Mazuel	1694
La Force	*Histoire secrète de Bourgogne*	Paris	Simon Benard	1694
d'Aulnoy	*Mémoires de la Cour d'Angleterre. Par Madame D****	Paris	Claude Barbin	1695
La Force	*Histoire secrète de Henry IV, roy de Castille*	Paris	Simon Benard and J. Collombat	1695
Bernard	*Histoire de la rupture d'Abenamar et de Fatime*	La Haye	Unknown	1696
La Force	*Histoire de Marguerite de Valois, reine de Navarre, sœur de François Ier*	Paris	Simon Benard	1696
Murat	*Mémoires de Madame la comtesse de M****	Paris	Claude Barbin	1697
La Force	*Gustave Vasa, histoire de Suède*	Paris	Simon Benard	1697–98
d'Aulnoy	*Sentiments d'une Ame pénitente, Sur le Pseaume, Miserere mei Deus, et Le Retour d'une âme à Dieu, Sur le Pseaume, Benedic anima mea . . . Accompagnés de Réflexions chrétiennes. Par Madame D****	Paris	Veuve de Théodore Girard	1698

Durand	*Voyage de campagne [Comédies en proverbes, par Catherine Bédacier, née Durand]*	Paris	Veuve de Claude Barbin	1699
Durand	*Les Mémoires secrets de la cour de Charles VII, roy de France, par Madame D****	Paris	Pierre Ribou	1700
Durand	*Histoire des amours de Gregoire VII, du cardinal de Richelieu, de la princesse de Condé, et de la marquise d'Urfé. Par Mademoiselle D****	Cologne	Pierre le Jeune	1700
d'Auneuil	*Nouvelles diverses du temps, La princesse des Prétintailles*	Paris	Pierre Ribou	1702
d'Auneuil	*L'inconstance punie. Nouvelles du temps*	Paris	Pierre Ribou	1702
Durand	*Les Petits Soupers de l'année 1699 ou Avantures galantes avec l'origine des fées*	Paris	Musier Rolin	1702
Durand	*Le comte de Cardonne, ou la Constance victorieuse, histoire sicilienne, par Mme D****	Paris	Pierre Ribou	1702
Lhéritier	*L'Apotheose de mademoiselle de Scudery. Par mademoiselle L'H****	Paris	Jean Moreau	1702
d'Auneuil	*Les Colinettes, nouvelles du temps*	Paris	Pierre Ribou	1703
d'Auneuil	*L'origine du lansquenet, nouvelles du temps*	Paris	Pierre Ribou	1703

Lhéritier	*L'Erudition enjouée, ou Nouvelles sçavantes, satyriques et galantes, écrites à une Dame françoise, qui est à Madrid*	Paris	Pierre Ribou	1703
La Force	*Anecdote galante, ou Histoire secrète de Catherine de Bourbon, duchesse de Bar, et sœur de Henry le Grand, . . . avec les intrigues de la cour durant les règnes de Henri III et de Henri IV*	Nancy	Unknown	1703
d'Auneuil	*Les Chevaliers errans, et Le Génie familier*	Paris	Pierre Ribou	1709
Lhéritier	*Mémoires de M. L. D. D. N. [Madame la duchesse de Nemours] contenant ce qui s'est passé de plus particulier en France pendant la guerre de Paris, jusquà la prison du cardinal de Retz, arrivée en 1652. Avec les différens caractères des personnes, qui ont eu part à cette guerre*	Cologne	Unknown	1709
Murat	*Les Lutins de château de Kernosy, nouvelle historique. Par Madame la comtesse de M****	Paris	Jacques Le Febvre	1710
Durand	*Les Belles Grecques, ou l'Histoire des plus fameuses courtisanes de la Grèce et Dialogues nouveaux des galantes modernes*	Paris	Veuve de G. Saugrain and P. Prault	1712

Durand	*La Vengeance contre soi-même, et le chat amoureux. Contes en vers, par M. D****	Paris	P. Prault	1712
Durand	*Henry, duc des Vandales, histoire véritable, avec un extrait des Histoires tragiques de Bandel, traduites par Belleforest . . . par M. D., auteur des "Belles Grecques"*	Paris	P. Prault	1714
Durand	*Amarante, ou le Triomphe de l'amitié. Par Madame ****	Paris	Claude Jombert	1715
Lhéritier	*Les Caprices du destin, ou Recueil d'histoires singulières et amusantes arrivées de nos jours. Par Mademoiselle l'H****	Paris	Pierre-Michel Huart	1718
Lhéritier	*Les Epîtres héroïques d'Ovide, traduites en vers françois par Mlle L'Héritier*	Paris	Brunet fils	1732
Bernard	*Laodamie, Reine d'Epire*	Paris	Pierre Ribou	1735 (staged 1689)

APPENDIX 5

Declarations of Love by Heroes

Author	*Tale*
d'Aulnoy	L'île de la félicité
	Gracieuse et Percinet
	L'Oiseau Bleu
	Le prince Lutin
	Le Rameau d'Or
	L'Oranger et l'Abeille
	Le Mouton
	Fortunée
	Serpentin Vert
	La princesse Carpillon
	La Biche au bois
	La Chatte Blanche
	Belle Belle, ou le chevalier Fortuné

	Le Pigeon et la Colombe
	Le prince Marcassin
	Le Dauphin
Bernard	Le prince Rosier
Lhériter	Marmoisan
	Les enchantements de l'éloquence
	Ricdin-Ricdon
	La robe de sincérité
La Force	Plus Belle que Fée
	Persinette
	L'Enchanteur
	Vert et Bleu
	Le pays des délices
	La puissance d'amour
	La Bonne Femme
Murat	Le parfait amour
	Le prince des Feuilles
	Le roi Porc
Durand	La fée Lubantine
	Le prodige d'amour
d'Auneuil	La tyrannie des fées détruite
	Le prince Curieux
	La princesse Patientine dans la forêt d'érimente

APPENDIX 6

Declarations of Love by Heroines

Author	*Tale*
d'Aulnoy	La Belle aux Cheveux d'Or
	La princesse Printanière
	Babiole
	La Grenouille bienfaisante
La Force	L'Enchanteur
Murat	Jeune et Belle
	Le père et ses quatre fils

NOTES

INTRODUCTION

1. "Choisissez d'une beauté parfaite et touchante, de l'esprit le plus grand et le plus aimable, ou des richesses infinies" (Murat, "Anguillette," 86). This and all subsequent references to Murat's tales and paratexts come from Patard, *Contes*.
2. "Je ne sais ce que je désire, répondit la charmante Hébé; je sens pourtant, continua-t-elle en baissant ses beaux yeux, qu'il me manque quelque chose, et que ce qui me manque est absolument nécessaire à mon bonheur" (Murat, "Anguillette," 91).
3. "Ah! s'écria la fée, c'est de l'amour que vous désirez, cette passion peut seule faire penser aussi bizarrement que vous faites. Dangereuse disposition! continua la prudente fée; vous voulez de l'amour, vous en aurez, les cœurs ne sont que trop naturellement disposés à en prendre; mais je vous avertis que vous m'invoquerez en vain pour faire cesser cette passion fatale que vous croyez un bonheur si doux, mon pouvoir ne s'étend pas jusque-là" (Murat, "Anguillette," 91–92).
4. "Jamais deux cœurs ne furent si promptement ni si vivement touchés" (Murat, "Anguillette," 92).
5. In this book I use the term *fairy tale* to emphasize the role of the conteuses' tales as important texts in the history of the fairy-tale genre. I use the term *contes de fées* to distinguish the conteuses' tales from the broad corpus of tales included in the genre.

6. But see Seifert and Stanton, who claim that préciosité is "an aesthetic category of dubious literary historical value" and instead identify the conteuses' work with the code of *galanterie* ("Editors' Introduction," 29n101).
7. Carter, "Introduction," x. Eichel-Lojkine emphasizes the fluid nature of the fairy-tale genre. Her comprehensive reexamination of the original sources of the literary fairy tale in sixteenth-century Italy and seventeenth-century France argues that it was produced by diachronic and synchronic processes of cultural dissemination and contamination (*Contes en réseaux*, 9–35, 39–51).
8. Warner, *Once upon a Time*, xviii–xix.
9. Haase, "Fairy Tale," I:322–25.
10. Bacchilega, *Fairy Tales Transformed?*, 1–7; Zipes, *Irresistible Fairy Tale*, 2.
11. Tatar, "What Is a Fairy Tale?," 16–17.
12. Warner, *Once upon a Time*, xvi–xxiv.
13. Zipes discusses the differences between literary fairy tales and oral wonder tales in a number of his books: *Breaking the Magic Spell*, 1–22; "Introduction," in *Oxford Companion to Fairy Tales*, xv–xxiii; *Happily Ever After*, 1–14; *Irresistible Fairy Tale*, 1–20. Bottigheimer's claims about the absence of a relationship between fairy tales and oral storytelling are set out most fully in *Fairy Tales*. Her position has provoked fierce debate, with a number of folklore and fairy-tale scholars questioning Bottigheimer's reasoning, in particular Seifert and Velay-Vallantin, "Comments on Fairy Tales," 276–80; Ziolkowski, "Straparola and the Fairy Tale," 377–97.
14. For a similar perspective, see Seifert and Velay-Vallantin, "Comments on Fairy Tales," 276–80.
15. Canepa, *From Court to Forest*, 16. Bottigheimer takes the opposite view in asserting that the fairy-tale genre was created by Straparola in the 1550s: *Fairy Tales*. However, Bottigheimer's definition of the genre is overly narrow as it is based solely on the "compact" model identified by Harries, whom she cites when discussing her definition of the fairy-tale genre in *Magic Tales and Fairy Tale Magic*, 7. For a critique of this position, see Zipes, *Irresistible Fairy Tale*, appendix A, as well as the discussion above in note 13.
16. Canepa, *From Court to Forest*, 16–19; Zipes, *Happily Ever After*, 17–28.
17. Verdier, "De ma Mère L'Oye," 185–202. See also Palmer and Palmer, "English Editions of French *Contes de Fées* Attributed to Mme d'Aulnoy," 227–32, and "English Editions of French *Contes de Fées* in England," 35–44.
18. Influential examples include Propp's identification of thirty-one basic functions of folk tales (*Morphology of the Folktale*), Lüthi's analysis of the aesthetic and anthropological implications of fairy tales (*Once upon a Time*; *Fairytale as Art Form*), and Bettelheim's assertion of the therapeutic value of fairy tales as a source of meaning for children (*Uses of Enchantment*; "Fairy Tales as Ways of Knowing").

On the limitations of these methods for examining literary fairy tales see Canepa, *From Court to Forest*, 19–23.

19. See, e.g., Walter Benjamin's 1936 essay "The Storyteller," 83–109.
20. Harries, *Twice upon a Time*, 6–18.
21. Seifert and Stanton, "Editors' Introduction," 3.
22. It is important to note that d'Aulnoy's tales, alongside Perrault's, exercised significant influence on popular print culture, the book trade, and the stage in nineteenth-century England (Schacker, *Staging Fairyland*, especially chapters 3 and 4). As Palmer and Blamires have shown, translations of d'Aulnoy's tales were republished frequently in England throughout the eighteenth and nineteenth centuries (Palmer, "Madame d'Aulnoy in England," 237–38, 250–53; Blamires, "From Madame d'Aulnoy to Mother Bunch," 69–72). Duggan's analysis of the publication history of d'Aulnoy's tales illustrates her ongoing popularity in nineteenth-century France ("The Reception of the Grimms in Nineteenth-Century France," 264, appendix 2).
23. Aarne and Thompson, *The Types of the Folk-Tale*; Propp, *Morphology of the Folktale*; Greimas, *Sémantique structural*.
24. Lundell makes a similar critique of the classification systems created by Aarne and Thompson (and arguably also the ATU) for failing to consider the influence of gender identity and therefore not including tale types that recognize active female characters ("Gender-Related Biases," 149–63).
25. In *Breaking the Magic Spell* and subsequent books, Zipes criticizes the modern culture industry for hijacking the subversive potential of fairy tales by creating homogenous cultural products that reinforce existing power structures (*Fairy Tales*; *Happily Ever After*).
26. Seventeen of the forty-one authors analyzed by Robert are women, and women writers produced half of the tales identified in her "Tableau général des contes de fées publiés de 1690 à 1778" in *Le conte de fées littéraire*, 75–82.
27. Other cultural histories from this period include Canepa, *Out of the Woods*; Tucker, *Pregnant Fictions*; Duggan, *Salonnières, Furies, and Fairies*.
28. Warner, *From the Beast to the Blonde*, especially xii–xxi, 48–50.
29. Seifert, *Fairy Tales, Sexuality, and Gender*, 1–18.
30. Hannon, *Fabulous Identities*, 16.
31. Seifert outlines the differences between their respective views in "On Fairy Tales, Subversion, and Ambiguity," 57–59.
32. Harries, *Twice upon a Time*, 3–6, 18.
33. DeJean, *Tender Geographies*, especially chapter 1.
34. Beasley, *Revising Memory*, chapter 2.
35. Goodman, *Republic of Letters*; Goldsmith, *Exclusive Conversations*; Beasley, *Salons, History*.

36. Stedman, *Rococo Fiction in France*, chapter 4.
37. Defrance, *Les contes de fées*, 22–27, 322–30; Mainil, *Madame d'Aulnoy*, 26–28, 35–38.
38. Jasmin, *Naissance du conte féminin*, 13–18.
39. Raynard, *La seconde préciosité*, especially parts 1 and 2.
40. Trinquet, *Le conte de fées français*, 19–43.
41. The limited existing analysis tends to assume that the meaning of fairy-tale love is obvious and therefore not worth defining: see, e.g., Benson, "Stories of Love and Death," 103–13; and McGlathery, *Fairy Tale Romance*. An exception is Lundskær-Nielsen, "'Love Is a Many Splendored Thing,'" 213–35.
42. Jasmin, "'Amour, amour,'" 213–34. See note 6 above on the category of préciosité.
43. Seifert and Stanton, "Editors' Introduction," 29–32.
44. Trinquet, *Le conte de fées français*, 19–43; Welch, "La femme, le mariage," 47–58.
45. Raynard, *La seconde préciosité*, 239–62.
46. Seifert, *Fairy Tales, Sexuality, and Gender*, chapter 4.
47. Seifert, *Fairy Tales, Sexuality, and Gender*, 116 (italics in original).
48. Hannon and Seifert cite Pelous, *Amour précieux, amour galant* in their discussions of seventeenth-century models of love (Hannon, *Fabulous Identities*, 97–98; Seifert, *Fairy Tales, Sexuality, and Gender*, 113–14). See also Duggan, *Salonnières, Furies, and Fairies*, chapter 2.
49. For an overview of the different methodological approaches in this emerging field, see Plamper, *History of Emotions*; Matt, "Current Emotion Research in History," 117–24.
50. Scheer, "Are Emotions a Kind of Practice?" 194.
51. Rosenwein, "Problems and Methods," 19–21. Rosenwein notes that Kaster also describes emotions as scripts in *Emotion, Restraint, and Community*, 8–9, 151n17.
52. Rosenwein, *Emotional Communities*, 199.
53. Rosenwein, *Emotional Communities*, 199–200.
54. Rosenwein has recognized the limitations of this explanation of change: "Theories of Change," 14. She proposes the metaphor of an open floorplan to explain how emotional communities "drew on the emotional repertories of past communities" in *Generations of Feeling*, 12–13. But this metaphor does not explain how or why emotional repertories change.
55. Scheer, "Are Emotions a Kind of Practice?" 194. Scheer borrows the phrase "acts of consciousness" from the work of Solomon, *True to Our Feelings*, 157.
56. Scheer uses the terms emotion and feeling interchangeably in "Are Emotions a Kind of Practice?" 198.
57. Rosenwein, *Emotional Communities*, 2.
58. Scheer, "Are Emotions a Kind of Practice?" 202.
59. Rosenwein, "Problems and Methods," 19–21.

60. Beasley, *Salons, History*, especially chapters 1 and 2; Goldsmith, *Exclusive Conversations*, especially 4–13.

1. THE CREATION OF A FEMALE COMMUNITY

1. "Les Contes de Fées sont devenus à la mode, et plusieurs personnes d'un esprit fort relevé, et très grande réputation, n'ont pas dédaigné d'employer du temps à nous en donner grand nombre dans le style simple et naturel que cette sorte de narration demande" (*Le Mercure Galant*, April 1698, 208–9).
2. There is little direct evidence connecting the 1690s literary fashion for fairy tales with oral storytelling traditions such as folklore or salon conversation (Hannon, *Fabulous Identities*, 11–12). However, there is evidence that parlor games involving tale-telling were popular in seventeenth-century salons and in the court of Louis XIV, and Zipes argues that storytelling games that used folkloric motifs as prompts were important antecedents to literary fairy tales ("Introduction: The Rise of the French Fairy Tale," 2–5). See also Seifert and Stanton, "Editors' Introduction," 5–6.
3. A particularly animated example is the controversy provoked by Bottigheimer's assertion that sixteenth-century Italian author Giovan Francesco Straparola invented the fairy-tale genre and that there is no evidence that the genre emerged from oral storytelling traditions. Zipes provides an overview of this debate in *Irresistible Fairy Tale*, appendix A. Folklorists who have contested Bottigheimer's claim emphasize the presence of numerous Latin antecedent texts, oral wonder tales, and storytelling traditions in other European, Asian, and African contexts; see, e.g., Ziolkowski, "Straparola and the Fairy Tale," 377–97; Vaz da Silva, "The Invention of Fairy Tales," 398–425; Ben-Amos, "Straparola," 426–46. Bottigheimer responds to their critique in "Fairy Godfather, Fairy-Tale History," 447–96.
4. Lhéritier, "Lettre à Madame D.G.***," 36. This and all subsequent references to Lhéritier's paratexts and tales come from Robert, *Contes*. I discuss Lhéritier's treatment of her medieval sources further in Reddan, "Translating Eloquence," 219–28.
5. "Si le peuple, ou les troubadours, s'étaient exprimés comme nous, leur contes n'en auraient que mieux valu" (Lhéritier, "Lettre à Madame D.G.***," 39).
6. "Mais avertissez vos amis qu'ils n'aillent pas juger de cette mode par les seuls ouvrages qu'elle m'a fait produire; ils lui feraient tort; ils en verront bien d'une autre délicatesse. Je ne sais que mettre les autres en train; n'est-ce pas beaucoup faire que de marcher des premières dans des routes nouvelles?" (Lhéritier, "Lettre à Madame D.G.***," 41, translation from Seifert and Stanton, *Enchanted Eloquence*, 293).
7. DeJean, *Tender Geographies*, chapter 1; Beasley, *Salons, History*, chapters 1 and 2; Goldsmith, *Exclusive Conversations*, 4–13.

8. Stedman, *Rococo Fiction in France*, chapter 4.
9. "Il tâcha de rappeler dans sa mémoire un conte approchant de ceux des fées" (d'Aulnoy, "L'île de la félicité," 129). This and all subsequent references to d'Aulnoy's tales and paratexts come from Jasmin, *Madame d'Aulnoy* unless otherwise indicated. My translation resists using the modern English term *fairy tale* for the phrase *ceux des fées* because d'Aulnoy does not refer to her stories as *contes de fées* until the publication of *Les Contes des Fées* in 1697.
10. Jasmin, "Notices des contes de Madame d'Aulnoy," in Jasmin, *Madame d'Aulnoy*, 1079.
11. Before 1695, Perrault composed three verse tales that fit within the *contes de fées* definition used in this book: "Grisélidis" in 1691, "Les souhaits ridicules" in 1693, and "Peau d'Âne" in 1694. All three tales were republished together in a small volume in 1694 and 1695. On Perrault's publication history, see Velay-Vallantin, "Tales as a Mirror," 93–95.
12. Although the title page of *Œuvres meslées* identifies the publication date as 1696, the *Extrait du privilege du roy* states that copyright was granted on June 19, 1695. The volume was first printed in Paris on October 8, 1695: *Œuvres meslées* (Paris: Jean Guignard, 1696).
13. "Les contes de Percinet, de l'Oiseau Bleu, et plusieurs autres qui sont du nombre qui furent si favorablement reçus du public l'année dernière, sont de la même Dame qui vient de donner les *Contes Nouveaux*. Tous ses ouvrages ont eu un si grand succès qu'on est persuadé qu'elle ne peut rien faire dont la lecture ne donne un extrême plaisir. Ces sortes d'ouvrages sont devenues fort à la mode" (*Le Mercure Galant*, February 1698, 239).
14. "Ainsi, une Demoiselle de qualité vient aussi de mettre au jour deux volumes intitulez *Les Contes des Contes*. S'il m'était permis de la nommer, son nom seul serait juger de la beauté de ces Contes, même avant que de les lire. Son bon goût est connu parmi les personnes qui se mêlent d'écrire, et plusieurs ouvrages d'une plus grande conséquence, et qui ont être fort applaudis dans les monde" (*Le Mercure Galant*, February 1698, 239–40).
15. See chapter 1, note 1.
16. "Les contes continuent d'être en vogue, et les *Contes Nouveaux, ou Fées à la mode, par Madame D*** sont du nombre de ceux qui ont le plus réussi. On n'en peut douter, puis que le public en a demandé une suite" (*Le Mercure Galant*, July 1698, 234–35).
17. *Le Mercure Galant*, February 1703, 387.
18. Here I prefer the term *conte de fée* to Bottigheimer's "fairyland fiction" because *conte de fée* is used by the conteuses to describe their tales. I have chosen to use this term rather than one of the other terms they used—*conte* (story), *bagatelle* (trifle),

nouvelle (novella), *histoire* (story or narrative), *récit* (narrative), and *peau d'âne* (tale of nonsense)—because *conte de fée* best captures the style of the genre created by the conteuses: cf. Bottigheimer, "Fairy Tales and Fairyland Fictions," 101–11.

19. Zipes, "The Meaning of Fairy Tale," 222.
20. Murat, "Voyage de Campagne," 367–68. Other examples include Lhéritier's "Marmoisan" and "La robe de sincérité." "Marmoisan" does not feature a marvelous setting, but it challenges male behavioral codes and, like Murat's "Le père et ses quatre fils," promotes free choice of marriage partner. "La robe de sincérité," which is a facetious version of ATU tale type 1620 (The Emperor's New Clothes), does not feature a fairy or a marvelous setting, but it includes a ruse about a supposedly magical object to explore ideas about female virtue and male jealousy. Like "Marmoisan," it reflects the gender politics in the conteuses' tales.
21. Appendix 1 and figure 1 fulfill different objectives. Appendix 1 shows the total number of tales produced between 1690 and 1709, and figure 1 illustrates when tales were published to show their dissemination beyond the salon context in which they were often circulated before publication.
22. Robert makes the same observation using similar data in *Le conte de fées littéraire*, 311–28.
23. Years in which no tales were published have been omitted from figure 2 to improve its readability.
24. An earlier version of this and the following paragraph appeared in *French History and Civilization* in 2017: Reddan, "Scripting Love," 95–97.
25. Marchal, *Madame de Lambert et son milieu*, 226–27.
26. Murat, *Journal pour Mademoiselle de Menou*, 180. Recent biographical research by Volker Schröder raises questions about whether d'Aulnoy did in fact compose tales in her salon as she spent close to a decade confined in a convent by order of Louis XIV dated 10 December 1686 ("Madame d'Aulnoy's Productive Confinement").
27. Piva, "A la recherche de Catherine Bernard," 42; "Eloge de Mlle l'Héritier de Villandon," *Le Mercure de France*, 539–41; "Eloge de Mademoiselle l'Héritier," *Journal des Sçavans*, 832–36.
28. "Sa maison était ouverte à tous les beaux-esprits et à toutes les femmes qui écrivaient" (Mayer, "Notice des auteurs, Mme d'Auneuil," in Mayer, *Le cabinet des fées*, 40).
29. Robert, *Contes*, 362n1.
30. Robert, *Contes*, 550n1.
31. I discuss both versions of the Riquet tale in chapter 4.
32. Stedman, *Rococo Fiction in France*, 146–63.
33. On the reputation of Claude Barbin, see Beasley, *Salons, History*, 148; Heidmann, "Madame de Murat: Contes (Review)," 280. Appendix 3 lists the publication details of early editions of the conteuses' tales.

34. Appendix 4 lists the publication details for early editions of works by the conteuses other than fairy tales.
35. Hannon, *Fabulous Identities*, 177–78. For another perspective on the modern literary community created by the conteuses and its links to seventeenth-century salon culture, see Böhm, "La participation des fées modernes," 119–31.
36. This journal was composed during Murat's exile in the region of Touraine at the Château de Loches following a public scandal involving accusations of moral debauchery and lesbianism: Clermidy-Patard, "Introduction," 11–17.
37. "Il est certain que c'est un très joli livre. Il est bien écrit, les sentiments en sont délicats et tendres" (Murat, *Journal pour Mademoiselle de Menou*, 154).
38. "Mme d'Aulnoy qui l'a fait, écrivait d'un air naturel, et quoiqu'elle n'eût pas dans son style autant d'élévation que Mlle de la Force, ni de pureté de Mlle Bernard, elle écrivait en femme du monde, et dans les choses où elle ne parle que sur ce ton-là, elle est inimitable" (Murat, *Journal pour Mademoiselle de Menou*, 179).
39. "Donner de l'esprit à ceux et celles qui n'en ont point, de la beauté aux laides, de l'éloquence aux ignorants, des richesses aux pauvres, et de l'éclat aux choses les plus obscures" (Murat, "Épître: Aux Fées Modernes," 199, my translation with reference to Tucker and Siemens, "Perrault's Preface to Griselda and Murat's 'To Modern Fairies,'" 129).
40. *Le Mercure Galant*, December 1701, 153–54. For the dates these prizes were awarded, see Seifert, "Catherine Bernard," 70.
41. *Le Mercure Galant*, December 1701, 155. See also Seifert and Stanton, *Enchanted Eloquence*, 62.
42. *Le Mercure Galant*, June 1699, 101–9; *Le Mercure Galant*, December 1701, 152–67.
43. In addition to the reports cited in chapter 1, notes 1 and 13–17, see *Le Mercure Galant*, December 1699, 221–22.
44. It was not uncommon for seventeenth-century women writers to publish works anonymously (DeJean, *Tender Geographies*, 1–5, 98). See also Hannon, *Fabulous Identities*, 168–71.
45. Timmermans, *L'accès des femmes à la culture*, 223.
46. Hannon, *Fabulous Identities*, 168–71; Seifert, "*Les Fées Modernes*," 134–44.
47. Chartier, "Du livre au lire," 79–80; Chartier, *The Cultural Uses of Print*, 183–240. Stedman has also used this concept to analyse the framing strategies used by the conteuses: "Charmed Eloquence," 107–21.
48. Ringham, "Les amantes de la fiction," 678–79.
49. "L'histoire que je viens d'écrire serait devenue la plus sérieuse occupation de ma vie, si j'avais osé me promettre qu'elle eût pu vous plaire; et bien que Votre Altesse Sérénissime m'ait fait l'honneur de s'arrêter quelques moments à la lire

je n'ai pas laissé d'hésiter à prendre la liberté de vous l'offrir" (d'Aulnoy, *Histoire d'Hypolite, comte de Duglas* [Paris: Louis Sevestre, 1690], n.p.).

50. According to Stedman and Gethner, the rondeau was a type of poem associated with the gallant, worldly culture of the seventeenth-century literary salon (Murat, *A Trip to the Country*, 23n2).
51. "L'Autre jour à mes yeux vint s'offrir une Fée, / Qui me dit avec un air doux: / «Vous vous seriez fort bien passée / De faire des Contes de Nous; / . . . / Je ne demanderais ni trésors, ni grandeurs, / Mon cœur de ces présents ne peut se satisfaire; / Je voudrais sur mes Vers, qu'épanchant ses faveurs / La Fée eût attaché l'heureux don de vous plaire" (Murat, "À son Altesse Sérénissme," 143).
52. "Vous n'offrez que des jeux, et votre unique affaire / N'est que de divertir en tâchant de lui plaire" (d'Aulnoy, "Épître," 725).
53. Murat, "Épître: Aux Fées Modernes," 200.
54. "Voici des reines et des fées, . . . viennent chercher à la Cour de Votre Altesse Royale ce qu'il y a plus illustre de plus aimable dans le nôtre. Elles savent que la France possède une grande princesse dont toutes les actions doivent servir d'exemple, et qui joint à la noblesse du plus auguste sang, une bonté et une générosité merveilleuse. . . . Ce sont sans doute de grandes princesses comme vous, Madame, qui ont donné lieu d'imaginer le royaume de féerie" (d'Aulnoy, "A son altesse royale Madame," 149).
55. Murat, "Épître: Aux Fées Modernes," 200.
56. Bottigheimer and Raynard, "Marie-Catherine d'Aulnoy," 169.
57. This dedication is addressed to "A Son Altesse Sérénissime Monseigneur Le prince de Dombes" (Bernard, *Inès de Cordoue* [Paris: Martin et George Jouvenel, 1696]).
58. "Vous avez eu la bonté de me permettre de vous dédier cette petite nouvelle; mais je tremble quand il s'agit de vous la présenter, et la délicatesse de votre goût me donne autant de crainte que votre auguste personne m'inspire de respect" (Bernard, *Œuvres, tome 1*, 175).
59. "L'accueil favorable que vous avez eu la bonté de faire à ma première nouvelle me fait espérer la même grâce pour celle-ci. J'ai même plus de besoin de votre protection que jamais" (Bernard, *Œuvres, tome 1*, 237).
60. "Je fais l'histoire d'un homme qui est assez généreux pour céder sa maîtresse à son rival; et comme il y a peu de gens capables des grands efforts, et qu'on n'est touché que des choses auxquelles on se sent quelque disposition, j'ai lieu de craindre pour le succès de ce livre. Mais, MADAME, les grands sentiments se trouvent dans les âmes royales. Ils sont surtout dans la vôtre au suprême degré et peut-être que par là le Comte d'Amboise pourrait vous plaire" (Bernard, *Œuvres, tome 1*, 237).

61. Seifert, "Marie-Jeanne Lhéritier de Villandon," 75.
62. Saupé and Collinet, "Charles Perrault," 50, 56n6.
63. Schröder, "Marie-Madeleine Perrault."
64. On Nemours's patronage of Lhéritier, see Seifert, "Marie-Jeanne Lhéritier de Villandon," 75. Lhéritier also edited the memoirs of the Duchesse de Nemours: *Mémoires de M. L. D. D. N.*
65. "Je contai celui de Marmoisan, avec quelque broderie qui me vint sur-le-champ dans l'esprit" (Lhéritier, "Marmoisan," 44).
66. "Ce que je viens de vous dire est toujours au fond bien naïvement le conte de Marmoisan, tel qu'on me l'a conté, quand j'étais enfant" (Lhéritier, "Marmoisan," 65).
67. Lhéritier, "Les enchantements de l'éloquence," 69; Lhéritier, "L'adroite princesse," 113.
68. "On écrit pour s'instruire et pour se divertir; on écrit aussi pour instruire et pour divertir ses amis. . . . Qu'importe que des gens sans goût soient peu contents d'ouvrages qui n'ont pas été faits pour eux" (Lhéritier, "Lettre à Madame D.G.***," 40, translation by Seifert and Stanton, *Enchanted Eloquence*, 291).
69. "Lettre à Madame D.G.***," 36.
70. Stedman, *Rococo Fiction in France*, chapter 4.
71. Stedman, *Rococo Fiction in France*, 135.
72. Like Lafayette's heroine in *La princesse de Clèves* (1678), Julie is determined to choose duty over her love for Hypolite. For a discussion of d'Aulnoy's framing narrative, see Stedman, "D'Aulnoy's *Histoire d'Hypolite*," 32–53.
73. "Elle loua beaucoup la manière dont il avait parlé . . . menez-lui [Hypolite], il la divertira beaucoup mieux qu'un livre, il vient de me faire un conte si agréable, qu'il faut qu'il ait la complaisance de le lui conter aussi" (d'Aulnoy, "L'île de la félicité," 145).
74. Stedman, "D'Aulnoy's *Histoire d'Hypolite*," 32–41; Stedman, *Rococo Fiction in France*, 130–38. Schröder has a different view; he suggests that d'Aulnoy composed *Histoire d'Hypolite* while she was confined in a convent by royal order ("Madame d'Aulnoy's Productive Confinement").
75. "Madame de Coulanges . . . voulut bien nous faire part des contes avec quoi l'on amuse les dames de Versailles . . . et nous parla d'une île verte, où l'on élevait une princesse plus belle que le jour; c'étaient les fées qui soufflaient sur elle à tout moment. Le prince des délices était son amant: ils arrivèrent tous deux dans une boule de cristal . . . ce fut un spectacle admirable" (Sévigné, *Lettres de Madame de Sévigné*, 259–60; translation from Stedman, *Rococo Fiction in France*, 130). Stedman acknowledges Faith E. Beasley for translation of the phrase "dames de Versailles" as "women of the upper nobility" (*Rococo Fiction in France*, 194n13).
76. It is not clear whether d'Aulnoy visited Spain or whether her account is purely fictional. Very little is known about d'Aulnoy's movements between 1672, when

it is claimed she fled France following her involvement in a plot to frame her husband for *lèse-majesté* (treason), and 1690. Duggan suggests that d'Aulnoy did spend time in Flanders, England, and Spain. This speculation is based on d'Aulnoy's publication of works including *Mémoires de la Cour d'Espagne* (1690), *Relation du voyage d'Espagne* (1691), and *Mémoires de la Cour d'Angleterre* (1695): "Aulnoy, Marie-Catherine d'," 80. Stedman suggests that these travel accounts should be read as "fictionally embellished narratives": *Rococo Fiction in France,* 130. For a summary of this debate see Ekman, "Concealing Identities, Revealing Stories," 59–61. More recently, Schröder argues that d'Aulnoy's literary production between 1690 and 1695, including *Mémoires de la Cour d'Espagne* (1690), was composed during her confinement in a convent in Paris, the Hospitalières de la Miséricorde de Jésus on Rue Mouffetard ("Madame d'Aulnoy's Productive Confinement").

77. D'Aulnoy's work was published during a travel writing vogue in late seventeenth-century France. Spain was a particularly important destination in true and imaginary travel accounts: Ekman, "Concealing Identities, Revealing Stories," 50.
78. d'Aulnoy, *Relation du voyage d'Espagne,* vol. 1, 142.
79. "Bien que je n'ai rien crû de tout ce que l'on me dit à Gargançon de Mira et de Nios, je ne laissai pas de prendre plaisir au récit de ce conte, dont j'omets mille particularités, dans la crainte de vous ennuyer par sa longueur" (d'Aulnoy, *Relation du voyage d'Espagne,* vol. 1, 147).
80. d'Aulnoy, "Saint-Cloud," 379–81.
81. The title "Le Nouveau Gentilhomme Bourgeois" alludes to Molière's *Le Bourgeois Gentilhomme* (1670).
82. Hannon makes a similar observation in *Fabulous Identities,* 188.
83. "La plus jolie romance du monde" (d'Aulnoy, "Don Gabriel Ponce de Leon," 425).
84. Response to "Finette Cendron": "il n'en avait jamais été une si galante, et surtout bien racontée" (d'Aulnoy, "Don Gabriel Ponce de Leon," 457). Doña Juana is an overly strict guardian entrusted with the care of her two nieces, Isidore and Mélanie, after the death of their mother. It is therefore entirely possible that the extravagant praise of her tale by Mélanie and the young man in love with her is flattery designed to appease an authority figure (d'Aulnoy, "Don Gabriel Ponce de Leon," 383–457).
85. Response to "Fortunée": "Moindres bagatelles" (d'Aulnoy, "Don Gabriel Ponce de Leon," 486).
86. d'Aulnoy, "Don Fernand de Tolède," 563, 605. This contrast is produced by the exaggerated ridiculousness of d'Aulnoy's frame-tale characters in *Le Nouveau Gentilhomme Bourgeois.* The newly wealthy hero, Dandinardière, and the thoroughly silly young ladies he attempts to impress, Virginie and Marthonide, are crazy about contes de fées. The fact that they are also represented as authors

of fairy tales is somewhat at odds with d'Aulnoy's use of frame-tale narratives to establish her authorial identity. As Hannon observes, this "ironic doubling" creates a critical distance from the conteuses' recreation of salon culture in their writing (*Fabulous Identities*, 189).

87. Response to "La Chatte Blanche": "il vit les [yeux] fermés, et qu'il ne remuait point" (d'Aulnoy, "Le Nouveau Gentilhomme Bourgeois," 791); response to "Belle Belle, ou le chevalier Fortuné": "qu'il pleurait tendrement" (d'Aulnoy, "Le Nouveau Gentilhomme Bourgeois," 841).
88. Response to "Le Pigeon et la Colombe": "un ouvrage parfait" (d'Aulnoy, "Le Nouveau Gentilhomme Bourgeois," 890); response to "La princesse Belle Étoile et le prince Chéri": "Il ne put s'empêcher, dans l'excès de son enthousiasme, de prendre le main de Virginie et de la tirer si brusquement, que n'y étant point préparée, elle tomba sur le vicomte de Bergenville, et le vicomte tomba rudement par terre" (d'Aulnoy, "Le Nouveau Gentilhomme Bourgeois," 949).
89. Response to "Le prince Marcassin": "Le conte avait paru assez divertissant à toute la compagnie pour faire attendre sans impatience que l'on servît le dîner" (d'Aulnoy, "Le Nouveau Gentilhomme Bourgeois," 997); response to "Le Dauphin": "Marthonide eut à peine cessé de lire, que chacun s'empressa pour louer le conte de Dauphin" (d'Aulnoy, "Le Nouveau Gentilhomme Bourgeois," 1037).
90. "Que les avantures fussent toujours contre la vraisemblance, et les sentiments toujours naturels" (Bernard, *Inès de Cordoue: Nouvelle Espagnole*, 7–8).
91. Durand, "La Fée Lubantine," in Robert, *Contes*, 445. All subsequent references to Durand's tales are to this edition.
92. Gethner and Stedman suggest that Murat's reference to the "noble residence" in which she heard the tale is an allusion to the Parisian salon of either d'Aulnoy or the Marquise de Lambert (Murat, *A Trip to the Country*, 51n46).
93. "Elle écrivait comme je fais par fantaisie, au milieu et au bruit de mille gens qui venaient chez elle" (Patard, *Journal pour Mademoiselle de Menou*, 180, translation from Stedman, *Rococo Fiction in France*, 163–64).
94. "Ressemblait parfaitement" (Durand, "La Fée Lubantine," 446). The narrator claims that the fairy, unlike the comtesse de Mortane, is a libertine who indulges all her desires (Durand, "La Fée Lubantine," 446–47).
95. "La feinte vicomtesse s'interrompit et dit à Madame de Mortane qu'elle aurait bien voulu savoir son goût pour donner à son héros la figure qui pourrait lui plaire" (Durand, "La Fée Lubantine," 452).
96. Murat, "Voyage de Campagne," 51, 63–64.
97. I discuss the significance of Lhéritier's self-representation as a historian and storyteller in Reddan, "Translating Eloquence," 219–28.

98. Lhéritier, "Les enchantements de l'éloquence," 77; Lhéritier, "L'adroite princesse," 113–14.
99. Lhéritier, "La tour ténébreuse," 116.
100. "Je raconte seulement ce que porte ma chronique; je suis historienne, et une historienne, aussi bien qu'un historien, ne doit point prendre de parti" (Lhéritier, "Les enchantements de l'éloquence," 77).
101. Lhéritier, "Les enchantements de l'éloquence," 70–79. However, as Seifert and Stanton note, Lhéritier's use of the term *chronique* is not entirely consistent with the association of this term with official historical records. In claiming that stories about women appear in her *chronique*, Lhéritier is expanding the definition of history to something more than stories about the heroism of great men (*Enchanted Eloquence*, 69–70n72).
102. "J'ai supprimé beaucoup de faits, et en ai ajouté encore un plus grand nombre d'autres qui m'ont paru plus amusants, et plus convenables au sujet" (Lhéritier, "Variantes de Marmoisan," in Robert, *Contes*, 66).
103. "Ces contes se sont remplis d'impuretés en passant par la bouche du petit peuple" (Lhéritier, "Lettre à Madame D.G.***," 39).
104. On the influence of Straparola on the conteuses' tales, see Trinquet, *Le conte de fées français*, chapter 3.
105. Murat, "Épître: Aux Fées Modernes," 200.
106. Murat, "Épître: Aux Fées Modernes," 200; Patard, *Contes*, 200n2.
107. "Si vous voulez, belle Comtesse, / Par vos heureux talents, orner de tels récits. / L'antique Gaule vous en presse" (Lhéritier, "L'adroite princesse," 114).
108. "J'en savais un [conte] depuis longtemps, qui avait autrefois été conté à un Hôtel fameux, dans un temps où l'esprit était un peu plus à la mode qu'à présent . . . que si on voulait j'en ferais part à la compagnie, pourvu qu'on voulût bien me permettre de ne suivre pas mon texte scrupuleusement, et que je pusse y mettre quelques embellissements que j'y croyais nécessaires" (Murat, "Voyage de Campagne," 355–56).
109. "Je l'ai narré à ma manière" (Murat, "Voyage de Campagne," 367).
110. These remarks appear in notice preceding "L'Enchanteur" in *Les Contes de Contes* (Robert, *Contes*, 339). Bottigheimer suggests that this claim applies to the style of La Force's tales rather than their plot as she identifies literary antecedents for all La Force's tales except "Tourbillon" ("Charlotte-Rose de La Force," 196).
111. The titles of these volumes are *Nouvelles diverses du temps, La princesse des Prétintailles* (1702), *L'inconstance punie. Nouvelles du temps* (1702), *Les Colinettes, nouvelles du temps* (1703), and *L'origine du lansquenet, nouvelles du temps* (1703).
112. "Je laisse au Mercure Galant le soin de vous instruire des conquêtes de notre grand monarque. . . . Pour moi je me charge de vous apprendre ce qui se passe dans les

ruelles des dames, et dans le cabinet des Muses" (d'Auneuil, "La princesse des Prétintailles," 711).

113. "Les Colinettes," 728; "L'origine du lansquenet," 743.
114. La Force, "Au lecteur," in *Les Contes des Contes.*
115. *Le Mercure Galant* (January 1700), 245–46; *Le Mercure Galant* (February 1703), 386–89.
116. "Ce livre est une fiction ingénieuse écrite dans le goût qui règne si fort depuis quelque temps parmi les dames, quoique ce dessein toutefois ne réponde pas à celui des autres contes des fées; puisque dans cet ouvrage l'on y détruit le pouvoir tyrannique de ces déesses imaginaires" (*Le Mercure Galant*, February 1703, 387).

2. A SHARED VOCABULARY OF LOVE

1. "Qu'on ne peut avoir de bonheur parfait sans amour, l'amour qui n'est pas réglé par la vertu cause tous les malheurs de la vie" (Durand, "La Fée Lubantine," 460).
2. "L'amour est une de ces passions turbulentes qu'on ne peut cacher que rarement sous le voile de la discrétion" (Lhéritier, "Ricdin-Ricdon," 161).
3. DeJean, *Ancients against Moderns*, 78–88.
4. See, for example, d'Aulnoy, "La princesse Carpillon," 659; d'Aulnoy, "Le Pigeon et la Colombe," 863; Murat, "Anguillette," 91, 110; Murat, "L'île de la magnificence," 248, 270; Murat, "L'Heureuse Peine," 191.
5. See, for example, d'Aulnoy, "La princesse Carpillon," 643; Murat, "Anguillette," 92, 94; Murat, "L'Aigle au beau bec," 376; Murat, "Le palais de la vengeance," 145; La Force, "La puissance d'amour," 400; La Force, "Vert et Bleu," 375; Durand, "La Fée Lubantine," 454; Durand, "L'origine des fées," 463; d'Auneuil, "La tyrannie des fées détruite," 522.
6. La Force, "Plus Belle que Fée," 321; La Force, "Le pays des délices," 392; Murat, "Le père et ses quatre fils," 362; Murat, "L'Heureuse Peine," 191; d'Aulnoy, "Babiole," 511; d'Auneuil, "La princesse Léonice," 571, 588.
7. Bernard, "Le prince Rosier," 280; Murat, "Le roi Porc," 211; Murat, "L'Heureuse Peine," 191; Lhéritier, "La robe de sincérité," 254.
8. Seifert identifies the elite class identity of the conteuses' protagonists as a sign of nostalgia. He suggests that royal protagonists are used as symbols of absolute perfection (*Fairy Tales, Sexuality, and Gender*, 111–13).
9. I discuss the representation of female agency in tales by Lhéritier, d'Aulnoy, and Murat in Reddan, "Thinking through Things," 191–209. I discuss the presence of mésalliances in conteuses' tales in chapter 3 of this book.
10. Finette's husband is also motivated by familial loyalty. He marries Finette to fulfill a promise to his dying brother that he will avenge him by marrying then killing Finette (Lhéritier, "L'adroite princesse," 109–12).

11. Robert, *Le conte de fées littéraire*, 35.
12. I discuss Rosenwein's methodology in the introduction under the heading "Interrogating Fairy-Tale Love."
13. d'Aulnoy, "Le prince Lutin," 237, 253; Murat, "Jeune et Belle," 122–23; Murat, "Anguillette," 94; La Force, "Tourbillon," 360; d'Auneuil, "La tyrannie des fées détruite," 521; Lhéritier, "La robe de sincérité," 224, 254.
14. DeJean, *Ancients against Moderns*, 78–88.
15. Gordon-Seifert, *Music and the Language of Love*, 245. See also Pelous, *Amour précieux, amour galant*; DeJean, *Tender Geographies*, chapters 2 and 3; Maclean, *Woman Triumphant*, chapters 5 and 6.
16. Descartes, "Les Passions de L'âme," part 2, 69, 79.
17. "S'il est vrai que je n'en parle pas mal . . . c'est parce que mon cœur m'a appris à en bien parler, et qu'il n'est pas difficile de dire ce que l'on sent" (Scudéry, *Clélie*, 1:390).
18. Although Lafayette is now the more well-known of the two, Villedieu's writing was extremely popular in seventeenth-century France with her historical novels, in particular the question of whether the confession scene in *Les Désordres de l'amour* served as a model for the one in *La princesse de Clèves*, the subject of contemporary literary criticism (Jensen, "Marie-Catherine Desjardins de Villedieu," 509–10). Moreover, Turnovsky argues that the publication history of *La princesse de Clèves* indicates that Lafayette's readership was smaller than the controversy in the *Le Mercure Galant* suggests, and that Scudéry's novels, including *Clélie*, were more widely read, particularly in the 1680s ("Literary History Meets the History of Reading," 436–39).
19. DeJean, *Ancients against Moderns*, chapter 3.
20. Much has been written about the origins of the concept of tendresse. See in particular DeJean, *Ancients against Moderns*, 84–88; Peters, *Mapping Discord*, 93–99; Pelous, *Amour précieux, amour galant*, 18–21.
21. DeJean cites Sévigné's February 9, 1671 letter to her daughter, and a 1692 sermon by Bourdaloue as examples of this semantic clustering (*Ancients against Moderns*, 86–87).
22. Dixon, *From Passions to Emotions*, 1–25.
23. DeJean, *Ancients against Moderns*, 79–82.
24. Murat, "Jeune et Belle," 121; Murat, "L'Heureuse Peine," 191; d'Aulnoy, "Le Pigeon et la Colombe," 863; d'Aulnoy, "Belle Belle, ou le chevalier Fortuné," 815; La Force, "Plus Belle que Fée," 321; La Force, "Le pays des délices," 392.
25. Perrault, "Grisélidis," 116. This and all subsequent references to tales by Perrault and other conteurs come from Gheeraert, *Contes Merveilleux*. Perrault, along with Fenelon and Préchac, uses the term *émouvoir* to describe the ease (or lack

thereof) by which a person is affected by emotion (Fénelon, "Voyage dans l'île des plaisirs," 414; Préchac, "Sans Parangon," 701; Perrault, "Grisélidis," 129).

26. Descartes, "Les Passions de L'âme," part 1, 28.
27. DeJean, *Ancients against Moderns*, 80–81; Dixon, "'Emotion,'" 340; Merlin-Kajman, "Introduction," 9.
28. The conteuses are not the only seventeenth-century women who questioned this aspect of Descartes's thinking. In Princess Elisabeth of Bohemia's correspondence with Descartes, she rebuffs the suggestion that thought alone can cure her vapors and argues that passion must be experienced before it can be subdued (Harth, *Cartesian Women*, 67–78).
29. I discuss the influence of this tradition on Perrault in Reddan, "The Battle for Control of the Heart," 79–94.
30. Alberti, *Matters of the Heart*, 3–4, 18–23; Jager, *The Book of the Heart*, 2–5.
31. Plato, "Timaeus," 1193–94 (70b–d).
32. Erickson, *The Language of the Heart*, 3–4. See also Jager, *The Book of the Heart*, xv, 4–5.
33. Erickson, *The Language of the Heart*, 11–12; Desjardins, *Le corps parlant*, 45–72.
34. Descartes, "Les Passions de L'âme," part 1, 31–33.
35. DeJean, *Ancients against Moderns*, 85.
36. Harth, *Cartesian Women*, 78–86.
37. Lhéritier, "Ricdin-Ricdon," 161.
38. "[O]n n'est guère maîtresse de soi lorsqu'on est agitée de cette passion [amour]": Durand, "Le prodige d'amour," 490.
39. Bernard, "Le prince Rosier," 279–85.
40. See, e.g., James, *Passion and Action*, 1–14; Paster, Rowe, and Floyd-Wilson, *Reading the Early Modern Passions*.
41. Love at first sight has had a profound influence on romantic literature in genres including the twelfth-century troubadour and *trouvère* tales and *amor de lonh* composed by the conteuses' literary ancestors. On the *amor de lohn*, see Asaro, "Unmasking the Truth about *Amor de Lonh*," 95–120. On the importance of the eyes and heart in Renaissance representations of romantic love, see Zarri, "Eyes and Heart," 53–69. Cupid, in his guise as the god of love, appears in several of the conteuses' tales. On the significance of the Cupid and Psyche myth in seventeenth-century French culture, see Birberick, "Rewriting Curiosity," 134–48.
42. Desjardins's interdisciplinary review of the medical, aesthetic, poetic, rhetorical, and ethical works on the passions published in France between 1640 and 1680 argues that the body was an essential site for theorization of the passions in seventeenth-century France (*Le corps parlant*).

43. Desjardins, *Le corps parlant*, 1–6, part 1. See also Descartes's typology of the external signs of the passions: "Les Passions de L'âme," part 2, 112–35.

44. "Ses yeux sont trop tendres pour que son cœur soit insensible" (Murat, "La fée Princesse," 385).

45. "Ilérie le regardant avec une tendresse qui marquait assez les mouvements de son cœur" (Murat, "Anguillette," 99); "elle paraissait regarder avec tendresse et vivacité un jeune pêcheur qui voguait autour de l'île" ("Le père et ses quatre fils," 359).

46. "[Le prince des Charmes] ne lui parlait que par ses regards. La princesse lui répondait, et ce langage si tendre leur avait appris qu'ils aimaient" (Murat, "L'Aigle au beau bec," 377); "Depuis ce jour où les cœurs de ces deux amants furent d'intelligence, leurs yeux le furent parfaitement aussi, et se donnèrent souvent de tendres explications de leurs sentiments secrets" (Lhéritier, "Ricdin-Ricdon," 161).

47. "Ils se regardèrent avec une joie brillante dans les yeux, et se tendant les bras, comme s'ils se fussent connus, ils s'embrassèrent et semblaient déjà, avec leurs petits bras, former une chaîne qui devait les attacher ensemble pour toute leur vie" (La Force, "Tourbillon," 359).

48. "Avouez la vérité, lui dit-elle, avec des yeux enflammé d'amour et de colère, votre cœur vous reproche les moments que les ordres du roi vous forcent de me donner? La trop heureuse Léonice vous occupe même jusqu'auprès de moi" (d'Auneuil, "La princesse Léonice," 575).

49. "La joie se répandit sur son visage: amour, amour, que l'on te cache difficilement!" (d'Aulnoy, "L'Oiseau Bleu," 193).

50. d'Aulnoy, "Le Pigeon et la Colombe," 859.

51. d'Aulnoy, "La princesse Carpillon," 643; Lhéritier, "La robe de sincérité," 201, 263; La Force, "Plus Belle que Fée," 315; Murat, "Le père et ses quatre fils," 362.

52. d'Aulnoy, "Le prince Lutin," 252; Murat, "La fée Princesse," 392.

53. Bernard, "Le prince Rosier," 282.

54. "Pourquoi me cacher vos sentiments, Constancia? lui dit-elle, votre visage trahit le secret de votre cœur, vous aimez" (d'Aulnoy, "Le Pigeon et la Colombe," 859).

55. See chapter 2, note 45.

56. "Leur conversation fut assez longue, ils se dirent pourtant peu de chose, leurs yeux et leurs soupirs se parlaient assez" (Choisy, "Histoire de la princesse Aimonette," 855).

57. Perrault, "Peau d'Âne," 161–68.

58. See, for example, Murat, "Le palais de la vengeance," 145; Murat, "L'Aigle au beau bec," 376; Murat, "Jeune et Belle," 121; Murat, "La fée Princesse," 383; d'Aulnoy, "La Biche au bois," 693; d'Aulnoy, "L'Oiseau Bleu," 191–92; d'Aulnoy, "La princesse Printanière," 269–71; Lhéritier, "Les enchantements de l'éloquence," 80–81; La Force, "L'Enchanteur," 346; La Force, "Vert et Bleu," 376; La Force, "La Bonne

Femme," 423; Durand, "Le prodige d'amour," 485; d'Auneuil, "L'inconstance punie," 722.

59. Bernard, "Le prince Rosier," 280; Murat, "Le roi Porc," 211; Murat, "L'Heureuse Peine," 191; Murat, "L'île de la magnificence," 270; Murat, "Peine Perdue," 397; d'Aulnoy, "La Biche au bois," 693.
60. La Force, "L'Enchanteur," 346. I discuss this tale further in chapter 3.
61. "Je vous trouve plus belle que le soleil" (d'Aulnoy, "La Belle aux Cheveux d'Or," 185).
62. "Je vous ai vu avec admiration monté sur votre beau cheval qui danse" (d'Aulnoy, "La princesse Printanière," 271).
63. Murat, "Jeune et Belle," 121.
64. "La noble éducation qu'elle avait eue la rendant beaucoup plus maîtresse d'elle-même que ne sont ces sortes de personnes, elle ne donna aucune marque extérieure de ce qu'elle pensait" (Lhéritier, "La robe de sincérité," 231–32).
65. "Notre héroïne n'était pas insensible, mais elle savait régner ses passions; et quand elle faisait réflexion à l'inégalité des conditions, elle se disait que le prince ne songerait à elle que pour se faire un amusement" (Lhéritier, "Marmoisan," 61).
66. Lhéritier, "Marmoisan," 61–64.
67. "L'histoire dit que les yeux de Blanche firent à leur tour une blessure au chasseur; mais j'ai peine à croire que ce fût dès ce premier moment" (Lhéritier, "Les enchantements de l'éloquence," 79).
68. "Aussi aisé à prendre feu que son fusil" (Lhéritier, "Les enchantements de l'éloquence," 79).
69. Characters who fall in love at first sight appear in tales by Perrault and Mailly: Perrault, "Grisélidis," 116; Perrault, "Peau d'Âne," 160–61; Perrault, "Riquet à la houppe," 234; Mailly, "Le prince Roger," 525, 531; Mailly, "La reine de l'île des fleurs," 566; Mailly, "Le Bienfaisant ou Quiribirini," 578, 581; Mailly, "La Supercherie malheureuse," 595; Mailly, "Le Favori des fées," 572.
70. Hearts are moved, touched, or made sensible by love in tales by Choisy, Mailly, and Perrault: Choisy, "Histoire de la princesse Aimonette," 851; Mailly, "Fortunio," 539; Mailly, "L'Île inaccessible," 606; Mailly, "La Supercherie malheureuse," 595; Mailly, "Le Favori des fées," 572; Mailly, "Le prince Guérini," 556; Mailly, "Le prince Roger," 531; Perrault, "Grisélidis," 116; Perrault, "Peau d'Âne," 161, 163; Perrault, "Riquet à la houppe," 240.
71. "Mais afin qu'entre nous une solide paix / Éternellement se maintienne, / Il faudrait me jurer que vous n'aurez jamais / D'autre volonté que la mienne" (Perrault, "Grisélidis," 124). For a different interpretation of this tale, see Jones, *Mother Goose Refigured*, 53–63. Jones argues that Perrault's conclusion of the tale with a loving marriage for Grisélidis's daughter proposes a balanced model of marriage as a replacement to the traditional, patriarchal union endured by Grisélidis.

72. I discuss the obligation of wifely obedience and the gendered experience of love in marriage in chapter 4.
73. Perrault, "Peau d'Âne," 153.
74. On feminist criticism of fairy tales, see Stone, "Feminist Approaches," 229–36; Haase, "Feminist Fairy-Tale Scholarship" (2000), 15–63; Haase, "Feminist Fairy-Tale Scholarship" (2004), 1–36; Seifert, "On Fairy Tales, Subversion," 53–71. Chapters 3 and 4 discuss the legal and social role of marriage in seventeenth-century France.
75. Préchac, "Sans Parangon," 693; Préchac, "La Reine des fées," 731–33.
76. Fénelon, "Histoire d'une vieille reine," 383–84.
77. Mailly, "Blanche Belle," 507; Mailly, "Le prince Roger," 531; Mailly, "Fortunio," 541.
78. "Si je consultais mon cœur, répondit la princesse, je n'en serais que plus malheureuse; laissez-moi je vous en prie, ajouta-t-elle, suivre une destinée que je ne puis changer sans m'exposer à trop de malheurs" (Mailly, "Le prince Roger," 527).
79. There is a lack of consensus about whether the appropriate term for the salon code of love is *précieux, galant, tendre,* or some combination of the three. Jasmin and Raynard use the concept of *préciosité* in their analysis of the conteuses' representation of love. Seifert and Stanton prefer the term *galanterie,* and they suggest that préciosité is an anachronistic and pejorative aesthetic category. Pelous claims that galanterie developed at the expense of sensibilité tendre, and Viala emphasizes the degree of overlap between the concepts of galant and tendre (Jasmin, "Amour, amour, ne nous abandonne point"; Raynard, *La seconde préciosité;* Seifert and Stanton, "Editors' Introduction," 29–30; Pelous, *Amour précieux, amour galant,* 148; Viala, *La France Galante,* 53–65). Given my focus on the conteuses' conversations about love and the shared emotional vocabulary they used to interrogate the gender politics of courtship and marriage, resolving the *précieux, galant, tendre* debate is beyond the scope of this discussion. It is, perhaps, instructive to note that the terms *tendre* and *tendresse* appear most often in the conteuses' tales. *Galant* or *galanterie* appear infrequently, and *précieux* rarely at all.
80. DeJean, *Ancients against Moderns,* 83–86.
81. See in particular Descartes, "Les Passions de L'âme," part 1, 45–50, part 2, 138, 144–48, part 3, 160. See also Brown, "The Rationality of Cartesian Passions," 270–75.
82. Duggan's reading of the *Carte de Tendre* emphasizes the appeal to reason in Scudéry's regulation of courtship practices (*Salonnières, Furies, and Fairies,* 62–90).
83. "Une certaine sensibilité de cœur" (Scudéry, *Clélie,* 1:211). This is the definition given by Clélie in her explanation of the towns one must pass through when navigating the *Carte de Tendre.*

84. This reading of the *Carte de Tendre* is influenced by Peters's excellent book *Mapping Discord,* in particular chapter 2, "Mapping Nonsense," 83–116, as well as Duggan, *Salonnières, Furies, and Fairies,* 62–77; DeJean, *Tender Geographies,* 55–57, 87–90.
85. Duggan, *Salonnières, Furies, and Fairies,* 66–77; Peters, *Mapping Discord,* 121.
86. Scudéry, *Clélie,* 1:407–11. Scudéry reportedly composed the *Carte de Tendre* following a conversation in her salon in which she told Paul Pélisson that he was not one of her *tendres amis* (Peters, *Mapping Discord,* 90–91, 238–39n35). Peters cites Tallemant des Réaux's *Historiettes* (1834–35) as his source for this claim.
87. Green, "Madeleine de Scudéry on Love," 272–81. See also Duggan, *Salonnières, Furies, and Fairies,* 68; Duggan, "Lovers, Salon, and State," 17–18.
88. Peters, *Mapping Discord,* 93–106.
89. The other towns on this route are Complaisance, Assiduité, Empressement, Sensibilité, and Tendresse. My translations are influenced by Duggan's translations in *Salonnières, Furies, and Fairies,* 249n10, and Peters's translations in *Mapping Discord,* 88–98.
90. This interpretation of the path to Tendre-sur-Estime draws on Duggan's analysis in *Salonnières, Furies, and Fairies,* 68–69. The other towns leading to Tendre-sur-Estime are Sincerité, Probité, Generosité, Exactitude, and Respect.
91. All the conteuses except for Bernard refer to love as a *sentiment* of the heart: see, for example, d'Aulnoy, "Le Rameau d'Or," 309; d'Aulnoy, "L'Oranger et l'Abeille," 338; d'Aulnoy, "Belle Belle, ou le chevalier Fortuné," 801, 823; Lhéritier, "Les enchantements de l'éloquence," 83; La Force, "La puissance d'amour," 400; Murat, "Anguillette," 110; Murat, "Jeune et Belle," 124, "L'Heureuse Peine," 180; Murat, "Le roi Porc," 211; Durand, "L'origine des fées," 463–64; d'Auneuil, "La princesse Léonice," 573.
92. See, e.g., d'Aulnoy, "L'île de la félicité," 140; d'Aulnoy, "Le prince Lutin," 243; d'Aulnoy, "La Belle aux Cheveux d'Or," 187; d'Aulnoy, "L'Oranger et l'Abeille," 362, 363; d'Aulnoy, "Fortunée," 485; d'Aulnoy, "Serpentin Vert," 594; d'Aulnoy, "La Biche au bois," 715; d'Aulnoy, "La Chatte Blanche," 763; d'Aulnoy, "Le Pigeon et la Colombe," 869; d'Aulnoy, "Le Dauphin," 1017; Lhéritier, "La robe de sincérité," 214, 222, 226, 249; Murat, "Le Sauvage," 300; Murat, "Jeune et Belle," 121, 122, 124, 127, 139; Murat, "Anguillette," 96, 97, 98, 110; Murat, "La fée Princesse," 385; La Force, "Persinette," 338; La Force, "L'Enchanteur," 355; La Force, "Le pays des délices," 397; La Force, "Vert et Bleu," 387; La Force, "La Bonne Femme," 426; d'Auneuil, "L'inconstance punie ou l'origine des cornes," 722; Durand, "L'origine de fées," 464.
93. "Le prince et l'aimable Irolite jouirent du rare bonheur de brûler toujours d'un amour aussi tendre et aussi constant dans une fortune tranquille, que pendant leurs malheurs il avait été ardent et fidèle" (Murat, "Le parfait amour," 83–84).

94. "Tout ce que l'amour le plus tendre inspire de plus fort était dans ces deux cœurs" (d'Auneuil, "La princesse Léonice," 583).

95. "Le tendre objet de mon amour" (d'Aulnoy, "Le Rameau d'Or," 327).

96. "Babiole avait un cœur, et ce cœur n'avait pas été métamorphosé comme le reste de sa petite personne: il prit donc de la tendresse pour le prince, et il en prit si fort, qu'il en prit trop" (d'Aulnoy, "Babiole," 511).

97. "La triste princesse ne pouvant contenir dans son cœur sa douleur et sa tendresse" (Murat, "Le père et ses quatre fils," 362).

98. "Les premiers mouvements de leurs cœurs furent donnés à l'admiration et à la tendresse" (Murat, "Le palais de la vengeance," 145).

99. Murat, "Le roi Porc," 211.

100. DeJean, *Tender Geographies*, 87–88. See also Peters, *Mapping Discord*, 112.

101. DeJean, *Tender Geographies*, 87–88.

102. Scudéry, *Clélie*, 1:412–25. See also Peters, *Mapping Discord*, 112–13.

103. DeJean, *Tender Geographies*, 87–88, 109–15.

104. See Lhéritier, "L'adroite princesse," 111; Murat, "Le Turbot," 348; d'Auneuil, "La tyrannie des fées détruite," 518.

105. "Une puissance secrète" (La Force, "L'Enchanteur," 339); "il se mit à genoux devant elle, lui dit qu'il aimait, et elle sentit une si grande inclination pour lui que toute la magie ne peut former rien de semblable, s'il n'est pris dans un sentiment naturel" (La Force, "L'Enchanteur," 340).

106. I discuss the tale of "Anguillette" in more detail in the introduction and in chapter 5.

107. "[Le mariage] était bien juste de récompenser une si longue amour, si ardente et si fidèle" (La Force, "L'Enchanteur," 354).

108. On the usage of *sentiment*, see Mailly, "La princesse délivrée," 624; Mailly, "Le prince Guérini," 550; Mailly, "Le prince Roger," 531; Mailly, "Le roi magicien," 515; Perrault, "Grisélidis," 136, 141; Préchec, "La Reine de fées," 732, 738, 745; Préchec, "Sans Parangon," 698, 700, 706, 708, 711, 728. On *tendre* and *tendresse* see Choisy, "Histoire de la princesse Aimonette," 851, 855; Mailly, "Blanche Belle," 507; Mailly, "Constance sous le nom de Constantin," 612; Mailly, "Fortunio," 541, 544, 545; Mailly, "La reine de l'île des fleurs," 559; Mailly, "La Supercherie malheureuse," 592; Mailly, "Le prince Guérini," 554; Mailly, "Le prince Roger," 526–27; Perrault, "Grisélidis," 111, 112, 123, 124, 128–33, 141; Perrault, "Le Maître Chat," 218.

109. The 1694 edition of the *Dictionnaire de l'Académie française* includes the following definitions for *inclination*: "Action de celuy qui incline sa teste, ou tout son corps" and "Disposition & pente naturelle à quelque chose." The term is used in this sense in tales by Mailly, Perrault, and Préchac: Mailly, "Blanche Belle," 507, "Fortunio," 533; Mailly, "La Supercherie malheureuse," 591; Perrault, "La belle au

bois dormant," 193; Préchac, "Sans Parangon," 696, 698, 703, 716; Préchac, "La Reine de fées," 734, 744.

110. Mailly, "La princesse délivrée," 623–24. In Mailly's "Le prince Roger," it is the hero's *inclination* that drives his pursuit of romantic adventure: 524–25.

111. Word frequency analysis on the ARTFL-FRANTEXT database identifies *passion*, with 104 occurrences, as the most frequently used emotion term in Lafayette's *La princesse de Clèves*. *Sentiment* is the next popular term with 61 occurrences, followed in descending order of use by *amour* (50), *inclination* (30), *tendresse* (9), *tendre* (5), *émotion* (1). *Amour* is the most frequently used emotion term in Villedieu's *Les Désordres de l'amour*, with 127 references. *Passion* is the next most popular term, with 29 occurrences, followed by *tendresse* (13), *tendre* (6), *émotion* (5), *inclination* (4), and *sentiment* (1). See ARTFL-FRANTEXT database, http://artfl-project.uchicago.edu/content/artfl-frantext (accessed October 23, 2019).

112. Lafayette, *La princesse de Clèves*, 38; Villedieu, *Les Désordres de l'amour*, 72, 123.

113. Lafayette, *La princesse de Clèves*, 199–200.

114. See in particular d'Aulnoy's "L'île de la félicité," "L'Oiseau Bleu," "L'Oranger et l'Abeille," "La princesse Carpillon," "La Biche au bois," "La Chatte Blanche," "Belle Belle, ou le chevalier Fortuné," "Le prince Marcassin"; and Murat's "Le parfait amour," "Anguillette," "Jeune et Belle," "Le prince des Feuilles," "L'Heureuse Peine," "Le père et ses quatre fils," and "La fée Princesse."

115. Murat, "L'île de la magnificence," 278–79.

116. d'Aulnoy, "Le prince Lutin," 258.

117. The relevant tales are "La princesse Rosette," "Finette Cendron," "La princesse Printanière," and "Fortunée."

118. "Vous ne savez pas s'il a toutes les qualités qui doivent animer sa beauté, s'il a de la naissance, de l'esprit, et surtout un cœur capable de répondre à votre tendresse" (Murat, "Le roi Porc," 211).

119. "Qu'il est impossible que l'intérieur d'un objet si accompli ne soit pas aussi parfait que l'extérieur est charmant" (Murat, "Le roi Porc," 211).

120. Premarital sex is the taboo La Force challenges in "Persinette"; infidelity is ultimately rewarded in "L'Enchanteur."

121. "Herminie épousa Léandrin qu'elle aima autant par inclination que par reconnaissance" (Lhéritier, "La robe de sincérité," 269); Lhéritier, "Marmoisan," 63–64.

122. "Enfin . . . il parla d'une manière si passionnée et si naturelle que la belle se laissa persuader que son amour était sincère et pur" (Lhéritier, "Ricdin-Ricdon," 160).

123. "Elle était bien en peine de savoir qui était ce chasseur; mais tous ses mouvements ne naissaient que de simple bienveillance et de curiosité" (Lhéritier, "Les enchantements de l'éloquence," 85).

124. Lhéritier, "Les enchantements de l'éloquence," 79.

125. d'Auneuil, "L'inconstance punie," 722–26.
126. d'Auneuil, "La princesse Patientine," 699–705.

3. COURTSHIP, CONSENT, AND DECLARATIONS

1. "Aimez-vous un cœur qui vous aime? / . . . / De mille et mille feux je me sens enflame / . . . / Jouissez du bonheur extreme / D'aimer et de vous voir aimé" (d'Aulnoy, "La princesse Carpillon," 654).
2. On the social implications of declarations of love in early modern courtship, see Barclay, *Love, Intimacy and Power*, chapter 3; Eustace, "'The Cornerstone of a Copious Work,'" 518, 524–37.
3. Lamaison and Bourdieu, "From Rules to Strategies," 110.
4. On courtship in seventeenth-century France, see Godineau, *Les femmes*, 27–32; Desan, "Making and Breaking Marriage," 2–10; Lebrun, "Amour et mariage," 306–10; Daumas, *Le mariage amoureux*, 38–49.
5. On the emotion scripts articulated in the *Carte de Tendre*, see the discussion in chapter 2 under the heading "Revising the Salon Legacy of *Galanterie* and *Tendresse*."
6. A key moment in this debate was the controversy inspired by the publication of *La princesse de Clèves* in 1678. The confession scene in Lafayette's novel, which emphasized the tension between virtue and passion in the female experience of a marriage was the subject of extensive discussion in *Le Mercure Galant* (DeJean, *Ancients against Moderns*, 59–63).
7. Daumas, *Le mariage amoureux*, 40–42; Burguière, *Le mariage et l'amour*, part 2.
8. Hanley, "Family and State," 64–65; Hanley, "Engendering the State," 6–11.
9. Brunelle, "Dangerous Liaisons," 75–103.
10. Godineau, *Les femmes*, 27.
11. Desan, "Making and Breaking Marriage," 3–9; Gibson, *Women in Seventeenth-Century France*, 42–45; Howell, "The Properties of Marriage," 31–54.
12. Hardwick, *The Practice of Patriarchy*, 51–75; Desan, "Making and Breaking Marriage," 3–7.
13. Desan, "Making and Breaking Marriage," 3–9.
14. Godineau, *Les femmes*, 31.
15. Pélissier et al., "Migration and Endogamy," 225–26.
16. Desan, "Making and Breaking Marriage," 2–9; Lebrun, "Amour et mariage," 300–312.
17. Howell, "The Properties of Marriage," 17–31.
18. Barclay, *Love, Intimacy and Power*, 87, 89–94.
19. Eustace, "The Cornerstone of a Copious Work," 522–37.
20. See, e.g., DeJean, "Introduction," 14; Lougee, *Le Paradis des femmes*, 21–25; Welch, "La femme, le mariage," 47–58.

21. Barclay and Eustace make similar observations. They differ in their interpretation of the agency of women in courtship but agree that the discourse of love did not alter the patriarchal structure of early modern marriage. Eustace suggests that courtship was a period in which the gender hierarchy was reversed, and women exercised more power than normal due to their ability to reject male suitors ("The Cornerstone of a Copious Work," 527–37). Barclay argues that the gendering of love as a gift offered by men to women meant that male victory over female reserve was inevitable, thus limiting the agency of women during courtship (*Love, Intimacy and Power*, 89–91).
22. Writers such as Lafayette and Villedieu contributed to the development of the genre of historical fiction during the 1670s. This genre was influenced by Scudéry's novels and criticized attempts by the French state to exercise control over marriage by codifying parental consent as a legal requirement (DeJean, *Tender Geographies*, 109–34).
23. The male writers identified by Carlin include anti-women satirists Nicolas Boileau-Despréaux and Jacques Losme de Monchesnay, and supporters of women such as Nicolas Pradon and François Gacon ("Imagining Marriage in the 1690s," 170).
24. Carlin, "Imagining Marriage in the 1690s," 167–72.
25. I discuss these unhappy endings further in chapter 5.
26. d'Aulnoy, "Finette Cendron," 456.
27. d'Auneuil, "La princesse Patientine," 709.
28. d'Auneuil, "L'inconstance punie," 726.
29. See, e.g., Mordicante in Murat's "Jeune et Belle," Ragotte in d'Aulnoy's "Le Mouton," and Berlinguette in Murat's "L'île de la magnificence."
30. This is shown most clearly in tales in which the absence of parental consent prevents union: Mailly, "Le roi magicien," 515–21; Mailly, "Le prince Roger," 526–30; Choisy, "Histoire de la princesse Aimonette," 851–58.
31. In Lafayette's novel, the Prince de Clèves, who had fallen in love with Mademoiselle de Chartres at first sight, declares his love to her before seeking consent for their marriage from her mother. Madame de Chartres tells her daughter that she will give her consent should she be inclined to marry the prince, and although Mademoiselle de Chartres does not object to the marriage, she has no particular affection toward her future husband beyond esteem and respect. The prince observes her lack of reciprocal passion before their marriage: "I have touched neither your inclination nor your heart, and my presence gives you neither pleasure nor pain" (Je ne touche ni votre inclination, ni votre cœur, et ma présence ne vous donne ni de plaisir, ni de trouble; Lafayette, *La princesse de Clèves*, 32).
32. d'Aulnoy, "La princesse Carpillon," 656, "Le prince Lutin," 257.

33. Murat, "La fée Princesse," 392–93.
34. Duggan argues that this type of mésalliance, a union between royalty and nobility, is the only type of unequal marriage found in d'Aulnoy's tales. To this end, d'Aulnoy elevates the status of characters borrowed from tales by Straparola such as "Le prince Marcassin," "Fortuneé," and "Le Dauphin" to avoid mésalliances between nobles and commoners: *Salonnières, Furies, and Fairies*, 205.
35. d'Aulnoy, "Le prince Marcassin," 973.
36. La Force, "Persinette," 335; Murat, "Le père et ses quatre fils," 365.
37. d'Aulnoy, "Le Dauphin," 1030, "L'Oranger et l'Abeille," 353.
38. Mailly, "Le prince Roger," 526–27.
39. Mailly, "Le roi magicien," 516.
40. d'Aulnoy, "La princesse Carpillon," 656; Murat, "Le père et ses quatre fils," 366.
41. d'Aulnoy, "Gracieuse et Percinet," 155–56.
42. Murat, "Le Sauvage," 283–84.
43. d'Aulnoy, "Belle Belle, ou le chevalier Fortuné," 837; d'Aulnoy, "Le prince Marcassin," 973; Lhéritier, "Marmoisan," 65; La Force, "Persinette," 338.
44. Fénelon, "Histoire d'une vieille reine," 383–84.
45. Mailly, "Blanche Belle," 507, "Le prince Roger," 531, "Fortunio," 541, "Le prince Guérini," 557. In Mailly's "Le prince Roger," the princess of Barcelona is embarrassed to have spoken first and refuses to contemplate resisting the marriage arranged by her father: 527.
46. Couples do not explicitly declare their love in Murat's "Le palais de la vengeance," "L'Heureuse Peine," "L'île de la magnificence," and "Le Sauvage"; or in d'Auneuil's "Agatie princesse des Scythes" and "La princesse Léonice."
47. "J'ai traversé l'univers pour venir admirer votre divine beauté, je vous offre mon cœur et mes vœux" (d'Aulnoy, "L'île de la félicité," 139).
48. "Voudriez-vous les refuser?" (d'Aulnoy, "L'île de la félicité," 139).
49. Prince Marcassin to Zélonide: "je t'aime, et je viens t'offrir de partager mon cœur et la couronne avec toi" (d'Aulnoy, "Le prince Marcassin," 981).
50. "Je suis à vous et je ne veux être qu'à vous" (d'Aulnoy, "Gracieuse et Percinet," 155).
51. "Un roi malheureux . . . qui vous aime et n'aimera jamais que vous" (d'Aulnoy, "L'Oiseau Bleu," 200).
52. The 1694 edition of the *Dictionnaire de l'Académie française* defines the word *laideron* as an insult given to a young woman who is ugly: "On appelle ainsi par injure une jeune fille ou une jeune femme qui est laide."
53. "Je vous ai vue, madame, répliqua l'invisible, je ne vous ai point trouvée telle que vous vous représentez, et soit votre personne, votre mérite ou vos disgrâces, je vous le répète, je vous adore" (d'Aulnoy, "Serpentin Vert," 586).

54. D'Aulnoy's tale rewrites the Cupid and Psyche myth, a story that was popular in seventeenth-century French literary and dramatic works (Birberick, "Rewriting Curiosity," 134–35).
55. "Une fée m'a donné cette figure et m'a prédit que je la garderais jusqu'au jour que je serais aimé de la plus belle personne du monde" (Bernard, "Le prince Rosier," 281).
56. "Il la persuadait qu'elle était très tendrement aimée" (Bernard, "Le prince Rosier," 282).
57. As I discuss in chapter 5, the marriage that follows this courtship is a cause of misery rather than joy.
58. The motif of a female utopia without men also appears in Murat's "Peine Perdue."
59. "Aimez, aimez tendrement, / Tout ici vous y convie; / Faites le choix d'un amant, / L'Amour même vous en prie" (d'Aulnoy, "Le prince Lutin," 243).
60. "Bienheureuse tranquillité / Qui régnez dans ce lieu champêtre, / Je perds chez vous ma liberté / Sans oser en parler, ni me faire connaître!" (d'Aulnoy, "Le prince Lutin," 247).
61. "Elle est mieux dans mon cœur" (d'Aulnoy, "Le prince Lutin," 248).
62. "Non, je ne suis démon ni fée; / Je suis un amant malheureux / Qui n'ose paraître à vos yeux; / Plaignez du moins ma destinée" (d'Aulnoy, "Le prince Lutin," 250). This note is written in response to the princess' fear that Lutin is a demon or a fairy.
63. d'Aulnoy, "Le prince Lutin," 256–57.
64. Another tale in which a declaration of love is made to a third party is Durand, "La Fée Lubantine," 352.
65. "Quelquefois que Lirette me regarde, elle me trouble entièrement; je me sens tout ému, et le moment d'après, ses mêmes regards me font un plaisir que je ne saurais dire; quand elle me gronde quelquefois, je suis très touché; mais qu'elle me dise enfin une parole de douceur, je me trouve tout joyeux" (La Force, "La Bonne Femme," 419).
66. "J'ai une ardente passion pour cette jeune beauté" (Lhéritier, "Les enchantements de l'éloquence," 90).
67. "J'ai pour elle l'amour le plus tendre et le plus ardent qu'on ait jamais eu" (Lhéritier, "La robe de sincérité," 249).
68. "Je ne veux, Madame, poursuivit-il, vous obtenir que de vous-même; ce n'est que par la respectueuse passion que j'ai pour vous, et par mes tendres services que j'ose aspirer à acquérir une place dans votre cœur" (Lhéritier, "La robe de sincérité," 201).
69. "Cet amant, qui s'était toujours contraint jusqu'à cet instant, ne put s'empêcher de dire tout bas à Herminie qu'en travaillant à sa liberté, il avait perdu la sienne" (Lhéritier, "La robe de sincérité," 263).
70. "Qu'on serait heureux, Madame, si toutes les blessures étaient aussi faciles à guérir que celle qui m'a fait verser des larmes pour vous! mais il en est de plus

dangereuses. . . . Je crains bien que vous n'ayez pas pour moi la sensibilité que j'ai eue pour vous, et que vous ne voyiez ce qu'elles me font souffrir sans en être touchée" (Lhéritier, "Marmoisan," 63).

71. La Force, "Persinette," 335, "L'Enchanteur," 340.
72. "Je ne suis pas un dieu, lui répondit-il; mais j'ai plus d'amour moi seul qu'il n'y en a dans le ciel ni sur la terre. Je suis Phraates, fils de la reine des fées, qui vous aime et qui veut vous secourir" (La Force, "Plus Belle que Fée," 313).
73. "Je n'ai rien à vous donner, lui dit-il; vous avez tout quand vous avez mon cœur" (La Force, "La puissance d'amour," 401).
74. "J'aspire à d'autres trésors, lui dit-il, et depuis que je suis frappé de l'éclat de vos charmes, je ne puis aimer que vous" (La Force, "Le pays des délices," 393).
75. "La proportion et les grâces de cette divine figure lui causèrent un si tendre transport qu'il ne put s'empêcher de lui dire avec impétuosité tout ce qu'il ressentait" (La Force, "Vert et Bleu," 379). La Force does not recount the words of Prince Vert's declaration.
76. "Ses sentiments paraissaient si nobles et si naturels que la princesse . . . ne douta pas qu'il ne fût celui que le ciel avait fait naître pour son bonheur" (La Force, "Vert et Bleu," 379).
77. Seifert and Stanton, *Enchanted Eloquence*, 31–32.
78. "Je viens vous offrir un cœur mille fois plus reconnaissant, un cœur vivement touché de vos charmes, et une fortune assez brillante pour devoir être désirée par toute autre que vous" (Murat, "Le palais de la vengeance," 148).
79. "Si Philax n'est pas assez sensible au bonheur d'être aimé de vous" (Murat, "Le palais de la vengeance," 148).
80. "Qu'il est inutile d'avoir de l'amour pour moi. Philax à qui j'ai donné mon cœur est trop aimable pour pouvoir cesser d'en être le maître" (Murat, "Le palais de la vengeance," 148).
81. As I discuss in chapter 5, Pagan gets his revenge on the heroic couple by destroying their love for each other.
82. Murat, "L'Aigle au beau bec," 377.
83. "Toute la nature s'élève contre moi en votre faveur; je connais même que j'ai tort de ne pas reconnaître votre amour, vous méritez un cœur tout entier" (d'Auneuil, "Le prince Curieux," 602).
84. "Si vous aviez voulu, je vous aurais fait roi, nous ne serions point partis de mon royaume" (d'Aulnoy, "La Belle aux Cheveux d'Or," 185).
85. "Je ne voudrais pas faire un si grand déplaisir à mon maître, pour tous les royaumes de la terre, quoique je vous trouve plus belle que le soleil" (d'Aulnoy, "La Belle aux Cheveux d'Or," 185).

86. The king applies what he thinks is *l'Eau de Beauté* (water of beauty) to his face so that he might become handsome enough to win his wife's love. Unbeknownst to the king, Belle's vial of this magical water was accidentally broken by one of her maids and replaced with a similar vial from his cabinet, which contained a deadly water used to execute princes and grand seigneurs (d'Aulnoy, "La Belle aux Cheveux d'Or," 186).
87. I discuss the social limits on Belle's agency in Reddan, "Thinking through Things," 197–99.
88. "Il faut que je vous avoue que vous êtes le seul que je peux souhaiter pour époux" (d'Aulnoy, "Babiole," 516).
89. Women who fall in love with metamorphosed heroes include Florinde in "Le prince Rosier," Merveilleuse in "Le Mouton," Livorette in "Le Dauphin," Marthésie in "Le prince Marcassin," and the hero's multiple brides in "Le roi Porc." Each of these women loves the hero before or without seeing his human form.
90. "Le roi lui dit que Moufette était maîtresse de se choisir un mari, qu'il ne la voulait contraindre en rien, qu'il travaillât à lui plaire, que c'était l'unique moyen d'être heureux" (d'Aulnoy, "La Grenouille bien-faisante," 680).
91. "Elle lui dit que s'il n'était pas son époux, elle n'en aurait jamais d'autre" (d'Aulnoy, "La Grenouille bien-faisante," 680).
92. "J'ai pour vous des sentiments que vous ne devineriez jamais, si je ne vous les expliquais moi-même . . . sachez donc, monsieur l'ambassadeur, que je vous ai vu avec admiration monté sur votre beau cheval qui danse; j'ai regretté que vous vinssiez ici pour un autre que pour vous; nous ne laisserons pas, si vous avez autant de courage que moi, d'y trouver du remède; au lieu de vous épouser au nom de votre maître, je vous épouserai au vôtre" (d'Aulnoy, "La princesse Printanière," 271).
93. d'Aulnoy, "La princesse Printanière," 268–84. I discuss the implications of this ending further in Reddan, "Thinking through Things," 198–99, 204–5.
94. "Voilà votre portrait, lui dit-elle, dès que je le vis, je vous aimai, et aussitôt, que je vous aimai, je me destinai à vous, et j'obtins de mon frère que je n'aurais jamais autre mari" (La Force, "L'Enchanteur," 346).
95. Murat claims that this relationship is not the mésalliance it would be if her heroine were human. Fairies, she argues, have the same privileges as goddesses: they can love shepherds who are worthy of love as easily as they can love kings because all men are beneath them (Murat, "Jeune et Belle," 121).
96. The 1694 edition of the *Dictionnaire de l'Académie française* identifies one of the definitions of *chiffre* as "l'arrangement de deux ou de plusieurs lettres capitales entrelassées l'une dans l'autre; & les premieres lettres de chaque nom sont d'ordinaire celles que l'on prend pour cet effet."

97. "Lorsque l'on veut brûler d'une ardeur immortelle, / Qu'un tendre cœur est alarmé! / Être charmant suffit pour être aimé; / Mais pour le rendre heureux, il faut être fidèle" (Murat, "Jeune et Belle," 122).

98. Jeune et Belle observes Alidor's indifference to the young and beautiful shepherdesses who visit to ask about the cause of marvels gifted to him (Murat, "Jeune et Belle," 124–25). She further tests him by appearing before him in the guise of a shepherdess and by giving him two portraits to see whether his feelings for her are genuine ("Jeune et Belle," 128–29).

99. "C'est moi qui vous ai donné des marques d'une tendresse qui fera à jamais, si vous m'êtes fidèle, votre bonheur et le mien" (Murat, "Jeune et Belle," 131).

100. Murat, "Le père et ses quatre fils," 365.

101. "Quitte pour moi cette jeune fée, je te vengerai de tes ennemis, et de tous ceux à qui voudras nuire" (Murat, "Jeune et Belle," 135).

102. "J'ajouterai vingt royaumes à celui que tu possèdes, cent tours pleines d'or, cinq cents pleines d'argent" (d'Aulnoy, "Le Mouton," 418).

103. "Il serait le plus heureux et le plus riche prince de la terre" (Murat, "L'île de la magnificence," 240).

104. Durand, "La Fée Lubantine," 456–60, "Le prodige d'amour," 490–94.

105. d'Auneuil, "L'inconstance punie," 723.

106. Unsuccessful male rivals appear in d'Aulnoy's "Le prince Lutin," "Le Rameau d'Or," "L'Oranger et l'Abeille," "La bonne petite souris," "Babiole," "Le Nain Jaune," "La princesse Carpillon," and "Le Pigeon et la Colombe"; in Lhéritier's "Ricdin-Ricdon"; in La Force's "Vert et Bleu" and "La puissance d'amour"; and in Murat's "Le palais de la vengeance," "Le prince des Feuilles," and "Le père et ses quatre fils."

107. The 1694 edition of the *Dictionnaire de l'Académie française* defines *bossu* as an adjective describing a person who has a hump on their back or stomach: "Qui a une bosse au dos, ou à l'estomac."

108. "N'étiez-vous pas bien malheureuse, madame Carpillonne, de refuser l'honneur que je voulais vous faire?" (d'Aulnoy, "La princesse Carpillon," 634).

109. When the princess attempts to refuse Bossu's wedding presents of gold, precious stones, clothes, and beautiful objects, he orders her to think of pleasing him: "vous devez songer à me plaire" (d'Aulnoy, "La princesse Carpillon," 635).

110. D'Aulnoy refers only to the hero as "le jeune berger" (the young shepherd), he is not given a proper name. Bossu's fears of disinheritance were well-founded as the king subsequently signed an act designating his youngest son the sole heir to the crown if he returned to the kingdom (d'Aulnoy, "La princesse Carpillon," 629–30).

111. "Le prince se plaignait toujours de l'indifférence de Carpillon parce qu'elle lui cachait ses sentiments avec soin" (d'Aulnoy, "La princesse Carpillon," 648).

112. “S’il est vrai . . . comment pourrais-je recevoir une telle déclaration? En me fâchant je le ferais peut-être mourir; en ne me fâchant pas j’aurais lieu de mourir moi-même de honte et de douleur. Quoi! étant née princesse j’écouterais un berger?” (d’Aulnoy, “La princesse Carpillon,” 646).

113. “En vain dans cet asile / Je vois avec la paix régner tous les plaisirs, / Où puis-je être un moment tranquille? / L’Amour même en ces lieux m’arrache des soupirs” (d’Aulnoy, “La princesse Carpillon,” 646). The practice of carving verses of love and lovers’ initials is a common trope in pastoral literature such as d’Urfé’s *L’Astree* (Seifert and Stanton, *Enchanted Eloquence,* 127n183).

114. “Vous voyez . . . un malheureux berger qui se plaint aux choses les plus insensibles, des maux dont il ne devrait se plaindre qu’à vous” (d’Aulnoy, “La princesse Carpillon,” 646).

115. “Je ne veux point aimer; j’ai déjà assez d’autres malheurs” (d’Aulnoy, “La princesse Carpillon,” 647).

116. “Je veux bien . . . convenir que vous avez un rival haï et abhorré” (d’Aulnoy, “La princesse Carpillon,” 647).

117. “Berger . . . si vous mourez, je vais mourir avec vous: en vain je vous ai caché mes secrets sentiments, connaissez-les, et sachez que ma vie est attachée à la vôtre” (d’Aulnoy, “La princesse Carpillon,” 649).

118. d’Aulnoy, “La princesse Carpillon,” 654. For the French text, see chapter 3, note 1.

119. “Vous ignorez sans doute que les filles des plus grands rois sont des victimes dont on ne consulte presque jamais l’inclination; si elles épousent un prince aimable et bienveillant, elles peuvent en remercier le hasard; mais entre un magot ou un autre, on ne songe qu’aux intérêts de l’État” (d’Aulnoy, “La princesse Carpillon,” 633).

120. “J’y consens . . . à condition qu’elle n’y aura point de répugnance” (d’Aulnoy, “La princesse Carpillon,” 630).

121. “Peut-on être heureux avec une personne qui ne nous aime point?” (d’Aulnoy, “La princesse Carpillon,” 633). As I discuss in the introduction, the fairy Anguillette also warns about the dangers of love (Murat, “Anguillette,” 91–92).

122. “Autant qu’il aimait, autant elle le haïssait: comme il ne lui parlait qu’en maître, et qu’il lui reprochait toujours qu’elle était son esclave, elle sentait son cœur si opposé à ses manières dures, qu’elle n’oubliait rien pour l’éviter” (d’Aulnoy, “La princesse Carpillon,” 630).

123. “S’il faut que je l’épouse, le jour de mes noces sera le dernier de ma vie: car ce n’est point tant la difformité de sa personne qui me déplaît en lui, que les mauvaises qualités de son cœur” (d’Aulnoy, “La princesse Carpillon,” 633).

124. “Je vous conjure d’y consentir de bonne grâce; la violence qu’il fait à vos sentiments marque assez l’ardeur des siens; s’il ne vous aimait pas, il aurait trouvé plus

d'une princesse, qui aurait été ravie de partager avec lui le royaume" (d'Aulnoy, "La princesse Carpillon," 633).

125. "Il ne veut que vous" (d'Aulnoy, "La princesse Carpillon," 633).

126. "Ne songez plus à la différence qui peut être entre lui et Carpillon, il est temps de les unir, songez . . . à leur mariage, je le souhaite, et vous n'aurez jamais lieu de vous en repentir" (d'Aulnoy, "La princesse Carpillon," 656).

4. MARRIAGE, GIFT-GIVING, AND OBLIGATION

1. "J'ai le pouvoir, Madame, dit Riquet à la houppe, de donner de l'esprit autant qu'on en saurait avoir à la personne que je dois aimer le plus; et comme vous êtes, Madame, cette personne, il ne tiendra qu'à vous que vous n'ayez autant d'esprit qu'on en peut avoir, pourvu que vous vouliez bien m'épouser" (Perrault, "Riquet à la houppe," 235).
2. Mauss, *The Gift*, 1–7.
3. Jasmin, "'Amour, amour,'" 227–32.
4. On the legal definition of marriage in seventeenth-century France, see the discussion in chapter 3 under the heading "Negotiating Parental Consent."
5. On the nature of salon criticism of marriage, see DeJean, "Introduction," 14; Lougee, *Le Paradis des femmes*, 21–25. On the presence of these ideas in the conteuses' tales, see Raynard, *La seconde préciosité*, 57–73; Warner, *From the Beast to the Blonde*, 167–70; Welch, "La femme, le mariage," 47–58.
6. For commentary on the rise of the companionate model of marriage in early modern France, see Goodman, "Marriage Choice and Marital Success," 26–61; Howell, "The Properties of Marriage," 17–61; Poska, "Upending Patriarchy," 195–211.
7. Davis, *The Gift in Sixteenth-Century France*, 124–29; Kettering, "Gift-Giving and Patronage," 131–32.
8. Mauss's essay, which remains the starting point for theoretical analysis of gifts in a number of fields, emphasizes the reciprocal nature of gift-giving (*The Gift*, 1–5, 13–14, 39–41).
9. Mauss, *The Gift*, 5. Lévi-Strauss also examines the strategic nature of gift exchange as a ritual establishing social bonds between gift-giver and gift-recipient ("The Principle of Reciprocity," 18–23). Gouldner interprets the cycle of exchange as the creation of indebtedness that structures social relations over time by maintaining social stability ("The Norm of Reciprocity," 63).
10. Desan, "Making and Breaking Marriage," 3–9; Gibson, *Women in Seventeenth-Century France*, 42–45; Howell, "The Properties of Marriage," 31–54.
11. Hardwick, *The Practice of Patriarchy*, 60–61.
12. Desan, "Making and Breaking Marriage," 2–9; Lebrun, "Amour et mariage," 300–312.

13. Gibson, *Women in Seventeenth-Century France*, 59–62; Wiesner, *Women and Gender in Early Modern Europe*, 296.
14. Davis, *The Gift in Sixteenth-Century France*, 124–29. Kettering's analysis of practices of gift-giving in patronage relationships in early modern France arrives at a similar conclusion to Davis about the symbolic significance of gift-giving ("Gift-Giving and Patronage," 131–32).
15. Davis, *The Gift in Sixteenth-Century France*, 27–29.
16. Davis, *The Gift in Sixteenth-Century France*, 9.
17. Davis, *The Gift in Sixteenth-Century France*, 8–9.
18. Bestor, "Marriage Transactions in Renaissance Italy," 26–31.
19. Klapisch-Zuber, *Women, Family, and Ritual in Renaissance Italy*, 215–39.
20. Davis, *The Gift in Sixteenth-Century France*, 28–29.
21. "Tenez, Ricdin-Ricdon, voilà votre baguette" (Lhéritier, "Ricdin-Ricdon," 150).
22. Lhéritier, "Ricdin-Ricdon," 149–50.
23. Lhéritier, "Ricdin-Ricdon," 175–76, 187–90.
24. Wiesner, *Women and Gender in Early Modern Europe*, 72; Goodman, "Marriage Choice and Marital Success," 30–40.
25. Howell, "The Properties of Marriage," 17–30. See also Barclay's study of the operation of power in elite Scottish marriages between 1650 and 1850, which argues that marriage discourses increasingly promoted the idea of love as a requirement for marriage during the eighteenth century: *Love, Intimacy and Power*, 61–64, 87–91. I discuss this further in chapter 3 under the heading "Negotiating Parental Consent."
26. Seifert, *Fairy Tales, Sexuality, and Gender*, 205–6.
27. Harries, *Twice upon a Time*, 35. Roche-Mazon is the strongest advocate for Bernard as the inventor of the tale ("De qui est Riquet à la houppe?," 404–11).
28. The opposition of male intelligence and female beauty evokes the Aristotelian association of men with the mind and women with matter that underpinned literary debate about the nature of women from the end of the fourteenth century: Hannon, "Antithesis and Ideology in Perrault's 'Riquet à la houppe,'" 106–7, 112–15. But see Ridley who argues that Perrault's tale inverts the Aristotelian mind-matter dichotomy: "From Perrault's 'Riquet à la houppe,'" 152–53.
29. Perrault, "Riquet à la houppe," 238–39.
30. "D'un époux odieux" (Bernard, "Riquet à la houppe," 289).
31. "Le plus heureux de tous les hommes" (Perrault, "Riquet à la houppe," 237).
32. "J'ai des choses fâcheuses à vous apprendre, mais j'en ai d'agréables à vous promettre" (Bernard, "Riquet à la houppe," 287).
33. "Son esprit, qui lui devenait un présent funeste, ne lui laissait échapper aucune circonstance affligeante" (Bernard, "Riquet à la houppe," 288).

34. "Vous avez le choix de m'épouser ou de retomber dans votre premier état" (Bernard, "Riquet à la houppe," 289).
35. "Il faut aimer Riquet à la houppe, c'est mon nom; il faut m'épouser dans un an; c'est *la condition* que je vous impose" (Bernard, "Riquet à la houppe," 287; my emphasis).
36. "Vous avez subi la loi qui vous était imposée. Mais si vous n'avez pas rompu notre traité, vous ne l'avez pas observé à la rigueur" (Bernard, "Riquet à la houppe," 291).
37. "Le gnome s'apercevait bien de la haine de sa femme, et il en était blessé, quoiqu'il se piquât de force d'esprit" (Bernard, "Riquet à la houppe," 290).
38. Mauss identifies generosity and gratitude as important elements of the gift-giver's reciprocal obligation (*The Gift*, 12–14, 19–41).
39. "Toi qui peux tout animer / Amour, si pour n'être plus bête, / Il ne faut que savoir aimer / Me voilà prête" (Bernard, "Riquet à la houppe," 288). The first two lines of this translation are influenced by Zipes's translation in *The Great Fairy Tale Tradition*, 718. The last two lines are my own translation.
40. "Quelqu'un qu'elle s'était engagée à épouser en acceptant ses dons qu'elle ne voulait pas lui rendre" (Bernard, "Riquet à la houppe," 288).
41. Douglas identifies the resentment felt by gift recipients who cannot provide a return gift as the reason why recipients of charity often dislike their benefactor ("Foreword: No Free Gifts," vii). See also Schwartz who argues that gift-giving creates a "balance of debt" that can never be repaid ("The Social Psychology of the Gift," 77–80).
42. Davis describes this type of failure as "gifts gone wrong" (*The Gift in Sixteenth-Century France*, 67–84).
43. "Quand je vous ai donné de l'esprit, je prétendais en jouir" (Bernard, "Riquet à la houppe," 291).
44. Seventeenth-century French women were legally subject to their husbands, who were allowed to correct their behavior with physical punishment as long as they did not draw blood or use a stick larger than the diameter of their thumb (Wiesner, *Women and Gender in Early Modern Europe*, 37; Gibson, *Women in Seventeenth-Century France*, 61).
45. "Les amants à la longue deviennent des maris" (Bernard, "Riquet à la houppe," 292).
46. "Ce que l'on voit dans cet écrit, / Est moins un conte en l'air que la vérité même; / Tout est beau dans ce que l'on aime, / Tout ce qu'on aime a de l'esprit" (Perrault, "Riquet à la houppe," 239).
47. "Dans un objet où la nature, / Aura mis de beaux traits, et la vive peinture / D'un teint où jamais l'art ne saurait arriver, / Tous ces dons pourront moins pour rendre un cœur sensible, / Qu'un seul agrément invisible, / Que l'amour y fera trouver" (Perrault, "Riquet à la houppe," 240).

48. I discuss salon counter-discourses about marriage in chapter 2 under the heading "Revising the Salon Legacy of *Galanterie* and *Tendresse*."
49. DeJean, "Introduction," 14; Raynard, *La seconde préciosité*, 44–66; DeJean, *Tender Geographies*, 21–22; Welch, "La femme, le mariage," 47–58.
50. DeJean, "Introduction," 4–6.
51. Montpensier and Motteville, *Against Marriage*, 26–29.
52. Montpensier and Motteville, *Against Marriage*, 43–49.
53. Carlin identifies d'Aulnoy's 1690 novel *Histoire d'Hypolite* and Murat's *Mémoires de Madame la comtesse de M**** (1697) as examples of 1690s texts supporting free choice of spouse ("Imagining Marriage in the 1690s," 170).
54. d'Aulnoy, "Serpentin Vert," 587–88.
55. d'Aulnoy, "Le prince Lutin," 246–52.
56. d'Aulnoy, "La Chatte Blanche," 764–65, 768–71, 789–91.
57. "Nous craignons, madame, que Rosette ne cause un grand malheur à ses frères; qu'ils ne meurent dans quelque affaire pour elle" (d'Aulnoy, "La princesse Rosette," 285).
58. d'Aulnoy, "La princesse Rosette," 286.
59. "Allons, lui dit-il, sortons de cette vilaine tour; le roi te mariera bientôt" (d'Aulnoy, "La princesse Rosette," 287).
60. "Mon papa, ma sœur est assez grande pour être mariée; n'irons-nous pas bientôt à la noce?" (d'Aulnoy, "La princesse Rosette," 286–87).
61. According to Defrance, peacocks are associated with Juno, Roman goddess of marriage and fertility. She suggests that Rosette's desire to marry the king of the peacocks is a coded representation of female sexual desire (*Les contes de fées*, 133–34).
62. "Je vous déclare que je ne me marierai jamais qu'au roi des paons" (d'Aulnoy, "La princesse Rosette," 288).
63. "C'est là . . . une malheureuse fantaisie" (d'Aulnoy, "La princesse Rosette," 289); "je ne sais où elle a été deviner qu'il y a dans le monde un roi des paons" (d'Aulnoy, "La princesse Rosette," 289).
64. "Elle est belle et bien sage, et nous lui donnerons un boisseau d'écus d'or" (d'Aulnoy, "La princesse Rosette," 290).
65. "Je l'épouserai de bon cœur . . . mais je vous assure que je veux qu'elle soit aussi belle que son portrait; et que s'il en manque la plus petite chose, je vous ferai mourir" (d'Aulnoy, "La princesse Rosette," 290).
66. "Elle ne manquera de rien avec moi, je l'aimerai beaucoup" (d'Aulnoy, "La princesse Rosette," 290).
67. "Elle jura qu'elle ne consentirait point à son mariage qu'ils ne rendissent les États de son père" (d'Aulnoy, "Finette Cendron," 456).

68. On the prince's lovesickness: "il la [la mule de Finette] fait ramasser, la regarde, en admire la petitesse et la gentillesse, la tourne, retourne, la baise, la chérit, et l'emporte avec lui . . . je n'épouserai jamais que celle qui pourra la chausser" (d'Aulnoy, "Finette Cendron," 453–54). His mother attempts to alleviate his despair by promising to acquire the wife he desires: "dis-nous qui tu veux et nous te la donnerons, quand ce ne serait qu'une simple bergère" (d'Aulnoy, "Finette Cendron," 453).
69. "Madame, ce sont mes sœurs qui sont fort aimables, je vous prie de les aimer" (d'Aulnoy, "Finette Cendron," 456).
70. "Pour tirer d'un ingrat une noble vengeance, / De la jeune Finette imite la prudence, / Ne cesse point sur lui de verser des bienfaits; / . . . / Que jamais un cœur magnanime, / Ne saurait se venger plus généreusement" (d'Aulnoy, "Finette Cendron," 457).
71. It is important to note the ambiguous nature of Grognon's claim to noble identity. As Duggan observes, d'Aulnoy's text states that Grognon is "*called*" a duchess, and her vulgarity and avarice suggest that her nobility is self-styled rather than innate ("Nature and Culture," 160, emphasis in original).
72. "Un millier de pistoles," "un boisseau de doubles louis d'or," "tant de perles et de diamants" (d'Aulnoy, "Gracieuse et Percinet," 153).
73. "Je vous en ferai le maître à condition que vous m'épouserez" (d'Aulnoy, "Gracieuse et Percinet," 153).
74. "Il y a encore une condition, c'est que je veux être maîtresse de votre fille, comme l'était sa mère; qu'elle dépende entièrement de moi, et que vous m'en laissiez la disposition" (d'Aulnoy, "Gracieuse et Percinet," 153–54).
75. "J'ai pris, dit-il, une colombe toute en vie" (d'Aulnoy, "Gracieuse et Percinet," 154).
76. "Il faut vous dire que j'ai rencontré la duchesse Grognon, et que je l'ai prise pour ma femme . . . je prétends que vous l'aimiez et la respectiez autant que si elle était votre mère" (d'Aulnoy, "Gracieuse et Percinet," 154).
77. d'Aulnoy, "Gracieuse et Percinet," 151–52. On d'Aulnoy's characterization of Grognon, see Verdier, "Gracieuse vs. Grognon," 13–21.
78. The moral of the tale praises Percinet's constancy and suggests that such a love will always be rewarded with perfect happiness: "Lorsque l'on aime avec constance, / Tôt ou tard, on se voit dans un parfait bonheur" (d'Aulnoy, "Gracieuse et Percinet," 174).
79. "Puisqu'elle était sa maîtresse, qu'il lui obéît en toutes choses" (d'Aulnoy, "Gracieuse et Percinet," 159).
80. "Ah! c'en est trop! Éloignons-nous de lui: il vaut mieux mourir que de l'aimer": d'Aulnoy, "Gracieuse et Percinet," 161.

81. "je suis comptable de mes actions au roi mon père" (d'Aulnoy, "Gracieuse et Percinet," 164).
82. "Si j'étais la maîtresse de ma destinée, lui dit-elle, le parti que vous me proposez serait celui que j'accepterais" (d'Aulnoy, "Gracieuse et Percinet," 164).
83. "Plus blanche que la neige" (Murat, "Jeune et Belle," 122).
84. "Oublie ses appas, ou ton amour sera funeste" (Murat, "Jeune et Belle," 129).
85. "Les fées ont les mêmes privilèges que les déesses: elles aiment un berger quand il est aimable, comme s'il était le plus grand roi de l'univers; car tout est au-dessous d'elles" (Murat, "Jeune et Belle," 121).
86. "C'est moi qui vous ai donné des marques d'une tendresse qui fera à jamais, si vous m'êtes fidèle, votre bonheur et le mien" (Murat, "Jeune et Belle," 131).
87. "Le destin a fixé le sort de Brutalis, / Il aura de l'esprit, il aura du courage, / Vous le verrez briller entre les plus polis; / Mais l'amour seul peut faire cet ouvrage" (Durand, "Le prodige d'amour," 479).
88. "Vous seule lui pouvez faire un don précieux, / Lui seul vous peut donner un sort doux et paisible" (Durand, "Le prodige d'amour," 493).
89. "Il la regardait avec une ardeur et un plaisir qui commencèrent d'ôter à ses regards cet air sombre et stupide qui voilaient toute leur beauté" (Durand, "Le prodige d'amour," 485).
90. Perrault, "Riquet à la houppe," 238.
91. The morals to Perrault's tale are discussed in chapter 4, notes 46–47.
92. Bernard, "Riquet à la houppe," 292.
93. "J'ai déjà déclaré . . . que mon dessein était de ne faire voir que des amants malheureux pour combattre, autant qu'il m'est possible, le penchant qu'on a pour l'amour" (Bernard, *Œuvres, tome 1*, 239).
94. "J'ai pensé qu'il valait mieux présenter au public un tableau des malheurs de cette passion que de faire voir les amants vertueux et délicats, heureux à la fin du livre. Je mets donc mes héros dans une situation si triste, qu'on ne leur porte point d'envie" (Bernard, *Œuvres, tome 1*, 177).

5. LOVE AFTER MARRIAGE

1. Raynard, "New Poetics versus Old Print," 93–106.
2. Boch, "Le conte en débats," 328–41. In addition to Villiers, *Entretiens sur les contes de fées* (1699), see Perrault, *Parallèle des Anciens et des Modernes* (1688–97); Faydit, *La Télémacomanie* (1700); Huet, *Traité de l'origine des romans* (1670); Bellegarde, *Lettres curieuses de littérature et de morale* (1702).
3. Villiers, "Entretiens sur les contes de fées," in Boch, "Le conte en débats," 387.
4. Villiers, "Entretiens sur les contes de fées," 386–87.

5. "Tous les contes de fées doivent renfermer par allégorie quelque vérité instructive . . . il n'y a à mon sens, de bons contes de cette nature, que ceux d'où l'on peut tirer de ces sortes d'instructions" (Villiers, "Entretiens sur les contes de fées," 391).
6. Villiers, "Entretiens sur les contes de fées," 391–92.
7. Raynard, "New Poetics versus Old Print," 94–99.
8. Jones, "The Poetics of Enchantment," 56.
9. This argument extends the position of Jones in "The Poetics of Enchantment (1690–1715)," 55–74.
10. Seifert, "On Fairy Tales, Subversion, and Ambiguity," 66–67.
11. For an overview of the key debates in the *Querelle des Anciens et des Modernes*, see DeJean, *Ancients against Moderns*; Fumaroli, "Les abeilles et les araignées," 7–218.
12. "Je prétends même que mes fables méritent mieux d'être racontées que la plupart des contes anciens, et particulièrement celui de la Matrone d'Éphèse et celui de Psyché, si l'on les regarde du côté de la morale, chose principale dans toute sorte de fables, et pour laquelle elles doivent avoir été faites" (Perrault, "Contes en vers," in Boch, "Le conte en débats," 362–63).
13. "Qu'ils doivent tenir un milieu qui soit plus enjoué que sérieux, qu'il faut un peu de morale, et surtout les proposer comme une bagatelle où l'auditeur seul a droit de mettre le prix" (d'Aulnoy, "Don Gabriel Ponce de Leon," 438).
14. "Tout ceci n'est rien qu'une fable, / Faite pour amuser quiconque la lira; / Toutefois on y trouvera une morale véritable" (d'Aulnoy, "La Bonne Petite Souris," 376).
15. "À qui t'a fait une faveur, / Montre une âme reconnaissante, / C'est la vertu la plus puissante / Pour toucher et gagner le cœur" (d'Aulnoy, "La Bonne Petite Souris," 376).
16. "Le seul mérite et la vertu, / Font la véritable noblesse. / Ô! toi qui d'honneurs revêtu, / Ne montres qu'orgueil et faiblesse, / Apprends de moi cette leçon: / En vain d'une antique famille, / Tu nous vantes l'illustre nom, / En vain sur toi la pourpre brille. / Quiconque a des vertus, malgré son humble état, / Passe pour noble, ou pour digne de l'être: / Mais tes honneurs et ton éclat, / Pour noble ne sauraient te faire reconnaître" (d'Aulnoy, "Fortunée," 485).
17. "Cent et cent fois ma gouvernante, / Au lieu de fables d'animaux, / M'a raconté les traits moraux" (Lhéritier, "L'adroite princesse," 113–14).
18. "Plus que ne font les faits et du singe et du loup" (Lhéritier, "L'adroite princesse," 114).
19. "Vous êtes en un âge où l'amusement et les jeux sont permis aux princes; mais en même temps vous devez donner quelques-unes de vos pensées à des réflexions sérieuses" ("A Monseigneur le Dauphin," in *La Fontaine*, 66).
20. "Ces puérilités servent d'enveloppe à des vérités importantes" (*La Fontaine*, 66).

21. "Il fait en sorte que vous apprenez sans peine, ou, pour mieux parler, avec plaisir, tout ce qu'il est nécessaire qu'un prince sache" (*La Fontaine*, 66).
22. "On voit de petites histoires répandues dans le monde, dont tout le dessein est de prouver agréablement la solidité des proverbes" (Lhéritier, "Lettre à Madame D.G.***," 35; translation by Seifert and Stanton, *Enchanted Eloquence*, 286).
23. Lhéritier, "Lettre à Madame D.G.***," 35–36. See also Raynard, "New Poetics versus Old Print," 97–98.
24. Montoya, "Contes du style des troubadours," 8–13.
25. "Semblent nous ramener le temps de fées, où l'on voyait tant de gens parfaits" (Lhéritier, "Lettre à Madame D.G.***," 36; translation by Seifert and Stanton, *Enchanted Eloquence*, 287).
26. In emphasizing the French nature of her sources, Lhéritier fails to acknowledge any intellectual debt to the sixteenth-century Italian tales by Giovan Francesco Straparola and Giambattista Basile (Bottigheimer and Raynard, "Marie-Jeanne Lhéritier de Villandon," 127–28, 137). See also Robert, "Les conteurs français lecteurs de Basile," 333–48.
27. On the inclusion of "Marmoisan" within the conteuses' corpus of tales, see chapter 1, note 20.
28. "On voit bien par de tels dictons / Que la sagesse de nos pères / Sans nous embarrasser de maximes sévères / Nous faisait ces belles leçons" (Lhéritier, "Marmoisan," 66).
29. On the didactic tone in Lhéritier's writing, see Seifert and Stanton, *Enchanted Eloquence*, 63–64.
30. "Doux et courtois langage / Vaut mieux que riche apanage" (Lhéritier, "Les enchantements de l'éloquence," 91).
31. "Étant entièrement assujettie à la vérité" ("Les Enchantements de l'Éloquence," 76).
32. "L'histoire peint les hommes comme ils sont, et les romans les représentent tels qu'ils devraient être, et semblent par là les engager d'aspirer à la perfection" (Lhéritier, "Les enchantements de l'éloquence," 76).
33. For a slightly different reading of Blanche's eloquence, see Seifert, "The Rhetoric of *Invraisemblance*," 121–39.
34. "Que les aventures fussent toujours contre la vraisemblance, et les sentiments toujours naturels" (Bernard, *Inès de Cordoue: Nouvelle Espagnole*, 7–8).
35. "Un amusement nouveau, d'imaginer des Contes galants; l'ordre fut reçu avec plaisir de toutes les Dames qui composaient cette petite Cour; on convint de faire des règles pour ces sortes d'Histoires" (Bernard, *Inès de Cordoue: Nouvelle Espagnole*, 7).
36. "On jugea que l'agrément de ces contes ne consistait qu'à faire voir ce qui se passe dans le cœur, et que du reste il y avait une sorte de mérite dans le merveilleux

des imaginations qui n'étaient point retenues par les apparences de la vérité" (Bernard, *Inès de Cordoue: Nouvelle Espagnole*, 8).

37. I discuss Bernard's authorial intentions further in the conclusion to chapter 4.
38. "Basses et puériles" (Murat, "Épître: Aux Fées Modernes," 199).
39. This is a reference to the manuscript title of Perrault's *Histoires, ou Contes du temps passé.*
40. Murat, "Épître: Aux Fées Modernes," 199–200.
41. DeJean, *Tender Geographies*, 90–93; Lougee, *Le Paradis des Femmes*, 138–70; Welch, "La femme, le mariage," 47–58.
42. Robert, *Le conte de fées littéraire*, 46–47.
43. Robert, *Le conte de fées littéraire*, 35.
44. Propp, *Morphology of the Folktale*, 63–64.
45. Robert, *Le conte de fées littéraire*, 46–47.
46. See also Thirard's analysis of "Le Nain Jaune" and "Le Mouton" as examples of d'Aulnoy's resistance of the implicit generic demand of a happy ending: "Les contes de Madame d'Aulnoy," 214–16.
47. Jasmin, *Naissance du conte féminin*, 480–94; Raynard, *La seconde préciosité*, 197–214.
48. Hannon, *Fabulous Identities*, 162–63.
49. These tales are "L'île de la félicité," "Le Mouton," and "Le Nain Jaune," which I discuss under the subheading "Separation, Death and Disappointment."
50. These tales are "Serpentin Vert," "Le Pigeon et la Colombe," and "Le prince Marcassin," respectively.
51. See especially the tale of "L'adroite princesse," which I discuss in the introduction to chapter 2.
52. d'Aulnoy, "L'Oiseau Bleu," 222; d'Aulnoy, "Le prince Lutin," 259; d'Aulnoy, "La princesse Printanière," 284; d'Aulnoy, "Le Rameau d'Or," 333; d'Aulnoy, "Babiole," 532–33; d'Aulnoy, "La princesse Carpillon," 661; d'Aulnoy, "La Grenouille bienfaisante," 686; d'Aulnoy, "La Chatte Blanche," 791; d'Aulnoy, "Fortunée," 485; d'Aulnoy, "Le prince Marcassin," 997; d'Aulnoy, "Le Dauphin," 1037; Lhéritier, "Marmoisan," 65–66; Lhéritier, "L'adroite princesse," 113–14.
53. On the use of the informal second person, see d'Aulnoy, "La Belle aux Cheveux d'Or," 187; d'Aulnoy, "Le Nain Jaune," 563; d'Aulnoy, "La Bonne Petite Souris," 376; d'Aulnoy, "Finette Cendron," 457; d'Aulnoy, "Fortunée," 485. For use of the formal second person, see d'Aulnoy, "Babiole," 532; d'Aulnoy, "Le Pigeon et la Colombe," 889; Lhéritier, "L'adroite princesse," 114; Lhéritier, "Ricdin-Ricdon," 192; La Force, "Plus Belle que Fée," 329; La Force, "L'Enchanteur," 355; La Force, "Tourbillon," 371; La Force, "Le pays des délices," 397; La Force, "La Bonne Femme," 434.

54. d'Aulnoy, "La princesse Printanière," 284; d'Aulnoy, "L'Oiseau Bleu," 222; d'Aulnoy, "Babiole," 533; d'Aulnoy, "La princesse Rosette," 298–99; d'Aulnoy, "Le Mouton," 425; d'Aulnoy, "Serpentin Vert," 604; d'Aulnoy, "Le Pigeon et la Colombe," 889; d'Aulnoy, "Le prince Marcassin," 997; d'Aulnoy, "Le Dauphin," 1036–37; Lhéritier, "Marmoisan," 66; Lhéritier, "La robe de sincérité," 270; La Force, "Plus Belle que Fée," 329; La Force, "L'Enchanteur," 354.
55. "Lorsque l'on aime avec constance, / Tôt ou tard, on se voit dans un parfait bonheur" (d'Aulnoy, "Gracieuse et Percinet," 174).
56. "Tendres époux, apprenez par ceux-ci / Qu'il est avantageux d'être toujours fidèles; / Les peines, les travaux, le plus cuisant souci, / Tout enfin se trouve adouci / Quand les ardeurs sont mutuelles; / On brave la fortune, on surmonte le sort, / Tant que deux époux sont d'accord" (La Force, "Persinette," 338).
57. "Ils partirent pour leur royaume, où le prince et l'aimable Irolite jouirent du rare bonheur de brûler toujours d'un amour aussi tendre et aussi constant dans une fortune tranquille, que pendant leurs malheurs il avait été ardent et fidèle" (Murat, "Le parfait amour," 83–84).
58. "L'amour, n'en déplaise aux censeurs, Est l'origine de la gloire; / Il sait animer les grands cœurs / À braver le péril, à chercher la victoire. / . . . / Mais un cœur ne craint pas les plus grands précipices, / S'il a pour l'animer, et la gloire et l'amour" (d'Aulnoy, "La princesse Belle Étoile et le prince Chéri," 945).
59. "Mais quand l'amour est pur, peines, inquiétudes, / Sont autant de garants des plus charmants plaisirs" (d'Aulnoy, "Le Pigeon et la Colombe," 890).
60. "Sans doute elle ignorait qu'un pareil marriage / Devi[e]nt un funeste esclavage, / Si l'amour ne le forme pas" (d'Aulnoy, "L'Oiseau Bleu," 222).
61. "Il vaut mieux manquer à l'amour, / Que de manquer à la sagesse" (d'Aulnoy, "Le prince Marcassin," 997).
62. "L'amour qui n'est pas réglé par la vertu cause tous les malheurs de la vie" (Durand, "La Fée Lubantine," 460).
63. "On n'est guère maîtresse de soi lorsqu'on est agitée de cette passion [amour]" (Durand, "Le prodige d'amour," 490).
64. "Pour un heureux amour sous votre empire, / On en voit mille malheureux" (La Force, "La puissance d'amour," 414).
65. "Avec un tendre amant, seule au milieu des bois, / Aimée eut en tout temps une extrême sagesse; / Toujours de la raison elle écouta la voix, / Et sut de son amant conserver la tendresse. / Beautés, ne croyez pas pour captiver les cœurs, / Que les plaisirs soient nécessaires; / L'amour souvent s'éteint au milieu des douceurs: / Soyez fières, soyez sévères, / Et vous inspirerez d'éternelles ardeurs" (d'Aulnoy, "L'Oranger et l'Abeille," 363).
66. d'Aulnoy, "La princesse Printanière," 263–84.

67. "Une noce est presque toujours une triste fête" (Murat, "L'Heureuse Peine," 196).

68. "Par différents chemins on arrive au bonheur, / Le vice nous y mène, aussi bien que l'honneur; / . . . / Aveugle déité, fortune trop cruelle, / Accordez mieux tout ce qui vient de vous; / Accablez les méchants d'une peine éternelle; / Donnez aux vertueux le bonheur le plus doux" (La Force, "L'Enchanteur," 354–55).

69. Propp, *Morphology of the Folktale*, 63–64. An earlier version of this section of chapter five was published in *Papers on French Seventeenth Century Literature* in 2015: Reddan, "Losing Love, Losing Hope," 327–39.

70. Trinquet provides a detailed analysis of unconventional endings in seventeenth-century French fairy tales by d'Aulnoy, Bernard, Perrault, and La Force in "Happily Ever After?," 45–54. Seifert reflects on the development of the marriage closure as the conventional fairy-tale ending, and on the difficulty of interpreting ambiguity in the conteuses' use of this ending in "On Fairy Tales, Subversion," 65–68. See also Jasmin on the theme of *les malheurs de l'amour* in the conteuses' tales in "Amour, amour," 227–32.

71. Trinquet, "Happily Ever After?," 45–46.

72. This calculation is based on the list of tales in figure 2 and my evaluation of the tales written by d'Aulnoy, Bernard, and Murat. I classified tales that ended with a favorable outcome for the heroic couple as happy endings, and tales that ended with death, pain or suffering for the heroic couple as unhappy endings.

73. Seifert, "On Fairy Tales, Subversion," 66–67.

74. DeJean, *Tender Geographies*, 90–93. See also Trinquet, "Happily Ever After?," 48–50; Raynard, *La seconde préciosité*, 197–214, 251–62; Seifert and Stanton, "Editors' Introduction," 29–32.

75. On the patriarchal legal framework of marriage in seventeenth-century France, see the discussion in chapter 3 under the heading "Negotiating Parental Consent."

76. Welch, "La femme, le mariage," 49–52.

77. See also Gélinas, "De quel type d'amour," 191–219.

78. "Qu'il ne se trouve point d'éternelles amours / Ni de félicité parfait" (d'Aulnoy, "L'île de la félicité," 144).

79. For a slightly different reading of "L'île de la félicité," see Duggan, "Feminine Genealogy, Matriarchy, and Utopia," 199–208.

80. "Souvent les plus beaux dons des Cieux / Ne servent qu'à notre ruine, / . . . / Le roi Mouton eût moins souffert, / S'il n'eût point allumé cette flamme fatale / . . . / Il haïssait sans feinte, aimait sans artifice, / Et ne ressemblait pas aux hommes d'aujourd'hui: / Sa fin même pourra nous paraître fort rare, / Et ne convient qu'au roi Mouton: / On n'en voit point dans ce canton / Mourir quand leur brebis s'égare" (d'Aulnoy, "Le Mouton," 425).

81. Jasmin, *Naissance du conte féminin*, 275–78. It is also possible that this moral satirizes the pastoral novel in the tradition of *L'Astrée*, which was an important literary influence on both d'Aulnoy and the contes de fées genre. On the role of the pastoral in d'Aulnoy's tales, see Thirard, "L'influence de la pastorale," 165–80.
82. "Mais le destin de Toute Belle / T'apprend à ne point t'engager, / Si ton cœur aux serments ne peut être fidèle" (d'Aulnoy, "Le Nain Jaune," 563).
83. "Belle âme dans un corps si parfait" (d'Aulnoy, "Le Nain Jaune," 549–50).
84. Carlin, "Imagining Marriage in the 1690s," 167–76.
85. The metamorphosis of people into trees is a motif in many mythological narratives, with the transformation of Philemon and Baucis in Ovid's *Metamorphoses* one of the most well-known examples. This trope also appears in Murat's "Anguillette" and in Bernard's "Le prince Rosier."
86. Murat, "Anguillette," 91–117.
87. "Pays des Injustices de l'Amour" (Murat, "Peine Perdue," 403).
88. "Personnes tendres, malheureuses et fidèles" (Murat, "Peine Perdue," 403). Peine Perdue's refuge does not have the same properties as l'Île Paisible, which is an island that has the power to cure "les passions malheureuses" (Murat, "Anguillette," 101–2).
89. "Florinde est née avec beaucoup d'appas, / Mais son malheur doit être extrême, / S'il faut qu'un jour elle aime / L'amant qu'elle ne verra pas" (Bernard, "Le prince Rosier," 279).
90. Bernard, "Le prince Rosier," 284–85.
91. "Le mariage, selon la coutume, finit tous les agréments de leur vie" (Bernard, "Le prince Rosier," 285).
92. "Les gens accoutumés à aimer ne sont pas si raisonnables que les autres et ne font guère l'exemple des bons ménages" (Bernard, "Le prince Rosier," 285).
93. I discuss Bernard's authorial intention in the conclusion to chapter 4.
94. "Les amants à la longue deviennent des maris" (Bernard, "Riquet à la houppe," 292).
95. "Avant ce temps fatal, les amants trop heureux / Brûlaient toujours des mêmes feux, / Rien ne troublait le cours de leur bonheur extrême; / Pagan leur fit trouver le secret malheureux, / De s'ennuyer du bonheur même" (Murat, "Le palais de la Vengeance," 158).
96. "Si vous voulez n'aimer que moi, il ne tiendra qu'à vous d'être le plus heureux et le plus puissant monarque de la terre; mais examinez bien le fond de votre cœur, et ne vous trompez pas vous-même en manquant de fidélité; je ne pourrais vous le pardonner, et ma vengeance égalerait mon amour" (d'Auneuil, "L'inconstance punie," 722).
97. "Il se jeta à ses pieds, et lui jura que jamais amant ne serait plus tendre et plus constant" (d'Auneuil, "L'inconstance punie," 722).

98. "L'indolence s'empara de son cœur" (d'Auneuil, "L'inconstance punie," 723).
99. d'Aulnoy, "La princesse Carpillon," 662, "La princesse Printanière," 284, "L'Oranger et l'Abeille," 363.
100. d'Aulnoy, "L'Oranger et l'Abeille," 362.
101. "Avec un tendre amant, seule au milieu des bois, / Aimée eut en tout temps une extrême sagesse; / Toujours de la raison elle écouta la voix, / Et sut de son amant conserver la tendresse" (d'Aulnoy, "L'Oranger et l'Abeille," 363).
102. Laideronnette's response to her unseen suitor emphasizes her inability to resist his courtship: "Quelque résolution que j'aie faite de ne jamais aimer, répondait la princesse, et quelque raison que j'aie de défendre mon cœur d'un engagement qui ne lui pourrait être que fatal, je vous avoue cependant que je serais bien aise de connaître un roi dont le goût est aussi bizarre que le vôtre; car s'il est vrai que vous m'aimiez, vous êtes peut-être le seul dans le monde, qui puissiez avoir une semblable faiblesse pour une personne aussi laide que moi" (d'Aulnoy, "Serpentin Vert," 587). D'Aulnoy's desire that reason (instead of passion) rule the the heart recognizes the commonplace nature of Printanière's lack of reason: "Et malgré le penchant qui souvent nous entraîne, / Je veux que la raison soit toujours souveraine: / Que toujours maîtresse du cœur, / Elle règle à son gré nos vœux et notre ardeur" (d'Aulnoy, "La princesse Printanière," 284).
103. Murat, "Anguillette," 101–2.
104. "Prenait de nouvelles forces" (d'Aulnoy, "La Grenouille bien-faisante," 676). The king's passion for the new bride he is supposed to marry weakens when he sees his wife.
105. Murat, "Le Turbot," 330–33.

CONCLUSION

1. "As children, we all hear fairy tales and read our lives into them. But we also want to see and realise our lives as virtual fairy tales even as we grow older. We never abandon fairy tales" (Zipes, *Happily Ever After*, 1).
2. See, e.g., "L'île de la félicité," "La princesse Printanière," "Le Mouton," and "Le Nain Jaune."
3. d'Aulnoy, "L'île de la félicité," 144.
4. La Force's unconventional morality appears in the tales of "Persinette" and "L'Enchanteur." Clandestine marriages also appear in tales by Murat and d'Aulnoy, although without the suggestion of authorial support for the heroine's transgressive actions. In d'Aulnoy's "La princesse Printanière," the heroine's parents cover up her affair with the ambassador to her husband so that she might marry the spouse they had chosen for her. In "Le père et ses quatre fils," the father of Murat's heroine retrospectively approves the union she consummated while

exiled on a deserted island. I discuss the unconventional features of both tales in chapter 3.

APPENDIX 1

1. Robert, "Tableau des contes de fées publié de 1690 à 1709," in Jasmin, *Madame d'Aulnoy*, 61–65; Robert, "Index des titres de contes (1690–1709)," in Boch and Rizzoni, *L'âge d'or du conte de fées*, 613–16.
2. Robert's table attributes Préchac's "La Reine de fées" and d'Auneuil's "Nouvelles diverses du temps" to Durand and does not include Durand's "La Fée Lubantine."
3. "La princesse des Prétintailles" and "Les Colinettes" are stories about fashion. "L'origine de l'Occasion" and "L'origine du lansquenet" are reflections about chance and the popularity of games of chance. "Les Chevaliers errants" reflects the style of oriental conte de fée popularized by the publication of Antoine Galland's translation of *Les Mille et une nuit, contes arabes* (The Thousand and One Nights) between 1704 and 1709.

BIBLIOGRAPHY

Aarne, Antti, and Stith Thompson. *The Types of the Folk-Tale: A Classification and Bibliography*. Helsinki: Suomalainen Tiedeakatemia, 1928.

Alberti, Fay Bound. *Matters of the Heart: History, Medicine, and Emotion*. Oxford: Oxford University Press, 2010.

Asaro, Brittany. "Unmasking the Truth about *Amor de Lonh*: Giovanni Boccaccio's Rebellion against Literary Conventions in *Decameron* I.5 and IV.4." *Comitatus: A Journal of Medieval and Renaissance Studies* 44, no. 1 (2013): 95–120.

Aulnoy, Marie-Catherine Le Jumel de Barneville, Baronne de. *Contes Nouveaux, ou Les Fées à la Mode. Par Madame D***. 2 vols. Paris: Veuve de Théodore Girard, 1698.

———. *Histoire d'Hypolite, comte de Duglas*. 2 vols. Paris: Louis Sevestre, 1690.

———. *Les Contes des Fées. Par Madame D***. 4 vols. Paris: Claude Barbin, 1697–98.

———. *Mémoires de la Cour d'Angleterre. Par Madame D****. 2 vols. Paris: Claude Barbin, 1695.

———. *Mémoires de la Cour d'Espagne*. Paris: Claude Barbin, 1690.

———. *Relation du voyage d'Espagne*. 3 vols. Paris: Claude Barbin, 1691.

———. *Suite des Contes Nouveaux, ou Les Fées à la Mode. Par Madame D***. 2 vols. Paris: Nicolas Gosselin, 1698.

Auneuil, Louise de Bossigny, Comtesse de. *La tyrannie des fées détruite: Nouveaux contes dédiés à Madame la duchesse de Bourgogne par Madame la comtesse D.L.* Paris: Veuve R. Chevillon, 1702.

———. *Les Chevaliers errants, et Le Génie familier, par Madame la comtesse D***. Paris: Pierre Ribou, 1709.
———. *Les Colinettes, nouvelles du temps, par Madame la comtesse D.L.* Paris: Pierre Ribou, 1703.
———. *L'inconstance punie: Nouvelles du temps, par Madame la comtesse D.L.* Paris: Pierre Ribou, 1702.
———. *L'origine du lansquenet, nouvelles du temps, par Madame la comtesse D****. Paris: Pierre Ribou, 1703.
———. *Nouvelles diverses du temps, La princesse des Prétintailles, par Madame la comtesse D.L.* Paris: Pierre Ribou, 1702.
Bacchilega, Cristina. *Fairy Tales Transformed? Twenty-First-Century Adaptations and the Politics of Wonder*. Detroit: Wayne State University Press, 2013.
Barclay, Katie. *Love, Intimacy and Power: Marriage and Patriarchy in Scotland, 1650–1850*. Manchester: Manchester University Press, 2011.
Beasley, Faith E. *Revising Memory: Women's Fiction and Memoirs in Seventeenth-Century France*. New Brunswick NJ: Rutgers University Press, 1990.
———. *Salons, History, and the Creation of Seventeenth-Century France: Mastering Memory*. Hampshire: Ashgate, 2006.
Bellegarde, Jean-Baptiste Morvan de. *Lettres curieuses de littérature et de morale, par M. l'abbé de Bellegarde*. Paris: Jean et Michel Guignard, 1702.
Ben-Amos, Dan. "Straparola: The Revolution That Was Not." *Journal of American Folklore* 123, no. 490 (2010): 426–46.
Benjamin, Walter. "The Storyteller: Reflections on the Work of Nicholas Leskov." In *Illuminations*, edited by Hannah Arendt, translated by Harry Zohn, 83–109. New York: Schocken Books, 1968.
Benson, Stephen. "Stories of Love and Death: Reading and Writing the Fairy Tale Romance." In *Image and Power: Women in Fiction in the Twentieth Century*, edited by Darah Sceats and Gail Cunningham, 103–13. London: Longman, 1996.
Bernard, Catherine. *Éléonor d'Yvrée*. Paris: M. Guérout, 1687.
———. *Inès de Cordoue*. Paris: Martin et George Jouvenel, 1696.
———. *Inès de Cordoue: Nouvelle Espagnole*. Genève: Slatkine Reprints, 1979.
———. *Le comte d'Amboise*. Paris: Claude Barbin, 1689.
———. *Œuvres, tome 1: Romans et nouvelles*. Edited by Franco Piva. Fasano: Schena, 1993.
Bestor, Jane Fair. "Marriage Transactions in Renaissance Italy and Mauss's Essay on the Gift." *Past and Present* 164, no. 1 (1999): 6–46.
Bettelheim, Bruno. "Fairy Tales as Ways of Knowing." In *Fairy Tales as Ways of Knowing: Essays on Märchen in Psychology, Society and Literature*, edited by Michael M. Metzger and Katharina Mommsen, 11–20. Bern: Peter Lang, 1981.

———. *The Uses of Enchantment: The Meaning and Importance of Fairy Tales*. New York: Alfred A. Knopf, 1976.

Birberick, Anne L. "Rewriting Curiosity: The Psyche Myth in Apuleuis, La Fontaine and d'Aulnoy." In *Strategic Rewriting*, edited by David Lee Rubin, 134–48. Charlottesville: Rookwood Press, 2002.

Blamires, David. "From Madame d'Aulnoy to Mother Bunch: Popularity and the Fairy Tale." In *Popular Children's Literature in Britain*, edited by Julia Briggs, Dennis Butts, and Matthew Orville Grenby, 69–86. Aldershot, England: Ashgate, 2008.

Boch, Julie. "Le conte en débats: Introduction." In *L'âge d'or du conte de fées: De la comédie à la critique (1690–1709)*, edited by Julie Boch and Nathalie Rizzoni, 327–51. Bibliothèque des Génies et des Fées 5. Paris: Honoré Champion, 2007.

Boch, Julie, and Nathalie Rizzoni, eds. *L'âge d'or du conte de fées: De la comédie à la critique*. Bibliothèque des Génies et des Fées 5. Paris: Honoré Champion, 2007.

Böhm, Roswitha. "La participation des fées modernes à la creation d'une mémoire féminine." In *Les femmes au grand siècle, Le baroque: Musique et littérature; Musique et liturgie: Actes du 33e Congrès Annuel de la North American Society for Seventeenth-Century French Literature*, edited by David Wetsel, Frédéric Canovas, Christine Probes, and Norman Buford, vol. 2, 119–31. Tübingen: Narr, 2003.

Bottigheimer, Ruth B. "Charlotte Rose de La Force, 'Notice Concerning the Following Story' in *The Tales of the Tales* (1698)." In *Fairy Tales Framed: Early Forewords, Afterwords, and Critical Words*, edited by Ruth B. Bottigheimer, 195–98. Albany: State University of New York Press, 2012.

———. "Fairy Godfather, Fairy-Tale History, and Fairy-Tale Scholarship: A Response to Dan Ben-Amos, Jan M. Ziolkowski, and Francisco Vaz da Silva." *Journal of American Folklore* 123, no. 490 (2010): 447–96.

———. *Fairy Tales: A New History*. Albany: State University of New York Press, 2009.

———. "Fairy Tales and Fairyland Fictions in France." In *Fairy Tales Framed: Early Forewords, Afterwords, and Critical Words*, edited by Ruth B. Bottigheimer, 101–11. Albany: State University of New York Press, 2012.

———. *Magic Tales and Fairy Tale Magic: From Ancient Egypt to the Italian Renaissance*. Basingstoke: Palgrave Macmillan, 2014.

Bottigheimer, Ruth B., and Sophie Raynard. "Marie-Catherine d'Aulnoy, *Tales of the Fairies* (1697) and *New Tales, or The Fashionable Fairies* (1698)." In *Fairy Tales Framed: Early Forewords, Afterwords, and Critical Words*, edited by Ruth B. Bottigheimer, 167–93. Albany: State University of New York Press, 2012.

———. "Marie-Jeanne Lhéritier de Villandon, *Diverse Works* (1696)." In *Fairy Tales Framed: Early Forewords, Afterwords, and Critical Words*, edited by Ruth B. Bottigheimer, 127–54. Albany: State University of New York Press, 2012.

Brown, Deborah. "The Rationality of Cartesian Passions." In *Emotions and Choice from Boethius to Descartes*, edited by Mikko Yrjönsuuri and Henrik Lagerlund, 259–78. Dordrecht: Kluwer Academic Publishers, 2002.

Brunelle, Gayle K. "Dangerous Liaisons: Mesalliance and Early Modern French Noblewomen." *French Historical Studies* 19, no. 1 (Spring 1995): 75–103.

Burguière, André. *Le mariage et l'amour en France: De la Renaissance à la Révolution.* Paris: Seuil, 2011.

Camus, Jean-Pierre. *Traité des passions de l'âme.* In *Les diversitez de Messire Jean-Pierre Camus.* Vol 9. Paris: C. Chappelet, 1614.

Canepa, Nancy L. *From Court to Forest: Giambattista Basile's* Lo cunto de li cunti *and the Birth of the Literary Fairy Tale.* Detroit: Wayne State University Press, 1999.

———. *Out of the Woods: The Origins of the Literary Fairy Tale in Italy and France.* Detroit: Wayne State University Press, 1997.

Carlin, Claire L. "Imagining Marriage in the 1690s." *Papers on French Seventeenth Century Literature* 28, no. 54 (2001): 167–76.

Carter, Angela. "Introduction." In *The Virago Book of Fairy Tales,* edited by Angela Carter, ix–xvii. London: Virago Press, 1990.

Chartier, Roger. *The Cultural Uses of Print.* Translated by Lydia G. Cochrane. Princeton: Princeton University Press, 1987.

———. "Du livre au lire." In *Pratiques de la lecture,* edited by Roger Chartier, 62–88. Paris: Rivages, 1985.

Clermidy-Patard, Geneviève. "Introduction." In *Journal pour Mademoiselle de Menou,* edited by Geneviève Clermidy-Patard. Paris: Classiques Garnier, 2014.

Coëffeteau, Nicolas. *Tableau des passions humaines, de leurs causes et leurs effets.* Paris: S. Cramoisy, 1620.

Daumas, Maurice. *Le mariage amoureux: Histoire du lien conjugal sous l'Ancien Régime.* Paris: Armand Colin, 2004.

Davis, Natalie Zemon. *The Gift in Sixteenth-Century France.* Madison: University of Wisconsin Press, 2000.

Defrance, Anne. *Les contes de fées et les nouvelles de Madame d'Aulnoy (1690–1698): L'imaginaire féminin à rebours de la tradition.* Geneva: Droz, 1998.

DeJean, Joan E. *Ancients against Moderns: Culture Wars and the Making of a Fin de Siècle.* Chicago: University of Chicago Press, 1997.

———. "Introduction: La Grande Mademoiselle." In *Against Marriage: The Correspondence of La Grande Mademoiselle,* edited by Joan E. DeJean, 3–25. Chicago: University of Chicago Press, 2002.

———. *Tender Geographies: Women and the Origins of the Novel in France.* New York: Columbia University Press, 1991.

Desan, Suzanne. "Making and Breaking Marriage: An Overview of Old Regime Marriage as a Social Practice." In *Family, Gender, and Law in Early Modern France*, edited by Suzanne Desan and Jeffrey Merrick, 1–25. University Park: Pennsylvania State University Press, 2009.

Descartes, René. "Les Passions de L'âme, 1649." In *Oeuvres Complètes de René Descartes*, edited by André Gombay. Charlottesville VA: InteLex, 2001.

Desjardins, Lucie. *Le corps parlant: Savoirs et représentation des passions au XVIIe siècle*. Sainte-Foy, Québec: Presses de l'Université Laval, 2001.

Dictionnaire de l'Académie française. Paris: 1694.

Dixon, Thomas. "'Emotion': The History of a Keyword in Crisis." *Emotion Review* 4 (2012): 338–44.

———. *From Passions to Emotions: The Creation of a Secular Psychological Category*. Cambridge: Cambridge University Press, 2003.

Douglas, Mary. "Foreword: No Free Gifts." In *The Gift: The Form and Reason for Exchange in Archaic Societies*, by Marcel Mauss, translated by W. D. Halls, vii–xviii. London: Routledge, 1990.

Duggan, Anne E. "Aulnoy, Marie-Catherine d' (1650/51–1705)." In *The Greenwood Encyclopedia of Folktales and Fairy Tales*, edited by Donald Haase, vol. 1, 79–81. Westport: Greenwood, 2008.

———. "Feminine Genealogy, Matriarchy, and Utopia in the Fairy Tale of Marie-Catherine d'Aulnoy." *Neophilologus* 82, no. 2 (1998): 199–208.

———. "Lovers, Salon, and State: *La Carte de Tendre* and the Mapping of Socio-Political Relations." *Dalhousie French Studies* 36 (1996): 15–22.

———. "Nature and Culture in the Fairy Tale of Marie-Catherine d'Aulnoy." *Marvels and Tales* 15, no. 2 (2001): 149–67.

———. "The Reception of the Grimms in Nineteenth-Century France." *Fabula* 55, no. 3–4 (2014): 260–85.

———. *Salonnières, Furies, and Fairies: The Politics of Gender and Cultural Change in Absolutist France*. Newark: University of Delaware Press, 2005.

Durand, Catherine Bédacier. *La Comtesse de Mortane par Madame* ***. Paris: Veuve de Claude Barbin, 1699.

———. *Les Petits Soupers de l'année 1699, ou Avantures galantes avec l'Origine des fées, par Madame Durand*. Paris: Musier Rolin, 1702.

Eichel-Lojkine, Patricia. *Contes en réseaux: L'émergence du conte sur la scène littéraire européenne*. Genève: Droz, 2013.

Ekman, Mary. "Concealing Identities, Revealing Stories: Marie-Catherine d'Aulnoy's *Relation du Voyage d'Espagne*." *Cahiers du dix-septième* 10, no. 2 (2006): 49–63.

"Eloge de Mademoiselle l'Héritier." *Journal des Sçavans*, December 1734, 832–36.

"Eloge de Mlle l'Héritier de Villandon." *Mercure de France*, March 1734, 539–41.

Erickson, Robert A. *The Language of the Heart, 1600–1750*. Philadelphia: University of Pennsylvania Press, 1997.

Eustace, Nicole. "'The Cornerstone of a Copious Work': Love and Power in Eighteenth-Century Courtship." *Journal of Social History* 34, no. 3 (2001): 517–46.

Faydit, Pierre-Valentin. *La Télémacomanie, ou la censure et critique du roman intitulé*. Eleuterople: Pierre Philalethe, 1700.

Fumaroli, Marc. "Les abeilles et les araignées." In *La querelle des Anciens et des Modernes: XVIIe–XVIIIe siècles*, edited by Anne-Marie Lecoq, 7–218. Paris: Gallimard, 2001.

Gélinas, Gérard. "De quel type d'amour les contes de Mme d'Aulnoy font-ils la promotion?" *Papers on French Seventeenth Century Literature* 34, no. 66 (2007): 181–219.

Gheeraert, Tony, ed. *Contes Merveilleux: Perrault, Fénelon, Mailly, Préchac, Choisy et Anonymes*. Bibliothèque des Génies et des Fées 4. Paris: Honoré Champion, 2005.

Gibson, Wendy. *Women in Seventeenth-Century France*. New York: St. Martin's Press, 1989.

Godineau, Dominique. *Les femmes dans la société française: 16e–18e siècle*. Paris: Armand Colin, 2003.

Goldsmith, Elizabeth C. *Exclusive Conversations: The Art of Interaction in Seventeenth-Century France*. Philadelphia: University of Pennsylvania Press, 1988.

Goldsmith, Elizabeth C., and Dena Goodman. *Going Public: Women and Publishing in Early Modern France*. Ithaca: Cornell University Press, 1995.

Goodman, Dena. "Marriage Choice and Marital Success: Reasoning about Marriage, Love, and Happiness." In *Family, Gender, and Law in Early Modern France*, edited by Suzanne Desan and Jeffrey Merrick, 26–61. University Park: Pennsylvania State University Press, 2009.

———. *The Republic of Letters: A Cultural History of the French Enlightenment*. Ithaca: Cornell University Press, 1994.

Gordon-Seifert, Catherine. *Music and the Language of Love: Seventeenth-Century French Airs*. Bloomington: Indiana University Press, 2011.

Gouldner, Alvin W. "The Norm of Reciprocity: A Preliminary Statement." In *The Gift: An Interdisciplinary Perspective*, edited by Aafke E. Komter, 49–66. Amsterdam: Amsterdam University Press, 1996.

Green, Karen. "Madeleine de Scudéry on Love and the Emergence of the 'Private Sphere.'" *History of Political Thought* 30, no. 2 (2009): 272–85.

Greimas, A. J. *Sémantique Structurale: Recherche de Méthode*. Paris: Presses Universitaires de France, 1986.

Haase, Donald. "Fairy Tale." In *The Greenwood Encyclopedia of Folktales and Fairy Tales*, edited by Donald Haase, vol. 1, 322–25. Westport: Greenwood, 2008.

———. "Feminist Fairy-Tale Scholarship." In *Fairy Tales and Feminism: New Approaches*, edited by Donald Haase, 1–36. Detroit: Wayne State University Press, 2004.

———. "Feminist Fairy-Tale Scholarship: A Critical Survey and Bibliography." *Marvels and Tales* 14, no. 1 (2000): 15–63.

Hanley, Sarah. "Engendering the State: Family Formation and State Building in Early Modern France." *French Historical Studies* 16, no. 1 (Spring 1989): 4–27.

———. "Family and State in Early Modern France: The Marriage Pact." In *Connecting Spheres: Women in the Western World, 1500 to the Present,* edited by Marilyn J. Boxer and Jean H. Quataert, 53–68. New York: Oxford University Press, 1987.

Hannon, Patricia. "Antithesis and Ideology in Perrault's 'Riquet à la houppe.'" *Cahiers du dix-septième* 4, no. 2 (1990): 105–18.

———. *Fabulous Identities: Women's Fairy Tales in Seventeenth-Century France.* Amsterdam: Rodopi, 1998.

Hardwick, Julie. *The Practice of Patriarchy: Gender and the Politics of Household Authority in Early Modern France.* University Park: Pennsylvania State University Press, 1998.

Harries, Elizabeth Wanning. *Twice upon a Time: Women Writers and the History of the Fairy Tale.* Princeton NJ: Princeton University Press, 2001.

Harth, Erica. *Cartesian Women: Versions and Subversions of Rational Discourse in the Old Regime.* Ithaca: Cornell University Press, 1992.

Heidmann, Ute. "Madame de Murat: Contes (Review)." *Marvels and Tales* 21, no. 2 (2007): 280–83.

Howell, Martha. "The Properties of Marriage in Late Medieval Europe: Commercial Wealth and the Creation of Modern Marriage." In *Love, Marriage, and Family Ties in the Later Middle Ages,* edited by Miriam Müller, Sarah Rees Jones, and Isabel Davis, 17–61. Turnhout: Brepols, 2003.

Huet, Pierre-Daniel. *Traité de l'origine des romans.* First published in *Zayde, histoire espagnole, par M. de Segrais,* by Marie-Madeleine Pioche de La Vergne de La Fayette. Paris: Claude Barbin, 1670.

Jager, Eric. *The Book of the Heart.* Chicago: University of Chicago Press, 2000.

James, Susan. *Passion and Action: The Emotions in Seventeenth-Century Philosophy.* Oxford: Clarendon Press, 1997.

Jasmin, Nadine. "'Amour, Amour, ne nous abandonne point': La représentation de l'amour dans les contes de fées féminins du Grand Siècle." In *Tricentenaire Charles Perrault: Les grands contes du XVIIe siècle et leur fortune littéraire,* edited by Jean Perrot, 213–34. Paris: In Press, 1998.

———. *Naissance du conte féminin. Mots et merveilles: Les contes de fées de Madame d'Aulnoy, 1690–1698.* Paris: Champion, 2002.

Jasmin, Nadine, ed. *Madame d'Aulnoy: Contes des Fées suivis des Contes nouveaux ou les fées à la Mode.* Bibliothèque des Génies et des Fées 1. Paris: Honoré Champion, 2004.

Jensen, Katharine Ann. "Marie-Catherine Desjardins de Villedieu." In *French Women Writers*, edited by Eva Martin Sartori and Dorothy Wynne Zimmerman, 503–12. Lincoln: University of Nebraska Press, 1994.

Jones, Christine A. *Mother Goose Refigured: A Critical Translation of Charles Perrault's Fairy Tales*. Detroit: Wayne State University Press, 2016.

———. "The Poetics of Enchantment (1690–1715)." *Marvels and Tales* 17, no. 1 (2003): 55–74.

Kaster, Robert A. *Emotion, Restraint, and Community in Ancient Rome*. Oxford: Oxford University Press, 2005.

Kettering, Sharon. "Gift-Giving and Patronage in Early Modern France." *French History* 2, no. 2 (1988): 131–51.

Klapisch-Zuber, Christiane. *Women, Family, and Ritual in Renaissance Italy*. Translated by Lydia G. Cochrane. Chicago: University of Chicago Press, 1985.

Lafayette, Marie-Madeleine Pioche de La Vergne. *La princesse de Clèves*. Edited by Emile Magne. Paris: Droz, 1946.

La Fontaine, Jean de. *La Fontaine: Œuvres Complètes*. Paris: Éditions du Seuil, 1965.

La Force, Charlotte-Rose de Caumont de. *Les Contes des Contes. Par Mademoiselle de ****. 2 vols. Paris: Simon Benard, 1697.

Lamaison, Pierre, and Pierre Bourdieu. "From Rules to Strategies: An Interview with Pierre Bourdieu." *Cultural Anthropology* 1 (1986): 110–20.

Lebrun, François. "Amour et mariage." In *Histoire de la population française*, edited by Jacques Dupâquier, Alfred Sauvy, and Emmanuel Le Roy Ladurie, vol. 2, 294–317. Paris: Presses Universitaires de France, 1988.

Le Mercure Galant (1678–1714). Bibliothèque nationale de France, département Fonds du service reproduction, 8-Lc2-33.

Lévi-Strauss, Claude. "The Principle of Reciprocity." In *The Gift: An Interdisciplinary Perspective*, edited by Aafke E. Komter, 18–23. Amsterdam: Amsterdam University Press, 1996.

Lhéritier de Villandon, Marie-Jeanne. *L'Apothéose de Mademoiselle de Scudèry*. Paris: Jean Moreau, 1702.

———. *La tour ténébreuse et les jours lumineux, contes anglois, accompagnez d'historiettes, et tirez d'une ancienne chronique composée par Richard surnommé Cœur de lion, roi d'Angleterre, avec le récit de diverses avantures de ce roy*. Paris: Veuve de Claude Barbin, 1705.

———. *L'Érudition enjouée, ou Nouvelles sçavantes, satyriques et galantes, écrite à une dame française qui est à Madrid*. Paris: Pierre Ribou, 1703.

———. *Les Caprices du destin, ou Recueil d'histories singulières et amusantes arrivées de nos jours. Par Mademoiselle l'H****. Paris: Pierre-Michel Huart, 1718.

———. *Le Triomphe de Mme Des-Houlières, reçue dixième muse au Parnasse*. Paris: Claude Mazuel, 1694.

———. *Mémoires de M. L. D. D. N. [Madame la duchesse de Nemours] contenant ce qui s'est passé de plus particulier en France pendant la guerre de Paris, jusquà la prison du cardinal de Retz, arrivée en 1652. Avec les différens caractères des personnes, qui ont eu part à cette guerre*. Cologne, 1709.

———. *Œuvres meslées contenant L'Innocente Tromperie, L'Avare puni, Les Enchantements de l'éloquence, Les Aventures de Finette, nouvelles et autres ouvrages en vers et en prose, de Mlle L'H***, avec Le triomphe de Mme Deshoulières, tel qu'il a été composé par Mlle L'H****. Paris: Jean Guignard, 1696.

Lougee, Carolyn. *Le Paradis des Femmes: Women, Salons and Social Stratification in 17th-Century France*. Princeton NJ: Princeton University Press, 1976.

Lundell, Torborg. "Gender-Related Biases in the Type and Motif Indexes of Aarne and Thompson." In *Fairy Tales and Society: Illusion, Allusion, and Paradigm*, edited by Ruth B. Bottigheimer, 149–63. Philadelphia: University of Pennsylvania Press, 1989.

Lundskær-Nielsen, T. "'Love Is a Many Splendored Thing': On the Treatment of Love in Hans Christian Andersen's Fairy Tales." *Scandinavica* 46, no. 2 (2007): 213–35.

Lüthi, Max. *The Fairytale as Art Form and Portrait of Man*. Bloomington: Indiana University Press, 1984.

———. *Once upon a Time: On the Nature of Fairy Tales*. Bloomington: Indiana University Press, 1976.

Maclean, Ian. *Woman Triumphant: Feminism in French Literature, 1610–1652*. Oxford: Clarendon Press, 1977.

Mainil, Jean. *Madame d'Aulnoy et le rire des fées: Essai sur la subversion féerique et le merveilleux comique sous l'Ancien Régime*. Paris: Kimé, 2001.

Marchal, Roger. *Madame de Lambert et son milieu*. Oxford: Voltaire Foundation at the Taylor Institution, 1991.

Matt, Susan J. "Current Emotion Research in History: Or, Doing History from the Inside Out." *Emotion Review* 3 (2011): 117–24.

Mauss, Marcel. *The Gift: The Form and Reason for Exchange in Archaic Societies*. Translated by W. D. Halls. London: Routledge, 1990.

Mayer, Charles Joseph. "Notice des auteurs, Mme d'Auneuil." In *Le cabinet des fées, ou, Collection choisie des contes des fées, et autres contes merveilleux*. vol. 37, 40. Amsterdam: Rue et Hôtel Serpente, 1785–89.

McGlathery, James M. *Fairy Tale Romance: The Grimms, Basile, and Perrault*. Urbana: University of Illinois Press, 1991.

Merlin-Kajman, Hélène. "Introduction." In *Les émotions publiques et leurs langages à l'âge classique*, edited by Hélène Merlin-Kajman, 5–27. Paris: Honoré Champion, 2009.

Montoya, Alicia C. "*Contes du Style des Troubadours*: The Memory of the Medieval in Seventeenth-Century French Fairy Tales." In *Medievalism in Technology Old and New*, edited by Karl Fugelso and Carol L. Robinson, 1–24. Cambridge: Brewer, 2008.

Montpensier, Anne-Marie-Louise d'Orléans, and Françoise de Motteville. *Against Marriage: The Correspondence of La Grande Mademoiselle*. Edited and translated by Joan E. DeJean. Chicago: University of Chicago Press, 2002.

Murat, Henriette-Julie de Castelnau, Comtesse de. *Contes de Fées. Dediez à Son Altesse Sérénissme Madame la princesse Douairière de Conty. Par Mad. La Comtesse de M*****. Paris: Claude Barbin, 1698.

———. *Histoires sublimes et allégoriques. Par Madame la Comtesse D**. Dédiées aux Fées Modernes*. Paris: Florentin et Pierre Delaulne, 1699.

———. *Journal pour Mademoiselle de Menou*. April 14, 1708–June 8, 1709. Bibliothèque de l'Arsenal, ms. 3471.

———. *Journal pour Mademoiselle de Menou*. Edited by Geneviève Clermidy-Patard. Paris: Classiques Garnier, 2014.

———. *Les Nouveaux Contes des Fées. Par Madame de M***. Paris: Claude Barbin, 1698.

———. *Mémoires de Madame la comtesse de M****. 2 vols. Paris: Claude Barbin, 1697.

———. *A Trip to the Country*. Translated by Perry Gethner and Allison Stedman. Detroit: Wayne State University Press, 2011.

———. *Voyage de campagne. Par Madame la Comtesse de M****. 2 vols. Paris: Veuve de Claude Barbin, 1699.

Palmer, Melvin D. "Madame d'Aulnoy in England." *Comparative Literature* 27, no. 3 (1975): 237–53.

Palmer, Nancy B., and Melvin D. Palmer. "English Editions of French *Contes de Fées* Attributed to Mme D'Aulnoy." *Studies in Bibliography* 27 (1974): 227–32.

———. "English Editions of French *Contes de Fées* in England." *Studies in Short Fiction* 11, no. 1 (1974): 35–44.

Paster, Gail Kern, Katherine Rowe, and Mary Floyd-Wilson. *Reading the Early Modern Passions: Essays in the Cultural History of Emotion*. Philadelphia: University of Pennsylvania Press, 2004.

Patard, Geneviève, ed. *Contes: Madame de Murat*. Bibliothèque des Génies et des Fées 3. Paris: Honoré Champion, 2006.

Pélissier, Jean-Pierre, Danièle Rébaudo, Marco H. D. van Leeuwen, and Ineke Maas. "Migration and Endogamy According to Social Class: France, 1803–1986." In *Marriage Choices and Class Boundaries: Social Endogamy in History*, edited by Marco H. D. van Leeuwen, Ineke Maas, and Andrew Miles, 219–46. Cambridge: Cambridge University Press, 2005.

Pelous, Jean-Michel. *Amour précieux, amour galant (1654–1675): Essai sur la représentation de l'amour dans la littérature et la société mondaines*. Paris: Klincksieck, 1980.

Perrault, Charles. *Histoires, ou Contes du temps passé. Avec des moralitez*. Paris: Claude Barbin, 1697.

———. *L'apologie des femmes*. Paris: Jean Coignard, 1694.

———. *Parallèle des Anciens et des Modernes*. Paris: Jean Coignard, 1688–97.

Peters, Jeffrey N. *Mapping Discord: Allegorical Cartography in Early Modern French Writing*. Newark: University of Delaware Press, 2004.

Piva, Franco. "A la recherche de Catherine Bernard." In *Œuvres, Tome 1: Romans et Nouvelles*, edited by Franco Piva, 15–47. Fasano: Schena, 1993.

Plamper, Jan. *The History of Emotions: An Introduction*. Translated by Keith Tribe. Oxford: Oxford University Press, 2015.

Plato. "Timaeus." In *The Collected Dialogues of Plato*, edited by Edith Hamilton and Huntington Cairns, translated by Benjamin Jowett, 1151–211. Princeton NJ: Princeton University Press, 1961.

Poska, Allyson M. "Upending Patriarchy: Rethinking Marriage and Family in Early Modern Europe." In *The Ashgate Research Companion to Women and Gender in Early Modern Europe*, edited by Allyson M. Poska, Jane Couchman, and Katherine A. McIver, 195–211. Farnham, Surrey: Ashgate, 2013.

Propp, Vladimir. *Morphology of the Folktale*. 1st ed., translated by Laurence Scott in 1958. 2nd ed., revised and edited by Louis Wagner and Alan Dundes. Austin: University of Texas Press, 1968.

Raynard, Sophie. *La seconde préciosité: Floraison des conteuses de 1690 à 1756*. Tübingen: Narr, 2002.

———. "New Poetics versus Old Print: Fairy Tales, Animal Fables, and the Gaulois Past." *Marvels and Tales* 21, no. 1 (2007): 93–106.

Reddan, Bronwyn. "The Battle for Control of the Heart in Charles Perrault's *Dialogue de l'Amour et l'Amitié* (1660)." In *The Feeling Heart in Medieval and Early Modern Europe: Meaning, Embodiment, and Making*, edited by Katie Barclay and Bronwyn Reddan, 79–94. Berlin, Boston: De Gruyter, 2019.

———. "Gift-Giving and the Obligation to Love in *Riquet à la houppe*." In *Emotion, Ritual and Power in Europe, 1200–1920: Family, State and Church*, edited by Merridee L. Bailey and Katie Barclay, 23–41. Cham, Switzerland: Palgrave Macmillan, 2017.

———. "Losing Love, Losing Hope: Unhappy Endings in Seventeenth-Century Fairy Tales." *Papers on French Seventeenth Century Literature* 42, no. 83 (2015): 327–39.

———. "Scripting Love in Fairy Tales by Seventeenth-Century French Women Writers." *French History and Civilization* 7 (2017): 93–107.

———. "Thinking through Things: Magical Objects, Power and Agency in French Fairy Tales." *Marvels and Tales* 30, no. 2 (2017): 191–209.

———. "Translating Eloquence: History, Fidelity, and Creativity in the Fairy Tales of Marie-Jeanne Lhéritier." In *Trust and Proof: Translators in Renaissance Print Culture*, edited by Andrea Rizzi, 209–28. Boston: Brill, 2017.

Ridley, Alison. "From Perrault's 'Riquet à la Houppe' to Buero Vallejo's *Casi un cuento de hadas*: The Evolution of a Formidable Female Voice." *Neohelicon* 39, no. 1 (2012): 149–65.

Ringham, Felizitas. "Les amantes de la fiction au tournant du grand siècle." In *Lectrices d'Ancien Régime*, edited by Isabelle Brouard-Arends, 677–86. Rennes: Presses universitaires de Rennes, 2003.

Robert, Raymonde, ed. *Contes: Mademoiselle Lhéritier, Mademoiselle Bernard, Mademoiselle de La Force, Madame Durand, Madame d'Auneuil*. Bibliothèque des Génies et des Fées 2. Paris: Honoré Champion, 2005.

———. *Le conte de fées littéraire en France: De la fin du XVIIe à la fin du XVIIIe siècle*. Rev. ed., with supplementary bibliography by Nadine Jasmin and Claire Debru. Paris: Champion, 2002.

———. "Les conteurs français lecteurs de Basile: Mlle Lhéritier, Mlle de La Force, un auteur anonyme, Cazotte." *Romanic Review* 99, no. 3/4 (2008): 333–48.

Roche-Mazon, Jeanne. "De qui est Riquet à la houppe?" *Revue des deux Mondes*. (July 1928): 404–36.

Rosenwein, Barbara H. *Emotional Communities in the Early Middle Ages*. Ithaca: Cornell University Press, 2006.

———. *Generations of Feeling: A History of Emotions, 600–1700*. Cambridge: Cambridge University Press, 2016.

———. "Problems and Methods in the History of Emotions." *Passions in Context* 1 (2010): 1–32.

———. "Theories of Change in the History of Emotions." In *A History of Emotions, 1200–1800*, edited by Jonas Liliquist, 7–20. London: Pickering and Chatto, 2012.

Saupé, Yvette, and Jean-Pierre Collinet. "Charles Perrault: 1628–1703." In *The Teller's Tale: Lives of the Classic Fairy Tale Writers*, edited by Sophie Raynard, 47–59. New York: SUNY Press, 2012.

Schacker, Jennifer. *Staging Fairyland: Folklore, Children's Entertainment, and Nineteenth-Century Pantomime*. Detroit: Wayne State University Press, 2018.

Scheer, Monique. "Are Emotions a Kind of Practice (and Is That What Makes Them Have a History)? A Bourdieuian Approach to Understanding Emotion." *History and Theory* 51 (2012): 193–220.

Schröder, Volker. "Madame d'Aulnoy's Productive Confinement." *Anecdota* (blog), May 2, 2020. https://anecdota.princeton.edu/archives/1182.

———. "Marie-Madeleine Perrault (1674–1701)." *Anecdota* (blog), December 31, 2017. https://anecdota.princeton.edu/archives/500.

Schwartz, Barry. "The Social Psychology of the Gift." In *The Gift: An Interdisciplinary Perspective*, edited by Aafke E. Komter, 69–80. Amsterdam: Amsterdam University Press, 1996.

Scudéry, Madeleine de. *Clélie, Histoire Romaine*. 10 vols. Geneva: Slatkine Reprints, 1973.

Seifert, Lewis C. "Catherine Bernard: 1663?–1712." In *The Teller's Tale: Lives of the Classic Fairy Tale Writers*, edited by Sophie Raynard, 69–73. New York: SUNY Press, 2012.

———. *Fairy Tales, Sexuality, and Gender in France, 1690–1715: Nostalgic Utopias*. Cambridge: Cambridge University Press, 1996.

———. "*Les Fées modernes*: Women, Fairy Tales and the Literary Field in Late Seventeenth Century France." In *Going Public: Women and Publishing in Early Modern France*, edited by Elizabeth Goldsmith and Dena Goodman, 129–45. Ithaca: Cornell University Press, 1995.

———. "Marie-Jeanne Lhéritier de Villandon: 1664–1734." In *The Teller's Tale: Lives of the Classic Fairy Tale Writers*, edited by Sophie Raynard, 75–80. New York: SUNY Press, 2012.

———. "On Fairy Tales, Subversion, and Ambiguity: Feminist Approaches to Seventeenth-Century *Contes de Fées*." In *Fairy Tales and Feminism: New Approaches*, edited by Donald Haase, 53–71. Detroit: Wayne State University Press, 2004.

———. "The Rhetoric of *Invraisemblance*: 'Les Enchantements de l'Eloquence.'" *Cahiers du dix-septième* 3, no. 1 (1989): 121–39.

Seifert, Lewis C., and Domna C. Stanton, eds. "Editors' Introduction: The Other Voice." In *Enchanted Eloquence: Fairy Tales by Seventeenth-Century French Women Writers*, edited by Lewis C. Seifert and Domna C. Stanton, 1–45. Toronto: Iter Inc., Centre for Reformation and Renaissance Studies, 2010.

———. *Enchanted Eloquence: Fairy Tales by Seventeenth-Century French Women Writers*. Toronto: Iter Inc., Centre for Reformation and Renaissance Studies, 2010.

Seifert, Lewis C., and Catherine Velay-Vallantin. "Comments on Fairy Tales and Oral Tradition." *Marvels and Tales* 20, no. 2 (2006): 276–80.

Senault, Jean-François. *De l'Usage des Passions, par le R.P.J.-François Senault*. Paris: Veuve J. Camusat, 1641.

Sévigné, Marie de Rabutin-Chantal. *Lettres de Madame de Sévigné de sa famille et de ses amis*. Vol. 5. Paris: Librairie de L. Hachette, 1862.

Solomon, Robert C. *True to Our Feelings: What Our Emotions Are Really Telling Us*. Oxford: Oxford University Press, 2007.

Stedman, Allison. "D'Aulnoy's *Histoire d'Hypolite, comte de Duglas* (1690): A Fairy-Tale Manifesto." *Marvels and Tales* 19, no. 1 (2005): 32–53.

———. *Rococo Fiction in France, 1600–1715: Seditious Frivolity*. Lewisburg PA: Bucknell University Press, 2013.

Stone, Kay. “Feminist Approaches to the Interpretation of Fairy Tales.” In *Fairy Tales and Society: Illusion, Allusion and Paradigm*, edited by Ruth B. Bottigheimer, 229–36. Philadelphia: University of Pennsylvania Press, 1986.

Tatar, Maria. “What Is a Fairy Tale?” In *Teaching Fairy Tales*, edited by Nancy L. Canepa, 15–23. Detroit: Wayne State University Press, 2019.

Thirard, Marie-Agnès. “Les contes de Madame d'Aulnoy: La tentation du merveilleux.” *Papers on French Seventeenth Century Literature* 29, no. 56 (2002): 197–221.

———. “L'influence de la pastorale dans les contes de Madame d'Aulnoy.” In *Tricentenaire Perrault: Les grands contes du XVIIe siècle et leur fortune littéraire*, edited by Jean Perrot, 165–80. Paris: In Press, 1998.

Timmermans, Linda. *L'accès des femmes à la culture (1598–1715): Un débat d'idées de Saint François de Sales à La Marquise de Lambert*. Paris: Honoré Champion, 1993.

Trinquet, Charlotte. “Happily Ever After? Not So Easily! Seventeenth-Century Fairy Tales and Their Unconventional Endings.” *Papers on French Seventeenth Century Literature* 37, no. 72 (2010): 45–54.

———. *Le conte de fées français (1690–1700): Traditions italiennes et origines aristocratiques*. Tübingen: Narr Verlag, 2012.

Tucker, Holly. *Pregnant Fictions: Childbirth and the Fairy Tale in Early-Modern France*. Detroit: Wayne State University Press, 2003.

Tucker, Holly, and Melanie Siemens, trans. “Perrault's Preface to *Griselda* and Murat's ‘To Modern Fairies.’” *Marvels and Tales* 19, no. 1 (2005): 125–30.

Turnovsky, Geoffrey. “Literary History Meets the History of Reading.” *French Historical Studies* 41, no. 3 (2018): 427–47.

Vaz da Silva, Francisco. “The Invention of Fairy Tales.” *Journal of American Folklore* 123, no. 490 (2010): 398–425.

Velay-Vallantin, Catherine. “Tales as a Mirror: Perrault in the *Bibliothèque Bleue*.” In *The Culture of Print: Power and the Uses of Print in Early Modern Europe*, edited by Roger Chartier, translated by Lydia G. Cochrane, 92–136. Princeton NJ: Princeton University Press, 1989.

Verdier, Gabrielle. “De ma Mère L'Oye à Mother Goose: La fortune des contes de fées littéraires français en Angleterre.” In *Contacts culturels et échanges linguistiques au XVIIe siècle en France*, 185–202. Tübingen: Papers on French Seventeenth Century Literature, 1997.

———. “Gracieuse vs. Grognon, or How to Tell the Good Guys from the Bad in the Literary Fairy Tale.” *Cahiers du dix-septième* 6, no. 2 (1992): 13–20.

Viala, Alain. *La France Galante: Essai historique sur une catégorie culturelle, de ses origines jusqu'à la révolution*. Paris: Presses Universitaires de France, 2008.

Villedieu, Mme de [Marie-Catherine Desjardins]. *Les Désordres de l'amour*. Edited by Micheline Cuénin, 2nd ed. Geneva: Droz, 1995.

Villiers, Pierre de. *Entretiens sur les contes de fées et sur quelques autres ouvrages du temps, pour servir de préservatif contre le mauvais gout. Dediez à Messiers de l'Academie Françoise*. Paris: Jacques Collombat, 1699.

Warner, Marina. *From the Beast to the Blonde: On Fairy Tales and Their Tellers*. London: Vintage, 1994.

———. *Once upon a Time: A Short History of Fairy Tale*. Oxford: Oxford University Press, 2014.

Welch, Marcelle Maistre. "La femme, le mariage et l'amour dans les contes de fées mondains du XVIIe siècle." *Papers on French Seventeenth Century Literature* 10, no. 18 (1983): 47–58.

Wiesner, Merry E. *Women and Gender in Early Modern Europe*. Cambridge: Cambridge University Press, 2000.

Zarri, Gabriella. "Eyes and Heart, Eros and Agape: Forms of Love in the Renaissance." *Historical Reflections* 41, no. 2 (2015): 53–69.

Ziolkowski, Jan M. "Straparola and the Fairy Tale: Between Literary and Oral Traditions." *Journal of American Folklore* 123, no. 490 (2010): 377–97.

Zipes, Jack. *Breaking the Magic Spell: Radical Theories of Folk and Fairy Tales*. 2nd ed. Lexington: University Press of Kentucky, 2002.

———. *Fairy Tales and the Art of Subversion: The Classical Genre for Children and the Process of Civilization*. New York: Methuen, 1988.

———. *Happily Ever After: Fairy Tales, Children and the Culture Industry*. New York: Routledge, 1997.

———. "Introduction: The Rise of the French Fairy Tale and the Decline of France." In *Beauties, Beasts and Enchantment: Classic French Fairy Tales*, edited by Jack Zipes, 1–12. New York: Meridian, 1989.

———. "Introduction: Towards a Definition of the Literary Fairy Tale." In *The Oxford Companion to Fairy Tales*, edited by Jack Zipes, xv–xxxii. Oxford: Oxford University Press, 2000.

———. *The Irresistible Fairy Tale: The Cultural and Social History of a Genre*. Princeton NJ: Princeton University Press, 2012.

———. "The Meaning of Fairy Tale within the Evolution of Culture." *Marvels & Tales* 25, no. 2 (2011): 221–43.

Zipes, Jack, trans. and ed. *The Great Fairy Tale Tradition: From Straparola and Basile to the Brothers Grimm: Texts, Criticism*. New York: W. W. Norton, 2001.

INDEX

Page locators in italics refer to figures. Page locators in bold refer to tables.

In the Women and Gender in the Early Modern World series:

Women and Community in Medieval and Early Modern Iberia
Edited and with an introduction by Michelle Armstrong-Partida, Alexandra Guerson, and Dana Wessell Lightfoot

Women's Life Writing and Early Modern Ireland
Edited by Julie A. Eckerle and Naomi McAreavey

Pathologies of Love: Medicine and the Woman Question in Early Modern France
By Judy Kem

The Politics of Female Alliance in Early Modern England
Edited by Christina Luckyj and Niamh J. O'Leary

Telltale Women: Chronicling Gender in Early Modern Historiography
Allison Machlis Meyer

Love, Power, and Gender in Seventeenth-Century French Fairy Tales
Bronwyn Reddan

www.ingramcontent.com/pod-product-compliance
Lightning Source LLC
Chambersburg PA
CBHW060806310726
48980CB00002B/253

* 9 7 8 1 4 9 6 2 1 6 1 5 1 *